The
Floating
Island

The Floating Island

A Tale of Washington

Garrett Epps

HOUGHTON
MIFFLIN
COMPANY
BOSTON
1985

A Richard Todd Book

Copyright © 1985 by Garrett Epps

Library of Congress Cataloging in Publication Data

Epps, Garrett.
The floating island.

I. Title.
PS3555.P63F55   1985   813'.54   84–25156
ISBN 0-395-37702-1

Printed in the United States of America

v   10   9   8   7   6   5   4   3   2   1

For Spen, the simple secret of the plot

Acknowledgments

The author would like to thank the following friends and colleagues who read this novel in manuscript: Liz Duvall, Judd Esty-Kendall, James Fallows, Katherine Fulton, Marc Granetz, David and Eve Ignatius, Spencie Love, Julia G. McLaughlin, Belinda Novik, Lee Smith, Richard Todd, and Wendy Weil. Without their help and encouragement, this book would never have been completed.

The reader can hardly conceive my astonishment, to behold an island in the air, inhabited by men, who were able (as it should seem) to raise, or sink, or put it into a progressive motion, as they pleased.
—"A Voyage to Laputa, Balnibarbi, Glubbdubdrib, Luggnagg and Japan" from *Gulliver's Travels,* by Jonathan Swift

Part One

His Majesty ordered that the island should stop over
certain towns and villages, from whence he might
receive the petitions of his subjects. And to this
purpose several pack-threads were let down with small
weights at the bottom. On these pack-threads the
people strung their petitions, which mounted up
directly like the scraps of paper fastened by school-
boys at the end of the string that holds their kite.
—"A Voyage to Laputa, Balnibarbi,
Glubbdubdrib, Luggnagg and Japan"

Chapter 1

WASHINGTON IS A MARKET. What is traded is reputation. This market clears daily; it has its booms, its panics, its frauds, its insider trading, its mighty rallies, and its overnight collapses; sometimes trading is slow, sometimes furious. All the energy that might be spent in governing the country is absorbed in the frenzy of the pit.

A tale of Washington, then, for all that it should contain dancing girls and passionate embraces, vows spoken in darkness and broken by day, explosions and electric bells, ghastly miasmas of dry ice, bold heroes swinging from ropes, and a live chicken, will be at its core a story not of power, destiny, or will but of reputation. Some will be made, and others lost.

The first player, a young man named Gerald Nash, wearing a tan suit, suede shoes, and small horn-rimmed spectacles, came suddenly to himself in a green cubicle. Had it not been out of keeping with his responsible position, he might have been considered to have fallen into a light doze before being awakened by the ringing of the telephone. Upon abstractedly lifting the receiver, he was unable to remember what an important official should say in such circumstances, so that what emerged was a faint, uncertain gurgle followed by, "Um . . . yesss — hello?"

"Is this Gerry Nash?" asked a voice, a flat, insinuating, feminine half-whisper.

"Yes," he said, recalled fully to himself. "Can I help you?"

"Of course you can," said the voice. "This is Diana."

Gerald was disquieted by how little surprise he felt at hearing, for the first time in seven years, the voice of the young woman he had once considered the love of his life. Her voice brought into his mind a flood of memories buried and half-forgotten, as if by simply calling she threatened to abolish the years passed and the distance traveled since they had last spoken. This sensation was unpleasant. For Gerald Nash, those years had been filled with striving and achievement, turns of fortune and rewards to merit, culminating in the creation of a successful and satisfying professional identity. His response must have sounded guarded in tone.

"Do you want me to hang up?" she asked.

"No, no, of course not," he said, with more certainty than he felt. He attempted to ask the usual questions — how she was, where she was living, what she was doing, and so forth — but she cut these off.

"Never mind that," she said. "I just want to know if you're still mad at me."

"Mad at you? We haven't seen each other in seven years."

"Then it makes sense for me to think you're still mad."

"I didn't know where you were — you just disappeared."

"Did you try to find out?"

"Well . . ." Gerald was suddenly assailed by vivid, incomplete, and conflicting snatches of memory — of the time, at the end of his first year of law school, when Diana had left, taking, it had seemed at the time, something small but central, like his shadow or the tune he whistled in the mornings or the patterns that floated before his eyes in the free, gauzy moment before dreaming. Where had she gone? Why had she left? Diana had always had precisely this effect on him at crucial moments: throwing him off balance, calling his assumptions into question, demanding to share his secrets. An image of Diana danced in the air before him, crossing her impossibly long, graceful legs as she perched on the corner of his battered GSA desk; he smelled her dark perfume, saw the delicate tracery of veins on her hands when she clasped them in front of her mouth or flung them into the air like hypnotic birds. The vision vexed him.

"You are still angry," she said.

He cast his eyes desperately around as if drowning, seeing his battered cork bulletin board, the framed signed photograph of himself and the President of the United States, and his prized window with its commanding view of an airshaft. "Diana, why are you calling me? Why now, after all this time?"

"I guess because it got to be pretty obvious you weren't going to call me," she said. "Anyway, I was going through some stuff over Christmas and I found the poem you wrote to me."

"I wrote you a poem?"

"Do you want me to mail it back to you so you can see?"

"No. You keep it."

She seemed to be unprepared for this answer. "Oh. Okay. Good-bye, then."

"Wait! Where are you? What's your address?"

"I'll call you sometime." She hung up, leaving Gerald in the green cubicle, confused and slightly dazed.

Gerald had allotted the next half-hour to a review of a departmental draft report entitled "Infrastructural and Training-Related Aspects of Interagency Solid-Waste Management Development Programs." The Assistant Secretary was to testify on this topic before the powerful Hench committee of the House of Representatives in a week's time. Being absent on a tour of departmental installations on the Gulf Coast of Florida, he had asked Gerald by phone to prepare a four-hundred-word memorandum, typed in upper-case letters, setting out the salient points of the subject and putting the Department's programs in the most favorable light possible.

But instead Gerald fell into a fugue state in which his dim cubicle, his dull memorandum, his sober professional identity dimmed and faded, displaced by extravagant images of pasts forgotten and futures never realized. Frightening lacunae loomed in his memory of the past decade, which ordinarily presented itself to him as a logical and resourceful progress through law school, private legal practice, and public-interest law into government service. There was a sudden shifting inside him, a sensation of danger and possibility lurking beneath the surface of his triumphantly mundane existence; and this shifting may account for some of the subsequent events of that peculiar day.

It had fallen to Gerald to represent the Division of Evaluation, Training, and Morale at the first annual National Conference on Further Alternatives, which was being held that week at an uptown hotel. Gerald was to appear at a session entitled "Eligibility Guidelines and Administrative Requirements for Direct-Grant, Block-Grant, Planning-Grant, and Matching-Grant Programs."

Gerald's division supervised a program called Community Action Training Allocations, designed by a previous administration to help struggling communities create new jobs. The Assistant Secretary was, in government parlance, on travel status; the Deputy Assistant Secretary, sensing political risk in the meeting, had put in for annual leave for that day on the grounds that her basil plants were going through a difficult germination; and the career civil servant actually responsible for the program had long ago declared a nonrecognition and nonintercourse policy toward the entire "public-interest" movement. It was for just such occasions that Gerald had been recruited, and he had promised to appear; but now he had floated in his mental Sargasso so long that it was already five to three, which was the time at which he was to speak.

Gerald quickly stuffed his notes into his attaché case, pulled on his tan suit jacket, and ran in his suede shoes along what was even by government standards an unusually long, confusing, and sad series of corridors and stairways. He burst onto the street, dashed three blocks to the nearest avenue, and hailed a taxi.

Even the hardiest urbanite will hesitate before urging a Washington cabbie to hurry. Near-lethal multilingual haste is the normal state of the hundreds of battered cabs that cruise the streets. Because a benevolent Congress supervises the taxi system, cabs are cheap: indeed, by a striking coincidence, the fare zones are drawn so that a small flat fare will take a passenger almost anywhere in the city that, say, a member of Congress might want to go. As a result, driving a cab is a dangerous, dirty, and difficult but unremunerative job. Hailing a cab in the District, a traveler may be sure he has engaged a driver whose chief purpose will be to deliver him rapidly (if not necessarily fully conscious) to his destination and then rush on to collect another meager fare.

Gerald's driver was identified by his hacker's license as Mustafa Abu Nasr. Gerald perched awkwardly on what remained of the rear seat as the cab sped past the White House and along the parkway; during the journey he was nearly deafened by an eight-track tape of an Islamic love ballad. The noise, and the three near-collisions, effectively prevented Gerald from using the trip to review his remarks and further contributed to his sense of events spinning somehow out of control. Arriving at the hotel (his tip earned him a muttered pleasantry from the driver that, had Gerald possessed the necessary Arabic camel-breeder's vocabulary, might have caused him some discomfiture), he dashed through the grand lobby to the door of a large, shabby ballroom, his tie, glasses, shoelaces, and attaché case askew.

"— had hoped to hear from Gerald Nash," an amplified voice was saying as he burst into the room, "but as he appears to have been detained, perhaps we'll —"

"Here I am!" Gerald intended to shout, although it emerged instead as an inaudible whoop or gasp. To attract attention he waved his arms in the air, and the sudden failure of the latching mechanism on his case caused his notes to scatter in a semicircle with a radius of six or seven feet.

"Here he is now," said the voice, as helpful onlookers returned Gerald's notes to him in jumbled order. "We're very pleased to have Gerald here today to speak about the CATA program. He's special assistant to the Assistant Secretary for Evaluation, Training, and Morale. I think some of you may have worked with him when he served on the interagency task force that drew up the guidelines for nonsexist federally funded pageants and parades. If you'd like to come up to the front, Gerald . . ."

The speaker, Gerald dimly perceived, was a tall woman with a mane of thick sandy hair, a fair complexion, and a wide, mobile mouth. She was waving him toward the podium, a welcoming smile on her face. Gerald found her face and gesture oddly but unplaceably familiar, which distracted his attention as he came into full view of the audience. Giving a weak smile and insufficient thought, he launched into his talk.

Disaster was averted, however, because Gerald had an all-purpose speech for such occasions, which he had given half a dozen times, so that he could run through it without calling on the higher mechanisms of consciousness at all. Briefly he explained the origins of the CATA grant program; cited favorable remarks made about it by the President, the Secretary, the Deputy Secretary, the Assistant Secretary, and (most important of all) the local morning newspaper; reviewed the increases in appropriations enacted by Congress for the past two fiscal years and the whopping increase requested by the administration in its budget proposal now pending before Congress; and closed with some stirring words which were the bureaucratic equivalent of what is known in evangelical churches as the altar call.

"So to sum up, I'd say that the CATA program is alive and well and here to stay, that this administration is committed to it, we believe in it, we think it's a good program, and that we at the ETM division are very much interested in getting word out about it. The money is there, the eligibility requirements are the same this fiscal year as they were last FY, and if anyone here has a project or knows of a project that he or she thinks may meet the guidelines, then I hope he or she will come forward and let us help him or her with his or her application. Or if he or she prefers, he or she can call us at the division, and in fact, I'd like to give him or her my direct phone number so he or she can talk to me directly about it." (During the entire speech, Gerald had, without fully knowing it, been scanning the audience as if looking for someone in particular, seeking something familiar in a look, a gesture, a facial feature. This half-conscious quest distracted him slightly, so that he inadvertently reversed two digits of his phone number; a dozen callers during the next week reached the Yam Disease Pavilion at the Beltsville Agricultural Research Center.)

Next Gerald called for questions, still scanning the crowd. A graceful hand was waving in the air; it turned out to belong to the woman who had introduced him. "Gerald, I wonder if you'd mind giving us a brief description of the ideal project you'd like to see apply for a CATA grant," she asked.

"That's a very good question," he said. "I'm not sure anyone has ever asked me to do just that, but I will try to give you an idea. What we're looking for would be a project which needs seed money in the range of $100,000 to $500,000, which is to be used not for capital expenditure or operating expenses but for start-up costs or training and development of a new or existing nonprofit enterprise. The enterprise should affect the entire community involved, and that should be demonstrated by support both from the local government and from a broad-based community group. CATA projects, of course, are supposed to relate to economic development, so we're particularly interested in communities that have been hit by adverse economic trends like plant closings. I think that if you could show me a project that met all of those criteria, I could almost promise you approval of the grant within thirty to sixty days."

Next he called on a chubby young woman in the second row.

"I'm sure we're all relieved to hear that the administration is committed to the CATA program," she sneered. "But when Bernard Weisman of Congressman Hench's staff spoke to us a little while ago, he pointed out that for the last FY, grants actually awarded amounted to only forty-seven percent of the funds authorized in the congressional budget. So if the problem isn't ideological, is it just inefficiency, or what?"

Even under today's relatively informal standards of behavior, it is not considered proper for a public servant to admit that his agency is inept, ill-managed, or unnecessary. The taxpayers deserve something better, and Gerald strove to give it to them.

"Well, of course I'm sorry to have missed any remarks by Bernard Weisman, who's a very knowledgeable observer and a good friend of mine," he began (thereby signaling to the audience that he considered Weisman a mendacious dolt and would go to almost any lengths to avoid speaking to or even seeing him). "I've learned not to argue with him about figures" (thereby calling him a liar), "and I'm going to accept that the figures you've cited are correct" (thereby implying that they were utterly false). "I would like to point out that during the fiscal year you cited, Mr. Weisman's boss, Representative Hench, and his committee in their wisdom decided to rewrite the eligibility guidelines in our authorizing statutes, and that there was a presidential veto of the departmental budget bill because one of the members from North Carolina attached a rider to the bill ordering the State Department to open diplomatic relations with the Dalai Lama. So we were operating under a continuing resolution containing a different set of guidelines for nearly half the fiscal year. Yes, we did fall short, and we're not making excuses for that" (a locution that praised the division for not doing what it had just done), "but I think you'll find that when the results are compiled for the current FY, our record will be much improved."

Seeing a thin young man in the back with his hand in the air and a broad smile on his face, Gerald made the not uncommon mistake of confusing a friendly appearance with a friend. "Next question?" he said, pointing at this young man.

The smile did not waver as the young man asked, "Tell us the real reason why you refuse to fund the Fourth Planet Harmony Incense Cooperative in Cranston, Rhode Island."

"I'm sorry, I really don't have specific grant requests with me —"

The young man mounted a chair and addressed the entire assembly. "Fools! Why do you not flee the wrath to come? The Ancient Ones of Mars know that you are given up to foul practices and negative thinking! Idolaters! Pharisees! Hypocrites! Wash pots of Moab! Neurotics! Overeaters! Yes, you smile in the faces of the people, but all the time you want to take their place! America must return to Ray! Only He offers the water of life —"

At this point the young man was seized by two hotel security guards, at the direction of the blond woman who had introduced Gerald. They carried him from the room, screaming as he went, "May you thirst for a thousand years! Sons of sandworms! Obsessive-compulsives!" and similar epithets that grew fainter as he receded into the distance.

The woman moved to the center of the room and said, "Now that Gerald has faced down the Temple of Ray, I think we should excuse him from any more questions. Thank you, Gerald — we're sorry for the interruption, and we appreciate your taking time

out to be with us. Don't forget tomorrow's panel on 'Plant Closings, Discouraged Workers, and the Power of Networking.' And
tonight there's a reception given by the Center for Citrus Product
Purity, at seven o'clock."

As the meeting rose, some half-dozen grant-brokers descended
on Gerald to request help with applications in various stages of
preparation, and by the time they had finished presenting him
with odd-sized and creased pieces of paper, the banquet room was
empty except for Gerald, the woman who had introduced him,
and a wary-looking young man who had recently been named
Washington correspondent for a Shreveport newspaper and who
was under the erroneous impression that the foreign minister of
Kuwait would shortly be holding a news conference in that room.

The woman now came toward him, wearing an expression that
Gerald was familiar with from dreams: a look of perfect intimacy,
as if they were old friends. "Gerry," she said, "I was hoping we
would get to talk before the meeting. I'm Margaret Luck. When
I knew you, my name was Margaret Gardner. I'm working for the
Coalition for Industrial Alternatives now."

"You're Jack's wife?" Like a stereopticon, his memory suddenly
superimposed another image on the woman in front of him. Jack
Gardner had been a lawyer in the suburban community in which
Gerald had grown up. It had been Jack Gardner, in fact, who had
interviewed Gerald when he had applied to the college he had
later attended.

"I was," she said. "I took my maiden name back after the divorce."

A decade ago, as a suburban wife, she had appeared to be a
settled matron of an older generation; but now he saw that she
was no more than five or six years older than he was. In fact, she
seemed to have gotten younger; there were a few gray hairs in her
shaggy mane and a few fine lines around her eyes, curving upward
as if she were used to laughing, but her clothes, which had been
of the pastel-skirt-and-blue-espadrille variety, were now the semi-
casual styles affected by sophisticated young women in the capital.

They traded intelligence of their old home town, and Gerald
was preparing to excuse himself politely when something happened to change his mind.

Ordinarily Gerald Nash prided himself on maintaining a neat appearance. His tan suit, canary-yellow foulard necktie, and blue oxford-cloth button-down shirt had been selected with an eye toward making a favorable impression on the audience at this conference. But after his hasty flight across town, Gerald had not been able to check his grooming before rushing into the meeting. He noticed Margaret looking at him with a slightly distracted look; after a minute or two she laughed apologetically and knelt at his feet.

"I'm sorry," she said, tying his shoelace. "I guess I'm a little compulsive about this kind of thing."

Gerald flushed; but then he noticed what a handsome woman was kneeling at his feet.

Dusting her hands, she rose and asked, "Are you on your way out?"

"Yes," he said without planning to. "Have you got time to go over to Dupont Circle and have a drink?"

"I have nothing but time," she said. "Would you mind if I just ran by my apartment and met you in, say, twenty minutes? I live very close by."

As he wandered across to the Circle, Gerald found himself repenting the invitation. On the one hand, it pleased him to appear before this woman, who had known him in awkward and squeaky-voiced adolescence, in his present aspect of an accomplished young man, but on the other hand, his friendliness seemed also somehow reprehensible — as if he were making himself a corespondent not only in her divorce but in the entire wasting blight of dissolution that had fallen over so many lovely tree-shaded communities like the one where he had grown up.

They had agreed to meet at a bar that doubled as a bookstore. As usual at this hour, it was thronged with young government workers, lawyers, journalists and political operatives, panhandlers, solicitors for cults, dancers in leotards, gay men on roller skates, and joggers in warm-up suits. With some difficulty Gerald got a glass of mineral water and established himself in front of a display of a book entitled *I'm Okay — You're Dead: A Guide to Creative Grief.* Here he stood, brooding over meanings and portents, until he caught sight of Margaret Luck.

She had changed into a soft flower-print skirt and an inviting white linen blouse. Had he been in the habit of looking at a woman from head to toe, he might have noticed these attractive garments first and been drawn as well to observe the delicate musculature of her neck, revealed because she had pinned her hair to the top of her head, and the ease and fullness of her figure. But, using a habit acquired during a shy adolescence, he began his inspection of Margaret with her feet, and so the first thing he noticed was her shoes.

These were a pale red. They would have looked correct on Minnie Mouse. The shoes seemed to belong to an earlier era, a time of fall leaf-burning and wood-paneled station wagons — a time, in short, to which Margaret belonged and he did not. He began blinking his eyes rapidly, as if the shoes were a piece of grit, and it was then that Margaret saw him and gave a cheery smile.

"Hi, there," she said. "Are you all right? You look like someone who has dirt in his contacts, but you obviously don't wear contacts."

Sometimes a chance remark, intended to be light or even affectionate, can put one person off balance and then set both people rocking back and forth in quest of equilibrium, like the drinking dolls sold at roadside stands. Gerald was sensitive about his glasses, and moreover he had a general aversion to looking silly, absurd, or at a loss. So without fully meaning to, he struck back in kind. "I was looking at your shoes," he said. "They remind me of what girls used to wear to the junior prom."

Margaret's face fell slightly. She lifted her foot and inspected one shoe critically. "They are a little old, I guess —"

"I'm sorry, I didn't mean —"

"I've had them a long time —"

"No, really, they look fine —"

"Shoes are so expensive these days —"

This exchange did give Gerald an opportunity to look closely at the leg in the shoe. It was solid, with a pleasantly rounded calf. This made him sorry he had mentioned the shoe.

"Cigarette?" Margaret was saying.

"No, sorry, I don't smoke."

"Lord, don't be sorry," she said, puffing smoke. "I wish to God I didn't. I've been trying to quit for years."

The young man next to Margaret pushed a pair of foam earphones back on his head and scowled at her. "Would you mind not holding that over here?" he demanded.

"Of course, I'm very sorry," she said. Trading drink and cigarette, Margaret managed to spill part of her gin-and-tonic on Gerald's foulard necktie, which gave rise to a concentrated burst of dabbing with napkins.

They began like drinking dolls to recover their balance. Gerald ordered another mineral water, and they began to talk that most soothing and comfortable of languages, Washington shop. Like all the traders on the reputation market, Gerald and Margaret regarded the United States government with the patronizing, impersonal malice of poor relations waiting by the bedside of a comatose rich aunt.

Prices rose and fell as they gossiped. The Secretary of Gerald's Department was up this week, as he was considered to have been the source of a news story favorable to his patrons in the White House; the Undersecretary was down, as he had delivered before the Hench committee a ringing defense of a departmental budget initiative disavowed by the White House the same day; journalists were going short in a third Department official, the Assistant Secretary for Field Operations and Applications Sequencing, because his patron, a cabinet secretary in another department, had been negatively portrayed in the story apparently leaked by the Secretary. Representative Buster Hench and his eagle-eyed assistant, Bernard Weisman, were up sharply, as they had discovered a $400,000 grant let by the National Endowment for the Arts as part of an ill-fated proposal to surround the entire city of Boise in a plastic shrink-wrapper.

This exchange of information is an immensely soothing pastime. By focusing their attention on the higher levels of the government, it reassures insignificant players of their own importance and gives them the illusion of involvement in great and mysterious decisions. In addition, the elaborate explanations advanced for each turn in the market make the process seem rational and sane, when the players secretly know it to be random and absurd. And most important for people like Gerald and Margaret, who spend most of their working hours dealing with the middle- and low-level bureaucracy (a cold, still region darkened by the shadows of sharks, lit by the brief flashings of electric eels, and agitated by the silent grouping and regrouping of shoals of small, colorless fish whose feeding and function are largely unknown), the exchange serves a function like professional sports, providing an escape from the tedium of their working hours.

The evening progressed; one drink, one cigarette, one item of gossip led to another. Without quite meaning to, they slid from after-work to early-evening drinking. At seven, Gerald looked at his watch and said, "Listen, I know you need to get back to the reception —"

"Not really," she said. "I'm off duty tonight. Those citrus people get on my nerves. They're always talking about pesticides for breakfast."

Perhaps it was the image of his roommate, Willys Handleman, stewing in rancor before the television, that made Gerald say, "I don't suppose you'd want to get something to eat? I've heard about a Spanish place somewhere around here."

"Sounds fine."

They left the bar for a seedy neighborhood of Victorian townhouses, shoe-repair shops, gay bars, and package stores. Spring is the one fragrant season in Washington; it was a clear, chilly night, and the wind smelled freshly washed. Margaret buttoned her sweater as they walked and then put her arm companionably through Gerald's. Her bold stride pulled him along slightly faster than he was used to going.

He had recently received from Handleman a detailed lecture on how to make a good impression at a new restaurant. Accordingly, he secreted a five-dollar bill in his right hand at the door, and when the headwaiter — a short, smiling man with an American accent and a Latin shirt — seated them, Gerald slipped him the money in the guise of a friendly handshake.

The little man recoiled. "God bless you, sir!" he cried. "We don't charge for our tables here!" Cackling with harsh laughter, he left them, and cold winds moved in his wake.

"What's wrong with him?" asked Margaret, who appeared not to have noticed the encounter.

"I don't know," Gerald said, quickly slipping the banknote

into his jacket pocket. "I think he just has an eccentric manner." He hid his flushed face behind a menu.

"Are you okay?" Margaret said kindly.

"Just — just your smoke getting to me a little," he retaliated.

"Heavens, I'm sorry, why didn't you say something?" She crushed her cigarette firmly.

They ordered wine and paella. As he had feared, she came to the topic of her marriage, and no soothing noises he made could dissuade her from talking about it.

"It must seem awfully strange to you, me popping up in another identity like this after all these years."

"Oh, don't be silly —"

"It feels strange to me too, a lot of the time. I mean, I thought my life was all taken care of the year I graduated from Hollins and married Jack."

"— seems perfectly natural —"

"And, of course, the night you came to see Jack for your interview I probably seemed about as old as your mother."

"— not at all —"

"But the truth is, I'm not, damn it. I wish I were. I'm not really as old as you are, in terms of living, of knowing the world. I spent ten years doing nothing in that house on Cedarview, waiting for new neighbors."

Now would come the tale: the bitter fighting, the husband's infidelity, the betrayals of the heart. He would be asked to take sides against Jack Gardner, against Cedarview Drive and Pinemount Crescent and Berrington Lane and Delmar Circle, against the ordered, somnolent, and once eternal-seeming world of his suburban childhood. "I didn't really know Jack very well."

"He's a hell of a guy," she said. "I miss him a lot. He writes to me, you know — writes letters by hand. He finally realized that I hated those dictated notes. That made me feel good. I enjoyed being married to Jack. Will it bother you if I smoke?"

"No, go ahead," he said, hoping to change the subject. "You said you've been trying to quit?"

"Our marriage didn't really break up. It just sort of disappeared. It was like one of those times when two people are pretending that something is true and thinking that the other person doesn't know it isn't, and then they suddenly just look at each other and crack up. It just never felt right somehow. At some point I realized I felt as if we were both dressing up in our parents' clothes. And then one night Jack stayed in the city, and it was like school was out, someone had declared a holiday. The next week I sold every stick of furniture we owned. I came here, and he stayed there."

The food arrived, and she stubbed out her cigarette. Acrid smoke wafted up from the smoldering butt, and she absently waved it away with her hand. Gerald reached out and ground out the butt, feeling annoyed. But she seemed to take the gesture for tenderness, and smiled, her eyes crinkling up at the corners.

She ate with a hearty appetite. "I'd love to know how you ended up with the Department," she said, cocking her head at him. "I used to try to predict what the boys would do when they came to Jack's. I had you picked for a film writer or something glamorous. Not that your job's not glamorous —"

"It's not," he said with the quiet pride of a man who does what must be done. "I just stumbled into it. I went to law school because . . . I guess because it seemed like a way to help people and get paid for it. Came to Washington to try to get involved in the country's problems, all that clean-for-Gene stuff. Got a job with a private firm. Corporate practice wasn't for me. So I worked in the President's campaign —"

"You did? Did you know Toad Earnshaw?"

"Know him? I roomed with him, for a while at least, at the beginning."

"What is he really like?"

He thought of explaining in detail: that Earnshaw was a young man in baggy khakis, with an overdrawn bank account and a rusty Ford pickup; that he was sometimes slow on the uptake, sometimes completely obtuse, often remorselessly self-seeking, occasionally intelligent. But he saw from her dilated eyes that his friendship with Earnshaw, who was trading at a premium in the market these days, gave him added luster in her eyes, so he answered, "Brilliant. And really a very fine guy when you take the time to get to know him."

"And after the election Toad got you a job with the administration?"

"Not exactly." In fact Toad Earnshaw had summarily fired Gerald after the election, a story not necessarily favorable to Gerald's standing on the exchange, so he skipped it. "I wanted to try the public-interest movement for a while."

"Really? Who were you with?"

"An outfit called the Equine Defense Fund. We were advocates for the horse — not for the industry but for the individual horse. We worked mostly with the Agriculture Department on things like horsemeat regulation. I was really shocked to see how hard some of the big food corporations are pushing for horsemeat in canned products and fast food. Sometimes we dealt with Interior on rules for wild-pony kills or recreational riding in national parks and wilderness areas. That's a scandal in itself — the conditions some of these concessionaires keep their horses under. We also lobbied for tax credits for horse-drawn farm machinery; I got to work with the Plain Churches Public Affairs Office on that one. And of course HUD and OSHA got into the proposed stall-and-stable regulations. I also helped a friend of mine, Willys Handleman, work on a book called *Unsafe at Any Gait*."

"I never saw it."

"It never got published. Willys quit in protest when we changed our position on dogfood deregulation."

"So how did that lead to this job?"

"Not very directly. They just needed somebody, and they knew me, and I was tired of the agency work at EDF."

"So what do you spend most of your time doing now?"

As if expressly to deflect this excruciating question, a mournful guitar chord echoed through the room. Gerald, who had taken the seat facing the wall, craned his neck and saw that a guitarist in a ruffled shirt and a tight black waistcoat had entered, followed by a flamenco dancer in a red dress. The guitarist began to play rippling chords, and the dancer lifted her skirts and began to dance.

Her hair was midnight black, coiled tightly at the crown of her skull and decorated with a rose. She held her shoulders high and smiled into the middle distance, as if at the memory of someone far away. Her pale red shoes struck loudly against the hardwood floor.

Gerald was absorbed by this unexpected performance, which struck him with the force that art can have when it comes upon us unawares. When the music stopped, he was vaguely surprised to come to himself in the restaurant again. He turned back to Margaret, who was lighting another cigarette. She burst into a series of racking coughs and began pounding herself on the chest. Tears gathered at the corners of her eyes. "Damn it," she said. "I swallowed some smoke the wrong way."

As was the custom, they split the cost of dinner evenly, but as Margaret was short of cash, she was forced to put the full amount on a credit card and collect from Gerald in cash. This was a normal transaction for their time, place, and class, but Gerald, his back to the room, was suddenly assailed by the notion that the flamenco dancer, the guitarist, and the mottled headwaiter were watching him scornfully as Margaret figured the tip, signed the bill, and tidily folded her copy of the receipt.

"Good night, sir," sneered the headwaiter as they left. "Come again soon. No charge for a table."

They walked among rows of upright, dull red and yellow houses with gabled windows and pointed roofs. On every block were proud signs announcing that one of the houses was being converted into luxury condominiums; on every window were heavy iron gates. Margaret slipped her sweater around her shoulders and folded her arms. Her red shoes flickered at the edge of Gerald's vision.

"I live a few blocks from here. I live in fear of the day I get converted," she said.

"Our apartment is a co-op, so it can't be converted."

"You have a roommate?" she asked.

"Yeah," he said, thinking of Willys Handleman, who was probably at home now in his sagging armchair, surrounded by books and papers and watching television. "How about you?"

"No," she said. "My place is really too small for two people who're not married to each other." She stopped before a corner row house, red brick with a dark shingled roof and a round turret pointing at the sky. "That's my place in the turret," she said. "I feel like an enchanted princess sometimes. Do you want to come in for a glass of wine?"

It is curious how a decision can be made at one level for rational reasons, in detail and precisely thought through, and yet be made at another level entirely in the opposite direction. So, for example, Gerald had decided to end the evening, go home, and watch Johnny Carson with Willys Handleman, because he knew that he could listen to Handleman's disgruntled chatter without taking energy away from sorting out the sensations of the day. So clear was this decision that as he heard himself say, "That sounds like fun," he had the incredulous feeling of watching a stranger disguised as himself floating with Margaret up the steep front stoop, past the dull brass mail slots, and up the dark stairs and into her tiny apartment.

The room he had seen, in different houses, a dozen times before: the ancient, intricate wallpaper, the tattered political posters, the blond wood coffee table with metal legs, the beanbag cushions. The bland white wine he had drunk at a hundred cheerless conferences, wine-and-cheese receptions, dinner gatherings, and late-night strategy sessions. The talk, of rents and apartments and real estate, neighborhoods, crime, restaurants, and taxis, was the ordinary chatter of Washingtonians.

And yet, despite his habit, inclination, and intention, Gerald Nash had a splendid night. When he decided that he would definitely leave, saying, "I have an eight o'clock meeting," which was a polite fiction, he found himself almost at once kissing Margaret, which did not seem to dismay or even surprise her, and in short order they were in her bedroom, a round chamber in which the light of a streetlamp glowed through the bars onto a Maxfield Parrish poster and a quilted bedspread, the sharp shadows of the bars crossing and recrossing the bright colors.

She unpinned her hair, which fell in a shadowy wave, and then kissed him again lightly. "Gerry, I don't usually pet on the first date," she said. "I don't know what you think. I've just been lonely here — I don't know what's going on, exactly . . ."

"Neither do I."

She laughed, indulgent and cynical, and kissed him again. "Oh, I think you do," she said. "Be kind to an old lady."

He had forgotten the difference in their ages. But whatever its intent, this remark set up a thrill — the lure of the forbidden.

He had never slept with a married woman before. He nuzzled the hollow of her neck, dimly relishing the excitement of infidelity, the delicious sense of barriers dissolving and hierarchies crumbling, of prohibitions and proscriptions fading into memory, and he was ravished by this sense as much as by her, giving himself to a world without order, memories, or rewards. Soon they lay on top of the quilt, crossed and recrossed by the bars, guarded by the streetlight. They joined in that fluid geometrical light, and she cried out softly as he moved inside her, and then cried out again, a sound at once lost and reassuring, as of a child in the forest who comes upon a trail of breadcrumbs.

He pulled the quilt over them both, and she nestled close to him, folding her solid body against his. Her breathing affected him like ether. He let sleep take him heavily, feeling that warm haze which is the beginning of a dream — that free, gauzy moment in which shapes and voices combine and recombine like shadows, then grow brighter and begin to move. He saw beneath his eyelids the blurred dim colors of the room, the two of them beneath the quilt; then the greens and yellows swirled and blended, and there rose before him the green grass of a meadow, the blue of a sounding stream. Enthroned before him was a woman in a red dress, who called to him in an emphatic, flat, intimate whisper; watching him with rapt attention, she rose to her feet, which, he noted in the deepening golden dream, were shod in pale red shoes.

Chapter 2

As THE LOVERS SLEPT, there occurred in the air above them a collision of forces in three dimensions, a churning of air and vapor so vast that it might have been supernatural — a delayed response to two centuries of prayers by hinterland evangelists for a cleansing baptism to wash away the sins of the scarlet capital.

The heavens rumbled once, and without further warning a cold spring rain burst over the city. It ran icy fingers down the tube tops of prostitutes, drowned the voices of drug-pushers in doorways, smeared the windows of limousines, and iced the rotors of helicopters. Dawn joggers, wrapped in oilskins, plunged and floundered in the grass of Arlington Cemetery. Rock Creek rose, driving raccoons and possums into the city's best neighborhoods. A mineral-water truck killed a fugitive deer on Military Road. The Eternal Flame went out.

From Anacostia to Anne Arundel, people woke and cursed the rain. Gerald Nash came awake with a violent start, reacting without knowing it to the silent crash of the streetlight going out. He heard the drumming raindrops and reflected bitterly that because

o question, but most people find them attractive in others.
sky's high school baseball coach, for one, was much taken
ne boy's spirit when he showed up for tryouts the following
g. "It's no such thing as a three-fingered pitcher, son," he'd
kindly.
got four," Zardovsky countered, holding up his thumb and
ers.
The coach counted. "Oh, yeah, so you do. Well, go on out and
ke a few warm-ups."

At season's end, when Bob Zardovsky had compiled a seven-and-one record and an earned-run average of 1.38, the coach repeated this exchange to a wire-service stringer as a joke on himself. The reporter gave Zardovsky the nickname "Three-Finger," which unfortunately stuck with him.

After two seasons at Gouge Eye High and one at Gouge Eye Bible College, Bob Zardovsky had lost a total of five games, two of them because of hangovers. He was offered a major-league contract and a bonus of $5000.

"I ought to get more than that," he protested.

"Sure you should, kid," said the scout who signed him, scratching the three days' growth of beard he maintained for professional reasons. "But they read them articles about you and they say, 'It's no such thing as a three-fingered pitcher.' "

"Goddamn it, I got four!"

"I know that and you know that, but that's what they believe. So finally I asked 'em, 'What if it was one, how much for the novelty value?' and they said, 'Five thousand,' and that's what you get. You want it or not? I gotta get down to Boise, I hear they got a third baseman in a iron lung."

The alternative was another year at Gouge Eye Bible, with a required seminar in Exodus, Leviticus, and Deuteronomy. Zardovsky signed.

Soon after, Zardovsky found himself with a farm team in Merida, where he tasted during the next three years his life's portion of glory. For those timeless seasons, amid the swelter of Gulf summer, he moved among American has-beens and Mexican rookies like a plumed serpent in pinstripes. In the square the old men spit-shined his hiking boots for free; in cantinas dark-eyed waitresses piled his plate high with venison and lobster.

of his needless lie about an eigh
to get up early, plunge into the ra
nowhere. Margaret stirred beside hi
and fine solid body were unguarded,
his face next to her perfumed shoulder a
into a confused half-dream of rotting pap

Less than a mile away, Gerald's roommate
Willys Handleman, woke to hear the rain sp
tongue. FAILURE FAILURE, it drummed, DESPAIN
man snorted, sighed, and flopped over in the tw
There would be no more sleep that morning. 1
would not be delivered for another hour; in the refr
a jar of mayonnaise, half a lemon, and two moldy slice
pizza. The hours stretched before him like a hallway
shadows and blind, bolted doors.

And on the southbound lane of a crowded highway nearb
Zardovsky woke from a happy dream of Mexico in the rainy se
to find himself slumped against the window of an intercity b

Zardovsky was a massive young man, with a physical self-assun
ance that made him seem even larger than he was. He had curly,
disorderly blond hair, cheerful protuberant blue eyes, and a
round, open face; he was dressed in patched blue jeans, a checked
flannel shirt, and brown lace-up boots with oil-resistant soles.
There hovered about him the air of open vistas, cold winds, and
smoky campfires. He had been born and raised in a town called
Gouge Eye, in the Pacific Northwest — a lumber-mill village beside a bold river, surrounded by fir, redwood, and pine and shadowed by snowy mountains and steep basalt cliffs.

At sixteen Zardovsky had taken a summer job at the Gouge Eye
Lumber Mill Number One, and within a few weeks he had managed to cut off the little finger of his right hand, which was the
hand he favored for eating, writing, and pitching a baseball. He
remembered little pain from the accident. But there was embarrassment. His elders usually worked for several decades in the mill
before cutting off parts of themselves.

After the accident Zardovsky had first displayed his most important character traits: eagerness to learn from mistakes and refusal
to be discouraged by setbacks. Whether these are useful qualities

But one day his odd mixture of deformity and balance disappeared. "You lost your drop ball, kid," said his manager after he had been shelled out of the fourth straight game.

"You going to take me out of the rotation, Skip?" he asked, forlornly easing his head against the greasy clubhouse wall.

"I wisht I could let it go at that. But see, the front office ain't never believed you was for real to start with. Shit, with your record they would of called you up for sure after last season, if you hadn't of had three fingers."

"I have f—"

"I know that, kid. But this came this afternoon."

The telegram granted Zardovsky his immediate, unconditional, and final release from his contract.

"That's it? Four years and that's all I get?"

"Hell, you're lucky they din't send it collect," said the manager, adding illogically, "Anyway, it's this kind of thing that makes it such a great game of ours. So long, kid."

The pale roofs and windmills disappeared; his Mexican fame tattered and disappeared, like old newspapers blowing across asphalt. But still before him then, as ever to come, gleamed like the lights of a city beyond the hills the distant, illusory glimmer of approaching good fortune. As many in Washington were about to discover, Bob Zardovsky was a hard man to discourage.

He came further awake and put a hand under the seat to touch a battered brown leather briefcase. In the case were the details of his mission and, he firmly believed, the hopes and future of his home town.

History had not been kind to Gouge Eye. In the days before white settlement, the local Indians had avoided it as a place unclean, naming it "The Place Where Snake Bites." The first party of white settlers had found themselves forced to consume a few of their companions while waiting for spring; Indians had then enslaved the nauseated survivors. Some years later a group from Pennsylvania had founded a commune devoted to generosity, Christian love, and the light within; the commune survived in a moribund lawsuit that still clouded some land titles in the western part of the county. Gold had been found in the foothills to the east, and for half a decade the town had flourished like a malodorous weed, acquiring, among other misfortunes, its name. Then the gold vein had given out. Since then the town had subsisted by cutting logs and working them in the Gouge Eye Lumber Mill, which had been owned since its inception by the Pearman family.

A decade before Bob Zardovsky was born, old Doc Pearman inherited the mill. He abandoned his career as an abortionist in Portland, hastened home, and optimistically renamed the mill Gouge Eye Lumber Mill Number One, in earnest of the glowing future he saw for the town. That bright future never dawned, though old Doc managed to lose most of his profits on projects designed to hasten it — a failed motel, a failed shopping center, a ghostly airport, a weedy industrial park. Each year the mill grew grimmer and dirtier and old Doc's dreams grew brighter, until finally he died.

Doc's heir was a nephew with a beard who lived on an island somewhere down the coast and made cherrywood mandolins. He appeared once, in faded blue jeans and a Harvard College sweatshirt, to promise the workers (and by this time Bob Zardovsky, back from Mexico, was one) that he would keep the mill going "come what may." Six months later a notice on the door announced that he had sold the mill to the Total Energy Corporation of Wilmington, Del., "who have promised to modernize, renovate, and expand it on scientific lines, which will ensure its future until the year 2000 and beyond."

Six weeks later there was another notice on the mill door, right above the shiny new padlock:

1. Due to overcapacity in the domestic pulp and paper industry, Gouge Eye Lumber Mill Number One will be closed as of above date.
2. Workers with five (5) years experience will receive two (2) weeks severance pay.

> Kindest personal regards,
> Jonas Catesby
> Assistant Vice President
> Pulp Processing Systems

"Had to come someday," said the old men, squatting in the shade of the covered bridge that led across the river to the foot of the mountains where the trout pools lay hidden and the streams had once been panned for gold. But some of the younger workers refused to accept it, and none was more vociferous than Bob Zardovsky. He was tired of anonymous dismissal; and besides, it had begun to dawn on him that his career in baseball was gone and that the only other thing he understood was working in the mill.

Because of his reputation for having traveled once before, Zardovsky had been chosen by the newly formed People's Lumber Mill Co-op as its ambassador to Washington. His briefcase (besides containing two Hershey bars, a dozen packs of Bubble Yum, and a change of underwear) was full of incorporation documents, tax-exemption statements, legal opinions, escrow receipts, balance sheets, testimonials, and financial projections, all aimed at getting a $250,000 grant from the federal government to reopen the mill.

The bus halted at a stoplight, then lurched forward, stopped again abruptly, and turned to the right. "Your next station stop will be Washington, D.C.," said the driver's public-address system. "Through passengers for Richmond, Greensboro, Jacksonville, and Miami will have a forty-minute rest stop. Passengers for other destinations change at this station. This coach will depart track seven in forty minutes." With a series of loud hisses, the bus slid into the track, and they had arrived.

Bob Zardovsky and the other passengers disembarked at a dangerous place in a dangerous city. Citizens of Washington passed this vicinity with downcast eyes. Certainly Bob Zardovsky's story would be a simpler one if he had done likewise as he walked past the lockers and the newspaper stand and the ragged files of suffering humanity standing in line for tickets like standby passengers across the Styx. But such was not his style.

Inside the glass doors he stopped, wedged his briefcase between his knees, adjusted the straps of his worn green backpack, yawned, ruffled his hair, and regarded his fellow travelers with a generous smile. Then he walked with wide, leisurely steps toward the door, and his passage was marked by acquisitive eyes.

He was standing at the door, puzzling out a taxi sign that said EZIKIAS OKAZAWEFO DIST. CAB, when a voice behind him said, "Excuse me, but are you from Virginia or Maryland?"

He turned to look down on (in decreasing order of solidity) a gelid smile, two glistening eyes, and a number of other features so weak as to verge on invisibility, all belonging to a pale young man in a narrow white rayon shirt.

"Nope," he said genially. "I'm from a long way off."

"Are you really? Me, too!" said this young man solicitously. "Where from?"

"Out west."

"Isn't that funny? So am I! Where out west?"

"Northwest, really —"

"Isn't that a coincidence?"

"Up in the mountains —"

"— amazing —"

"— little place called Gouge Eye."

"I'm from not far away!"

The bus trip had tired Bob's eyes. No matter how he squinted, this odd, soft little fellow would not come into full focus. As soon as one feature was clear, another blurred, though in the middle of his pale face, always dominant, was that dazzling and secretive smile.

"Huh? You are?"

"You betcha! Say, isn't this great, meeting somebody from home!"

"Where-all exactly are you from again?"

"Oh, a little place, I'm sure you've never heard of it —"

"Try me, friend, I've hunted all over the valley."

"I live here now," the stranger said. "I'm Lightning. What's your name?"

"I'm Three-Finger Zardovsky. Say, did you go to Consolidated High? Seem like I've maybe seen your face."

"That's right — just for a little while. What a fascinating name. Where are you staying, Three-Finger?"

"Isn't that the goddamned question? Say, did you have old Miz Barefoot for your homeroom teacher?" Zardovsky was trying to remember where he had seen the stranger's face before and was encountering difficulty because he never had. He almost missed the next remark, which seemed so opportune that it was like the fairy tale where a talking fish gives the hero a wish.

"— seeing as how you're from near my home town, if you want to crash with us . . ."

"Are you kidding? Fuckin' A!"

Nothing rippled Lightning's smile after that, even when, as they were passing through the outer door into the rain, a plump, bearded young man ran up behind them, puffing heavily, and shouted, "Hey, buddy, don't go with him, he's an agent of a reactionary puppet exile regime!"

Lightning, not as weak as he appeared, urged Zardovsky firmly out the door.

"What was his problem?" Zardovsky asked.

"I think he's some kind of Communist," said Lightning, opening an umbrella. A battered Plymouth drove up; Lightning urged Zardovsky into the front seat, then pushed in after him so that the new arrival was wedged between Lightning and another young man in a similar white shirt. The car sped off in a strong perfume of motor oil. "This is Cloud," said Lightning. "Cloud, meet Three-Finger."

"What a fascinating name," said the driver.

"It ain't a patch on you guys," said Zardovsky. "I'll just hold on to that," he added to Lightning, who was helpfully trying to relieve him of his briefcase.

They turned onto a proud avenue that led past ruined buildings and weed-grown vacant lots, then prosperous office buildings, handsome embassies, and exclusive clubs. A streetlight halted them at a traffic circle. Around them slogged a miserable army of pedestrians, glaring at each other and at the sky. There was a sharp rap at the window. Lightning opened it slightly and a third young man, wearing a yellow rain slicker and a familiar smile, thrust in a thick manila folder. Lightning nodded slightly and rolled the window up. "What brings you to town, Three-Finger?" he asked, looking straight ahead.

"That's a long story."

"How fascinating," his companions both replied as the car lurched up a narrow street.

"Wait now, lemme tell you about it. Hell, if you went to Consolidated, I know you remember old Doc Pearman that used to run the mill?"

"How fascinating," said Lightning. "Here we are."

There was something delightfully familiar about the scene into which they disembarked. It was a broad, dirty street with scrubby boxed saplings at intervals along the sidewalk. Far-off sirens were wailing, and there was the distant echo of conga drums. Tin signs proclaimed the names of stores and cantinas: Mercato Caribe, Bodega, Rincon Habana, Casa Chiapas. Smudgy signs were stapled to the trees: ¡BOX! said one, and next to it another proclaimed, ¡GRAN MANO A MANO BAILABLE! *Intipuca City v. Billo's Bogota Boys!* He had stepped into the car in Washington, but he was getting out in Merida.

"This is our house," Lightning said with more pride than seemed strictly justified. SUNRISE HOUSE, as a sign proclaimed it to be, was a dingy, narrow, three-story brick structure crowned with turrets and merlons of brick. The lower windows were boarded over, and those higher up were crossed by iron bars. The tiny front yard was piled with bricks, wire, and dog droppings. VISI-TORS WELCOME said a sign across the bolted front door.

The dark front hall was full of smiling people of several sizes, who made soothing noises, proffered towels, and sought with eager hands to divest him of his rain parka and backpack. "Thanks," he said, "I'll just keep the briefcase."

Lightning presented a tall smile and a short one. "This is Open," he said, gesturing at a tall, bearded youth. "He's our elder brother."

"Sunrise welcomes you, Three-Finger."

The shorter smile belonged to a blond girl with plump cheeks and an underfed body, who to Zardovsky's surprise reached up and hugged him around the shoulders. "Welcome home, Three-Finger," she said warmly.

Zardovsky was touched. "You can call me Bob," he said.

"What a fascinating name."

"Sunshine will stay with you until lunch," Lightning said. "I've got to go back out."

Sunshine caught Zardovsky's arm and breathed, "Come into the New Living Room."

They sat on worn pillows and listened to the rain dripping. "Did that guy mention lunch?" Zardovsky asked.

"Plenty of time," Sunshine said vaguely. "What brings you to town, Bob?"

This time he got to tell the whole story. He began with old Doc's passing and worked forward, but Sunshine, who though skinny and pale was also a pleasant little bundle, watched him with her unwavering smile and whispered at every pause that it was fascinating. He began to warm to the material. The raindrops stopped drumming in his ears; his stomach fell silent; he led Sunshine — so interested, so admiring, so small and deferential and blond — through the history of the town, into the oil-and-sawdust reek of the mill, beside the still waters of the crater lake. So engrossed did he become in his tale that it came as an unwelcome interruption when a smiling woman put her head in the door and brightly called, "Lunchtime!"

But Zardovsky was a man of physical vigor and hearty appetite — qualities that have more than once saved their possessors from subtle spiritual traps. Nothing Sunshine said could keep him from noticing that his lunch was not enough to keep a cat alive. There was a dab of soggy brown rice, a few antisocial kidney beans, a despairing flap of lettuce, and an odd-tasting cup of fruit punch. "Is this all?" he asked in dismay.

Around him were three or four other wayfarers, each eating with a smiling, admiring friend. They seemed unaware of each other, lost in parallel firmaments of acceptance and love. "It's good for you, Bob," Sunshine said.

"You think I could get some more of these beans?"

Sunshine looked disappointed. "Rainbow's only cooked enough for us and the ones who are at work. Would you really want them to go without?"

Somehow he had been put in the wrong. But still, like Oliver Twist, Bob Zardovsky wanted more.

"Look!" cried Sunshine. "The rain is stopping!"

At that moment, with the cheerful light of an interior sun, Bob Zardovsky remembered the edibles stashed in his briefcase. This was to set off a major crisis in the odd household in which he had come to rest.

Zardovsky had begun to think he had had the good fortune to stumble into a nest of radicals on his first day in town. Radicals, he thought, would be secretive, purposeful, gregarious, and weird — and the people of Sunrise House were all of those. In addition there was the name, which suggested that they were involved in the movement for alternative sources of energy. But in fact the people of Sunrise House were not political activists but (in descending order of spiritual merit) priests, deacons, acolytes, and disciples of the Temple of Ray.

Little was known to the public of the doctrine and organization of this spiritual army. But one of its foremost elements was strict adherence to a set of dietary restrictions that banned almost every kind of food and allowed only small amounts of those that were licit. Most of the membership was constantly in a state of acute malnutrition. Newcomers were often induced to accept certain ideas they might have rejected on a full stomach; long-term disciples hardly noticed their hunger except for a dull ache that took the place of such habits of mind as doubt and critical thought. When Zardovsky had been welcomed into the commune, deft and holy fingers had searched his backpack; but his briefcase had so far escaped the examination. As he and Sunshine stepped onto the decrepit back porch, he casually fumbled out a chocolate bar.

Almost at once the atmosphere around him changed.

"Say, Bob —" Sunshine breathed. Saliva filled her mouth; she swallowed and began again. "Could I have — a piece — of that?"

"Sure you can, little darlin.'"

The candy disappeared between them. When it was gone, Bob Zardovsky gave a grunt of animal satisfaction and stepped into the wet spring sunshine. Meanwhile, inside his companion's brain a biochemical revolution was under way. Her blood sugar rose to unprecedented heights. Spots danced before her eyes; unearthly music filled her ears; buried memories and impulses stirred. Before her guilty, swimming eyes, she saw a handsome, large young man who seemed likely to possess courage, sensitivity, wisdom, and more food. It was not strange that these impressions combined into a brief stab of sexual attraction — nor that, in someone of Sunshine's mystical temperament, this feeling in turn masqueraded as awe and worship.

Thus was born the persistent heresy that Bob Zardovsky was not a washed-up ballplayer but an Angel of the Lord.

"Let's play *volleyball!*" cried a cheerful voice from the back door.

The other guests stumbled into the watery sunshine, each with a smiling, hungry ghost in close attendance. A scuffed volleyball appeared, skidding through the puddles of the flagstone yard.

Gay, faintly martial music tinkled from an upper window. The games began.

The Temple of Ray found its main congregation in the flabby children of the middle class, for whom the next few hours of strenuous exercise, punctuated with odd group cheers, chants, songs, and folk dancing, were designed to finish the work of the scanty lunch and the mesmeric attention; exhaustion and confusion would render these unfortunate pilgrims docile and receptive. But to Bob Zardovsky the sports were a mere physical distraction that freed his mind to make serious plans for the coming days. He planned to confer as soon as possible with Open, who was apparently the head radical. Tomorrow he would set out early and cover the government offices before nightfall. Figure a couple of days to get the paperwork straight, and there should be good news to report home by the weekend.

Bob Zardovsky was wrong about so many things.

Meanwhile the smiling acolytes ran and jumped and chanted and danced; everyone was having such a fine time, everyone was so happy and healthy and wise. One by one the troubled children in the Temple's net quieted and turned their thoughts to their new friends, wrapped in an ambiance of smiling interest and oddly ravenous love.

After the games, to the strains of soothing music, the players were led into the house. Like children at a strange, dingy day camp, they were separated, fed punch and cookies, distracted with games and toys, gentled and petted and soothed into delicious inactivity. But between Zardovsky and Sunshine there had occurred a subtle readjustment of roles. As evening shadows lengthened, they sat comfortably on the back porch. He was leaning against the splintery rail, whittling and thinking of nothing in particular; she, disobeying all her training, was telling him the story of her life.

Sunshine's story — an ordinary tale of lower-middle-class life culminating in banal but terrible spiritual catastrophe — was illuminated like a medieval manuscript with glowing angels, fiery demons, and odd flying objects. Her oblique account of Temple initiation practices had elements of interest. Her summary of instructions given to Temple members sent to work for the government might have explained in advance certain troubling later events. And her assessment of Open, her spiritual guide, was somewhat less than charitable.

But Zardovsky did not listen to a word she said. His years in Mexico had convinced him that verbal communication between men and women was often not only unnecessary but undesirable. He planned to direct careful attention toward Sunshine later. But for now he occupied himself with planning strategy, nodding his head whenever her voice paused and saying, "That sure is interesting."

"— and we were warned to beware of hypocrites and sepulchers and those who sacrifice with strange fire, for they are not sincere," Sunshine was saying. "And that's right on for sure, because we had this brother here in the nest who everybody thought was real sanctified and had wholly like cast off the cloak of his former life, but one night he woke us all up by shining his flashlight in our eyes and saying it was the Archangel Michael, and that was blasphemy for sure. So Open and Lightning took him into their room and you could hear him yelling all up and down the hall but they couldn't cast out the demon and he just kept returning to his folly like a dog to its vomit and the last state of that guy was worse than the first for sure. So Open had to send for Mr. Chin and he said we should put this brother in St. Elizabeth's because he was like wholly given up to foul practices and poor mental hygiene. I think Mr. Chin was real mad at Open because he warned us all against questioning the words of Ray which is the sin that hath like no forgiveness, and he said that Open —"

"*Sunshine!*" said an angry voice. Boring through the rusty mesh of the screen door were the angry eyes of Open himself, and below them his smile was twisting itself into grotesque and threatening forms. "Go inside and help Rainbow make the supper."

Mortally afraid, the little blonde darted through the door. Bob Zardovsky smiled and said, "That's a good idea, buddy, I need to talk some things over with you."

These words worried Open. The Temple of Ray was suffering from some internal disorganization. Headquarters — the Ninth Nest — was in Idaho, and as the Ninth Nest did not trust the telephone, all communication took place by short-wave radio. But the set was old and balky; for the past three weeks he had been out of communication with Idaho.

Meanwhile the Washington nest was undergoing unwelcome theological ferment. The incident that Sunshine had been relating to the heedless Zardovsky had been the culmination of a very serious challenge to Open's authority, and though it had ended happily, with the heretic in a barred ward, it had brought on Open the wrath and suspicion of some in the Ninth Nest. For weeks he had feared that they might send a messenger to tempt him, perhaps in disguise.

Though Zardovsky seemed an unlikely messenger, the universe in which Open lived was not an orderly world of probability but a jagged plain of omens, signs, flashes of revelation, and sudden, impenetrable darkness. Every event was scanned for its hidden significance, and now the elder was determined to discover — without revealing anything himself — the meaning of this unwelcome visitor.

"What do you want here?" he demanded coldly.

It was clear to Zardovsky that these radicals were suspicious of outsiders, who might be police informers. "Look, don't be worried. I know what's going on here," he said. "I'm not here to make trouble. Some mighty good folks out west sent me here with an important job to do."

The message was clear: the stranger was a messenger. One false step would be fatal. "I've been expecting you," Open lied.

"You have?"

"I got word from out west."

"How in hell . . . oh, it must be from that guy Lightning. I figured he had to know about it."

Open's face flushed with triumph and anger. He had given away nothing and had already learned something important: Lightning, his second-in-command, was in contact with Ninth Nest. He had trusted Lightning, and once again trust had been a mistake.

"Damn!" Zardovsky was saying. "It's good to have friends in this town! The way things are going, we'll get that money in no time!"

Again Open was learning valuable information. The operation

involved money. Until now the main activity of the Washington nest, aside from recruitment and selling wilted flowers, had been infiltrating government departments and stealing documents. Now the strategy must be changing. Something was up, all right, and Open could turn it to his advantage. "It is best we do not speak of these things now," he said. "You will join me for dinner tonight; after the Sharing, we will talk."

"Fuckin' A!" said Zardovsky. "I'm hungry as a hog, too! When do we eat?"

"I must first do a few needful things."

Open found Sunshine cowering in the fetid pantry.

"Little sister," Open said sternly, "what does Three-Finger have in his briefcase?"

Sunshine looked at Open's piercing eyes and was sure that he had discovered her fatal dalliance with chocolate. Her training and inclination were to throw herself at his feet, beg forgiveness, and weep bitterly. But the serpent tempted her again, and she fell.

"I don't know, elder brother," she said.

He smiled gently at her and said, "Sister, we need to know what's in that briefcase. I want you to take care of this man while he is with us. Do you understand me?"

In the delicate liturgical tongue of the Temple, Lightning had just ordered her to perform an office she had been chosen for before, when entertaining an important visitor from Ninth Nest or a particularly wealthy or prominent recruit. Temple prostitution, of course, is recorded in the most ancient of chronicles, but rarely could a priestess have accepted her duty more willingly than Sunshine. To have our most shameful desires suddenly sanctified by divine authority is an intoxication few mortals ever know.

Dinner was a severe disappointment to Bob Zardovsky. After the vegetable loaf and lentil soup, Open asked each newcomer to stand and share his name. Emboldened by the friendly atmosphere, Zardovsky stood and said, "I'm Three-Finger Zardovsky from Gouge Eye. I'm glad I found all you good folks, and with the help of my little buddy Open, here" — he warmly clasped the high priest by the shoulder — "I'm going to get some results for all the folks back home."

This impudent familiarity with the leader impressed the faithful and convinced the newcomers that Zardovsky had at least semiofficial status. As for Open, he was worried. This Zardovsky, or whatever his real name was, acted as if he knew a secret — and from this, for Open, it was a short step to concluding that he knew the only kind of secret worth knowing, that is, a secret about Open.

Now the room was darkened for Open's sermon; as he stood he distractedly considered his options. In plainer language than he used, here is a brief summary of his gospel:

Somewhere in Asia is a tiny landlocked people whose major activity has always been misinterpreting foreign ideas. In ancient times they eagerly adopted the Chinese state, with divine emperor, silk robes, Confucian etiquette, fireworks, and the binding of feet. But they omitted such elements as roads, taxes, armies, and schools. As a result they were frequently overrun by ill-mannered barbarians.

After the Second World War they adopted a version of democracy that included uncontested elections, mandatory voting, and freedom of speech enforced by torture and firing squad. More recently they had come under a version of communism that included animal sacrifices before pictures of Marx, hereditary succession to the party leadership, and reverent obeisance to the Politburo's food.

In the last years of the democracy, a young mission student somewhere in the upland savannas had brought the national genius to bear on Christianity. In the school library he had found the King James Bible, the works of the late Dale Carnegie, and several dog-eared volumes of popular science fiction. The young divine constructed a theology embracing all three and set forth to evangelize the world. Those who joined him were given much love, little food, and no freedom; they gave up such encumbrances as their names, their pasts, and any cash, securities, or bearer bonds. They lived in squalor and millennial hope, and all present were cordially invited to join.

At an early stage of the homily Zardovsky lost consciousness.

Many in the congregation were in a light doze, a state that enhanced the force and beauty of Open's words. But Zardovsky, exhausted by his travels and the meager meals, plunged directly into

a plenary sleep. His dreams on scented wings carried him to
Mexico again, where, on a sweltering July night, he was holding
Tapachula to one hit in seven innings. He felt the humid breeze
on his arms, smelled tortillas and beans from the grandstand,
heard the home crowd exhorting the batter to knock the big
gringo out of the box. Cars honked in the distance, and from
beyond the bullpen came the cackles of fowl, who from time to
time interrupted play by wandering into left field and pecking at
the outfielders. Zardovsky had fallen behind the Tapachula Terror, "Hubba Hubba" Hernandez, on a count of three and one. So
there were two choices: the spitter, or go for the head. But his
mouth was dry. Then a hand from behind the mound shook him
and someone said, "May you never thirst, Three-Finger."

"Say what?" Coming awake in the stuffy dining room, he
rubbed his gummy eyelids and blinked.

"Share the water of life," said Open's voice.

"Yeah, thanks a lot," Zardovsky said. With one gulp he dis-
patched the chalice of holy water that had been consecrated for
the entire group.

An appalled silence followed.

Zardovsky rubbed his face, yawned again, and looked at the
solemn congregation, who were regarding him variously with
indignation, puzzlement, and fear.

"This party is dying fast," he said. "Come on, Sunshine, we got
to do something about this."

He led the priestess toward the front door. Open rushed to
block his path, but Zardovsky, assuming that his friend wanted to
pay for part of his beer run, disabled the elder with a good-
natured slap on the back. Clutching his briefcase in one hand, he
led Sunshine into the rain-washed city street.

Down the block was a small glass-fronted store with a sign that
read CHONG'S BODEGA Y GOURMET SHOPPE. When they entered, a
small Oriental man came hurtling from behind the meat counter,
pointing an accusing finger at Sunshine and screaming, "Out! I
tell you before, stay out! Alla you Temple creeps stay away! Get
out or I call cops!"

"Whoa up, cowboy," said Zardovsky genially. "You musta got
me mixed up with some other four-fingered lumberjack."

"You come from Temple?"

"Hell, no, I'm not even Jewish. I been eating with the folks at that solar-energy house down the block."

"I knew it! Temple! I know you bastards from way back!"

"Look, friend, you're getting a little worked up about all this. I just want some beer and Fritos and stuff to take to my buddies back there."

"You take beer to Temple?" The little man seemed richly amused by this notion. He began scurrying around the aisles with them, laughing quietly. Soon they had assembled three cases of Miller High Life, two giant bags of Fritos, a half-gallon of assorted bean and sour-cream dips, five jars of salted peanuts, and six enormous Hershey bars that Sunshine seemed to find irresistible. As Zardovsky signed his traveler's check, the little grocer added three quart bottles of pink wine, saying, "This onna house. Little present from Chong."

The refreshments made the evening. Temple members were magnetically drawn to the high-carbohydrate snacks, and the prospective converts lined up for beer, which Zardovsky dispensed with the blessing, "This'll cure your thirst for sure." Several recruits regained their senses and departed forever, others threw up, and still others fell asleep. Among the faithful, the food and the blasphemous alterations made to their eucharistic service gave rise to a spirit of theological excitement bordering on orgy. Buried doctrinal disputes and personal quarrels surfaced in a welter of acrimonious Biblical citations. Much of the anger centered on Open's strict conduct as elder brother — so much, indeed, that when the elder ordered an end to this heretical riot, no one obeyed him or even acknowledged his presence.

Pity Open; he felt as Moses must have when he saw the Israelites dancing around the golden calf. After ten years in the Temple, his mind had become a dim place, a haunted tower of shadowed cul-de-sacs, crumbling stairways, clouded mirrors, and hidden passages. Zardovsky was his private nightmare — a stranger with powers greater than his who would dethrone him from his place of power.

Overmastered by the stranger, spurned by his flock, Open repaired, like Moses, to the mountaintop, or more properly to the communications room, a dark, blind closet on the top floor where the war-surplus short-wave radio set squatted uselessly on a table. The radio had died some weeks ago, but Open still from time to time turned the set on in hopes that a miracle might have restored it to service. Lights came on; there was a hum, but there was no signal. He could not call the Ninth Nest.

At length, in the extremity of fear and desperation, Open tried the radical measure of talking to God directly in timeless terms. *Oh Lord,* cried his soul, *what would you have me do?*

Perhaps Heaven, unable to help Open directly, sent him for consolation the dull, dreamless sleep that stole over him while downstairs the apostates danced around the maypole.

When he woke again, it was a few minutes before dawn. He crawled to the door. The stranger must be sleeping now, and off his guard. If prayer would not serve Open, cunning must. Shoeless, he tiptoed down the stairs. In the New Living Room the faint glow of a streetlight glinted off the scratched clasp of Zardovsky's briefcase; next to it was a dark mass: Zardovsky, sleeping in a heap, one arm clasping a well-fed, well-satisfied Sunshine.

It was Open's chance; but luck was not with the elder. As he fumbled with the clasp, he felt a large though incomplete hand clutching his collar.

Bob Zardovsky knew how to handle thieves. Cursing loudly in the half-darkness, he dribbled the intruder like a basketball, strode with him to the front door, and hurled him bodily off the porch, over the scrubby hedge, and onto the dirty sidewalk.

He turned to see the acolytes of the Temple, unsteady on their feet and sketchily dressed, peering silently at him. "Somebody wake up that guy Open," he said. "A burglar got into the house, and he was trying to steal my stuff."

"That was Open," said Sunshine, with a faint note of satisfaction. "You just threw him over the hedge."

Zardovsky peered at the elder brother, elbows and dignity in tatters, moaning moistly on the pavement. Dimly he began to realize that this episode might complicate his efforts to enlist Open's help. "Is that right?" he said. "Who would of thought Open was a burglar?"

He tucked in his shirt and retrieved his jacket and backpack.

The light was beginning to rise on the gray neighborhood. "I gotta get some breakfast," he said. "I'll check you later."

Hearing the word *breakfast*, Sunshine ran forward, close to tears. "I want to come with you," she said.

Zardovsky only smiled, kissed her lightly on the forehead, and uttered one of mankind's most venerable false prophecies. "I'll see you real soon, honey," he said, and set off in the dirty urban dawn.

Chapter 3

BEFORE HIS ELECTION THE PRESIDENT, an obscure provincial official, had promised to reorganize the federal government along unspecified modern lines. After the inauguration he had sent forth like doves a crew of Ivy League MBAs to reconnoiter the moldering federal mansion — to open the closets, cupboards, attics, and vaults, inventory the decaying contents, and then rearrange them in more pleasing order.

These emissaries had swept, dusted, stacked, chopped, lopped, reupholstered, and rearranged what they found, shifting whole suites of antique furniture from room to room, adding several imposing new wings and fire escapes, and demolishing one or two drafty old towers. But as so often happens during housecleaning, a certain disorder began to creep into the process at about the halfway point. Various oddments, curios, sundries, and knick-knacks — in fact, even a few forgotten houseguests long ensconced in undesirable bedrooms — began to collect in awkward heaps. Among this debris were offices with no known function, surviving divisions of defunct agencies, boards created by dead Presidents to handle forgotten emergencies, and some organizations arising from causes so long forgotten that no one could remember a time when they had not been or a reason why they still should be.

The reorganizers had opened a commodious closet, stashed the rubbish in it, and locked the door. Thus was Gerald's Department born.

The Secretary was a retired Air Force general whose career had followed the postwar pattern of upward failure. As a major in Vietnam, he had led his squadron in a picture-perfect air attack that had utterly destroyed an undefended farm village densely populated with peasants loyal to the Saigon government. "We have been forced to attack our friends," he said in a widely quoted aphorism, "because we couldn't find the enemy."

His superiors had promoted him to colonel and assigned him to command an obscure missile base where, it was devoutly hoped, he would never be heard from again. But two years later one of the superannuated missiles under his command had exploded, burning 140 acres of prairie and hurling its nuclear warhead into the rec room of the bachelor officers' quarters. Before a congressional committee, the colonel blamed the disaster on declining standards in U.S. high schools.

The colonel had been promoted to general and given responsibility for a five-year, multibillion-dollar effort to develop the world's first plutonium-powered helicopter. On its maiden flight the prototype had soared to an altitude of sixty yards, turned gracefully upside down, and plowed into the desert. Several minor Indian tribes downwind had been largely obliterated by the gas plume. Taking off his uniform, the general had repaired to that modern monastery, the academic research institute, where he wrote an article blaming this catastrophe on a failure of national will.

Political figures, who often lack the time and inclination to read books, are sometimes profoundly moved by articles, particularly those that are short and make sweeping charges with a minimum of documentation. The general's article found its way into the hands of the President-elect, and his appointment followed.

The Secretary spent most of his time placing Department field representatives in U.S. embassies in Warsaw Pact nations. From them he received dozens of obscurely worded cables almost every day. This sort of diffident executive behavior is far from unknown in official Washington. To deal with it, management specialists have devised the deputy system. Just as each human body has a soul, each key government official has a deputy who can exercise the powers of office in the absence, boredom, or abject stupidity of his or her superior.

There are three sorts of deputies. The first is appointed to work beneath a politically connected chief who has little interest in or qualification for his job. This type of deputy is career-minded, self-effacing, and nonpolitical; he keeps things running, avoids disaster, and thinks up plausible explanations for the ignorant policies handed down from above. When these policies fail, this type of deputy is blamed, denounced, and fired, going on to obscure but lucrative work in private industry.

The second type is named to work beneath the occasional chief who is actually qualified for his job. Such an appointee must be balanced by a deputy who can be counted on to spy upon, confuse, and impede his superior at every opportunity. When policies fail, this type of deputy becomes an ambassador to a nonaligned nation or a candidate for the House of Representatives.

The third type of deputy combines the disadvantages of the first two. He or she is someone who must be given a job of some kind because of political credentials, but who lacks qualifications for any job at all. These deputies are stuck randomly on the underside of the bureaucracy like lumps of chewing gum, where they dry and harden. When policies fail, they must usually be scraped off.

The Deputy Secretary was of this third type. He had pursued a career on Wall Street, then given it up to pursue his passion for conservation. He had moved back to his native New Hampshire, where he had raised $200,000 for an obscure provincial candidate who had a sound position on the prothonotary warbler. After the election he had confidently put in his name for administrator of the Environmental Protection Agency, then deputy administrator, and so on down until he was at last jammed into Gerald's Department, where he spent his time peering out of his office windows through binoculars.

The Assistant Secretary for Evaluation, Training, and Morale, Gerald's nominal superior, had served two terms as mayor of Magic City, Kentucky. One day he had received a visit at the town hall from an emissary from the White House, who conveyed the President's personal invitation to consider a candidacy for the U.S. House of Representatives in the off-year election. With the support of the White House, the stranger suggested, the mayor should better the party's traditional showing in that district considerably.

And so he had. Instead of the usual third of the vote, the mayor had received nearly forty percent. Soon after, the same emissary had appeared in an air-conditioned pickup to offer the ex-mayor a key role in the creation of a new cabinet department. So, like the hero who traded his cow for a handful of magic beans, the ex-mayor had found himself unexpectedly and with mixed feelings transported to a wild and mysterious land.

The Assistant Secretary was conscientious, according to his lights. When he happened to be at his desk, he read any letter or statement written for his signature. When it contained figures, he checked the arithmetic; when there were names, he checked their spellings; when it contained the words "I feel," he changed them to read "I think." But early in his tenure he had found in the departmental budget a line item for "site visits" by senior officials to departmental field offices, and he had quietly decided that now was his chance to fulfill a childhood ambition of visiting all the states and Guam.

The Deputy Assistant Secretary for Evaluation, Training, and Morale was a woman named Nancy Quoin, proud holder of a B.A. in communications and a master's in business administration, and for two and a half years coauthor of the popular column "My Status, Myself," in *Bosslady* magazine.

Below these appointees, and occasionally in contact with them, was a large and diverse swarm of career civil servants grouped variously in offices, bureaus, sections, task forces, and administrations. There were clerks, typists, receptionists, messengers, guards, mail sorters; budget analysts, policy analysts, economic analysts; equal employment opportunity specialists, minority contract compliance specialists, publications specialists; environmental impact technicians, administrative law judges, hearing officers, referees, and masters; educational administrators, professional educators, and adjunct faculty; psychologists, psychiatrists, and social workers; public affairs officers, public relations officers, community relations officers, minority relations officers, congressional relations officers, and the few forlorn employees of the Inspector General's office, who walked to and from the cafeteria in a group to avoid assault.

This diverse staff wrote handbooks, periodicals, guides, and brochures; compiled rosters, analyses, and statistical abstracts; issued guidelines, suggestions, and criteria; accepted comments and interventions; held meetings, conferences, and workshops; issued press releases and held media briefings; developed policy guidance; issued advisory and binding opinions; granted technical assistance; disbursed grants, allocations, and subsidies, audited the grantees and recipients thereof, and sometimes demanded refunds, penalties, and interest; brought, defended, and settled civil actions; demanded and distributed rebates; administered direct- and block-grant programs, and conducted public, community, foreign, and inter- and intragovernmental relations. And yet of all of them, only one could be said to have been a figure of importance: Baxter Muntin, director of the Office of Personnel and Program Evaluation (OPPE).

This resplendent personage was known by name to perhaps twenty people outside the federal government, yet all twenty agreed that he was the most powerful person in the division. Among other things, he was responsible for the odd organization and swollen size of the division, which had originally been planned as a small administrative addendum to the office of the Deputy Secretary. But when the new Department was begun, the Secretary-designate, who had known Baxter Muntin when both were at the Pentagon, asked him to assume command of assembling its lost bureaucratic tribes, bringing them forth from dusty basements, dry archives, and forgotten annexes to the Department's commodious but dingy new headquarters.

The office Muntin had picked for himself was sandwiched safely in the middle of the largest division of the entire Department, buffered by its own assistant secretary and charged with a mission so muddled that no one would know it was failing to perform it.

It was located in its own wing of the building, farthest of all from the Secretary's office, so that prying political appointees would seldom venture there.

In short, under Muntin's skilled stewardship, the Division of Evaluation, Training, and Morale had assumed the form of one of the larger, less intelligent dinosaurs: it had a pea-sized brain in the tiny, vulnerable head and a larger, more influential cortex in the padded, impervious rump.

It was to the small head of the dinosaur that Gerald Nash repaired on the gusty spring morning two days after his dinner engagement with Margaret Luck. He had slept at home and breakfasted with Willys Handleman on instant coffee, gossip, and the morning papers. It was well past nine as he strolled down the sad corridors to the Assistant Secretary's suite, at the far end of which he had his own office (reached through a featureless frosted-glass door that bore the painted image of a hand and the words "Enter through 409," indicating the janitor's closet).

This morning his tidy desk was disfigured by pink message slips scattered across it like autumn leaves, which said in no particular order, "Ms. Quoin called"; "Call Nancy Quoin"; "NQ must see you ASAP," and so on, all with the same grim import.

Gerald did not rate even partial custody of a secretary. The Assistant Secretary had offered to let Gerald share his, but Ruby Fentress considered Gerald a personal affront aggravated by the insult of being asked to take his telephone messages. Thus even before arriving he had begun the day in ill favor with Ruby.

Storm warnings from the Deputy Assistant Secretary were always a bad sign. Gerald sighed as he thought of the morning ahead. But dealing with Nancy Quoin was (insofar as the term had any meaning) his job.

His intercom buzzed angrily, like a bee trapped in a jar. "It's *that woman* on line two," Ruby's voice hissed.

"Thanks, Ruby."

"Oh, don't mention it. I'm sure I don't have anything else to do."

Nancy Quoin's voice filled the line. "Glad you could make it to work," she said. "Would you mind stepping around to my office?"

Quoin's office had two windows, doubling the amount of airshaft in view. Almost every available inch was filled with the curling, delicate fronds and tendrils of green plants, ferns, and herbs in earthenware pots. After a few minutes in the verdant jungle twilight, however, a newcomer's eye might also have picked out a large sign thanking visitors for not smoking, a framed signed photograph of the President, and a tattered poster that began "Go placidly amid the noise and haste . . ."

Upon Gerald's arrival, Quoin lunged at him across her desk like a starving wolverine, barking, "Have you seen what that bastard is doing now?"

"Which bastard is it today?"

"Very funny. Verrry funny. You know goddamned well I mean your drinking buddy Baxter Muntin. That son of a bitch! Why do I have to put up with this shit?"

The source of these ripe oaths was an oddly demure figure. Nancy Quoin was a slender, youthful-looking woman. Below her flaring nostrils, brown hair, and red-rimmed hazel eyes, she wore a pale beige blouse with matching bow at the neck, a plaid skirt with ornamental brass pin, and tasseled loafers. The effect was that of a convent-school senior who had spent her summers in the merchant marine.

The offending memo had been sent under the initials of Muntin. It described procedures to be followed by OPPE personnel seeking approval of travel requests. The division's travel budget was strained, it explained (though it did not explain that most of the strain came from the Assistant Secretary's expeditions). Accordingly, vouchers were to be submitted in advance and in triplicate to Muntin, whose office would ensure that they met a new series of criteria, outlined in items 1 through 19 of the enclosed sheet. It seemed unexceptionable, even praiseworthy, to Gerald.

"What's the problem with this, Nancy?" he asked mildly.

"This travel downhold is my project and those vouchers ought to come here, and you know it and so does your friend Muntin."

"To tell you the truth, I didn't know that."

"We decided it at the senior staff meeting last month. I sent you a memo."

"I must have forgotten, then."

"Maybe Muntin just forgot too. But I doubt it. That bastard

never forgets anything. This time he's pushed me too far. I'm going to the AS with this."

"I'm not really sure the AS wants to deal with this," said Gerald with considerable understatement. In fact, a large part of his job involved forestalling Quoin's frequent threats to storm into her superior's office during his infrequent visits, which he preferred to keep tranquil.

"I'll write Muntin a memo and copy you and the AS, then."

"Look, Nancy, do we have to go the whole memo route on this? Muntin is a genius at memos. He'll snow us all under, and the AS will be on my — on our backs about it. I tell you what. I've got a meeting with him at eleven-thirty. Why don't you let me bring it up with him, just feel him out a little?"

"You've got a meeting with him?" Her face was suspicious and alert. "What's that all about?"

"It's an interim report from something called the Fungibility Task Force. The AS wants me to develop some guidance about it before it comes up with Hench. Why don't you sit in? We'd be glad to get your input too."

"I'd love to, Gerald, but I'm just snowed under with the travel vouchers from the other offices." Quoin scurried away from anything that smelled like controversy. Travel vouchers, being at once important and completely routine, were the sort of task that filled her days. "So you'll talk to Muntin?" she continued.

"I'll see if I can work it out."

At this, Nancy Quoin brought into operation her smile, a high-wattage cold-light unit that she considered the most powerful tool in her equipment locker. "That's marvelous," she said. "But Gerald, I hope you'll be tactful about this. Don't go charging in and throw your weight around. I'm trying to nurture a more positive atmosphere around here."

And so Gerald Nash left, having agreed to do what he had originally intended to do, leaving Nancy Quoin congratulating herself on having manipulated him into doing it.

In the Assistant Secretary's anteroom, Ruby was holding a brightly colored postcard. "Greetings from Turkey Bend, Ark.," it said. Gerald assumed this was her regular set of instructions from the Assistant Secretary. "Anybody call me?" he asked warily.

"Some *girl*." Ruby sniffed. "She couldn't be bothered to leave a name."

Gerald decided to return Margaret's call after lunch. "I've got a meeting with Baxter Muntin," he said. "I'll be back after lunch."

Muntin's office suite had no windows at all; he used this sacrifice to justify its size, which dwarfed that of the Assistant Secretary's suite. In his outer office this morning sat a pale woman of indeterminate age, with drab brown clothes and watery pink eyes.

"Where's Mrs. Mills?" Gerald asked.

"Who?"

"The lady who usually works here."

"Oh, yeah, for sure. She's sick or something like that."

"I see. I'm Gerry Nash. You're . . ."

"Filling in for that other lady."

"I know that. I meant your name."

"I'm . . . Gloria. I'm Gloria." She buzzed her boss. "There's some guy here to see you. I'm going to send him in."

Muntin's private office contained a matching wall set of American and departmental flags; a small bronze replica of the Iwo Jima Memorial; framed citations from seven patriotic, civic, and veterans' organizations; a blond wood desk and matching coffee table; thirteen keepsake ashtrays; a scale-model prototype turbine-powered battle tank with cigarette lighter and weather radio inside; a dark leatherette couch; a handsome breakfront jammed with budget documents; framed photographs of the President (small), the Secretary (larger), and the chairman of the House Appropriations Committee (largest of all); and a file cabinet containing a bottle of unblended Scotch whisky and six glasses. Behind the desk, oozing self-assurance, good will, and cigarette smoke, sat Baxter Muntin himself.

Muntin was a man of slightly above medium height, wearing a gray suit and matching thin gray-brown hair. His stomach had swelled above and below the waistband of his trousers, but there was nothing to account properly for the impression of size but his unusual degree of contentment, animation, and amour propre.

He hustled Gerald to a chair and flung him into it with a motion of the wrist. "May I offer you something?" he asked, hovering massively. "A cigarette? No? A cup of coffee? A glass of ginger ale? A cracker?" Like the ancient god of the underworld, Muntin believed that a guest who had eaten or drunk under his roof would be his forever. Gerald asked for coffee.

Muntin stepped to the door and called, "Gloria, my dear? Yes, you. Would you mind stepping down to the cafeteria and getting Mr. Nash a cup of coffee? And ask the gentlemen in the conference room if they'd like anything, would you?"

He paced behind his desk and sat down. "The gentlemen from the Fungibility Task Force are setting up in the conference room," he said comfortably. "How much do you know about this particular vital arm of the Department's doings?"

"Almost nothing."

"I was in that blissful state myself until I sent one of my people out to the Records Center. It took him three days and he nearly died of microfilm shock, but he got the goods." Muntin delicately realigned the keepsakes on his desk, like a general readying for battle. "Gerald, do you know what is the major difference between economics and everything else?"

"Money, I guess."

"Brilliant! It's the concept of money — the fact that a dollar in your pocket is the same dollar as it is if it's in my pocket. You can spend it, I can spend it, anyone can spend it for anything they want. And that means money is fungible — transferable, interchangeable, nondifferentiated. So a whole mathematics can be built around it. Do you follow so far?"

"Yes, as far as it goes."

"You're quite right to be skeptical, because as soon as we leave the marketplace, all this ease of transfer disappears. Perhaps I cherish the clean air of my home town, while you cherish your job as a steelworker. These desires may conflict. How do we solve these conflicts? By an orderly mathematical process? No! By a clumsy, unpredictable, subjective process —"

"You mean politics?"

"Just so — all this fanfaronade on Capitol Hill. Economists have concluded that if they could find a mathematical way to reconcile these conflicts, politics wouldn't be necessary anymore. So fifteen years ago, they persuaded the government to set up the

Ad Hoc Fungibility Study Group. This in turn became the Fungibility Working Group, the Fungibility Feasibility Study, and finally the Fungibility Task Force. In the interim the originators of the idea have died or come to their senses, the original commissioning agency has been abolished, and to us has fallen the privilege of evaluating the preliminary report of the task force."

"After fifteen years?"

"You young people are always impatient. We have to brief our superiors on whether to continue with the project or send it to the Records Center, never to return. Try not to fall into a coma and to ask a minimum of one question. These gentlemen have come a long way to brief us, at government expense. We damn well owe it to our country to be briefed. Come along, Gerald."

In the green-paneled conference room, Muntin introduced the members of the task force. Professor Farben was head of the Center for Creative Social Science; he wore a close beard and plastic-rimmed glasses so large he seemed about to jump through them and land on the table, croaking academic jargon. Dr. Trivet, a psychoeconometric consultant to one of the Department's more obscure bureaus, carried a fringed buckskin briefcase that went well with his tailored suede leisure suit and driftwood pipe. Mrs. Guttmacher, who studied communications and public-policy interface for a market-research firm, was unavoidably absent on a sabbatical to research political advertising in Peru. At the head of the group, glowing with parental pride, was Henry Palmer, a fresh-faced economist from OPPE's Impact Projection Branch and *ex officio* secretary of the task force.

Palmer presented each visiting savant, summarizing his background and recent accomplishments. The visitors treated Gerald with delicious deference, complimenting him on his tender age, elite education, and experience with the Equine Defense Fund.

As the meeting convened, Gloria reappeared, balancing cups of coffee and doughnuts, which she was regarding with horrified distaste. Her delivery of refreshments was somewhat cavalier; though Dr. Trivet assured the group that a competent dry-cleaner could remove most of the stains on his suede suit, the drenching of Professor Farben's notes gave a slightly disjointed air to his subsequent presentation.

In summary form, that presentation was as follows:

1. *Historical review of fungibility concept:* Early attempts rudimentary: Mosaic code's "eye for eye, tooth for tooth," etc. Progress of mankind (interruption from Dr. Trivet to point out that task force had agreed to nonsexist language in draft document; reply by Dr. Farben that he personally did not regard *mankind* as a sexist usage; hastily interrupted by Mr. Palmer) thus conceptualized as progress from non-, a-, or infungibility ("barbarism") to fungibility ("civilization"). Review of economic thought on this concept from Adam Smith to Hayek and Galbraith; Prof. Farben encounters increased difficulty reading notes.

2. *Fungibility in everyday life:* Popular sayings embody notion: "six of one, half a dozen of the other," "all the same to me," "grist for the mill," etc. Slide presentation of rudimentary fungibility systems already in use, e.g., dollar signs, smile faces, forks in restaurant reviews.

3. *Alternative models independent of fungibility concept:* Ruined beyond recall by coffee stains.

4. *Conclusions:* Fungibility is a social good and its extension is a central task of enlightened government.

5. *Recommendations:* Five-year Fungibility Project (FP) with staff of thirty-eight, budget of $13.7 million in constant dollars, leading administrative role for Henry Palmer, hefty contracts for all present. Objective: Computerized "fungibility index," updated constantly on real-time basis, containing state-of-the-art numerical index capable of reducing any complex decision to three nine-digit numbers.

6. *General feeling of personnel at conclusion of this phase of project:* Positive. Grateful. Eager for challenge ahead.

7. *Reaction of group to presentation:* Profound silence broken by rumble from stomach of Mr. Muntin.

8. *Question asked by Mr. Muntin:* Whether constant-dollar budget projection not slightly optimistic. Answer in negative. Questioner referred to supplementary documentation, citing expected dollar benefits to follow from increased fungibility dissemination. Implementation proposals include computer terminals in departmental field offices giving readouts on as-needed basis to federal, state, local governments, private industry, nonprofit sec-

tor. Delicate suggestion advanced that this will improve visibility and public acceptance of Department. Mr. Muntin's stomach rumbles again.

9. *Question asked by Mr. Nash:* Whether popular saying "You can't compare apples and oranges" illustrates opposing counterfungible tendency. Energetically refuted by Dr. Trivet, who suggests that proverb in fact represents affirmation by denial. Begins disquisition on "blood from turnips"; hastily concludes when Mr. Muntin offers to send out for coffee. Group adjourns.

"Good God," said Gerald reverently when he and Muntin were alone again. "What a turkey that thing is! Can you imagine what Hench would do to the AS at a hearing on that line-item?"

Muntin's smile was unusually generous and complacent. "Are you acquainted with Bernard Weisman?"

"Hench's LA? Yeah, I know him. He gave me a hotfoot at a panel just this week. Who do you think I'm worried about?"

"It may interest you to know that Weisman prevailed upon the Congressman to read Samuelson's *Economics* over the winter. I'm not sure Hench's read a book since Ian Fleming died; this one has had an enormous impact on his thinking. Weisman tells me that his boss is deeply interested in this project."

"Well, somebody would still have to sell it to the Secretary's office."

"Whatever Buster wants, Buster gets — within reason, of course. How about a cup of coffee?"

"Good God, no! Where did you dig up that space cadet, anyway?"

Muntin chuckled. "She is an unusual specimen, no doubt about that. She seems to have trouble remembering her own name —"

"I noticed that too."

"— but she is the temporary secretary assigned to me, and it would be unprofessional of me to quibble. It's a sacrifice we civil servants have to make, Gerald. It wouldn't happen in private industry. It wouldn't be *permitted* in private industry. They follow a ruthless standard in private industry, Gerald." Muntin tapped the ash from his cigarette with a delicate movement of his spatulate fingers. "But I could not speak harshly to that young lady if, God forgive me, I wanted to. And as for firing her, Gerald, you know how hard it is to fire a junior civil servant."

"Or, for that matter, a senior executive."

"Of course, of course," Muntin agreed. "But there are other things you can do to a senior executive. You could thrust him into, let's say, a chaotic situation, you could tie his hands, you could second-guess him endlessly and subject him to abusive and petty criticism from above. Which reminds me, do you have something else you wanted to talk to me about?"

Muntin had a preternatural talent for knowing when Gerald was on a mission from Nancy Quoin. "That's a tough introduction to follow, Baxter," Gerald said.

"I was speaking hypothetically, of course."

"Of course. Well, changing the subject entirely, the DAS is very anxious that everybody on the senior staff follow up on the procedures established in last month's staff meeting."

"Okay, it's the travel vouchers, is it?"

"Yes."

Muntin levered himself out of his chair and paced to the breakfront. "Gerald," he said plaintively, "when I took on this assignment, it was my understanding that the Assistant Secretary and his senior staff would, after a period of orientation, move on in God's good time to the arena of policy, which is the area for which senior appointees are uniquely suited. The mundane running of the office, I supposed, would be left to career civil servants. Was that so terribly naive on my part?"

"Baxter, no one wants to take over your job. It's a question of style —"

"Style! Merciful God! If it's a question of style, of course I can't hope to compete with the DAS. What a woman! So elegant — and what a command of the language! Why, some of the things she's said to me I haven't heard since I left the Marine Corps! But you know, I have to wonder how this office is going to function if I can't send my secretary to the water cooler without a note from the principal."

Fuming and smoking, Muntin padded across the gray office carpet, raising a supplicatory hand to heaven. "What next?" he asked. "Hall passes? Mandatory phys. ed.? Where is it all going to end?"

"Baxter, you're overdramatizing. After all, these procedures were worked out at the senior staff meeting —"

"That drum-head court-martial! Who was there? Just the Iron Lady and us helpless bureaucrats! She just talked about nurturing and humanism until she had rammed every point down our throats. Gerald," he said, looming over Gerald's chair with an accusing finger, "if I weren't a gentleman, or if she were, well, long before now I would have —"

"Sit, Baxter, sit," Gerald urged, moving out of reach. "Can't we work something out? Isn't there anything you feel good about sending her?"

Muntin dropped into his chair. "You know, Gerald," he said, "if I were to send her all the travel vouchers that come through this office, she'd suspect me of faking them. We clear dozens a week — Richmond, Baltimore, Philadelphia, Atlantic City, Martinsburg, and so on. Nickel-and-dime stuff. What she wants is the major expenses, am I right?"

"I'm not so sure of that."

"So what I'll do is issue an update to my memo announcing that major trips will require her signature. How's that?"

Those long-distance, big-ticket trips would worry Nancy Quoin the most, for they could become targets of newspaper columnists or congressional investigators. For the second time that day, Gerald Nash had the sensation of seeing the person in front of him maneuver, with the agonizing roars of a professional wrestler, into a position prepared long in advance.

"Just tell her I'm redrawing the policy. Then I'll send her my substitute. Maybe she'll want to change it later. We'll see." Muntin delicately ground out his cigarette. "Gerald, what would you say to a little lunch?"

The two passed companionably out of the office. True, Gerald had not achieved everything Nancy Quoin wanted. But he had averted open warfare between appointee and civil servant, feminist and sexist, veteran and pacifist, new consciousness and old bureaucracy. It was his job.

A few minutes later, the office door swung halfway open; the dim light revealed a narrow, wedge-shaped face with a fixed smile and a pair of lifeless eyes. Then the door swung shut, and Gloria, Muntin's temporary secretary, stood in the darkness, gurgling faintly. Gloria was not the name she had been born under. Her friends at the Temple of Ray called her Daybreak.

Still in the dark, this hungry ghost dashed to the file cabinet, which opened with a clatter of glassware and was hastily closed. There was a panicky scuffling, as of someone feeling along unfamiliar surfaces, then footsteps, and again the half-light from the door, revealing Daybreak leaving the room at high speed, carrying Baxter Muntin's fat leather briefcase.

Open's Washington nest had a special mission: to pilfer every government document it could. The objective was to deflect a huge conspiracy against Ray himself. It had begun with the Internal Revenue Service, which had demonically blocked tax-exempt status for the Temple's kosher delicatessens in Chicago, then had spread to the Immigration and Naturalization Service, led by the Evil One to question certain statements on Ray's visa application. The perceived plot included the Justice Department, the National Institute of Mental Health, the Federal Aviation Administration, the Central Intelligence Agency, the National Weather Service, the U.S. Coast and Geodetic Survey, and, in its most shadowy and terrifying reaches, Gerald's Department.

A federal worker attracts little attention carrying sheaves of papers, which can often be copied and returned before they are missed. But in her befuddlement, Daybreak had taken the case itself, which could be swiftly missed and easily traced to her. She quailed under the bored gaze of the departmental security guard at the front entrance. The spring breeze seemed to echo the shrilling of police whistles. She began running toward the subway, intending to take a train uptown and give her burden to an elder. But then she saw, coming from the station with another briefcase, a figure she loved and respected. Surely this was a sign from heaven. Without a word she thrust her burden on him and fled.

Bob Zardovsky was startled when a young woman came running up, hurled a briefcase into his arms, and disappeared into the crowd. He tried to dash after her, but the case crashed against his left leg and threw him sideways into the path of a party of Japanese orthodontists, who wobbled and crashed around him like duckpins. "Sorry, sorry, excuse me," he muttered as they ceremoniously helped him to his feet; by the time they had finished bowing, the fugitive had disappeared.

This was only the latest in a series of confusing events. Many things, large and small, puzzled Bob Zardovsky about the capital. There was the subway, with fare machines that one needed computer skills to operate; there was the confusing street layout, which doubled certain streets and quadrupled others, while the grand avenues angled in and out, appearing and vanishing into circles and cul-de-sacs. But most puzzling of all was the difficulty he encountered in meeting or speaking to anyone actually involved with the government. The United States seemed to be run by an entity as elusive as the Jesuit God — everywhere at once and yet nowhere in particular, impossible to converse with or interrogate.

At the first office on his list, the responsible official was "on travel status"; at the second the entire staff was at a training seminar in Virginia; and the third had ceased to exist.

He was going to Gerald's Department when the stranger thrust upon him the briefcase — a case of sleek maroon leather, with the initials B.L.M. inscribed on a brass plate below the combination lock. As he examined it, the Japanese tourists began taking his photograph, as if he were a monument or a cherry tree. On one side of the case was a frayed paper airline baggage label with the cryptic legend "B.L.Muntin, Diroppe, Fall N304A, D.C." This Fall Building was the address he had been given for his destination, something called the ETM division.

Bob Zardovsky decided to return this briefcase. No such good impulse ever goes unpunished.

The Albert B. Fall Building was a huge gray structure half a block wide and seven stories high, with rows of square windows glaring onto the street as if in chronic pain. Zardovsky had by now become used to the routine of entering a federal office building. He signed his name, his affiliation ("Lumber Co-op"), and the time of entry, then presented both briefcases for inspection. "Where'd you get this case, man?" the guard asked.

"It belongs to this guy Muntin," Zardovsky hedged. "I'm just delivering it to him."

"Okay, go on up."

Nothing is sadder than a government corridor, particularly on a breezy spring day more suited for hitting fungoes or hiking by the crater lake. Floor and ceiling stretched ahead and behind

Zardovsky, meeting at infinity; the ceilings muffled all sound —
the languid murmur of voices, the clanking of copying machines,
the bereaved ringing of unanswered telephones. Time, motion,
progress seemed to stop, caught in a static web of disorder. An
infinity later, he arrived at a featureless door marked B.L. MUNTIN,
DIRECTOR, OFFICE OF PERSONNEL AND PROGRAM EVALUATION. Putting down his double burden, he threw open the door and nearly
knocked down a woman who was trying to come out.

She fell back gasping, as if mortally frightened.

"I'm looking for Mr. Muntin," Zardovsky said. "Are you his
secretary?"

Her nostrils flared and she bit her lip, looked suspiciously behind her, and smiled. Her complexion had the tint of a cleaned
raw walleye pike. "Mr. Muntin's at lunch just now," she said.
"Can I help you?"

"I just brought him his briefcase."

"Thank you, I'll see he gets it." Grabbing the case, she disappeared behind the door like a jumping jack, leaving Zardovsky
unable even to ask directions to his real destination.

After fifteen minutes of wandering, he finally found it, only to
be told that the Assistant Secretary for Evaluation, Training, and
Morale was "on travel status."

"I don't reckon he'll be back for a week or two," a pleasant
gray-haired lady drawled at him.

"Is there anybody else I could talk to?"

"Usually you have to have an appointment, sugar. Sometimes
we let Mr. Nash handle this kind of thing, but he's not in." A
mischievous look crossed her face. "You know what, though? The
Assistant Secretary's deputy is eating lunch in her office right now.
She just might be able to help you, if she was of a mind to. Her
name is Nancy Quoin."

He paced down another sad corridor and through an empty
anteroom filled with muffled chamber music from an FM radio,
and found himself face to face with the same pale, strange woman
he had seen on the floor below.

Once again his appearance seemed to terrify her. "What are
you doing here?" she demanded, hastily putting down a yogurt
carton and plastic spoon.

"Is this the right office? I'm looking for somebody named Nancy Quoin."

As she went through another set of odd facial gymnastics, Bob Zardovsky began suddenly to feel a slight uneasiness, a pitch and roll in his stomach. This Washington was a damned weird place, he thought.

Meanwhile Nancy Quoin was plotting her escape. She had gone to Muntin's office innocently enough, hoping to hear that the voucher issue was settled and intending to do away with any residual bad feeling by insincerely flattering Muntin and dishonestly blaming Gerald. But finding the office empty, she had formed the correct suspicion that the two males were lunching together without her, which convinced her at once that they must also be plotting against her. She had been storming out when temptation (which seemed to delight in taking on the form of Bob Zardovsky) had thrust the unlocked briefcase into her hands. All the modern management books agreed that she would be a fool to pass up this opportunity to divine the secrets of her adversary, so she had looked inside and, to her guilty surprise, found something that seemed to promise rich opportunities for revenge. She had assumed that Zardovsky, with his informal clothes and rough manners, was a menial, without eyes, ears, memory, or consequence; but just as she was gloating over her guava yogurt, he rose before her, knowing her name, her office address, and her guilty secret.

"Okay, what is this?" she barked.

"Is this Quoin lady around?"

"I'm Nancy Quoin."

"But didn't I just see you downstairs? I thought you were —"

"Look, I don't know who you are or what you want, but I'm Nancy Quoin."

Swallowing his bewilderment, he began again. "Sorry, I must of got you mixed up with somebody else."

"Well, what is it?"

He explained his errand, and a smile spread across the pale woman's face. Here, he thought, was at last the sympathetic ear of a helpful government, though in fact the smile was simply one of relief, as Quoin realized that she might get away with it after all.

"So anyway, I was hoping you could help me get the application going," he concluded. "I have the documents in my briefcase if you'd like to look at them."

"Oh, please, Mr. Zardovsky, don't get out those papers, because if I looked at them here and now it would ruin everything. You see, it wouldn't be constitutional."

"Say what?"

Nancy Quoin rose and walked to the window. This raised her above the head of the other party and was recommended for putting across a difficult (or, as in this case, wholly dishonest) point. "You see, Bob, the problem is that as a federal agency, we can only step in if the case involves interstate commerce."

"That's no problem, ma'am, half of the wood we process goes down to California for drywall and the rest gets shipped straight to Japan."

"We aren't talking about the logs, Bob, we're talking about your application. You see, if you hand it over here in the District, that's hardly interstate, is it?"

"Geez, I brought all this stuff from the West Coast —"

"I know, these legal technicalities probably sound ridiculous. I *could* just take the application and brazen it out. But unfortunately, that might leave us vulnerable to a court challenge down the road. I've seen multimillion-dollar projects tied up for years over just this issue. Do you want to take that chance?"

Something about this broad was way off base, Zardovsky concluded; any paperwork he left with her would probably disappear without a trace. "That sure is interesting," he said, sidling toward the door. "I tell you what. I'll just grab a bus back where I came from and we can get this thing started right."

Alone again, Quoin dipped a spoonful of guava yogurt and plotted her next move. The formidable Baxter Muntin was delivered into her hands. The old-boy network was in for a hell of a shock.

On the street again, Zardovsky looked at his list of addresses. He wasn't sure whether the next one was a government office or what. It was up in Northwest, a place called the Coalition for Industrial Alternatives. The contact was someone named Margaret Luck.

He would try it. He could use a little luck right now.

Chapter 4

NORTH OF DUPONT CIRCLE, in a neighborhood of Latin grocery stores, ethnic restaurants, and forgotten governments-in-exile, stands the Park View, the cooperative apartment building in which Gerald Nash lived. Like a once-lovely dowager in mean surroundings, the old building turns toward the neighborhood a pale, genteel appearance — pastel red-and-gray stone façade, carved marble entrance, and a dim lobby with a tile floor, gleaming brass letter slots, a mahogany grandfather clock, and a wilted fern in an earthenware pot.

The owner of Gerald's apartment worked for a dubious branch of the State Department and had been in Central Africa so long he had no idea of the present grotesque level of rents in Washington. Gerald paid the meager sum of $500 for two bedrooms, this rent theoretically to be split between himself and his roommate, Willys Handleman. Handleman usually managed to come up with $100 or so.

Most of the other residents owned their apartments. They were for the most part prosperous middle-aged civil servants who had acquired from long use the look and feel of old documents. An unwritten code severely restricted fraternization between these lofty proprietors and mere tenants like Gerald. His only commerce with the *haute monde* of the Park View had been a notice in his mailbox informing him that the co-op board had voted five to one to ask him to be quicker in removing from the lobby his subscription copies of *The National Journal*.

The lobby was empty and silent. Gerald buzzed for the elevator. For a few minutes nothing happened, except that he began to feel the skin-crawling sensation that someone was watching him. Turning quickly, he caught a glimpse of a thin metal tube poking up through the bars of the wrought-iron stair railing; it disappeared downward, and the ancient elevator wheezed into action.

"Hello, David," Gerald said when the doors opened. "Was that you peering at me through the railing?"

"You saw me? Damn, Rambler, I thought I had rigged up that periscope out of sight." The operator was a young black man of roughly Gerald's age, size, and build, dressed in black wrestling shoes, black Levis, and a black turtleneck sweater. There was an eerie resemblance in their two faces — both delicate, studious, and bespectacled — as if they were distant cousins in a family of pensive intellectuals.

Gerald stepped into the elevator. From the instrument panel protruded a tangled mass of wire. "Good God, David, what are you doing, rigging a bomb?"

"See, that's why I need the periscope. If one of the board members saw this shit they'd get on my ass. I knew you'd be cool."

"What is it, though?"

"See, Rambler, I'm trying to wire up the elevator buzzer to set off an alarm back in the little TV room in the basement. That way I can go back there and sack out when I'm doing the late shift."

"David, if you had the right equipment, you'd be dangerous."

"You got that right. All I ever needed was some decent hardware. Like in Vietnam, this buddy of mine sneaked me into this comm center in Saigon. I damn near died. All these white guys running around with videotape cameras and satellite downlinks and me with that shit-ass little hand-crank radio. Him and me wired up the board so the satellite dish would pick up Radio Moscow and blast it over the Armed Forces Radio right in the middle of the Pro Bowl. You talk about some brass *pissed off* . . ."

They reached the top floor and Gerald stepped out. "You'd better get those wires out of sight," he said. "All the big shots are due home any minute."

"Yeah, I don't want to lose this good gig. If I work here twenty years they might put me on the morning shift." The door closed on his dark, discontented form.

Gerald's bachelor quarters were at the end of the hall. It was a spacious apartment with high ceilings and fine views on three sides. Gerald let himself into the hall and heard the television blaring: "— the administration's new wage-price guidelines succeed? Only time will tell. But one thing is certain: pressure is building for change. This is Ed Hackett, at the White House."

"You disgusting idiot!" blared another voice, followed by a heavy thump.

"Hold your fire, Handleman!" Gerald called. "I told you not to throw things at my TV!" He burst into the living room to find Willys Handleman threatening the screen with a copy of the *Federal Register.*

People often thought that Willys Handleman was fat, but he was merely ill-dressed and unhappy. His dark hair fell over his forehead in an unruly forelock, and his dark eyebrows hovered like thunderclouds over his suspicious eyes. Waves of disorder radiated outward from his tousled head and youthful face: to the cheap, ill-fitting khaki shirt, the torn blue jeans and worn-out jogging shoes; to the dirty and semicollapsed whitish-gray reclining armchair that had been his main contribution to the apartment; and to the untidy piles of books and newspapers surrounding it and the detritus scattered across the rug — old yogurt cartons, take-out food containers, sweat socks, broken pens, and crumpled wads of yellow lined writing paper.

"I am now willing to consider a constitutional amendment abolishing freedom of the press," Handleman announced solemnly, "if that's what it takes to get Ed Hackett off the air."

Television broadcasters, even more than most people, attracted Handleman's wrath. One he would damn for his toupee, another for her red lipstick, a third for his pudding face and avuncular manner. Television stardom involved no talent or intelligence, he reasoned, but brought a great deal of money and fame; thus he saw no reason why others should be warmly ensconced behind the screen while he remained out in the cold.

"It's almost over," said Gerald. "Let's turn it off."

"Hey, no, Andy Griffith is next." Handleman's workday, such as it was, was spent in the crumbling chair in front of comedies, game shows, and serials, with irregularly spaced interruptions for meals at an Indian restaurant two blocks away. Bathed in the babble of daytime programs, Handleman wrote reviews of obscure political books for formerly left-wing magazines. This week's quota was scattered across the rug: *I Found My Thrill on Capitol Hill*, by a former congressional page turned porno star; *Sanity in America's National Security, Nuclear Arms, Military Procurement, Diplomatic, and International Economic Policies: A Modest Proposal*, by two Harvard sophomores; and *Dying by Inches: Crisis in the Bureau of Standards.*

"What's the count for this week?"

"Six."

Every six months or so, Handleman delivered a major article, designed to shoot him upward like a rocket in Washington's skies. His current project was to be called "Ten Things Big Government Does Well," and he had hopes for it: a lucrative book contract, a newspaper column, dinner at the White House, even an interview on National Public Radio. The problem was that to date he had thought of only six things, a dilemma he seemed to blame on Gerald.

"Was there any mail for me?" Gerald asked.

"Yeah, I think I put it on top of the refrigerator."

Handleman began watching the television comedy. Even his laughter had a grudging sound, as if he were sure he could write a better program if he ever got the chance.

On top of the refrigerator Gerald found a Visa bill and a postcard that read in its entirety: "1) Your brother has decided to get married July 4. You must come. 2) Your father is in good health. 3) My promotion came through. YOUR MOTHER. P.S. Write."

The refrigerator was virtually empty. "What are you going to do for dinner?" Gerald called to Handleman, whom he could hear angrily disputing the claims of a roach-killer commercial.

"I've got some *paneer mattar* and lemon pickle. I'll split it with you."

Gerald sincerely intended to shop for groceries. Often he marked on his calendar a time to do it. Once he got home, however, the calendar was still at the office and he was usually tired. Besides, there was almost no restaurant in the neighborhood too dirty, small, or ethnically obscure to take his Visa card.

With the special guilt of the affluent but insolvent, he hastily carried the bill, unopened, to the scarred writing desk in the hall and shut it in the center drawer. At that moment the phone on the desk rang.

Despite his general air of torpor, Handleman could reach a ringing telephone in almost no time at all. He might pass weeks without departing from his usual round of the apartment, the 7-Eleven store, and the Indian restaurant, but a steady flow of gossip marched into his ears over the phone, as if he were the digestive endpoint of an enormous peristalsis that embraced the entire city. He materialized between Gerald and the telephone now with the quivering instantaneousness of the roadrunner in animated cartoons.

"It's for you," he said accusingly to Gerald.

"Gerry, hi, it's Maggie." Her voice blew over the wire like a familiar, friendly perfume.

"I'm expecting a call," Handleman claimed, and padded back to the living room.

"Let me tell you what happened at the office today." She seemed to expect Gerald to be amused by her favorable description of the visiting athlete who had appeared at her office babbling about solar energy and Nancy Quoin, and who was now crashing on her couch.

"That sounds cozy," he said.

"Don't worry, Gerry. I never was one for jocks, as a rule. Why don't you come out with us for a pizza and we'll play Space Invaders?"

"What, the three of us?"

"Gerry, if you're jealous, I'm flattered."

That settled the matter in Gerald's mind. "No, thanks," he said.

"I've got to go through some reports tonight. I'm supposed to brief the AS on a new project Muntin has sold to Hench."

"Okay," she said wistfully. "If you change your mind, we're going to the pizza place in a half-hour or so. I really would like to see you."

Gerald hung up. "Hey, Handleman," he called. "You still got that *paneer mattar?*"

Spicy food had no effect on Handleman beyond a few beads of sweat on his upper lip, a slight increase in eyebrow mobility, and a general rise in his spite level.

Some years earlier Handleman had been a joyful participant in the antiwar movement of the sixties, but all that remained of his radicalism was obsessive self-absorption, consuming suspicion, and utter unwillingness to serve any corrupt institution at less than the top level. While in Washington Handleman had been press officer for the Equine Defense Fund (resigned in protest), managing editor of a public-interest news service (bankrupted by a staggering coffee bill), press critic of a counterculture weekly (closed when the Toiling Masses League occupied its offices), and book reviewer for the breakfast program of a listener-supported FM jazz radio station (abandoned when a tape recorder broke down and the management asked Handleman to come in at 6:00 A.M. once a week).

His present work as a free-lancer barely kept him in curry, but he could work at his own pace without leaving the apartment or even getting fully dressed. But no matter where Handleman was, like a powerful AWACS plane patroling the frontiers of ambition, he maintained a close and caustic watch on his contemporaries who were burrowing upward in the bureaucracies of the Congress, the press, the agency bar, the public-interest movement, and the federal government. For none of them (except, so he claimed, for Gerald) did he feel anything but a generalized obsessive contempt.

Gerald had come to depend on the pinpoint accuracy and extravagant malice of Willys's ratings of people. On the Washington stock exchange Handleman was something between E. F. Hutton and Joe Granville.

"What do you know about Bernie Weisman, Willys?" Gerald asked.

"What, Hench's whiz-kid LA?" Handleman's eyebrows darted back and forth suspiciously. "Not much, really. A toad, of course.

From the Bronx. Special fellowship at Yale. Got beat out for a Rhodes by some Columbia rugby player. Joint M.B.A.–J.D. from Stanford. Supposed to be a big intellectual, but I think he's a phony. He writes about economics for law journals and vice versa. His big bug is regulatory reform. Hench hired him because of some piece he did on risk analysis."

"I heard he got Hench to read Samuelson's *Economics*."

Gerald could see Handleman filing this information behind his eyebrows. "If true, he's smarter than I thought," he said. "Now lemme ask you something. Are you going out with this broad? What's her name again, anyway?"

"Who says there's only one?"

"Go fuck yourself." In no area was Handleman's envy more active than in sex. Periodically he fell heavily for some long-legged twenty-two-year-old *Congressional Quarterly* researcher or assistant press secretary. His wooing usually involved custom-tailored suits and Hungarian restaurants, and always ended badly.

"What are you going to do tonight, Willys?"

"I guess I'll keep reading these books. 'Charlie's Angels' is on later, then there's that guy that says 'Hey' on the late news."

Gerald considered the prospect. "I think I'll go out after all," he said.

"It isn't that many girls that've heard of Pistol Pete Reiser," said the big stranger, lounging on the other side of the Formica table with a narrow-waisted beer glass in his hand.

Maggie Luck laughed ruefully. "To begin with, I'm hardly a girl —"

Zardovsky hooted and popped his bug eyes out even further.

"I'm serious," she said. "I'm old enough to have seen some of these guys. I think my dad only had a child to have an excuse to go to the ball park. Christ, I can almost remember the Streetcar Series."

"Browns and Cardinals? Gimme a break, you weren't born then?"

"To tell the miserable truth, I was a year old. Sometimes I think I can remember those games, I heard my dad talk about 'em so much. He saw them all. Later on he took me to see Jackie Robinson, Joe DiMaggio, Satchel Paige —"

"Eddie Gaedel?"

"Bill Veeck's midget? No — didn't he only bat one time? Oh, I get it, you were testing me. Did I pass, smart-ass?"

Zardovsky laughed. "You do know your baseball pretty good. Let's get us some more beer."

He flipped a paw, and the waitress, a tough-looking brunette a couple of years and many pounds older than Maggie, appeared almost at once. Zardovsky seemed to have established some occult power over this woman, who gazed at him with the rapt look of a rabbit that has met the snake of its dreams. "We'll take another big pitcher of this good draft, darlin'," Zardovsky said, and she hastened off.

Maggie fished a cigarette out of her purse and put it in her mouth. Zardovsky's hand appeared in front of her face, clicking her plastic lighter with such force that the flame nearly burned her eyebrows off. She took the lighter away, turned down the flame, and lit up.

"Sorry," Zardovsky said. "I'm not used to these things." He let his eyes wander around the bar: sawdust on the wooden floor, old movie posters on the paneled walls, pinball machines and video games, a vintage jukebox pumping old rock music. "This is a nice place," he said. "Reminds me of home. I guess most of these folks work at factories around here?"

Maggie laughed, which sent her into one of her choking fits. "I'm sorry, Bob," she said when she could speak again. "To begin with, there aren't any factories in Washington. And if there were, these folks wouldn't work in them, believe me. Though they do try to look like factory workers — in their off hours."

"Who are they, then?"

"Let's see if I can give you some examples. The girl in the overalls is deputy counsel to the Senate subcommittee on biomass energy. The guy with wings on his hat is some kind of economist at the White House — I forget whether he does trigger-price strategies or reindustrialization. The guy in the Steelers jersey is TV critic for one of the papers. The fat fellow with the beard studies the CIA for one of the think tanks, or maybe it's the other way around. The girl in the peasant skirt and pigtails is research director of the municipal workers' union. The black guy in the silk shirt — no, don't point, he's not near as drunk as he looks — is a C.P.A. and management consultant and could probably buy and sell the bar and everybody in it. You begin to get the picture?"

Zardovsky scratched his blond curls and wrinkled his forehead. "Hell, these folks are running the government!" he said.

"They think they are, anyway."

"They're so young!"

"Yeah, but they make up for it by not being qualified for their jobs."

He guffawed. "Damn, Maggie, you're a character, you know that? I get a kick out of you."

Maggie wondered if all this eye-rolling was meant to be amorous. The notion discouraged her; not that the big jock was exactly unattractive . . .

"Okay," Zardovsky said with a sarcastic smile. "Take this nerd that just came in, with the slick hair and the tee-nancy eyeglasses. What does he do?"

With an odd, pleasant shock she saw Gerald, blinking in the dim light like a silly little owl.

"He's my boyfriend," she said coolly. "Any other smart remarks?"

Zardovsky's face flamed red. Gerald started across the floor, picking his way as carefully as if it were a minefield. Maggie watched, half-amused, and wondered exactly what about him had attracted her so. Partly, she thought, it was because he reminded her of her husband, Jack, who had also been a thoughtful soul. Margaret, in contrast, made a lifetime career of rushing into things. Another part of it, though, was precisely that he seemed different from Jack, who (she had realized after she married him) thought deeply and then always came to the most conventional conclusion possible, while inside Gerald, she thought, there was something a little more surprising, though it was well concealed. And partly, of course — this new thought broke in, making her blush — in his mixture of callowness and self-assurance, in the seriocomic independence that overlay his need for love, he reminded her of the boy-child she had wanted and never had.

"I got finished early," Gerald was saying. He looked suspiciously at Zardovsky and put a hand, at once proprietary and tentative, on Margaret's shoulder.

"Gerry, this is Bob Zardovsky."

"Gerald Nash."

"It's a pleasure, buddy."

"I understand that you met my colleague Nancy Quoin," Gerald said as he slid into the booth.

"Ah, yeah," Zardovsky said with an uncertain smile. "She sure is an . . . interesting lady."

"You think so? I've always been able to stifle my fascination with her," Gerald said. "Did she really tell you to mail your application across a state line?"

Zardovsky nodded sheepishly. "She must of thought I was right off the bus. And of course I am. Say, let's get you a beer glass and we can all split another pizza. Hey, good lookin —"

"Don't order pizza on my account," Gerald said. "I ate some curried peas a while ago."

"Curried peas? You serious? Honey, just bring my little buddy here a glass, will you? You got to eat more than that, Gerry. Maggie says they have good sausage heros."

"No, thanks, the sausages here stay with me for days and days."

"You a regular here, too? Maggie was explaining about how all you high-powered types hang out in this place."

"I don't exactly hang out here — they don't take credit cards."

"You're a character too," Zardovsky said. Reaching this conclusion about people seemed to reassure him.

Margaret suddenly jumped to her feet and waved at someone across the room. "Bernie!" she called. "Come over here a minute!"

From the entrance came a short, slender young man with small, suspicious eyes and fine dark hair. He wore Levis and a denim jacket; these garments sat on his body as if rented for the occasion.

"Hi, Maggie," he said. "I'm sorry I didn't get back to you today. The hearing ran long."

"No problem, Bernie," she said. "What's this T-shirt?" He was wearing a silk-screened shirt that bore two outlines of nuclear-power cooling towers, with a black X drawn through one. Beneath it was the stenciled slogan FEWER NUKES.

"I got it at your conference. Weren't you at that workshop on 'Middle-of-the-Road Energy Paths'?"

"I missed it."

"Catchy slogan," Gerald said.

"How are you, Gerry?" The young man extended a hand toward Gerald with equal parts of unwillingness and condescension. "I thought we were going to lock horns at the panel, but you didn't show up."

"Always sorry to miss hearing you speak. What was your hearing?"

"Just cleaning up some odds and ends on interagency aspects of metric conversion."

"Anyone there from our shop?"

"No, but I gather we're going to hear from your boss next week."

"Bernie," Margaret said, "I want you to meet Three-Finger Zardovsky."

Weisman gave a scornful laugh as they shook hands. "Sounds like some kind of baseball player or something."

"I played for Merida."

"Bernie is Buster Hench's legislative assistant," Margaret said. "Bob is a constituent of yours, Bernie. He's here with a CATA grant application."

The small eyes took on a hostile and disapproving glint. "I'd love to hear all about it," Weisman said, "but I've got some people waiting for me. Come up to the Hill sometime and we'll discuss it."

"You be in tomorrow?"

"I should be. Maggie knows the way." Weisman clapped Gerald awkwardly on the shoulder. "If the Secretary saw you drinking with Maggie here, he'd use you for helicopter fuel, Gerry."

As the denims retreated stiffly across the room, Gerald eyed Margaret with surprise. "I didn't know you were so buddy-buddy with Bernie Weisman," he said.

"He owes me a favor," she said. "The coalition helped him out with some research on the Rigid Airship Corporation bill."

"You *are* an enemy of the Department, then."

"Oh, come on, Gerry, we were only against it because the Secretary wanted to defund CATA to build dirigibles. You weren't really for it, were you?"

Gerald felt constrained to defend administration policy in public. If he failed to defend the administration's stupid mistakes, people might forget what a key post he held. "Oh, never mind," he said. "So, Bob, you're from Hench's district?"

"So Maggie says. We haven't seen him in so long, we'd more or less forgotten he existed."

"If you get Hench on your side, you don't have to worry about Nancy Quoin or anybody else."

"I'm going to see this boy Weisman first thing tomorrow morning. You know if he's a baseball fan, Maggie?"

"Not exactly. He likes the Yankees."

"I guess that's close enough. I know a couple of those guys."

"No kidding?"

The two glided back into their baseball conversation. Gerald sullenly drained his beer. He was piqued to see Margaret so familiar with Weisman, his rival and a thumping ass. He had also taken a shamefaced dislike to this big popeyed baseball player, who seemed like a decent fellow but had a way of monopolizing the conversation. He peevishly decided that if the grant could be approved — which would send Zardovsky back to the West Coast — he would not be sorry.

"I'd better get on home," he said, sliding out of the booth. "Good luck with Hench."

"Say, thanks, little buddy."

Margaret's face fell. "Don't you want to come to my place and drink cheap wine for a while?"

"I'd better not. Bob, let me know if you run into any more problems."

To leave the bar, Gerald had to detour around the substantial form of the waitress, who seemed to be glaring at Margaret and Zardovsky with an expression of fierce jealousy. That was ridiculous, Gerald thought. He must be projecting.

As he let himself into the hallway, he again heard Handleman's voice over the babble of the television. "False conflict!" it said. Then, after a few seconds, "Cliché!"

Handleman the critic was massacring "Charlie's Angels."

But Gerald entered the room to see not the shabby, unhappy figure he had left behind, but a resplendent stranger, preening before the television in a blue three-piece suit with a faint red stripe. Handleman had outdone himself this time: the new suit had three-button, double-vented styling, a four-pocket vest, and pleated trousers with double watch pockets.

Sartorially at least, Willys Handleman was two people. In his normal shabby attire, he was routinely offered small change by warm-hearted pedestrians, stopped and asked to identify himself by police officers, frisked at airport security checkpoints, and refused service at package stores. But from time to time he risked prison for check-passing and credit-card fraud to acquire a custom-tailored suit, and such a garment served him as a magic cloak of respectability. Wearing one, he was likely to be mistaken for a junior member of Congress or one of the better class of white-collar criminal defendants.

"What is this, Willys? Are you dressing up to impress Farrah Fawcett?" Gerald asked.

Handleman whirled angrily. "What are you doing sneaking up on me?" he demanded. "I thought you went out to dinner."

"This is nice goods, Willys, very nice indeed. I thought the tailor had cut off your privileges until you paid him."

"There's a new shop up on Jefferson Place. The poor guy looked so eager when I went in, I couldn't resist ordering something to make him feel good."

"How did he feel when you asked him to bill you?"

"I didn't have to — I got my American Express card back. What do you think?"

"I think you won't have it long."

"I mean about the suit, asshole."

"Looks great. What's the occasion? Willys, are you looking for a job again?"

Handleman blushed. "Of course not."

"Then who's the lucky girl?"

"Fuck you, smart-ass. By the way, that girl called again."

"While I was out?"

"Yeah. She wouldn't leave a message."

A nameless foreboding stole over Gerald, as if some thought he had been trying to ignore were growing until he could no longer control it. Something seemed to be hovering in the air just behind his back, regarding him with unpitying malice, about to swoop.

That was ridiculous. He was having an anxiety attack of some kind. Hastily he changed the subject. "Is the news on?"

"Yeah, it's on the other channel. Don't you want to watch 'Charlie's Angels'?"

"No, let's switch."

He slumped on the couch while Handleman adjusted the set. What could he be so worried about? Life was progressing just as he had planned it. His job was serene, and his personal life was definitely looking up. This new affair was a marvelous example of the irresistible attraction, amounting almost to a *droit de seigneur,* that everyone in Washington agreed power conferred on its possessor. He was worrying for nothing.

"Look at this," Handleman was saying. "It's just a few blocks from here."

The screen showed police cars drawn up outside a decaying townhouse and searchlights playing over the façade while officials parleyed with someone barricaded inside the front door. A woman's voice, flat and emphatic, was saying, "Officials of the Temple vowed to resist any move to inspect Sunrise House by force. One spokesman, who identified himself only as Open, called the Health Department's action, quote, an infringement of the Bill of Rights and an insult to the Ancient Ones of Mars, unquote."

The camera cut to the reporter on the street, microphone in hand, staring out at the camera with her lovely head held to one side and a glance so bold it suggested that between her and the viewer there already existed an intimate and unsatisfactory understanding, a long history of heartbreak and betrayal.

"For now," she said, "the situation is a standoff. But Health Department officials vow that unless they are admitted soon, they will use force." A soundless weight crashed down on Gerald from behind as the reporter added, "This is Diana Cazadora, Reaction News Squad, in Adams-Morgan."

Chapter 5

GAMALIEL ("BUSTER") HENCH had once been an insolvent lawyer in the Pacific Northwest, specializing in personal-injury suits against insurance companies. He had enjoyed shuttling from country courthouse to country courthouse, interrogating his clients about the most disgusting details of their injuries and drinking steam beer in roadhouses that smelled of pine-oil disinfectant. But he had foolishly put up his name as a congressional candidate for the same reason he had adopted his self-bestowed manly nickname: as a way of advertising his law practice. In one of the common spasmodic displays of disgust for an incumbent President, he had been, to his horror, elected.

At first Congress had borne some pleasing resemblances to his former life. Avuncular committee chairmen made the decisions; senior figures in each party told him how to vote. The local fishing was not much; neither was the beer; but at least no one asked his opinion, paid attention to anything he said, or ever put his name in the papers.

That golden way of life crumbled. The great chairmen died; the senior figures were disgraced; and the newspapers began to print all sorts of things that really seemed none of their business. At some point he mislaid his wife and children and sold his old house in the Pacific Northwest. His hair turned iron-gray. He gave up beer and began to drink martinis whenever he could get them.

Without his conscious volition, meanwhile, Buster Hench was becoming a fearful name. He had one overriding virtue as a legislator of the new style: a limitless tolerance for subcommittee hearings. No one could sit out a longer or duller hearing than Buster Hench. Colleagues dubbed him "the Iron Bladder." Let others make speeches, write bills, or travel to tropical climates; Hench doggedly filled white printed booklets with incomprehensible testimony. When Gerald's Department was born, Hench was the only member of Congress who could tolerate overseeing it, and he was promoted to full-committee status and found himself at an eminence that rendered cabinet members, lobbyists, and susceptible reporters nearly mute with awe.

Life had equipped Buster Hench for such duties as drinking, washing his car, and watching the Sunday football games; a brutal and exploitative political system had robbed him of these joys. (A summary of football scores was placed on his desk every Monday.)

Like many public men who live constantly swathed in flattery and deference, Buster Hench felt the cares of his office to be uniquely difficult. The arrival of Bernard Weisman on his staff did nothing to lessen this feeling. True, Weisman was original and brilliant. But he was also chilly, distant, and demanding. Weisman had begun chivvying Hench to read massive technical tomes in his leisure time; he tried to monitor the Congressman's social invitations, and even frowned on Hench's harmless daily dozen martinis. Now, when the Hench committee produced some new and complex amendment, blocked some foolish proposal, or demolished some moronic administration official, colleagues said, "Brilliant young man, that Weisman. Wish I had him on my staff."

Weisman's fatal flaw, in fact, was his inexperience in the ways of flattery and self-effacement. He had a suitably elevated view of his own stature. This took the form of a sense of wrong nobly born; like hundreds of his coevals on Capitol Hill and in the bureaucracy, Weisman reasoned that he had placed his country and its people in his debt by accepting his modest $35,000-a-year salary. In recompense Weisman asked only one thing: sweeping and unchallengeable power.

Not, however, the old-fashioned, cumbersome retail type of power, once treasured by congressmen and their aides, of helping individuals with trifles like pension checks or veterans' benefits. What Weisman coveted, along with many others of his time and station, was something at once less personal and larger, sweeping but abstract, involving huge but subtle changes in tax laws or gargantuan government programs. These actions might or might not impinge on the lives of ordinary citizens — Weisman did not know or care. But they were appreciated and respected in Washington, which was the home of everyone who really counted — indeed, of almost everyone he knew.

This explains why Weisman had no interest in helping Bob Zardovsky with his CATA grant.

With obnoxious directness, Zardovsky appeared the morning after they had met. He jammed his bulky form into Weisman's corner of the office, spilling over the tiny wooden chair grudgingly kept for visitors. Weisman regarded him with disdain; in his size, athletic self-assurance, and sunny expression, he reminded the young aide uncomfortably of the rugby player who had (as Willys Handleman, with his usual accuracy, had reported) beaten him out of a Rhodes scholarship some years before.

Weisman reminded himself that Margaret Luck, for reasons of her own, was sponsoring this cretin's quest and seemed to expect Weisman to help him as a favor to her. Margaret had helped him block the Rigid Airship bill (the kind of exercise of power of which he approved). Margaret was a very useful person to work with. True, she possessed no advanced degree or prestigious job experience. But she attempted to atone by being thorough, original, and clear-headed. Even better, she was slightly diffident, and so did not object when someone like Bernard Weisman appropriated her research for his own glory.

Weisman nurtured less professional designs on her as well, designs that had previously been repulsed with such good nature that Weisman (who had the common tendency to mistake good humor for weakness) assumed victory was only a matter of time.

So Weisman was by his own standards positively expansive with

Bob Zardovsky, favoring him with a chilly nod and the words, "I'll be with you as soon as I finish this."

The memorandum Weisman was reading addressed the subject of elections. It reminded staff members that there would be the formality of a general election the following November. Hench's pride dictated that each reelection victory be more crushing than the one before. So members of the staff who had never visited Hench's home state and district were urged to memorize such pertinent facts as their size, location, and principal cities. This information was to be put to use in creating press releases and speeches that would appeal to the distant and primitive natives of this terra incognita.

A less confident man than Weisman might have wondered if a slight touch of sarcasm in Hench's writing style might not be directed at himself. A few days before, Weisman had confidently but erroneously identified the capital of Hench's home state. Weisman raised his eyes to the gaping lummox before him. Perhaps Zardovsky could be an instrument for demonstrating to Hench his responsiveness to direction from above.

He laid the memo to one side. "Now," he said languidly, "what seems to be your problem?"

Powerful people often form a habit of demanding that petitioners tell their stories over and over, and always from the very beginning. A certain number of supplicants simply give up at the prospect of beginning anew the nineteenth time; others tend to fall into self-contradiction or to reveal extraneous information that can be used to refuse or, better yet, delay their requests.

But this technique was ill adapted to discourage Bob Zardovsky, who responded to each impatient interruption, deliberate misunderstanding, and obfuscatory question with patience and crushing detail. Weisman survived Zardovsky's synopsis of the growth and collapse of the Gouge Eye Lumber Mill Number One, the minute-by-minute recapitulation of the formation of the People's Lumber Co-op, and the garbled summary of Zardovsky's eventful few days in Washington. But he crumbled during the season-by-season account of Zardovsky's career in organized baseball. In fact, he did not make it past the top of the sixth inning of the annual Gouge Eye Bible – Salmon Falls Vocational diamond classic; that is to say, he did not listen long enough to correct the misapprehension that Zardovsky was a well-known, popular figure in Hench's home state.

"This is all very interesting," he said, partially covering a yawn, "but getting your grant will not be quite as easy as you may think. I'm sure that back in your home town, you people picture us here in Washington as simply waiting for any chance to give away the taxpayers' money, but the reality is a bit more complex. As you may or may not know, even with the CATA program, for example, an application must meet some fairly strict requirements to be considered, which may take some time to get together —"

"If you mean the DE234, the certified audit, the community reference, and the planning go-ahead, endorsement, and statement of need by local authority and state officials, I have them in my briefcase."

"Who briefed you on those requirements?"

"One of the boys — he worked as timekeeper, he had dropped out of law school up to the state university. He hitchhiked up to the state capital and looked up all that shit in the *Federal Register*. Here, lemme show you." With a flourish, Zardovsky reached into the briefcase and produced a pair of jockey shorts. "Hold the phone," he said, hastily stuffing the underwear in a jacket pocket, then bringing out a thick sheaf of documents.

At this point Zardovsky began to notice a curious paradox about the federal government. It was reputed to have an insatiable appetite for documents, but whenever he produced his own small scrap pile, people seemed oddly reluctant to accept it. Weisman raised an eyebrow and with a desultory gesture indicated a low table where Zardovsky might discharge his uneasy burden.

"If you have all the materials together," he said, "why don't you just make them available to the new Department? As you may or may not know, the applicable division is that of evaluation, train—"

"I tried that once," the big stranger replied, and launched into a bone-numbing account of mistaken identity, exchange of hand luggage, and bizarre theories of the interstate commerce clause.

"Okay, okay," said Weisman, not far from coma. "Leave it there, for what it's worth. I'll see if I can get someone to take a look at it."

"We'll take anything you can do for us," Zardovsky said. "You know, when I first got here, I really figured this whole business would be fairly straightforward. But I've run into a lot of jerk-offs since then, pardon my French. It's beginning to piss me off, frankly."

Weisman glanced at his watch. "Be that as it may, Bob, we don't have much time. I'm going to try to get you in to meet the boss. To be perfectly frank, I'm sticking my neck out doing even this much. But as a friend, I have to tell you that Congressman Hench has a bad temper. It would be absolutely fatal to your project if he got the idea you were abusing your access to pressure him. If I were you, I wouldn't even mention it. Just leave all that to me."

"What, you mean don't say nothing to him about the grant?"

"It's completely up to you. I could just let you go in there and, as you would probably say, piss him off. Then your grant might not have any chance. But suit yourself."

At that moment, in the inner office the great man himself was in the grip of profound melancholy. The day before, he had presided over a hearing designed by Weisman. He remembered everything about it — the overheated, largely deserted committee room, the procession of smug academics and civil servants reading polysyllabic statements, the endless documents submitted by witnesses and whisked away by the staff, the flat silences as each witness realized that the members of the committee were either unconscious or too ignorant to ask even a single question. But nowhere in his memory could he find a clue to what the whole exercise had been about.

Today, as often in recent months, Buster Hench was assailed by the sense that some key to life's mystery had slipped from his grasp.

So his mood was one of absent-minded irritation when the intercom produced Weisman's smug voice, saying, "Congressman, in line with your memo, I've already set up a photo session. It's a baseball player, very well known in the district. It'll just take five minutes."

He squinted at the rugged young fellow who followed Weisman through the door.

"Congressman, this is Three-Finger Zardovsky," Weisman said.

"It's a pleasure," said Hench. The big man seemed oddly reticent, almost nonverbal. Hench had noticed that many people he met recently, since he had assumed the chairmanship of the full committee and hired Weisman, were like this. He tried to put the stranger at ease. "I've certainly heard your name —"

"You have?"

"Tell me again which club you're with."

"Right now I'm with Sturgis Sporting Goods."

"Sturgis Sporting Goods?"

"Truth is, I'm in the lumber business, mostly."

"Smile," said a voice. There was a flash.

"I used to play for Merida."

"It's a National League expansion team, I think, Congressman," Weisman said proudly.

"Merida is in Mexico, you idiot," Hench said calmly.

"Hispanic vote . . ." Weisman gurgled, with the expression of a man drowning in thin air.

"There aren't fifteen Mexicans in my whole district, Weisman!"

Bob Zardovsky saw another opportunity to do a good turn. He put a friendly hand on the Congressman's elbow. "See, I live in Gouge Eye, Mr. Hench," he said. "The reason I'm here —" Weisman began making motions to him to be quiet. "Look, Bernie," Zardovsky said, "let me just explain this situation. Hell, Mr. Hench don't seem like such an asshole to me. I think you've got him all wrong."

"What is going on here, anyway?" Hench asked.

"Mr. Hench," Zardovsky said earnestly, "you've got this poor little guy so scared he can hardly see straight! You got to learn to take it easy on the folks that work for you. It's like old Doc Pearman always used to say before he died, life is too long to be a son of a bitch full-time."

Some Americans regard politicians as lacking inner poetry. If these philistines could have seen into Buster Hench's soul at that moment, how humbled they would have been! The name Doc Pearman, like Proust's immortal madeleine, summoned up an explosion of memory — colors, sounds, smells, and emotion coruscating together like a tropical sunrise. He had sued Doc Pearman half a dozen times, had drunk with him a dozen more — indeed, had been carried home a few times by this worthy adversary, the biggest drinker for miles around the confluence of the river and

Walnut Creek. These memories came flooding out from the melancholy and suppressed store of those forgotten times, with a force more poignant as he learned that another of his friends, half-forgotten, had died and left him isolated in the white marble of Washington.

"Did you say Doc Pearman was dead?"

"Yeah, see, that's why I'm here, Congressman —"

"Sir," Weisman interrupted, "you have a meeting scheduled with Dr. Capello of the National Scalp Institute on the *alopecia aereata* bill."

"Ask him to wait, Weisman," Hench said. "Son, tell me how Doc Pearman died."

"And that was it?" Maggie Luck asked wonderingly.

"Yep. He just listened to the story, and after a while he called up some guy named Munson —"

"Baxter Muntin?"

"Yeah. And this guy said to have somebody check over the papers and then send them to him and he'd take care of it."

They were gathered in Margaret's apartment for a celebration dinner: Gerald, Margaret, Zardovsky, and Willys Handleman. All afternoon Zardovsky had been bustling in the kitchen, leaving not one pan unsoiled; the result, which he called chili, bubbled on the stove.

Gerald was sitting in a corner of the living room, glued to the seven o'clock news. Maggie poked his shoulder gently. "Gerry, did you hear that?"

"What?" He looked unwillingly away from an exclusive interview with the mayor of Washington, who was explaining that while the city and its people faced many serious problems, there was absolutely nothing the District government could do about any of them.

"Hench just called Muntin and put the grant through," Maggie said.

"It seems out of character for Hench to help anybody out," Gerald said. "He must be having some kind of breakdown."

"You're really down on the guy," Zardovsky said. "He was pretty decent to me."

Handleman popped like a champagne bottle. "That toad

Hench? Decent? If Buster Hench's grandmother was on fire, he wouldn't piss on her unless he got something in return." Slumped on the sofa in his khaki shirt and cutoff jeans, he managed to deliver this opinion without shifting a single muscle of body or face.

"You seem to feel kinda strongly about it, old son," Zardovsky said gently.

"Don't be silly," said Gerald with a half-smile. "If Willys calls somebody a toad, he doesn't feel strongly about him. You have to go up through bastard all the way to asshole before you get to the people he dislikes."

"Oh, for Christ's sake," said Handleman, his eyebrows diving over his nose. "I just call a spade a spade. Most congressmen are bastards. It's stupid to pretend they're not. But most people in this town do."

Pungent vapor drifted from the kitchen. "Hot damn," Zardovsky said, sniffing the air. "That chili is just getting right."

They ate sitting on the floor. "You guys sure are cynical," said Zardovsky as he ladled out the chili. "Hell, I think things aren't too bad. I figured when I came here, all I had to do was get somebody to listen to the situation and they'd help us out, and see, that's just what's happened."

This remark, like an off-color joke, produced an awkward silence. At this moment Willys Handleman took a long swig of beer from the can. As sometimes happens when cold beer hits a dry throat, this produced an internal spasm that emerged audibly as a burst of hiccups. Bob Zardovsky turned to Handleman and with his huge right hand delivered a brisk therapeutic thump between the shoulder blades, but instead of curing Willys, this kindly meant gesture doubled him over where he sat and produced the uniquely embarrassing phenomenon known as "nose shoots." The spectacle of Handleman hacking and gasping but somehow trying to maintain a dignified mien reduced Margaret to laughter; Gerald, watching Margaret, also began to giggle.

Embarrassment was a felony in Handleman's statute book. As he wiped his face with a checked cloth napkin, he fixed Zardovsky with a hostile stare that made even the big ex-ballplayer uneasy.

To bridge this awkward moment, Margaret asked, "Did he really invite you to go drinking with him, Bob?"

"Yeah, next week. He said he'd announce the grant the next day. He's going to some nightclub some friend of his is opening."

Handleman popped again. "What? You're going to the opening of Status?"

"What do you know about it, Willys?" Gerald asked.

"It's Honest John LaVache's new toy."

"What, LaVache from the artificial sweetener subcommittee?"

"Yeah. What an asshole!"

"See what I mean?" Gerald said to Zardovsky.

"That guy's got a finger in every sleazy deal in this town," Handleman continued. "He's from Louisiana, his father's real rich. He owns oil tankers or something; got his start in the slot-machine business. Honest John tried to practice law down there, but he screwed up so bad the father had to buy him a House seat to get rid of him. He hasn't done a thing up here except play the real-estate market and screw anything that moves."

"How do you know all this stuff?" Zardovsky said in genuine admiration. "You're like some kind of encyclopedia."

Handleman again looked baleful, as if this were an insult.

Meanwhile, Gerald noticed that Maggie had dropped out of the conversation altogether and was emptying her bowl of chili. She seemed unaware of what was going on around her, absorbed in her own animal high spirits. In the same moment he became aware of a gaze directed at him. Bob Zardovsky's eyes had fixed on him; now they swung over to Margaret, still heedlessly eating, then back to Gerald, as if something about the two people puzzled him.

"Hey, Bob," said Margaret at that moment. "This stuff isn't bad at all."

"People think a congressman has no feelings," said Buster Hench.

He and Bob Zardovsky were sitting at a glass table. The night-club was furnished in black-and-silver art deco style, with mirrored walls and a silvery dance floor illuminated by dazzling lights.

"This is some fancy beer garden," Zardovsky said.

Hench seemed not to hear. From his jacket pocket he took a large green cigar; he bit off the end and lit it with a Zippo lighter. "People," he went on implacably, "think congressmen are some low form of life. Ah, but when they want something, they sing a different tune. 'It's Tommy this and Tommy that and Tommy go away, but it's "Thank you, Mr. Congressman" when the band begins to play.' "

Disco music began to blare from a sound system. "You feeling okay, Mr. Hench?" Zardovsky said above the din. "You sound like you bit down on a rotten taco."

An elegant figure in an Italian suit hurried up to their table. "Buster, Buster," he said. "What an honor! Your man Weisman seemed to think you wouldn't be able to make it tonight."

"Weisman doesn't know as much as he thinks," Hench said. "I'd like you to meet one of my constituents. Bob Zardovsky, Honest John LaVache. Bob's a professional baseball player."

"Is that right?" asked LaVache, squinting at Zardovsky through a health-club suntan. "What club are you with?"

"Sturgis —"

"Bob's with the New York Yankees," Hench said quickly.

"I want you gentlemen to meet Tatiana," LaVache said.

A slender, dark young woman in high heels and a short black dress appeared. "So pleased to meet more of John's friends," she said in a Slavic accent. "You are congressman, yes?" she said, batting her eyes at Hench. Then she turned to Zardovsky. "And even you, too? It is so wonderful! In America anyone is congressman!"

LaVache led her away. "Enjoy yourselves," he called over his shoulder. "I'll send the girl around."

"Going back to what I was saying," Hench said inexorably, "you take that guy there. He was on a subcommittee about Russian emigration policy. You might think he'd be bored. But Honest John LaVache has a real gut understanding of the personal side of a problem. He got this subcommittee to hold special hearings about this ballet dancer who couldn't get a visa to leave Russia. Month after month he hammered away on that one case, to drive home to people the terrors of a totalitarian system. So finally the Russians let her go. Was this some shallow desire to get his name in the papers? Hell, no! He's screwing her every night! Don't get me wrong — it's all honorable. He left his wife and everything. But still, a lot of people wouldn't understand the kind of passion that a guy like John LaVache brings to his duties, and if they did, well, all I can say is, there'd be a lot less yap, that's all I can say."

An attractive young woman with dark hair came up to the table; Zardovsky concluded that she must be the waitress. "Hello, little darlin," he said with a smile. "We'll have two mugs, a big pitcher of draft, and some barbeque Fritos."

She looked at him with disgust. "Congressman," she said to Hench, "I'm Debby Vartan, director of public relations for the club. I'd like to present you with your honorary lifetime membership card, compliments of Congressman LaVache. And would you mind if I got a photograph of you for our wall display? You might want to ask your, ah, friend to step away from the table."

"Don't be silly," said Hench, smoothing his iron-gray hair. "This is a constituent and a personal friend of mine, Three-Finger Zardovsky of the New York Yankees."

When she had gone, Zardovsky said, "Why do you keep telling people I play for the Yankees?"

"You know your problem?" Hench answered. "You sell yourself short. You could have been with the Yankees if you'd had the breaks. Anyway, who's going to know? There hasn't been a ball club in this town for ten years."

Hench seemed intent on matching Zardovsky drink for drink. He was drinking martinis and Zardovsky was drinking beer. Zardovsky was half listening to Hench's chorus of complaints and half goggling at the crowd. Past their table strode a tall, silver-haired man in a smart gray suit. A small group of shabbier men were jumping around as if desperate to catch his attention. "I'm afraid I can't answer any more questions tonight," the tall man was saying.

"That guy must be a senator," Zardovsky said. "Those reporters are really pestering him."

"Senator?" Hench said incredulously. "Are you kidding? That's Joe Powers — Joe *Powers,* the columnist. The men with him are the minority members of the House Judiciary Committee. Joe's a close personal friend of mine, you know."

"Is that right?" said Zardovsky.

"Sure. Known him for years. He lets me be a source every now and then. He hasn't let power go to his head. He still treats a freshman congressman with the same courtesy he'd give an important anchorman."

Bob Zardovsky felt that now-familiar sense of disorientation — a sense of living in a place where the normal order of things was reversed or scrambled or set at oblique and shifting angles, as if the capital were the kind of carnival whirligig in which eccentric ovoid plates are set on a round tilting surface, accelerating and decelerating in unpredictable bursts. Buster Hench seemed actually to think in this kind of elliptical pattern; his unceasing monologue had fragmented into a series of unintelligible phrases: "optimated interface . . . accelerated sign-off . . . integrated minimax . . . direct-drive trigger-price mainframe . . . decoupled disincentives . . . Zardovsky, my boy, if you want my opinion, it's all a bunch of shit."

"What is, Congressman?"

"All of it. The whole shooting match. Old Uncle Tom Cobbly and all. The entire fucking nine yards. What we ought to do is pack it in and move back to Gouge Eye, don't you think?"

"I already live in Gouge Eye, Congressman."

"See? What did I say? Sure, let old Hench do it, who cares about Hench, let him save the country. Why don't you be a congressman and I'll go work pulpwood for old Doc Pearman?"

"Doc Pearman is dead, Congressman."

"Oh, yeah, I forgot." He drained his glass, then rose ponderously. "Order some more of these, will you? I'll be right back."

As the Congressman disappeared, an unknown voice next to Zardovsky's ear said, "Would you bring us a telephone, please?" Once again Zardovsky noted the unique ability people in Washington seemed to have to appear and disappear in unexpected ways. At his elbow had materialized a little man with bright, knowing, mischievous eyes. "You must be the baseball player," he said.

"I didn't catch your name . . . ?"

The telephone arrived. "I hope you'll forgive me," the little man said. "I've got to make one quick call."

He plunged into a rapid-fire conversation. "Hi . . . yes . . . ummh . . . uh-uh . . . ahem . . . okay . . . mmmph . . . right . . . check . . . up to a point . . . roger."

His eyes were his most striking feature, large and light, their irises a pale robin's-egg blue. A sharp thin nose jutted over a mouth that seemed to have at least half-a-dozen corners, out of any of which he could mutter at will. His hair was so thin as to be largely a courtesy, and a large dark vein crossed his scalp diagonally, as if the activity inside his head were so intense that a special blood supply had been brought in to feed it.

"Wilco and out," he concluded, just as Buster Hench returned to the table. "Congressman, always an honor," he said, grasping Hench's hand. "You may not know this," the little man said fiercely to Zardovsky, "but Buster Hench is a pretty big man around this town."

"I am?" Hench said, sitting down. "You're a big fellow too, big fellow. And my friend Zardovsky is a big fellow too. He's a professional baseball player —"

"For the New York Yankees," said the little man, winking at Zardovsky.

The little man's forgiveness somehow put Zardovsky at a disadvantage, so that he confined his participation in the conversation that ensued to a series of nods, winks, and shrugs of agreement. That conversation consisted largely of the little man's amplification and gloss of his original thematic statement, that Buster Hench was a really big man in this town (the latter phrase, recurring in the Homeric discourse with near-hypnotic regularity, was intended to dignify the capital with its coyly modest diminution). Accompanying this central theme — praise of the big man by the little man — was an epic catalogue of Hench's specific qualities and accomplishments, organized under such headings as Not Afraid of Presidents (his courage in defying the powerful dirigible lobby cited here), Far-Seeing Economic Thinker (Weisman's hard-hitting report on "Economic Implications of Metric Conversion in the Container-Cargo Sector" deftly summarized and credited to Hench), and Friend of the Little Man (great, almost undue, stress laid here on Hench's willingness to help the ordinary guy who had a problem with, say, the Immigration and Naturalization Service). Hench seemed to relish the performance; because of the nature of his record, he seldom met anyone who knew it in its full incoherence.

As Zardovsky was finishing his thirteenth beer, he noticed in himself the most common symptom of heavy drinking, a sudden hunger. "Hey," he suggested, "what do you say we order some meatball sandwiches and onion rings?"

Hench answered with a hollow groan.

"You feeling a little squirrelly, Mr. Hench?" Zardovsky asked solicitously. "I don't blame you — all this loud music and smoke and stuff. Only thing for it is to get you something to eat. You know if there's a Pizza Hut around here?"

Hench groaned again, and the little man sprang into action. "I think we could all use some fresh air," he said, laying a pile of bills on the table. "Whaddaya say, big fellow? How about a little walk around the block, clear the old noggin, huh?"

They made their unsteady way past the dance floor, on which Honest John LaVache was executing the "disco rope" with Tatiana, and into the smoky-mirrored atrium. Hench seemed to be having a mild intestinal seizure. "Where's the head?" he muttered between his teeth.

"Right this way," said the little man with an air of command. To Zardovsky he said, "Look, pal, you get us a cab and I'll bring the Congressman out in a minute."

Zardovsky flagged a cab ("Abu al-Fezzan Serving the District"). He and the driver engaged in bilingual, oblique, and increasingly acrimonious discourse until it dawned on Zardovsky that the other members of his party were not coming.

As reconstructed later, what happened was as follows:

The resourceful little man, for reasons then obscure, led Buster Hench out by another exit and into a different (though equally battered) taxicab, which sped them off to a house in the wilds of upper Northwest. Hench's recollections of this trip, assembled later under great pressure, remained somewhat hazy. Oh, fatal haze, formless graveyard of reputation! Had Hench been more alert — had he been in the company of a sharper-eyed companion, like Zardovsky — he might have noticed something amiss about this destination before it was too late.

The little man proposed meeting some friends of his who lived in this house. Hench could never pinpoint what had given him the impression that these friends would be complaisant female lobbyists of the kind he had read about in the Sunday color supplements but never actually met. Imagine his confusion when the occupants of the later-famous little house turned out to be not courtesans but turbaned Hindu merchants.

Those Brahmans! Those turbans! Those obsequious bows and

melodious accents of Hind! Sharper vision might have shown Hench the labels on the turbans and robes reading "Garment Care Instructions"; sharper hearing might have let him discern in the merchants' speech faint echoes not of Lahore, Madras, and Goa but of Gary, Cleveland, and Medford, Mass. He might have wondered about their deferential pleas for help with their business, their sales of braided rugs, of gold and frankincense and myrrh — worthy enterprises obstructed by slight misunderstandings about visas. He might not have been so ready, remembering the little man's praise, to promise his help, and might not have accepted, with lopsided smiles and slurred but circumstantial promises of service, all recorded so clearly by the videotape cameras behind the gilt-framed living-room mirror, the fatal attaché case of cash.

Sobriety returned in queasy waves at the evening's close, as the Hindus identified themselves as FBI agents. The little man had disappeared; many things disappeared in the ensuing hours and days, in the rush of bail hearings, arraignments, pleadings, press conferences, discovery proceedings, and votes of censure that dominate the life of an overworked modern legislator. One of the things was Bob Zardovsky's CATA grant, which was indefinitely postponed.

Part Two

Those people suppose, that because the smallest
circle hath as many degrees as the largest, therefore
the regulation and management of the world require no
more abilities than the handling and turning of a globe.
—"A Voyage to Laputa, Balnibarbi,
Glubbdubdrib, Luggnagg and Japan"

Chapter 1

THE TEN O'CLOCK NEWS became Gerald's secret vice. No one, not even Handleman, knew of the bond of memory and desire between him and the image on the screen. Once, as if idly, he asked Margaret, "Do you think that girl is attractive?"

Margaret was reclining at his feet, her thick blond hair in sweet disorder against a fat India-print cushion, her fine legs sprawled before her in tight, frayed blue jeans, a cigarette between her lips and a glass of white wine balanced on her stomach. She too spoke as if idly, after studying Diana, who was introducing a three-part exposé of glue abuse at inner-city playgrounds. "I think so, if you go for that type."

"What type is that?"

"Dark and dangerous — you know, malign allure."

"I'm not sure I follow."

"That's because you go for my type."

"Which is what?"

"I'm not sure, but nobody has thought I was dangerous since I gave up playing the trumpet."

Gerald's cheeks burned, unseen; and, unseeing, Diana's dark, dangerous eyes met his. Those eyes seemed now to be watching him almost all the time: from televisions in store windows, from promotional placards on buses, from newspaper advertisements. Diana was at city council meetings, housing project murders, Virginia political rallies, municipal union bargaining sessions, antique steamboat races.

Time after self-hating time over the course of weeks, Gerald left his name and number for her at the television station. But no answer came from the flickering image.

One morning Gerald walked to work under limitless blue skies, along wide, rain-washed avenues framed by delicate flowering trees; the next he crawled through soupy smog, along steaming sidewalks, under a sky the color of dried fat. Summer had come to Washington.

It was Gerald's custom several times a week to run two miles. He enjoyed the blank frame of mind it brought on — like the effects of marijuana but without the tendency toward inappropriate laughter. Once summer arrived the park was unbearable, and Gerald was thrown on the facilities of the Washington YMCA.

Those unfamiliar with this institution may associate these four initials with a decaying structure smelling of sweat socks and offering the use of a freezing swimming pool, a patched medicine ball, half-a-dozen antique Indian juggling clubs, and a threadbare towel. But the Washington Y was the kind of sports facility Mussolini had once wanted every young Italian to have.

Gerald's membership entitled him to gymnasium, weight room, swimming and racket-sport facilities, and to a specially carpeted locker room and padded exercise area with color television, telephone cabin, and fruit-juice vending machine, and to the whirlpool bath, steam room and sauna, suntan room, and optional massage service. (Willys Handleman had come to the Y to write a scathing exposé for an underground newspaper. After the tour, however, he began to badger Gerald to lend him the four-figure sum needed to join. When Gerald pointed out that Handleman's idea of a brisk workout was nine innings of dice baseball, Handleman broke off negotiations on the grounds that Gerald was an elitist.)

One morning Gerald strode in through the double glass doors.

He was due shortly at a divisional senior staff meeting, a prospect of such agony (especially now that the simmering feud between Quoin and Muntin had erupted into full-scale war) that he intended to run nearly twice his usual distance and then fry himself to catatonia in the steam room. He dressed in Tigers running shoes, blue knit shorts, and a white T-shirt that showed a drawing of the Capitol dome flanked by a red heart and a green dollar sign, below which was the inscription WASHINGTON IS FOR LAWYERS.

The jogging track was on the top floor. From its slow lane a runner commanded a view of the gymnasium floor below. During certain hours of the day the gym floor was crowded with young women in leotards doing dance routines. At these times the slow lane was crowded. At other hours there were basketball games in which lawyers, lobbyists, journalists, and endocrinologists attempted to maim each other with their elbows while shouting imitation ghetto slang (to the ill-concealed amusement of the cleaning staff). During these hours male joggers preferred to battle for possession of the fast lane. These contests could turn bitter, with polysyllabic insults, veiled criticism of running style, and threats of legal action. Gerald preferred to run in the early mornings when the track was nearly empty.

As on many mornings, Gerald knew everyone on the track by private nickname. There was Horns, who ran in a billed cap decorated with soft stuffed-cloth antelope's horns, with a pair of foam earphones wired to a cassette tape recorder strapped to his back and a solid-state wristwatch designed to give a constant digital readout of his pulse. Coke Bottle, an appropriately shaped young woman, covered enormous distances by flinging her flabby legs outward while clutching her hands tightly to her chest. Crane, a tall, thin man with prematurely gray hair and a limitless number of pastel running suits, performed an elaborate set of stretching exercises, flung his beaky nose forward, and staggered after it for ten or twelve laps before collapsing in a tangle of knees.

Gerald began his running routine, clicking off the laps on his counter. The trivial and self-absorbed quality of his thoughts ("Strike, roll, push, knees loose, hands loose, strike, roll, push," and so on) partly accounted for the soothing effect that running had on him. After ten laps or so, mental activity slowed to a delicious ooze.

So Gerald at first did not react when from the region of his right ear he heard a familiar voice say, "Where have you been lately? I've been looking for you all over the place."

At the edge of his vision flickered impossibly long legs, and Diana pulled abreast of him, running effortlessly.

"Don't let up," the vision cried, clapping her hands in exhortation. "A good runner can carry on a conversation at a steady pace. I was wondering when I'd see you here."

"I've been calling you," Gerald said.

"I know."

"Why didn't you call back?"

"I'm sick of the telephone. You're always so buttoned-up and official when I call you."

"Always? You've only called me once in seven years!"

"That's why. Are you glued to the TV set daily at six and ten?"

"No," he lied.

"I must be slipping," she said complacently. "I'll have to talk to makeup about it."

"Let me check," he said, dropping back. This brought him into collision with Horns, who had been running right behind Diana to get the best view and who now ricocheted into a corner, cursing, to adjust his headphones. Gerald regained his stride and looked at her — long midnight-black hair, graceful arms, lithe, elegant legs, "No. You look fabulous. You've filled out some. This job must agree with you."

"I like it — for now. But there's one problem."

"What's that?"

"How do you get a date in this lousy town?"

So, ignoring what breathlessness and nostalgia had left him of his better judgment, Gerald invited her to the movies and dinner that evening.

They met after work at a grubby film theater off Connecticut Avenue. Diana came straight from the station, flying out of the taxi in a silk blouse and fashionably slit skirt, her face dramatic in camera makeup.

"Are you still on duty?" Gerald asked.

"Not tonight. Anyway" — she indicated the black radio beeper strapped to her belt — "they can always reach me if something breaks on one of my stories."

The film told the story of a tribe of psychic mutants who were seeking to control the world by telekinetically exploding their enemies' heads from the inside. This was shown in admirable detail, full color, and slow motion. The rowdy audience applauded each eruption; Diana slumped in her seat, and only the glittering of her eyes showed she was awake. Gerald felt a puzzling sympathy for the victims.

After the film they walked through Adams-Morgan in search of a restaurant — a happy task in Washington. The determination of successive postwar administrations to give vocal but insufficient support to unpopular governments around the world has given the capital a rich and varied choice of ethnic cuisine. The restaurant Diana selected served the cuisine of a small nation in northeast Africa, which consisted of chicken or beef, sometimes cooked and sometimes raw, doused in sauces with many exotic names but all consisting of red pepper.

At the table she fixed him with her dark eyes. "You haven't turned into a vegetarian or anything, have you?"

"Christ, no."

"Do you smoke?"

"No."

"You still don't have any bad habits?"

"I watch a lot of television."

Years before, he had been struck by her ability to create intimacy simply by assuming it, so that those on whom she wove her spell found themselves treating her not only as an old friend but as their best or even only friend. It was a matter of accepting no limitations — of unbounded self-confidence and curiosity that dissolved the usual barriers of shyness or diffidence.

Had Gerald had a chance to see Diana as she really was, he would have seen a tall young woman with olive skin, a heart-shaped face, a full mouth, and sardonic eyebrows. Wherever she walked or sat, male eyes turned toward her irresistibly, drawn by her physical beauty, her sulky grace, and her smile, which gave her the look of a stock trader who has obtained advance copies of the next year's *Wall Street Journals*. When she flung herself into an encounter, waving her long, slim hands, reaching across space and time with her dark, almond-shaped eyes, a man would have had to be a saint or a fool to notice as she turned him into a swine.

"What about you — do you still do horoscopes and all that parapsychology stuff?" he asked.

Her languid hand in the air dissolved the question. "We'll get to me later. Do you still have a motorcycle?"

"No."

"Do you still sing to yourself while you're working?"

"No," he said after a minute. "I don't guess I do."

Gerald ordered cooked chicken; Diana, raw beef. They ate their meals with spongy flat bread and washed them down with honey wine. The bread was utterly tasteless but was handy for cooling the mouth after a violent dose of red pepper — which was fortunate, because the wine was so thick that it was impossible to drink.

"Okay, now," said Gerald after a speechless period in which the combination of gummy bread, gluey wine, and searing sauce had made him wonder whether he would ever be able to breathe again. "What about you?"

"What do you mean?"

"You know damn well what I mean. We broke up, you dropped out of school to become a warlock or whatever, and I just never fucking heard from you again. Seven years later you call me on the phone to ask me about some poem. Then you turn up on TV. Where the hell have you been all this time? Why didn't you ever call me — or else, why call me now?"

She rolled her wineglass between her hands, throwing shadows on the white tablecloth. "I wanted to call you. But I felt ashamed. I didn't really understand why it didn't work with us. Can you remember why?"

The question sent loose pebbles rattling in dark caves of memory: of nights spent smoking marijuana and drinking cheap Portuguese wine, days walking picket lines; of the electric intensity of extreme youth. There were bright spots — shouted slogans, whispered words — and dark, impenetrable gaps. "No. I never knew," he said.

"I just felt like everything had turned to shit without any reason.

I felt like I had to go somewhere and start over before I saw you again, so you'd know I wasn't the same old person. I thought if I got to the West Coast I would acquire magical powers or something and they would let me win you back, wipe out whatever it was that went wrong.

"Thank God I didn't get there at the time. I probably would have joined the Manson family or something like that. But instead I ran out of money in Yuma. I thought about calling you for help — you were a sucker for a damsel in distress — but it didn't feel right. So I got a job as a cocktail waitress at this motel. I figured I could get some money together, get out to the Coast. But it turned out part of the job was turning tricks for the manager. All the other girls there were hookers. Stupid me, I hadn't even suspected. There was this magician working the lounge, and I sort of came on to him and told him all about how I'd studied parapsychology in college, so he hired me as his assistant, shilling for him in the mind-reading act and all this jazz. I kept having this vision of you coming into one of these podunk motel lounges and seeing me stooging in black stockings for this moron. So when I got to Vegas I left him — didn't say anything, just ducked out. I had about sixty dollars. I figured that since I believed in telekinesis and synchronicity and all that shit, I should go into the casino and put it all on twenty-six. So I stood by the table for an hour, waiting for the vibrations to speak to me. And then I suddenly realized that all that shit I was always spouting off about — I didn't believe in it to amount to sixty dollars. Best thing that ever happened to me. I bought a bus ticket to L.A. Figured I'd become a movie star, you'd see me on the screen, call me up, there we'd be. I got a part, too — in something called *Night of the Bat People*. Third vampire girl from the left — you ever see it?"

"Well, I don't get to many movies."

"That's good. It means you weren't taking girls to the drive-in. That was my whole film career. I got a job at an all-night radio station, very important work, keeping the Procol Harum records out of the Iron Butterfly jackets. But one night the news guy got sick and they got me to read the AP wires. Next thing I know, I get a message about somebody wanting me to take a screen test. It was this two-candle TV station out in the valley. Their FCC license was up for renewal and somebody had complained that they didn't have women on the air.

"So I took the job. What a dump that place was! I was supposed to make coffee and type and read the morning news. Then they started talking about giving me the Suzy Homemaker show — you know what a joke that would have been. The only recipe I knew was for macrobiotic massage oil. But the farmworkers' strike came along, and guys from the nets were coming through. I latched onto a stringer slot and ended up with a job at one of their affiliates in Houston. By that time I didn't know where you were or what you were doing. Then this job came along. It's the last stop before the net, and they let me use their research computers. I put your name in the hopper and out came your phone number. So here we are."

"I still don't see why you never called or wrote or anything," he said. "Just to say you were alive, if nothing else. I've been thinking — all this time, I've been thinking . . ."

"What did you think?"

"Oh, Christ, I can't remember anymore. I guess it doesn't matter."

"Damn you, there you go again!" She threw her hands on the tabletop. "I knew you would do this — you've always been like a little clam or something, with your secrets, you always slip away or close up. That's why I didn't want to call you — I was afraid you'd just mumble at me and I'd end up feeling terrible about everything I was doing. I was still scared of you."

Few things are better calculated to disarm a young man (particularly one whose personality is an uneasy blend of aspiration and insecurity) than for an attractive woman to claim to be afraid of him. Whether by design or in sincerity (the difference often being less marked than most of us admit), Diana followed this surprising admission with one of these few things. "You could have hurt me, Gerry. I loved you so much. I'm not sure you ever believed that."

Inside Gerald there was a loose, settling sensation, as if ice blocks were melting. The conversation had gotten wholly out of control. The few pebbles of memory became an avalanche, breaking soundlessly over him. He tasted the thing that, without knowing it, he had spent years trying to avoid: the bitter ichor of regret, of sorrow for his youth and hopes and for the heart-whole certainty of his lost love for Diana.

"You don't want fried prunes, do you?" she asked. "That's all they serve for dessert. They come with sweet goat yogurt."

In the street she slid her arm through his. "You live around here, don't you?" she said casually.

What followed can be readily imagined.

Luckily, Handleman had gone to a Humphrey Bogart double feature, leaving a note: "Margaret called." Gerald crumpled this into a ball. He felt an uncharacteristically firm resolve not to think about what he was doing. After the requisite hypocritical interval, he led Diana into his bedroom. Her legs were at least as long as he had remembered, her lean body as supple and surprising, her mouth as sweet and yielding. Her breath was like a wind from distant worlds of possibility; he felt a rushing sensation, as if he were traveling at unimaginable speed, faster than light, into remote regions or backward in time . . .

Much later, in the dark, cluttered bedroom, there was an electronic beep. Diana rose and dressed with silent haste, then furtively felt in the pocket of Gerald's suit jacket, extracted a key, and glided out the door. Gerald slept like one bewitched.

Willys Handleman spent the night dreaming uneasily of himself as Sam Spade, sending women to prison; of himself as Richard Blaine, packing them onto the Lisbon plane; of himself as Peter Lorre, fleeing from them into shadows and shame. He woke early, pulled on a pair of cutoff jeans, and staggered into the living room to watch the early news. There was a brief recap of the preliminary motions in the Hench prosecution; then an account of the mayor's fact-finding mission to Hong Kong; then a report on a police raid at a Temple of Ray commune, which had netted ten thousand pages of stolen but unimportant government documents. During the latter report his mind wandered, as it often did, to the small but finite possibility of something happening that would transform his life at one triumphant stroke. He could not choose between a phone call from the President to offer him a joint appointment as chief speechwriter and Secretary of State, a letter from the Pulitzer Prize board apologizing for inadvertently dropping his name from the last list of winners, and an amorous telegram from Meryl Streep.

He was roused from these delightful imaginings by the sound of a key in the apartment door. He hurried to the hall, where he saw an attractive, oddly familiar young woman with long dark hair.

"Hi!" she said placidly. "You must be Willys. I'm Diana, Gerry's friend."

From where he was standing, Willys could see Diana both in the hallway and on the screen of Gerald's television set, in a bizarre stereo effect that led him (not for the first time) to question his own sanity.

"You," he gurgled, "aren't you —"

"Yes," said Diana, who was used to having this effect, "I'm Diana Cazadora."

"I'm watching you right now!"

"Don't wake Gerry," she said contentedly. "How am I?"

"Great! I mean, good. Fine, I mean. Not bad at all."

"You sure you want to stop there? You won't go as low as *fair,* or *passable?*"

Willys kept goggling. "Haven't I seen you someplace else? Wait a minute — you were in *Night of the Bat People!*"

"Good God," she said. "No one has ever recognized me from that picture before. What are you, some kind of computer?"

"I have a good memory for, ah, faces," Handleman said proudly. In truth, dark and dangerous ladies formed a prominent part of his rich fantasy life.

Willys found the real Diana uncommonly easy to talk to. He was vexed that she was so interested in Gerald rather than in himself, but he gave her the information she wanted, starting with every scrap he knew about Gerald's love life and progressing to his work at the Department.

"What does he do over there, anyway?" she asked.

"His main job is to keep the whole thing from blowing up and landing on the front page of the morning paper. The people over there hate each other."

"That's fascinating," Diana breathed, honing in on Willys with her dark eyes. "Can you give me any examples?"

"Sure. Take right now. The Deputy Assistant Secretary — her name's Nancy Quoin — is trying to get one of her subordinates fired. It's driving Gerry crazy."

"That doesn't sound like such a big deal. Why doesn't she just fire him?"

"If you'll excuse my saying so, Diana, you haven't been in this town quite as long as I have. Firing a civil servant is hell, no matter who he is. And this guy is extremely powerful and has a lot of friends. Somehow Nancy got hold of proof that his résumé has a lot of mistakes in it. It says he graduated from Notre Dame, but it turns out he dropped out and finished at Pawnee Professional Institute or someplace like that."

"How in the world did she find that out?"

"Nobody knows. She thought it would be a snap. She filed her complaint with the Office of Personnel Management and leaked it to somebody on Hench's staff. But Hench self-destructed, and now Quoin's out on a limb. If she fights the thing through the OPM and MSPB procedures, it could take years. And meanwhile Muntin is gunning for her — he figures if she goes, the whole thing will blow over. Poor Gerald spends all his time trotting back and forth, carrying messages between the camps."

"That's fascinating," Diana said. The dark eyes took on a sheen of worship. "You certainly are well informed."

"Well, I've been around this town a long time."

"Could I ask you a favor? I'm new here and I don't know the territory. Would you mind if I called you from time to time to talk things over?"

"Sure, go ahead," Handleman said magnanimously. "Of course, I can't reveal some of my sources —"

"Of course not. I understand that."

"And I'm out on interviews —"

"Maybe it wouldn't be convenient."

"No, no, no, as long as you call in the mornings. Or the afternoons, too. I go out for lunch a lot. Do you like Indian —"

From the other room came the sounds of Gerald waking from vivid, rushing dreams. Diana covered Willys's mouth with her hand. "Do me a favor," she said. "Don't tell Gerry I had to go out, okay?"

Handleman nodded without hesitation. Thus began a fateful alliance between these two pilgrims in the sunless desert of ambition, in appearance so different, in spirit so attuned.

Chapter 2

THE EARLY WEEKS OF SUMMER were not shaping up as a good period for Margaret Luck. Bernie Weisman was no longer speaking to her. Gerald seemed to get more nervous and elusive every day. But the thing that really bothered her was that she had not stopped smoking.

Every summer the cycle of resolutions, remedies, and self-loathing repeated itself. In her college days she had played tennis, climbed mountains, and ridden horses. She still had a kind of outdoor look, the loose, confident stride of someone at home with her body. But the athletic exterior was a sham. She could barely make it up the stairs to her apartment without wheezing like a manatee; in the mornings she coughed and retched for minutes at a time. Every time she switched to a lower-tar cigarette, her consumption rose proportionately, until she found herself near financial ruin because of the expense of smoking huge numbers of weirdly named cigarettes she hated.

A year before, she had tried behavior therapy, which had required her to keep voluminous notes on each cigarette she smoked; the note-taking had nearly cost her her job. Then she had tried acupuncture, which hurt miserably, failed to slow her smoking, and left her with the recurring sensation that one of her earlobes was misshapen. So this June she had answered an ad from the Women's Mental Health Collective for a sixty-dollar, three-session course of feminist hypnotherapy.

The hypnotist operated out of a row-house office on Capitol Hill. She saw Maggie after work on Friday night. She was a squat, middle-aged woman with a lisp. "Hypnothith ith nothing mythtical," she told Maggie. "Itth a method of reaching a new thtate of conthiouthneth, a different thychic thpathe." The lisp struck Maggie as so ludicrous that she was shocked when it sent her drifting into a semiconscious, buzzing state. Her right arm snaked in the air on command; her head lolled in the chair; her eyes rolled up in her head. The hypnotist evoked images of her life as a nonsmoker; she saw herself turning down cigarettes at parties, after meals, at coffee breaks, at work, on airplanes. She would not smoke again for five days, the hypnotist told her; now she would wake up, feeling refreshed and confident.

At home again, she drifted lazily around her apartment, watering the plants and tidying the kitchen, feeling graceful and effectual. Gerald had more or less said that he would almost certainly call her for dinner that night. Her chores finished, she curled up on the sofa with a glass of wine and the afternoon paper. The headlines were about Buster Hench's attempts to devise a novel plea to the bribery charges: neither "guilty" nor "not guilty," but "alcoholic."

There was also news of the primaries, which (as far as anyone could tell) the President was winning. Maggie had not read far, however, before she drifted into a placid, blissful state that seemed to be an aftereffect of hypnosis, in which she happily chased butterfly wisps of thought through green meadows until something — maybe the distant yodel of a siren, or the blast of a car horn, or someone upsetting a garbage pail in the alley — made her start awake. She was aware simultaneously that Gerald had not called her and it was now too late to expect him to, and that she had managed even in her half-trance to light and smoke two successive cigarettes.

Her evening, her hopes, her self-respect lay in shards around her; she was a mush-headed moron addled by hypnotic commands that didn't work, smoking automatically beside a telephone that wouldn't ring. And the same self-hating logic made it appropriate that at the height of her fury and self-disgust, the telephone did ring, bringing on an involuntary surge of surreal hope that if she had been wrong and Gerald was calling, then maybe the two cigarettes didn't count and her new beginning could begin again.

"Hello, Gerry?"

A voice, familiar but definitely not Gerald's, said, "Hey, Maggie? Is this Maggie Luck?"

"Yeah."

"Zardovsky here."

"Oh."

"I do something wrong?"

"No. I'm sorry. I was expecting a call from . . . somebody else."

In the brief pause that followed, Maggie managed to marshal arguments on both sides, capitulate abjectly, locate and light a cigarette, and then say, "What can I do for you, Bob?"

"I just got back in town. The co-op voted to try this whole thing over again. I was just wondering if I could crash on your couch tonight."

Zardovsky was a cheerful presence, but he was given to guffawing late at night at jokes on the Carson show and to leaving his socks in corners of the room. Just then the thought of cheerfulness outweighed her fastidiousness, and she said, "I guess it'll be okay for a day or two. Where are you?"

"I'm at the bus station. I'll get a subway up to Dupont Circle."

"Have you had dinner?"

"I got some raisins and peanuts and stuff in my briefcase."

"How disgusting. Why don't we go out and get something?"

"That's real nice of you."

"And don't speak to strangers this time, okay?"

Waiting for Bob, she fell sound asleep. When she came to, he was knocking at her apartment door, looking like Barnacle Bill the Sailor in his blue T-shirt and backpack. He lurched into the room, hurling his backpack and briefcase into opposite corners as if to claim as large a piece of territory as possible. "Damn, it is hot in this town," he said. "I wake you up? You feeling okay? You look like you got the bong-bongs or something."

"I'm all right. Do you want a beer?"

"Does a bear shit in the woods?"

She explained why she seemed so close to catalepsy. "No kidding — hypnotized?" Zardovsky said, delighted. "Did you cluck like a chicken or anything?"

"I would have, I think. I would have done just about anything except give up smoking."

"Yeah, that's about the toughest thing there is. We had this guy on the ball club down in Mexico who tried to quit for ten years. He'd been a big base-stealer but he started getting kinda windbroke. Finally he went to a Mexican faith healer."

"Maybe I should do that," Maggie said, settling comfortably on the huge pillow. "The problem is, I don't have any faith."

"Neither did this guy I'm talking about. The old man said it didn't matter — he would cure him by his own spiritual power. He danced around and squawked in Maya and then he told this guy he had plucked the bad demons out of his lungs and he wouldn't want to smoke no more. Then he charged him two hundred pesos."

"So did your friend quit smoking?"

"Shit, no. The next month he burned down a hotel in Durango by mistake."

Zardovsky seemed to expand to fill the sofa. He yawned and stretched his arms over his head. "Listen," he said. "I don't want to ruin your evening or nothing. You're probably planning to go somewhere. Don't worry about me. I'll just get a hamburger and sack out."

"Fat chance of me going anywhere tonight."

"No date or nothing?"

"Not even one."

"What happened to that ner— I mean, that guy Gerry?"

"I'm asking the same question. He's been appearing and disappearing lately, like a lightning bug."

"Fuck him then. Pardon my French. What I mean is, why don't you tell him to take a hike?"

"Did you say you had nuts?"

After a great deal of chewing, she continued. "The thing is, Bob, men are not all that plentiful around this town. I don't mean attractive men or men who aren't married or men who aren't gay —

I just mean men in general. I read somewhere that there are two
and a half women for every man working for the government."

"Holy shit, no wonder all these guys want to be in Congress!
What do all these women do?"

"I think they mostly work for the FBI. Anyway, maybe it sounds
stupid, but you don't throw something away, even if it's not ideal."

"Aw, bullshit. Pardon my French again. You don't believe that
yourself. You just like this guy and you're embarrassed to admit it."

She felt herself flushing and looked down at her hands while a
laugh forced its way up from her solar plexus. This hulking ex-
jock, she suddenly realized, was not as dumb as she had thought.

"You want some dinner?" she asked.

"Hell, yeah." With the energy and mass of a breaching whale,
he flung himself to his feet, yawning, hitching up his jeans, stretching, and in general managing to radiate a huge warm aura of male
complacency. "I ain't got much money on this trip. We're really
getting strapped back home," he said.

"Well, up on Columbia Road are some cheap Cuban joints, if
you like black beans."

"Sure — used to eat 'em all the time in the Yucatan. It made for
a long bus ride home."

The walk led them through a series of dark streets. As they went,
he explained the situation back in Gouge Eye. The co-op had
bought an option on the mill, which would expire at the end of
the year. Three weeks ago some local residents had spotted two
late-night hikers carrying plastic gasoline jugs near the mill. They
had frightened these sportsmen off, but some in the town had concluded that the corporation would not be grief-stricken if the old
mill burned down, which would allow them to collect the insurance money. So the co-op board had set patrols around the property to watch for comings and goings.

As this explanation ended, Zardovsky and Maggie found themselves on a particularly empty and cheerless stretch of street. One
block away, visible in the distance, was Columbia Road, the noisy
boulevard that Zardovsky had on his last visit mistaken for Calle
Sesenta in Merida.

For the past half-block or so, Margaret had been dimly aware of
raucous Latin music. Quite suddenly the music switched off. She

put her arm through Zardovsky's in an attempt to urge him forward. She did not want to vocalize the strange tickle she was feeling between her shoulder blades, so she said apologetically, "It's not far now. I'm hungry, aren't you?"

With the precision of a nightmare, a shape flowed out of an entryway and said, "Hey, man, you got a cigarette?"

Don't stop, don't look, she begged Zardovsky silently, tugging on his arm, deliberately not seeing the stranger, willing him out of existence. Bob flipped his free hand nonchalantly at the shadow and said, "Sorry, buddy, don't smoke 'em."

"How 'bout fifty cents?" It was a young voice, with a strong Spanish accent.

"Wish I could help you," Zardovsky said.

"You better hole on," said the stranger with the helpful tone of someone settling a nagging argument. "I got a gun."

Zardovsky raised his hands smoothly, and Margaret did the same. "The two of us are looking at the trees," Zardovsky said. "We ain't seen you, amigo, we don't remember what you look like. Matter of fact, we probably won't even remember that we ran into you tonight. You just take whatever you need and then we'll walk on like nothing happened."

"Shut up and gimme the wallet, man," said the voice. Margaret, even in her nauseated panic, recognized the sense in what Bob had said. She lifted her eyes and saw the streetlight casting a globe of light on the pale leaves of a tall walnut tree. "Gimme the purse, lady," said the voice. Concentration on her breathing carried her through the next half-minute or so, the longest she had ever endured. A dozen breaths later the voice said, "Okay, you guys get outta here now, and no screamin, 'cause I gonna be watchin you."

They ran, but they had not covered five steps before they heard the stranger running behind them and an ominous metallic click. "Freeze, goddamn it! *Freeze,* you mothers, or I blow you fuckin knees off!" cried the voice. "Now turn around, goddamn it!" The voice had a frenzied sound, and as Margaret turned she saw the young man's long face, handsome clear Latin features, curly black hair, an angry scar over his left eye. He was shaking. He was going to kill them; she had no hope left.

"Goddamn it! Goddamn it!" he yelled. "I knew it!" He began

leaping up and down gracefully, the gun, a snub automatic, waving back and forth between them. "Goddamn it! It is you, man!" he shouted. "I thought I knew you from someplace, then I saw from your wallet, man! You're Tres-Dedos Zardovsky! Shit, I saw you pitch a no-hitter against Tapachula six years ago! Here's your stuff back. I din't take nothin. I'm sorry I bother you guys, I din't know who you were." He slipped the pistol into the pocket of his jeans. "You were great, man," he said to Zardovsky. "I never forget — Hernandez was O for four. You struck him out lookin in the ninth."

"Yeah, Hubba-Hubba was pretty bent outa shape about the whole thing," Zardovsky said, lowering his hands to his sides. "He busted his bat in the clubhouse afterwards. It took my team five innings to get me one run. Those shitheads — nobody would talk to me between innings, either."

"Listen, I'm sorry I took your wallet — you too, lady. I wasn't going to hurt you for real, no matter what. Shit, I don't even got bullets in the gun."

"What?" Zardovsky asked amiably. "You mean to say the pistol never was loaded?"

"Naw, man."

"Show me, amigo."

The mugger pulled out the automatic and flipped open the clip, showing that it was empty; then he pointed it above his head and pulled the trigger, producing a soft, harmless click.

"Well, you son of a bitch," said Zardovsky. Pivoting slightly on his left foot, he directed at the smaller man a killer gut-punch that would have doubled up a much larger opponent.

But the mugger took this blow with an expression of mild surprise and no discernible pain; he laughed, raised his hands over his head, and called, "Hey, that was good! Try another one, come on, take your best shot, man!" Then he noticed Zardovsky shaking his fist and became solicitous. "Careful, man, you can't take no chances with your hands," he said. "You could break a finger or somethin."

"You wearin some kinda lead corset?" Zardovsky grumbled.

"Naw, I was flyweight champion of my province, man. Shit! I coulda beat Duran. Listen, don't be mad no more, I said I was sorry, din't I? I tell you what — lemme buy you some beer or somethin, okay? You like Latin food?"

"We were going to some Cuban joint," Bob said.

"Aw, shit, that stuff is for rich people. You could spend four, five dollars in one of those places — each. You come with me, I know a real people's place — you too, lady, sorry I scared you, no hard feelins, okay?"

Maggie found herself shaking the little man's hand. She and Zardovsky fell into step behind the mugger, who was jubilantly executing dance steps down the sidewalk; after a few paces he switched on a tape deck and the salsa music resumed.

"We'll run away at the traffic light and lose him on Eighteenth Street," she whispered to Zardovsky.

"You kidding? Pass up a free meal?" he whispered back, with his maddening popeyed grin. "Anyway, you got any idea how long it's been since I met somebody who saw me pitch?" Zardovsky threw his big arm around her shoulders and squeezed her not unpleasantly breathless. "Oh, come on, honeybunch," he said. "I won't let nothin bad happen to you."

So she ended up on a dim side street in a corner of the neighborhood she had never seen before. MA DZUDZ SANITARY CAFÉ said new lettering on the building's dingy windows. MARIACHI EVERY NITE. Inside was a tiny lunch counter and two Formica-and-vinyl booths.

A small, dark waitress brought them three bottles of a black, thick beer with the label "Leon Negra." The first few sips had a galvanic effect on Maggie's nervous system. The combination of her earlier nap and the adrenalin rush of the mugging merged to produce an almost painful awareness of the world around her, which was familiar and yet eerily transformed, as if life were a barge that with no warning had torn loose from its moorings and begun slipping, unpiloted, downstream.

Soon there appeared huge plates of fried cornmeal dough, some kind of crude coleslaw, and refried beans, which Bob began eating voraciously while the mugger talked.

"My name is Paco Sanchez," he said. "My father ran the dock union in Belize until the British threw him out. Then he went to Tegucigalpa and bought a cigar store. One day when I was little the soldiers came and killed him. So I promise myself that when I grow up I will make a revolution. Now I am a minister."

"A minister?" Zardovsky said. "What-all denomination are you affiliated with?"

"Hey, you mean like a priest? No, man, I mean *minister* — okay, Vice Minister for Tourism, Sport, and Foreign Affairs of the Frente para Liberación Armada de la Nación — you know, the FLAN. You probly heard of us. No? Okay, maybe we ain't done much so far, but we will. We got a government in the hills, radios, jeeps, everything. We even got our own lottery. They send me over the border into Mexico and I hitch a ride up to the States with some coyotes. I'm supposed to start our information office. But I got no money left, and those bastards in the government devalue the balboa again. So that's how come I was tryin to rob you, see? I din't really want to do it. So this is like a sign, 'cause I finally get my nerve up and the first people I rob is Tres-Dedos Zardovsky, like one of my idols, you know. So, okay, *basta*, no more robbin with guns for me no more. I got to think of somethin else for sure. Maybe you can help me. Maybe I help you. You come here anytime and ask for Paco. Okay? I do anything for Tres-Dedos. Okay? Friends maybe a little, lady?"

Four men with guitars burst into the room and began playing the opening chorus of "Volver, Volver." A fifth man stood outside playing a trumpet, as if afraid the full power of the instrument would shatter the plate-glass window. Margaret shook hands with the little maniac who had threatened to kill her half an hour ago. She looked from his face to Bob's: goofy, grinning, smeared with hot sauce and sweat. Whatever else had happened, she admitted to herself, the evening had been considerably less dull than she'd expected.

Chapter 3

IN THE DAYS that followed his reunion with Diana, Gerald found himself prone to gusts of inappropriate emotion, as if his mind were a boarding house in which a twenty-one-year-old lodger had begun loudly playing the guitar, cooking aromatic meals, and leaving motorcycle boots on the front stairway.

Diana was seldom to be reached, unpredictable in her phone calls, and irregular in her appearances at his door after the ten o'clock news, which she had been picked to coanchor while a colleague was on vacation. Once she appeared she conveyed the intoxicating impression that given a choice of all men on earth, she had chosen to exist only for him. It was only when she disappeared again that he found himself formulating questions for which there was never time when she reappeared.

Willys Handleman meanwhile seemed to regard this new affair with the odd satisfaction he ordinarily reserved for things that might bring personal advantage to him. He even began to throw away his empty curry cartons and pop bottles, revealing parts of Gerald's rug not seen for nearly a year.

With the thoroughness of his legal training, Gerald had re-hearsed an exhaustive catalogue of reasons why he and Margaret should stop seeing each other, including every reason but the real one. But when he saw her, he found himself listening sympatheti-cally to her complaints about quitting smoking. In his guilty com-passion, he began lighting her cigarettes for her, and this small ges-ture of intimacy somehow led him directly back into her barred bedroom.

So for the rest of June, Gerald was tormented by his hyper-trophied conscience. To it he threw the sop of a short memo to the Assistant Secretary, urging him to stop in Gouge Eye at the end of his midsummer tour of departmental installations in Alaska. *"The proposed CATA grant is of an intriguing and unusual nature,"* he wrote, adding the unemphasized clause, "and its development po-tential is reportedly enhanced by the first-rate freshwater fishing in the immediate area."

All in all, Gerald welcomed the Fourth of July weekend, which was the date set for his brother's wedding.

One of the joys of living in the nation's capital is the extreme convenience of National Airport, only ten minutes from down-town. This demands some minor sacrifices by the capital's residents, of course; often they must replace windows and eardrums cracked by the roar of the planes, and occasionally houses themselves blunder into the path of an airliner. But the Congress regards these as acceptable sacrifices to be made by people who have no voting congressman and thus no human worth.

Gerald battled his way through a throng of travelers, airline per-sonnel, security guards, and solicitors for the Temple of Ray and the Toiling Masses League. One of the latter for some reason marked Gerald as a lively prospect and pursued him across the terminal with peremptory demands that he buy a bumper sticker with the message OPPRESSED WORKERS NEVER HAVE A NICE DAY.

Gerald took refuge in the newsstand, where he bought a paper-back novel to read on his flight. The book was called *Blood Breth-ren*, and its cover billed it as "a searing tale of top-level terror by the best-selling author of *The Ruling*." Reading it in the depar-ture lounge, Gerald gathered the following: Fentley Van Helsing V, thoughtful young Supreme Court law clerk, was disturbed. New

Chief Justice H. Harrold Jorga insisted that the Court hold all sessions after sundown. And when the liberal Justice for whom Van Helsing worked fell ill with a strange anemia, Van Helsing was forced to a chilling conclusion: *the Chief Justice of the United States was a vampire.*

At this point Gerald's flight was called. Gerald ordered a martini and passed the rest of the flight so deep in thought that he might have been thought asleep.

Gerald's mother was at the arrival gate. She was a spare woman with short gray hair, and she was wearing a brown raincoat and a watchful expression. In recent years she had apparently decided to treat Gerald as one of many interesting but unfamiliar persons with whom she had occasional contact.

"Everybody's waiting for us at the house," she said crisply. "I want to get back before your father burns it down."

She had traded her worn blue station wagon for a tiny white Chevette. "By the way," Gerald said as they sped away, "am I correct in assuming that Lem is marrying Audrey? You didn't mention any names on your postcard."

"Lem is strictly a one-woman man."

The little car whined along tree-shaded avenues as Gerald's mother outlined the wedding plans. A quiet family dinner tonight; the ceremony in the back yard at noon tomorrow, with a reception to follow; the bridal pair off that evening on a five-day honeymoon canoe trip. "The wedding itself is mostly just the families, but there will be a lot of people you know at the reception." She scooted the little car into the driveway. "About the reception, son . . ."

"What about it, Mom?"

"I hope you don't mind — most people will think you're still working for that horsemeat lobby. It seemed better. It's . . . I mean, it's an election year, after all."

Gerald puzzled over this cryptic statement, then forgot it as he looked at his boyhood home, an oblong fieldstone house with a gray hipped roof, white gables, and a square white screened side porch. It was set back from the quiet suburban street by a broad lawn and shaded by a tall chestnut tree. On the east side of the lot ran a quiet stream.

"Everybody's out back," his mother said. "I don't intend to let any of these festivities into the house if I can avoid it."

Behind the house was a flagstone patio overlooking another lawn, bordered on two sides by hedges and on the third by the stream. A blue-and-white canopy was set up on wooden poles for the next day.

"Hey, Champ!" called Gerald's father, who was presiding over a charcoal grill as complex as a small nuclear reactor. Gordon Nash was a youthful-looking man just past middle age, with a crew cut and the fixed, faintly apologetic smile that is the hallmark of the lesser ranks of America's executive corps. The nickname referred to Gerald's triumph a decade and a half earlier in the finals of the all-state junior high school spelling bee, when, after flawlessly rendering *ambivalence, supercilious,* and *debilitating,* Gerald had nearly stumbled over *ecstasy* but had gone on to score a knockout blow with *valetudinarian.* Over the years the salutation had acquired, to Gerald's ears, a slightly derisive sound.

"You remember Mr. Jakes, Gerald," his mother said.

The bride's father was a massive man with thick white hair and a beet-red complexion. He owned a swimming-pool company, and he kept his eyes fixed on a point beyond Gerald's right shoulder, as if measuring the greensward for a kidney-shaped model. "Hey, buddy, good to see ya again," he said. "I hear you're giving those horsemeat bureaucrats a hard time."

"Actually —" Gerald began. His mother began gesturing at him to be quiet. "We, ah, just try to keep them honest."

"That's my boy! I don't think you've met my wife, Domenica, Gerry."

Gerald had met Mrs. Jakes before, but that had apparently been one or more wives ago. Domenica was a small woman with dyed blond hair who was wearing a blue muumuu cut to reveal shoulders tanned to the color of a baseball glove. "What's this about horsemeat?" she said. "You in the hamburger business?"

"Hell, no, Dom," Harold Jakes said. "Gerry is one of those Nader Raider types. He raises hell with the people who grade horsemeat or something."

"No kidding? I hope you can straighten 'em out fast, then. You got any idea how much a can of Alpo goes for at the Piggly Wiggly these days?"

Gerald had the uneasy feeling that his mother, not for the first time, had dealt him a losing hand, but he played it as best he could. "Our position is that dogfood would be cheaper and more healthful if it contained less horsemeat," he said. "Commercial dogfood preparations high in saturated fats of the type contained in less desirable cuts of horsemeat are more expensive and bad for your pet's health. In fact, some of the all-time top money-earners among A.K.C. champion studs are fed on a high-fiber, meat-free diet, using a mix of complete proteins and complex carbohydrates like millet and barley."

She considered this for a minute, then said, as if to herself, "Aw, what a load of crap."

Gerald's father, not for the first time, came to the rescue. "You folks excuse me, I've got to talk to the prodigal." He led Gerald over to the grill. "Don't pay any mind to Domenica, son," he said in a low voice.

"Would you tell me why Mom wants me to pretend I'm still with Equine Defense?"

"We'll talk about that later. Have a beer." He handed Gerald a can. "Listen, just between us, son, I wonder if you know what the hell is going on with these concrete-housing standards over at HUD? Are they trying to put the small manufacturer out of business altogether?"

"Since I'm supposed to be staff counsel for the Equine Defense Fund, I'd just better say I don't know, don't you think?"

"Maybe so. It's just —"

"Where're the guests of honor?"

"Where they usually are, sacked out in the hammock. Go on over and say hello."

Lemuel Nash and Audrey Jakes were reclining indistinguishably in a Sea Island rope hammock stretched between two metal poles. Their mass stirred lazily as Gerald approached, and a familiar voice called, "Hey, Gerry." Lem was a rangy young man. Where Gerald's features were serious and pensive, Lem's face customarily wore a look of bemused nonchalance, as if he had some idea of what was going on but didn't consider it a threat. He wore his unruly hair in no discernible style, largely because Audrey, who had been his girlfriend since puberty, cut it for him. She was a short blonde with a face chiefly organized around freckles and an inquisitive nose. She seemed to perfume the air around her with suntan oil and Packer's Pine Tar Soap.

Lem lazily unwound his arm from Audrey's shoulder and pulled something from the pocket of his khakis. "Catch, Gerry," he called, and threw his brother a small object that caught the twilight with a bold sparkle: a gold wedding band.

"Why are you giving this to me?"

"Because you're the best man, dummy."

"What do I have to do?"

"Just hand me that."

"You two come get your dinner," Gordon Nash called to the bride and groom.

"These old folks'll poop out pretty soon," Lem said to Gerald out of the corner of his mouth. "Then we can smoke some dope."

Over the steaks, coleslaw, and potatoes there was loud, jocular talk of the wedding and its putative aftermath; then, over bricks of Neapolitan ice cream, the conversation turned nostalgic.

Gerald, in his new dignity as best man, felt that he should offer a toast. At first, though, his brain would only produce the standard speech: *This administration is committed to the CATA program, we feel it's a good program* . . . Then he said, "I guess one of my big memories about high school is how much time people spent worrying about college boards and grades and beating the Russians. Lem and Audrey just took life as it came, and it doesn't seem to have hurt them much. I know you two will be happy. Good luck, and I hope we'll all see more of each other."

After he had finished, Domenica Jakes smiled graciously at the groom and said, "All I can say is, Lem, everybody seems to think you're a big fuck-up, but you're not such a bad guy."

"That was real nice, Champ," Gerald's father said as they were crushing paper plates into the garbage can.

But his mother turned from the garbage disposal with tears of vexation in her eyes. "How could you say we made you worry all the time?" she said. "And in front of that horrible woman, too!"

"What are you talking about? And speaking of not understanding, why am I not supposed to tell people what I do for a living?"

"See what I mean? Go ahead! Do what you want! Ruin your brother's wedding, I don't care!"

Slightly at a loss, Gerald went into the back yard, where a quarter-moon was shining on Lem and Audrey rocking peacefully in their hammock, as if the whole dreary revel had never happened. His brother leaned out of the hammock and thrust under his nose a marijuana cigarette slightly smaller than a Montecristo Corona Corona.

Gerald puffed gingerly. "Mom seemed pissed off at me," he said.

"She's just uptight in general," Lem said. "I think she's actually pissed at me. She thinks I should be more serious about things. She wants me to buy some life insurance or something like that. Hey, try again. This is good stuff. And now it's my wedding and she thinks I ought to be worried about that. Instead, she has to do all the worrying. I think I burned out my uptight center with mescaline or something."

It occurred to Gerald that there was something true, even profound, in this statement, something that had to do with the sound of the July wind high in the willow branches and the chuckle of water in the stream and the far-off babble of a television set on which he could hear faintly the menacing tones of Johnny Carson's monologue. But as he opened his mouth to say so, he found that he could not remember his planned response or even (taking a step backward) exactly what he had planned to respond to. So his remark ended up (as such remarks end up a million times a night across this fortunate land) with the simple observation, "Hey, this *is* pretty good stuff."

Margaret rose to reproach him, Diana to tempt him; Willys watched him with a look of suspicion, anger, and something else, half ashamed and half triumphant, although Gerald was not sure that the expression was not on his own face, as if he were seeing Willys in a mirror . . .

He woke in his gabled bedroom. His heart hammered, his breath came in short gasps, and all this worry came to a halt on one awful suspicion: Where was the wedding ring?

He cursed himself as an obsessive fool. A normal person would turn over now and pursue the fading wisps of dream, curl them around him warmly, and give up this idiotic self-doubt.

Ten minutes later, sighing, he got out of bed, upsetting and breaking a plastic scale model of *PT-109* on which, as a fourth-grader, he had spent weeks of loving assembly. He picked his way across the half-lit room and felt in the pocket of his jacket, at first confidently, then with annoyance, then with despair. He had lost the ring.

Wild with self-loathing, he surveyed his options. Suicide seemed most appropriate, but it would mar the nuptials. He could sneak out, make a search of the back lawn, and then, when that failed, wait for daylight and make a lightning raid on a jeweler's store. If he was calm and discreet, no one need know of his failure in the family trust. He confidently grabbed the doorknob and tiptoed into the hall.

A siren sounded, a bell rang, a bright carbon light came on, and every member of the household awoke at once. As if in a miserable dream, Gerald found himself half-dressed, the center of attention in his home at 3:00 A.M.

"What is it?" his mother's voice called.

"Somebody set off the burglar alarm," his father said.

"Okay, Gerry, let's kick his ass!" Lem yelled. "I've got my softball bat."

The telephone rang.

"That's the police," Lem called to Gerald. "If we don't give them the right code number, they send a car out."

"Officer, this is Gordon Nash," his father was saying. "No, everything's all right, I've got it here somewhere."

Gerald crept down the stairs.

"You freaking out?" Lem whispered on the landing. "I've still got some Quaaludes stashed somewhere, if the maid hasn't popped them. No thorazine, though."

"No, really, I just wanted to walk around."

"I appreciate that, officer, but I assure you it's not necessary," his father's voice was saying as Gerald stole out. "I've got the number here somewhere . . ."

Fifteen minutes later, in the faint glow of the setting moon, Gerald found a token that there is order in the universe, and grace, and mercy as well, even if they often come in humiliating forms. There by the metal hammock pole, like a circlet of fairy gold, gleamed his brother's wedding ring. He held it on his palm and felt a wave of peace and comfort, and then he collapsed in a happy heap in the rope hammock, all sins temporarily absolved, and slept the night away amid the gentle chorus of the frogs.

Of the ceremony itself, from Gerald's point of view, the less said the better.

The bridal couple read antiphonally from *The Hobbit*. A Unitarian cleric discoursed on the theme of happiness, beginning with Need for and progressing through Inevitability of. One small cousin was sick in the ironwood bush. Gerald felt only an overwhelming pride as he handed over the ring.

Afterward, a swarm of guests in all shades of pastel descended on the buffet under the canopy. The band struck up a heavy-metal version of "The Lion Sleeps Tonight."

Gerald found himself wedged next to his father. Gordon Nash eyed his elder son warily, as if gauging his chances if he made a break for freedom. "Say, Champ," he said, "your mom was a little on edge last night —"

"No harm done."

"Say, that's great. Between us, I think she's done a hell of a job on this wedding."

"It was a nice ceremony."

"Glad you thought so, Champ. Oh, I guess Lem and Audrey are a little eccentric, you know, but between us, I think Lem's all right these days."

"I agree, Dad. I think Lem is happy and I think he's going to do a good job for you down at the plant."

Gordon Nash's jaw dropped in surprise. "Do you really mean that, Gerry?"

"Sure. Why shouldn't I?"

"Christ, I don't know. I mean, you always used to . . . anyway, say, that's great! First-rate! Listen, I hope you don't have to hurry back to D.C., 'cause I sure would like to get you over to the plant, show you some of the changes Lem and I have in mind. I really think you'd be impressed with the old place. You know, I still think you'd do a hell of a job if you came in with us, and I know Lem feels the same way —"

Gerald's mother appeared and kissed his cheek without warning or mercy. "Gerry, your friend Don Worbush is looking for you. He was married four years ago. His wife's name is Betty. Now remember what I told you yesterday."

"Mom, I still want to know —"

"*Not* now, dear. Run along."

He found Don Worbush engulfing roast beef and wearing white trousers and shiny white leather shoes. The two men greeted each other with the shamefaced enthusiasm of people who have no intention of renewing their friendship.

"Christ, Don," Gerald said, pumping his friend's hand, "I haven't seen you since — when was it? — freshman year. Where's Betty?"

"That's some memory you've got there, Gerry. She's over there mooning at the wedding cake. She's got our little girl with her — see, in pink?" Gerald made appropriate, insincere coos of pleasure. "What about you, Gerry? Whatever happened to that girl you had with you, what was her name? Dana?"

"Diana."

"Yeah, Diana — what a piece of ass she was! Oh, say, sorry, you didn't marry her or anything, did you?"

"No," said Gerald, with the assurance of a big-city bachelor. "She's a TV reporter in Washington now. We go out from time to time — nothing serious. So what are you doing these days?"

"We've got a practice out near Village Square Plaza Mall, two partners and myself. We're doing pretty well."

"What specialization did you go into, after all?"

"Oh, just general dentistry. Orthodontics didn't suit me — too many kids whining about how you're ruining their sex lives."

There is danger in seeing an old friend who has become a stranger. Old habits of tactless intimacy can persist after the affection that spawned them is gone. Gerald blurted without thinking, "Dentistry? I thought you were going to be a doctor!"

Worbush smiled gently. "Oh, when it came down to it, I didn't really want to hack up all those dead bodies. What about you, big fellow? I thought you'd be in Congress by now. You still in horsemeat marketing or whatever the hell it was?"

Gerald saw no reason to pretend to hold this garbled job, whatever his mother's overanxious concern for the partisan sensibilities of her neighbors. Don Worbush was an old friend. "No," he said. "I left there a year ago. I'm with the administration."

The effect was suitably dramatic. "No kidding? What do you do?"

Gerald named the Department he worked for. "I'm special assistant to the Assistant Secretary for Evaluation, Training, and Morale."

"What the hell does that mean?"

"We handle mostly internal affairs: effectiveness monitoring, personnel problems, office design, communications enhancement and clarification — that kind of thing. As you know, the President wants to open up the bureaucracy to a more flexible, task-oriented approach. For example, one of our task forces has just finished a report on open-plan office design and its effect on worker satisfaction. This kind of thing helps us develop a data base on some questions that can be applied not only to other government agencies at the federal, state, and local level but also to the private sector. We also have a task force — this is pretty interesting, really — working on a concept we call global fungibility, which —"

"Are you in charge of affirmative action?"

"Well, nominally, yes, it is monitored by one of our offices in terms of procedures and —"

"So I guess you make sure a lot of dumb spades get fat jobs?"

This question extinguished Gerald's discourse altogether, leaving only a damp hiss and gurgle, followed by a nervous laugh as he realized that his old friend must be making a clumsy attempt at humor. "You'd be surprised how many people think that kind of thing, even in Washington," he said tactfully.

"Why shouldn't they? It's true, isn't it?"

"Quit kidding around, Don."

"Kidding around? Kidding around?" Worbush's voice rose, attracting attention from the guests near them. "Do you think I was kidding around all those fucking hours I put in at the organic chem lab? You're goddamn right I wanted to be a doctor, Gerry-boy. And so what happens? I get turned down so some dude from the ghetto can have my place — some pimp who doesn't know hemoglobin from heroin!"

"Oh, Don, you don't really believe that —"

"Don't tell me what I believe, goddamn it!" Worbush shouted. He and Gerald were suddenly the center of a knot of curious onlookers. "You people in the government think you know what I believe?"

"Government?" called a voice from the crowd. "Who's with the government?" Gerald recognized Bob Krupinski, a neighbor with whom he had never discussed anything more consequential than the local pro football team. Behind him Gerald could see friends and neighbors whispering to each other the dread word *Government,* as in a simpler time they might have whispered, "Plague!"

"Listen," Krupinski said, "would you mind explaining to me what the hell you people think you're doing with the new sewage treatment plant? First you tell us we have to build it, then you tell us we have to shut it down. Can't you make up your minds?"

Gerald saw heads turning as word spread from the knot of onlookers to more remote corners of the party that a government official had been brought to bay. There was a discordant hard-rock guitar fanfare, and Gerald's mother's voice squealed over the public-address system: "If everyone would gather around, we're about to cut the cake!"

Much relieved, Gerald said, "I guess I'd better join the wedding party." He was completing a successful withdrawal when his way was blocked by his first-grade teacher, whom he had assumed to be long dead. "You tell those people you work for that this bilingual education program is a *disgrace,*" she said in a voice that brooked no contradiction.

This delay was fatal. Suddenly he was surrounded by a small knot of people who until seconds ago had been his childhood friends, neighbors, and distant cousins and were now transformed into a snapping, snarling pack, barking complaints. Beyond them he could see other guests trying to pretend that nothing unusual was going on as Gerald's tormentors howled their complaints:

"What about the McLaughlin Reservoir?"

"— two hours for a tank of gas!"

"— how much baling wire is up since January —"

"— food stamps —"

"— Russia —"

"Please everybody, the cake!" Gerald's mother's voice called from miles away. It was no use. More and more numerous, louder and angrier, the pack pressed around Gerald until he began to give way, first a half-step backward, then a full step, then a double-time backward rout, by the hammock pole and past the willow trees, until, in a moment that was all that anyone would ever really remember of the wedding of Lem Nash and Audrey Jakes, Gerald's left foot felt the ground give way beneath it; he scrabbled ignominiously for purchase on the sandy bank, his right arm shot wildly above his head, his mouth gaped in a silent *O* of embarrassment and alarm, and he rolled in agonizing slow motion headfirst into the stream.

Chapter 4

Not long after the wedding, in a city to the north of
Washington, the duly elected governor of an official state of the
American Union strode to a large rostrum and said, with a more
or less straight face, "I am pleased and proud to place in nomination for reelection the name of the President of the United States!"

The immediate reaction to this announcement was twofold. The
television cameras gave it their usual respectful, unnerving attention. The delegates beyond and below the cameras executed,
in contrast, a series of variations on the themes of boredom and
inattention. They read newspapers, balanced their checkbooks,
played games of chance, slept, performed glassy-eyed Transcen-
dental Meditation exercises or discreet yoga postures, leaned forward in positions designed to lengthen their Achilles tendons,
arranged or consummated sexual assignations, constructed and
waved crude banners saluting television newscasters, listened to
the Orioles–Red Sox game, or paid their Visa bills. One delegate
from Maine had prepared for this moment by dressing as a lobster
at his own expense, but owing to a misunderstanding on the part

of the security staff, he spent most of the evening's session in the admitting wing of a nearby teaching hospital.

Amid such rejoicing the President was renominated by his party. Gerald Nash watched the convention with the sound off, preferring the commentary of Willys Handleman, but after the President's triumph he left a number of phone messages for a man named Toad Earnshaw.

Gerald and Toad were professional acquaintances and fellow acolytes at the President's feeble flame. Earnshaw modestly bore the nickname "the Mid-America Mastermind," earned when he rose in a fifteen-month period from assistant manager of a whole-sale mobile-home parts distributorship to chief adviser to the President of the United States.

By a pungent irony, Willys Handleman had been the instru-ment of Gerald's acquaintanceship with Toad. It had happened some five years or so earlier, shortly after Gerald, fresh from law school, had begun a career as a corporate lawyer. His firm had assigned him to a task force defending a corporation that manu-factured artificial-insemination devices for thoroughbred mares. These devices had the unfortunate defect of causing multiple sub-normal births, miscarriages, sterility, or all three in sequence; the result was an epic series of lawsuits, administrative hearings, rule-makings, and legislative inquiries at the state and federal levels. The case promised to last a generation; Gerald would thus get to study the legal, medical, and political implications of horse-breeding for most of the rest of his life.

Willys at the time was press officer of the Equine Defense Fund, which had intervened in the court proceedings as *amicus curiae*. Shortly before the presidential primary season, Toad Earnshaw had appeared in Washington and called Handleman from a pay phone to suggest a meeting. Unbeknownst to Earnshaw, Handle-man had a few days previously accepted a job as youth coordinator for another presidential candidate, who was considered at that time to have the inside track on the party's nomination.

Handleman invited Gerald as a witness, then donned a pearl-gray, two-button, flared herringbone suit with a pair of red sus-penders. They met Earnshaw in the bar of a hotel on Sixteenth Street; Toad offered Handleman a job and in return received a masterly Washingtonian tongue-lashing. With irrefutable logic, Handleman made clear that Earnshaw's scheme to elect a little-known, penniless provincial governor President was not only impossible but also reprehensible. Then, with such majestic tolerance that, to Gerald at least, he resembled King Babar the Elephant, Handleman departed, pursued by the headwaiter, who had mistaken him for the Finnish ambassador.

"Your friend doesn't seem overwhelmed with the brilliance of my campaign strategy," Earnshaw said to Gerald.

"Apparently not."

"How 'bout you? You want to work for us?"

"What does it pay?"

"Fifteen dollars a month plus all the Cheerwine soda-pop you can drink."

Gerald weighed this against the prospect of a lifetime as a wealthy horse-contraceptive lawyer. "I'll take it," he said after three and one-half seconds.

A few weeks later, Handleman's candidate, in conversation with a seemingly sympathetic reporter for the morning paper, casually mentioned that he believed that space aliens in UFOs would shortly land to save mankind and that he had learned this information in a conversation with his dead father. This platform powered the candidate to a two percent showing in the New Hampshire primary and left Willys out of a job.

After the election Gerald had with some justification expected to move to an elevation only slightly lower than Toad's own; but at a crucial point — in the magic weeks between election and inauguration day — Earnshaw had rather regretfully fired him. With the perverse politeness that many from his home region bring to unpleasant or pointless acts, Toad had explained that Gerald, being a Washingtonian, had to be fired lest people not understand that Toad was in control. Two years later Earnshaw had recruited Gerald again, explaining that with the new Department in chaos, he needed a Washingtonian lest people not understand that Toad had not lost control.

Almost against his will, Gerald found Earnshaw an engaging presence on the Washington scene, largely because of his habit of dropping out of sight for weeks at a time and reemerging with a bold new strategy designed to salvage what was left of the President's popularity. Gerald seldom spoke with Toad (though he was careful not to let this be known around the Department), and he was not even sure his calls would be returned at all.

Gerald was sitting in his office unenthusiastically drafting yet another memo to the Assistant Secretary, suggesting how to operate a division in which the Deputy Assistant Secretary was not only not speaking to the senior civil servant but actually considered herself, with some justification, to be in physical danger from him. The intercom buzzer sounded and Ruby's voice, normally so grudging, gushed over the wire like a blast of honeysuckle perfume. "Gerald, honey," she said, "your friend Mr. Earnshaw is calling you *from the White House.*" There was a sound of lines coupling, and then she said, "Mr. Nash is now ready to speak with Mr. Earnshaw."

"One moment for Mr. Earnshaw."

"Hello," said Toad's voice, "who the hell is this?"

"It's Gerry Nash, Toad."

"Why in the foggy blue-eyed morning am I calling you?"

"I think you're returning my call."

"I am? How come? Oh — Gerry, damn, sorry, I was just spacing out there for a minute, how the hell are you, old buddy?" Earnshaw's voice, as always, had the casual judiciousness of a man who sat beside a gas pump and gave inaccurate directions. "Listen, I got your message. Took me a day or two to get squared away after the convention. What can I do for you?"

"I just had something I wanted to tell you about the campaign. Is this a good time to talk?"

"Never too busy to talk to an old friend. Tell you what, if you can tear yourself away, why don't you come uptown and have a sandwich with me? I'd like to hear what's on your mind. We can duck out to that place on Connecticut Avenue."

"Sure, Toad."

"See you about twelve-fifteen, then. You don't mind eating early? Us country folks get hungry."

Gerald's taxicab, spewing Haitian music from the in-dash stereo, pulled up in front of the restaurant to find Earnshaw lounging casually against a mailbox, hands in pockets, ignoring a small knot of gawking admirers, including two retired school-teachers from Omaha and the Argentine naval attaché in his dress whites.

The object of all this attention was a lanky figure given to khaki trousers, penny loafers, and shapeless blue blazers; he had recently grown a neat goatee, which together with his thick bowl haircut and long bony face gave him the look of a Mexican rock musician.

"Hello, Toad," said Gerald. "I like your beard."

"Damn thing grew in all gray. I grew it so congressmen would stop calling me 'Sonny.' Now Boy Scouts keep offering to help me cross the street."

There was much speculation in Washington on the question of who actually owned the restaurant at which they were to eat, some favoring the Mormon Church and some the Bahraini government. The restaurant would not take reservations, which left its head-waiter free to exercise exquisite discrimination in who was seated, where, and how quickly. Insecure Washingtonians had been known to schedule a lunch there simply in order to get a quick reading of their current standing in the status line-up.

Its foyer was dark, smoky, and crowded, as if it were the ante-room of hell. Anxious men in gray suits jingled coins as they waited to be called; the beefy maître d'hôtel guarded the entrance to the basement dining room with a clipboard and a huge smelly cigar, repelling all inquiries by snarling, "Don't rush me, Mac, I'll fit ya in somehow." This unhappy crowd parted around Earn-shaw (and Gerald, in his wake) like the Red Sea. The huge head-waiter, his face wreathed in malodorous smoke, condescended to greet the great man with his well-known humor. "Glad to see you can afford lunch out once in a while, fuzz-face. Who's ya sidekick?"

Toad ceremoniously presented a folded five-dollar bill, which the other man accepted, not as if intending to render service for it but rather as if ennobling the donor. With a mock-threatening flourish, he pulled aside the velvet rope.

The landing had a view of the large, high-ceilinged dining room. Gerald paused there for a moment: the low, rhythmic rumble of conversation, the sober gray dress of the male crowd, and the bald spots on the tops of their heads gave the room the look of a refectory for an order of worldly tonsured monks. "Praise lunch from which all blessings flow," they seemed to be chanting. "As it was yesterday, is now and ever shall be, lunch without end, amen."

"Quit woolgathering, Gerry," Toad said. "We got some serious eating to do."

They were seated at a banquette in the center of the floor. "You must really rate around here," said Earnshaw with the pachydermatous irony that in the powerful passes for humility. "I never got such a good table before. Look over there; they've put us next to the Ambassador. Not bad for a couple of country boys, what d'you say, Gerry?"

The revered figure to whom Earnshaw referred was seated in a matching banquette, separated from theirs by a funereal display of flowers. He was the legendary elder statesman and living symbol of the President's party, an upright patrician figure who had twice been elected governor of Illinois (acquitted on all counts), once nominated for Vice President of the United States (defeated in a historic landslide), and once appointed ambassador to the Court of St. James's (all but bankrupted by the social demands of the post). Over the years the Ambassador had grown old, thin, and slightly confused. He was at present fiercely gumming *blanquettes de veau,* respectfully flanked by liberal figures in bow ties, one of whom was cutting up his meat.

These two tables were the epicenter of the room; around them in concentric circles, closer to the wall as they descended in importance, lunched and babbled the near-great, the powerful, the influential, the well-known, the rising, the declining, the forgotten, the obscure by choice, and the obscure despite desperate efforts to emerge. Dozens of eyes noted Earnshaw, and then, like those of crocodiles basking in Nile mud, slid lidlessly over to note the hitherto insignificant features of Gerald Nash.

"I'll have a chicken salad sandwich on white bread and a can of Pearl beer," Earnshaw told the waiter. "Just leave it in the can, why don't you?"

"I'll have steak gaucho and a glass of red wine," Gerald said.

"Hot damn, I'm lunching with the quality folks today," Earnshaw said, lighting an Old Gold cigarette.

"Give me a break, Toad. Junior cabinet staffers have to order wine here or they'll throw us out. Only senior White House people can get beer still in the can."

"You figure?" Earnshaw had the gift of appearing deeply fascinated by his lunch companion while actually scanning the crowd around him. "Gerry, ole buddy, you know you're a hell of a good fellow," he said in a tone that suggested that this thought was a wholly novel and surprising one. "We appreciate the good work you've been doing at the Department. I can imagine that from your point of view it's probably not the job you've always dreamed of, but you've knuckled down and done it. And He has noticed, too."

"He spends a lot of time thinking about our division, does He, Toad?"

A smile broke through the goatee, giving Earnshaw's face an expression at once sheepish and wily. "Guess I can't bullshit you too damn much, can I? You knew me when I was still knocking manure off my boots. But you'd be surprised how much He really does care about details like that. Reorganization is His baby, you know — He really is interested in how it's going at the new departments."

"It isn't going at all where I live."

"Gerry, I sympathize with your situation. We're trying to get some help for you folks over there. But these folks are good people. The Secretary, your boss, Nancy Quoin — they helped us out when we needed help and we're going to stick with 'em. You know, down home we always say that if you lie down with dogs, you get up with fleas."

Gerald noticed that a party of men with gray suits and hair had approached the table in deferential silence; Earnshaw had evidently interjected the last sibylline utterance for them to overhear. He rose with courtly, self-deprecating grace. "Counselor, how are you today? Judge, always a pleasure. Commissioner, good to see you. Do you gentlemen know Gerry Nash? He's the brains over at our new Department."

"Don't hold me to such a low standard, Toad," said Gerald, juggling shiny faces and empty titles. For their part, these latter-day Magi paid little or no attention to him, focusing in religious awe on Toad, to whom they babbled an unintelligible round of powerful phrases:

"— matter straightened out —"

"— speak to the girl —"

"— meeting early next week —"

"— let's have lunch —"

These incantations complete, the three departed in an ecstasy of self-abasement, backing away from the presence. The waiter carrying lunch to Gerald and Toad was nearly floored during this minuet; he redeemed his honor later by pouring half a bottle of Perrier water on an inoffensive Commerce Department economist in another part of the room.

"So, I gather you want to do a number on my head," said Toad as he bit into his sandwich. "What's agitating you?"

Gerald baldly recounted the events of his brother's wedding, culminating with his baptism in the stream.

Earnshaw hooted. "Sounds like you're a popular fellow, Gerry," he said. "Maybe you shoulda stayed here in town and come down to the House for the fireworks display."

"Well, Toad, these are actually pretty decent people, and most of them like me well enough," Gerald said. "They just couldn't control themselves, they're angry about something. That seems politically significant to me."

"I'm not sure I follow," Earnshaw said. His face became a blank mirror of incomprehension. Gerald remembered that he could maintain this expression throughout a meeting, meanwhile hearing, refining, and preparing to steal every good idea within a fifteen-foot radius.

"This wasn't a personal thing," Gerald said. "They're just angry at the government — in a way, I think, at the very idea of government. It seemed to cut across party and age lines. I think it might have some implications for the election. The President is the incumbent, obviously, and he might be the target for this kind of thing."

"Gerry," Earnshaw said, "I want you to know I appreciate your coming to talk to me today. You are a very loyal friend, and the President appreciates that kind of loyalty. There's damn little of it in this town, that's for damn sure. This place is worse than we

ever thought it was — vultures everywhere, vicious assholes . . .
I swear —" With a visible effort, Earnshaw retrieved his thoughts
from whatever dark chasm they had tumbled into. "But I think
it's possible to overreact. All of us who work here in this town
sometimes find that when we go home, a few old friends may
treat us differently — they're jealous of what we've done, maybe
they have an ax to grind, some special interest they're involved in.
I'm not sure there's any great significance in that. Our pollster —
you remember Clark Guppy — has been running tracking polls
every week for the last eight months. If this deep feeling was
there, he'd have picked it up."

"I remember Clark. How's he doing, by the way?" Gerald asked.

"Great — complexion's pretty much cleared up. Just between
us, Gerry," Earnshaw went on, placing a hand on Gerald's elbow
in the gesture that indicates that a powerful man is about to
bestow on one less powerful one of the prefabricated confidences
such men carry about like John D. Rockefeller's dimes, "I think
the President is in a very strong position as we begin the campaign. We couldn't have asked for a better opponent — a washed-
up former governor, no Washington background, no foreign-
policy experience. He looks pretty on TV, but there's no substance
there, and we plan to exploit that fact. And we don't like to talk
about it, of course, but we have the resources of incumbency to use,
within limits, between now and November."

"I'm just playing devil's advocate, Toad," Gerald began cautiously, "but doesn't it occur to you that people said exactly the
same things about us four years ago, and we still managed to win
the election?"

"Goddamn it, Gerry, that is outrageous and you ought to know
it! There's no comparison between the two men. This guy is a
fool and a dangerous fool at that. And we have a solid record to
defend, with some damn fine accomplishments in both the foreign-
and domestic-policy areas."

"Just as an exercise in campaign strategy, Toad, let's list the accomplishments that are going to make a difference to the people
at my brother's wedding."

"Well, for one thing —" Earnshaw was rescued by the appearance of Baxter Muntin, who padded to their table, beaming

benevolently with a face whose faint oily sheen betrayed a recent and enthusiastic rendezvous with steak, fried potatoes, mixed green salad, and English-style trifle.

"Mr. Earnshaw, Mr. Nash," said Muntin, "may I present Miss Cazadora?"

There followed a frozen moment from which each participant carried away a radically different image. Earnshaw, shaking Muntin's hand, watched Gerald's nod of recognition to Diana; Diana shot a speculative look from Gerald to Toad and back again; Gerald looked from Muntin to Diana in formless but acute anxiety; and Muntin beamed over the whole encounter, missing nothing at all.

"Baxter," said Toad, "Gerald tells me you've been single-handedly keeping things flowing at the OPPE shop."

"Sir," said Muntin, "we civil servants ask no more than a chance to be useful, as long as we are *permitted,* as long as we are *suffered to remain.* Will you have a cigarette?"

"I'd admire a cigarette," Earnshaw said. Muntin ceremoniously lit it for him.

If only there had lived in the Washington of that time a sculptor capable of capturing in bronze or marble the resonant intricacies of that moment: Earnshaw dully radiating self-esteem and satisfaction, Muntin vibrating with obsequious pleasure. *Political Appointee and Civil Servant,* our sculptor might call the masterpiece — although just as apt would be the title *Roman and Parthian* or *Crusader and Levantine Merchant* or *GI and Neapolitan Procurer.* Look here, before the image fades: picture Toad dressed in chain mail bedizened with the arms of the Knights of Malta, as he politely begs service of the Levantine before him; see his solicitous good manners, his satisfaction at his own noble conduct, yet see also the practiced eye with which he looks from his own sharp blade of Toledo steel to the plump neck of his new subject, reflexively gauging the distance and angle. See the eternal Muntin in his flowing robes, bowing as he offers his jars of oil, his dates, his carpets; yet see too how the hooded eyes measure the distance between the new conqueror and the ancient cedar tree, as if wondering how long before some new conqueror, equally welcome, equally hated, strings the old one from its limbs.

But it is not permitted to see these visions behind the solid granite of American reality, in which two men meet always and only as fellow passengers in the tourist class of history; and so Gerald Nash turned from this tableau to the absorbing sight of Diana.

"Diana Cazadora from Reaction News," she said, smiling at Toad with an air that suggested that she had been looking forward to this meeting for some time, less with yearning than with quiet, prophetic certainty.

Under her worshipful gaze Toad put a proprietary hand on Gerald's elbow. "You know Gerry Nash, here? He's been telling me how to get the President reelected."

"How do you do?" Diana said smoothly, slipping him a nearly invisible wink with her off eye, which bound his tongue by suggesting that the two of them shared a rich secret.

"I'd like to know what that one's up to," Toad said after Muntin and Diana had gone.

"Baxter?" Gerald said, his head still vibrating with the suspicion, akin to the power of our most vivid nightmares, that people he knew separately were swirling together in ominous conspiracies behind his back. "Fighting for survival, right now."

"I meant the girl. What a sweet piece she is! Half the guys in the press office are hot for her."

"I didn't know she covered the White House."

"Why would you? She does weekends now and then for the net. Damn, I'd like to go on deep background with her!"

This distressing conversation was interrupted by the sight of the Ambassador arising from his meal. He was helped by his lunch companions, who had to be reinforced by two busboys and a sommelier. The symbol of Gerald's and Toad's party passed their table, directing at Earnshaw a stiff, vague nod of patronage as he rattled painfully toward the exit.

As if by prearrangement the waiter fluttered up with their check, which Earnshaw, shooting presidential cufflinks, signed without reading. "I want you to know how much we all appreciate your giving us the benefit of your wisdom, Gerry. I've always said your political instincts were good."

"Even when you fired me?"

"Don't hold grudges against your friends, old buddy, just your enemies. Let me think about all this and get back to you. There's a few things in the works you ought to appreciate. Say, how's your buddy Handleman these days, speaking of political instincts?"

There was no satisfactory answer. They rose and passed among the gray-clad monks. Gerald went first; behind his back, a head taller, strode Earnshaw, basking in the attention of a hundred eyes and directing between Gerald's shoulder blades an oddly avaricious gaze.

Chapter 5

DIANA BECAME PART OF THE CITY'S summer landscape. By day Gerald walked on steaming streets among people who seemed to be restraining only by superhuman effort their desire to maim and murder each other, and Diana walked beside him, her musky perfume at the base of the city's explosive smell. He ran at the Y and Diana's legs flickered at the edge of his sight, pacing him to near exhaustion; in the drab quiet of his office, Diana's voice bounced at him from the ceiling and the corners, making suggestions he could not quite hear or resist. At night he sat in the apartment beside Willys Handleman, torpid and panting in his crumbling armchair like a great mournful sheepdog. Around them Washington quivered in the heat like a brushed drum, and Diana hovered somewhere in the darkness. Gerald began to feel as if he had fallen into a silent and glassy well; as if small invisible fetters were fretting his flesh; as if he had lost himself in a world as like the one he knew as the room beyond the mirror, and yet like that one oddly twisted and distorted at its edges.

Willys, meanwhile, seemed to have found for the first time some fragments of peace, cheer, and hope. He stopped throwing books at Gerald's TV set; his showers, meals, and haircuts became more regular; like a huge infant, he began sleeping through the night.

One late-August night they sat dripping in the living room, absorbed in boring tasks. Willys was reading a book entitled *The Coming Crisis in U.S.–Albanian Relations,* snorting every few pages at the author's naiveté. Handleman maintained a keen amateur interest in Balkan affairs, because he was unlikely to meet anyone who knew as much about the subject as he did.

Gerald was staring at a wilderness of intradepartmental memoranda, draft reports, and proposed policy guidance documents, his eyes traveling the lines at the same pace as the sweat droplets crawling down his neck. Every half hour or so he dialed Margaret's number, holding the phone through a precise ten rings and hanging up. Bob Zardovsky, spouting boisterous gratitude, had hopped a bus west the week before to prepare a reception for the Assistant Secretary in Gouge Eye. Tonight Gerald wanted to see Margaret with a force amounting to dread, as if her barred bedroom were a refuge into which he could escape from the oily menace in the summer air. But the phone rang unanswered, leaving him annoyed because he knew he had no moral claim on her fidelity or time.

"Give it a rest, Gerry," Handleman said after the fourth attempt. "I'm expecting a call."

"You're always expecting a call."

Handleman's eyebrows danced. "I'm not a bureaucrat," he said. "I don't work nine to five."

"Where's your call coming from — Albania?"

"Hardly likely. It's four A.M. in Tirana just now."

"Handleman, you are amazing. How many people in Washington do you suppose know Albanian standard time off the top of their heads?"

As usual, Handleman reacted badly to praise. "Oh, for Christ's sake," he said. "That's what's wrong with Washington. Here America is supposed to be a responsible world power and we don't know the simplest things about the rest of the world. This book, for example — it makes some pretty good points. Of course, it's a little superficial in its discussion of Albanian ideology, but I've got to admit it's pretty sophisticated when it comes to the foreign-policy implications of the Albanian–Chinese split. Even after all this time, most Americans still think of Enver Hoxha as a Mao-ist —"

"When they think of him at all."

The telephone managed to gasp out a quarter of a ring, then Handleman levitated from his chair and snatched up the receiver. "Hello," he barked. "Oh, yeah? Great! . . . Uh-uh, like I told you . . . yeah, he's here." He thrust the phone at Gerald, saying grudgingly, "It's for you."

Like a hot wind from the east, Diana's voice floated over the line. "Are you going to be around later? I'd like to come by."

"Sure. If you can stand the heat."

"That's never been my problem. Would you do me a favor?"

"Anything within reason."

"Only that far? I just wanted you to watch the show tonight. It'll interest you, I think."

"Listen!" Handleman said as Gerald hung up. "The crazy guy is out again!"

Echoing off the nearby buildings was the voice of a neighborhood lunatic who at irregular intervals apostrophized the D.C. police force with details of an obscure grievance. "You overpaid, underworked, officious fascists!" he was screaming.

Gerald and Willys crept to the window. The aggrieved party was a middle-aged white man, dressed neatly but informally. His voice was commanding — it permeated the block, boring straight through walls. "Blood-stained parasites! Bureaucratic oafs!" he was shouting. "Liars! Degenerates! Jacks-in-office! Deviates! Double-dippers!"

"Are you sure there's nothing we should do?" Gerald whispered.

"I called the police once. They told me they knew all about him." As if to confirm what Handleman said, a scout car drove by the lunatic, blinked its blue light in salute, and passed out of sight. The lunatic seemed to take this as completion of his task and departed with hands in pockets, whistling a pleasing tune.

"I guess he's harmless," said Gerald.

"Harmless? He's scaring everyone to death!" Handleman retorted. "Get out of here, you bum!" he shouted out the window. "Noise polluter! Sorehead! Paranoid!"

"Christ, it's after ten," Gerald said.

Handleman dived for the TV receiver, which winked into life, blaring: "— and a special segment introducing Diana Cazadora's Searchlight Team, with a report on cult infiltration of government bureaus. But first, these headlines."

There were the obligatory murders, rapes, arsons, and abductions; a cheerful announcement by the mayor that he was striking a blow at the housing shortage by accepting a low-rate mortgage on a $180,000 mansion; a report on the arrival of riot police to subdue 3700 black teenagers who had all been notified that the mayor's summer job program had placed them in seven temporary fish-feeding jobs at the National Aquarium; and a debate over the craze for jogging shoes made from the fur of endangered species.

Then the male anchor said, "Federal authorities are increasingly concerned about infiltration of government departments by political extremists and religious cultists. Reaction News's Diana Cazadora has done some infiltration of her own to learn how one cult has become involved in the top-level battles of the new Cabinet Department. Here is her report."

Shortly after Diana began to speak, Gerald was assailed quite powerfully by a sense of alienation, as if he had moved to some vantage point from which he could watch both the TV and himself at the same time, or as if he had become part of the news program, scripted by an unknown hand like the other two parts of the show:

AUDIO	VIDEO	NASH
DIANA: Bill, insiders who follow the affairs of the Department are buzzing over the recent attempt by Deputy Assistant Secretary Nancy Quoin to oust Baxter Muntin, career civil servant and one of the most powerful figures in Washington's "permanent govern-	*Diana* at desk, cool and dark, with secret smile in alarming flower. *Photo slides* of Muntin and Quoin, arranged as if glowering at each other.	Involuntary twitching of arms known to psychologists as "startle reaction"; unsuccessful attempt to catch eye of Willys Handleman. Squirming in chair as if too hot.

AUDIO	VIDEO	NASH
ment." The dispute centers on a government personnel form which falsely says Muntin graduated from Notre Dame instead of Pawnee Professional Institute in 1949. But Searchlight has learned that the dispute is actually linked to a shadowy campaign by the Temple of Ray, a cult group with Asian origins, to purloin government documents. One of the Temple's former members, arrested recently for shoplifting in a D.C. candy store, has told federal prosecutors of her role in the operation. She spoke with Searchlight in return for a promise that her real name not be used. STRANGE ME-CHANICAL VOICE: We were told to go into the offices and get any papers we could. DIANA: And you worked for the Department as a temporary secretary? S.M.V.: That's right.	*Photo slide* of diploma bestowing Pawnee's B.S. in personnel on Muntin. *File film* of Sunrise House during police raid, with officers emerging carrying cartons of paper. *Mystery woman,* in three-quarter c.u., lit to conceal her face. *Slide:* "Voice Electronically Disguised" Cut away to *Diana,* directing at M.W. a familiar look of fascination.	Inarticulate sounds denoting surprise. Silence and near-total disorientation. Slight, unfocused nausea. Desire to reach into television, shake pictured shoulders, and demand explanation.

AUDIO	VIDEO	NASH

DIANA: And did you take any papers?

S.M.V.: *(faintly)* Yes.

Cut back to M.W.

DIANA: From whom?

S.M.V.: From Mr. Muntin. I took his briefcase.

Slide: "Former Temple Member"

DIANA: In that briefcase, Searchlight has learned, were Muntin's prized press clippings from his two years as "Crazy Legs" Muntin, the all-time greatest gridiron ground gainer in the history of Pawnee Professional — clippings that reveal Muntin's connection to the school. Our source told us that she passed the briefcase on to a mysterious senior figure in the Temple hierarchy, whom she could identify only as "Three-Finger." These photos, coincidentally shot by Dr. Hirusuko Hasegawa of Osaka, Japan, and obtained exclusively by Searchlight, show the actual transfer of the stolen documents. They reveal that the indi-

Diana at news desk, secret smile mixed with standard reporter's prosecutorial smirk.

Sense of generalized regret such as may accompany but does not necessarily cause religious or political conversion; desire that things had been better managed and that certain errors, beginning with own conception and birth, had been conclusively avoided.

Series of slides made from fine-grained black-and-white photos shot with motor-driven Nikkormat by Japanese orthodontist, showing *indistinct figure* rushing in from l., thrusting briefcase into hands of *Bob Zardovsky,* and blurring off, r. Sequence edited to omit Zardovsky's oxlike look of surprise and subsequent fall onto pavement.

AUDIO	VIDEO	NASH
vidual code-named "Three-Finger" is actually Robert Zardovsky, an obscure former professional athlete who lists his address as Postal Drawer D, Gouge Eye, but whom several sources have confirmed as an important messenger who visited Sunrise House shortly before the theft of the briefcase.	Close-up of *Zardovsky* beaming at tourists with two briefcases in hands. *Diana* at desk, signaling by raised eyebrow that ridiculous address and town name clearly suggest guilt of something.	Attempts to make sense of new information producing rapid sequence of mutually incompatible and uniformly erroneous conclusions.
These photocopies of departmental visitor logs show that just minutes after the photos were taken, Zardovsky checked in — and listed as his destination the division in which Nancy Quoin works. And	*Slide* of entry book showing Zardovsky's signature.	
Mr. Y. Y. Chong, proprietor of Chong's Bodega y Gourmet Shoppe in Adams-Morgan, confirms that just the night before, Zardovsky was purchasing supplies for a Temple service. ORIENTAL ACCENT, INTERRUPTED BY CHUCKLES: He say he take beer to zombies in Temple. He have little girl from	*Medium close-up* of Chong, posed proudly before dingy shop front. *Slide:* "Y.Y. Chong, Store Owner"	

AUDIO	VIDEO	NASH

Temple with him. They buy beer, Milk Duds, bean dip. He say big party for alla Temple people.

DIANA: Attempts to reach Zardovsky in Gouge Eye were unsuccessful. An individual at Zeke's Tackle Shop and Post Office said that Zardovsky was, quote, at a clambake for some guy from Washington, unquote.

Quoin also did not return Searchlight's calls. However, Baxter Muntin agreed to speak with Searchlight at his modest home in northern Virginia.

Diana at desk, now with both eyebrows raised to indicate that something sinister must be up.

MUNTIN: Obviously, I'm not proud of this aspect of my personnel record. It's clear that an unfortunate mistake has occurred. But I have tried to make a career as a civil servant that would be valuable to the agencies I have served and the country I love. I can't help feeling that there has been an attempt to politicize the civil service under cover of this type of allegation.

Muntin fills screen in tight c.u., his usually jovial features set in pained but determined lines.

Itchy sense in small of back, as of pricking of ectoplasmic knives.

AUDIO	VIDEO	NASH

DIANA (off camera): Do you feel that your difficulties are part of a larger conspiracy to infiltrate and paralyze the government? And how do you explain the apparent involvement of such high administration officials as Nancy Quoin?

MUNTIN: I hope you won't put words in my mouth. I can't explain any of this. All that I can really say is that as a career civil servant, I find the whole business distressing.

Tight c.u. of Muntin looking grave; extremely faint version of his most mischievous twinkle in eye.

Sudden realization that Muntin is, as usual, at least two steps ahead of this game.

DIANA: Unanswered questions about the Briefcase Affair remain. But observers feel that it does shed a much-needed ray of light on the shadowy web of connections between cults and the federal bureaucracy. A spokesman for the U.S. attorney's office refused to comment, but sources at the Justice Department told Searchlight that the investigation is continuing. We'll be back after this.

Medium c.u. of Diana at news desk, with satisfied air of prosecutor who has snuck double first cousin onto jury in murder case.

Dawning realization that report is almost over; intense relief; stirring in bowels; dash for bathroom.

Cut to commercial for roach killer.

Difficult as it may be to believe, some who knew Gerald Nash were inclined to dismiss him as lacking in spirit and élan. But Gerald felt the full gamut of emotions, from tender yearning to violent rage. In recent years he had devoted little of this emotional range to what might loosely be called his personal life. He had concentrated on his work, of which, beneath his conventional self-deprecating irony, he was quite proud indeed. He believed that it was he, with his appeasement of Baxter Muntin, his self-abasement before Nancy Quoin, and his uncritical protectiveness of the Assistant Secretary, who served more than anyone else as nurse and attendant to the ETM division in its invalid state, flexing its limbs to keep blood flowing, turning its palsied body to prevent bedsores, whispering soothing words when it cried out in troubled twilight sleep.

Reappearing from nowhere, Diana had spread her tendrils first to enslave his senses and then to engulf his work in her own dark designs. He felt it as an alarming assault on the fortress of his identity.

No instrument could have registered the reaction; Gerald himself was at best half aware of it. But somewhere deep inside him there was a change, as if a weary traveler carrying a burden through lightless vistas had stopped at the edge of a chasm that might lead to rescue or ruin and cast into it speculatively a stone, whose long, silent fall would gauge the depths beneath.

By the time Gerald emerged from the bathroom, Willys Handleman was on his way to an all-night Mysore-style cafeteria, where he intended to make a light collation of *idli, sambar, pongal, basmati* rice with cashews, onion *raita,* curried chickpeas, Madras *masala dosa,* sweet *lassi,* and *gulab jamun.*

At length Gerald heard the elevator door opening and the indistinct melody of Diana's voice. He burst out of the apartment to find her deep in conversation with David Beaufort, the elevator operator.

"I'm not really sure what they believe in," she was saying. "Half the time they sound like fundamentalist Christians and the rest of the time they're babbling about the Ancient Ones of Mars. One girl told me that Ray has a dish antenna he uses to talk to Mars, but I think that's just a rumor."

"Well, shit, you could do it easy enough," David said. "Technically, I mean, it's no big deal. Tell you the truth, if I had the right equipment —"

"But there's nobody on Mars to talk to, David!" Gerald broke in.

"Yeah? You been there, Rambler?"

Diana turned, her expression uncertain but energetic, her smile exquisitely suggestive. "Hi, Gerry! David saw my report and he was asking about the Temple of Ray."

"I saw it too," Gerald said. "I have a couple of questions myself."

"Is Willys here?" she asked.

"He just went down," David said. "He said he was *beaucoup* hungry."

"Oh. Gerry, do you have a beer for me? I'm pretty blitzed out. See you later, David."

"Yeah, take it easy. You, too, Rambler." The doors closed and he sank glumly out of sight.

Diana grabbed a Carta Blanca beer from the refrigerator and threw herself onto the couch. She was dressed in a pale pink cotton print skirt and a black tank top. Her legs were gracefully stretched before her, her arms embraced the back of the couch, and her long dark hair fell in pools and eddies. Her makeup was more dramatic than usual, highlighting her high cheekbones and drawing the onlooker's eyes toward hers, which glittered enticingly.

Gerald paced back and forth, uncertain whether to throttle her or ravish her. "Why in hell didn't you tell me you were going to do that report?" he asked.

"I called to tell you to watch it."

"Diana, don't play around." Gerald felt that one false move would plunge him off the tightrope into the weightless void of words where she soared with such elusive grace. "Here you've just blown the roof off the thing I've been working on for the last three months, and you didn't even think to mention it to me beforehand."

"I figured that people might know that you and I are seeing each other. I try to play it down, like when Baxter and I ran into you at lunch. But it's hard to keep a secret in this town. You know that. So I figured that your only defense if anybody asked you about it would be that you didn't know anything about it beforehand. Was that wrong?"

"Diana, what's really bugging me is that you got all this from me first."

"That's not true."

"Oh, come on — if not me, then who?"

"I can't tell you that. You know that part of the game as well as I do. But it wasn't from you. You hardly tell me anything except how far you jog in the mornings. Anyway, this whole business isn't exactly secret. I've been on the cult beat since I got here. I tried to do the whole thing in a professional way. If you think I've done anything wrong, or if I've hurt you or made you angry, all I can say is that I'm really sorry."

This sentiment was so becoming that Gerald sat down — not next to Diana, which would have signaled complete cease-fire, but in Handleman's armchair, which sagged and groaned as if protesting this usurpation. They looked at each other warily for a few minutes; then over their two faces, as over one face regarding itself in a mirror, stole two small and rueful smiles, like those of children who, having passed the afternoon playing pirates, at last find the pretense too much to be maintained.

For Gerald it was a vivid moment. Every angle of the room leapt out at him in the dim light of the electric chandelier, of whose six bulbs only two were still burning. In one corner of the rug was a McDonald's hamburger carton that Willys had brought in a week ago, and next to it were three crumpled sheets of yellow legal paper and a No. 2 pencil he had apparently snapped in two in frustration. On the wooden coffee table was the afternoon paper, with a three-column picture of Toad Earnshaw, to which Handleman had added an eye patch and a pair of drooling fangs; above it was the headline "White House Aides in Reelect Huddle; Earnshaw Seeks New Campaign Team." Beside the paper was a letter addressed to Gerald from the Visa company, stamped in red URGENT AND PERSONAL and with the additional penciled notation "Gerry, I opened this by mistake, better pay it — W." On top of the envelope was a plastic souvenir paperweight featuring the

President's daughter, an excruciatingly bad country-and-western singer; beneath it was a scrap-paper memorandum in Handleman's script that read, *"To do:* 1. Pay tailor bill. 2."

Gerald's eye marched over these familiar things; Diana appeared to him in memory, in imagination, and in reality, and at that minute he felt the power to send her away or bind her to him. Such feelings of freedom and power may be wisdom or folly, but few of us, having experienced one, do not yearn for it again, whatever the price, whatever the result.

"Diana," he said at last, "why did you come back to me after all these years? Was I just something you hadn't finished? Is that it?"

She had been watching him with an intent gaze that blended the look of a cat watching a mouse hole and that of a child in a stroller afraid that an adult is about to walk away. "I told you, Gerry."

"You said you loved me."

"There you are."

"It was in the past tense, I recall. Why now? Why here? Why me?"

These riddles silenced her. She opened her hands to reveal emptiness. Gerald stood, feeling tall and remote. "Come on, old girl," he said. "It's time for bed."

He led, and meekly she followed. But as she walked behind him, bound by his riddling, her submissive hands were balanced by her watchful eyes. Finding herself in the unfamiliar, not wholly unpleasant but in the long run unsatisfactory, position of being subordinated to Gerald, she knew that such victories do not always last.

Later that night, entangled in indistinguishable dreams, they woke to hear Willys Handleman's inconsolable typewriter keeping the dog watch before dawn. The sound seemed to vitalize Diana, who turned to Gerald with a submissive fierceness that surprised him, while he was able to think about it.

Chapter 6

DAVID BEAUFORT, the night elevator operator at the Park
View Apartments, rose early the next morning in the trim Georgia
Avenue row house where he lived as a lodger, renting the back
bedroom from a widow who operated a nearby dry-cleaning shop.
His landlady's business was declining on a parallel with her
strength and memory, and she had formed the fixed notion that
David was about to come to work for her. So David had begun to
refuse her offers to fix him breakfast; he suspected that she kept
an account of these small favors, hoping to place him under a
lifelong obligation. He leaned out the window and ate a sausage
biscuit he had bought the night before, idly counting the bottles
that winos had thrown over the wooden fence into the landlady's
prized rhododendron bushes.

He had worked the night shift, arriving home a little before
two. But David had promised the superintendent of the Park
View to help clear out a basement storeroom jammed with cartons and papers, the life's work of a deceased archivist at the Department of Agriculture: nine cartons of notes, diagrams, and

documents for an unwritten work which was to have been entitled
The Life Cycle of the Humble Soybean. David needed the money
to buy a new derailleur for his racing bike, the one piece of precision machinery he could afford.

As the greasy red sun was beginning to torch the sidewalks,
David eased the wheels down the back stairs, hoping to escape
Mrs. Carter, the landlady.

"Is that you, David?" she called as he was quietly opening the
back door.

"Yes, Mrs. Carter, I'm on my way to work."

"Work? You just got home a few hours ago!" She fluttered into
the kitchen, her head cocked to one side like a robin's: a spare,
dark black woman in a severe gray blouse and pale slacks.
"David . . ." she said uncertainly.

He wondered what new obligation she had laid on him while
he slept. "What you got on your mind?"

"Don't forget what I told you about my pants-pressing machine."

David was used to these imaginary conversations of hers, which
usually ended in his promising to perform some messy piece of
repair or yard work. "What *about* your pants-pressing machine,
Mrs. Carter?"

"Well, like I told you, it's still smoking some. And you did say
you could fix it. Today?"

"Mrs. Carter, that thing is shot. What you need is a new
machine."

"But David, you're so good with things like that — and you did
say you could . . ."

Mrs. Carter was attacking David's weakest spot: he could fix
almost anything, and improve it. But he got only the detritus of
technological civilization on which to use his skills — ancient
toasters, rusty sedans, Mrs. Carter's moribund pants-presser.
Though he yearned (sometimes lying awake with the frustration
of a man who knows his talents could change the world) to get his
hands on something big and powerful — computers, jet aircraft,
Formula One racers — he would settle for the pants-pressing machine. "All right, Mrs. Carter, I'll try to get by around four
o'clock. I'll pay you the rent then too."

"Don't be later than that," she said, uncompromising in victory. "I like to watch 'The Jeffersons' at five."

"All right, Mrs. Carter."

He walked the bike cautiously down the alley and then pedaled off across Northeast. This part of Washington is a tragic patchwork of decency and danger: streets of painfully tended brick homes crossed by arteries of murder and crime — grim boulevards, side streets, and cul-de-sacs where pimps and drug dealers hawk their merchandise; streets of neat, fading barbershops, grills, rib shacks, cleaners, furniture stores, and small groceries alternating with blocks of shattered, barred storefronts, bricked-up poolrooms, social clubs, and package stores specializing in chilled fruit-flavored wine.

David rode along a broad avenue that angled into Adams-Morgan. Winos were grouped on stoops in fraternal ease; middle-aged women, wearing their respectability like invisible armor, waddled along the sidewalk or waited at bus stops; street vendors offered watches and lewd greetings to passing women; Muslims and Adventists hawked periodicals; beer deliverymen serviced taverns; soul and disco rose and fell as teenagers passed with stereo boxes on their shoulders; a sprayer truck browsed the gutter.

Something stirred in David's soul as he watched this unruly promenade. Perhaps it was the boys with boxes, who reminded him of himself when he had carried a radio through the jungles of Vietnam; or perhaps it was the children who squatted gravely in the entries between houses and on the sewer gratings, talking or throwing balls or playing with dolls. Since his return from Vietnam David had felt like a wanderer on the earth, akin to no one, speaking in an unknown tongue to the empty air — a man making a sacrifice no one had asked for and no one would profit from. But like millions before him, he took solace in the children. His muscles warm, feeling the sweet responsive equipoise of his bicycle beneath him, he blessed the sights around him and felt, for this moment, reconciled to the blind turnings of his subterranean life. On his solemn face flickered an unaccustomed smile as he turned from the avenue into a side street that led uphill toward the Park View.

On that quiet block, as if conjured by his mood, sat a young boy, no more than ten or eleven, huddled on the curb, weeping over an ice-cream cone spilled in the gutter before him. David slowed the bike and called, "What's wrong, little brother?"

The boy looked at him with wary greed. "I dropped my ice cream."

David worked his hand into the pocket of his tight jeans. "Shit, don't be crying about that," he said. "I got me some money here for another one."

But when he looked up, the boy was coming toward him, carrying a big switchblade knife.

"Gimme the bike, Jack," he said.

David began to pull his hand from his pocket. He half-laughed at the boy's audacity and tensed himself to pedal away.

"Look out!" called a voice. David turned his head in time to glimpse another young boy behind him, swinging a huge spanner wrench that burst his vision into a red shower of pain and sent him sprawling against a fender. Small hands bundled him from the bike and might have stabbed him if the same voice, drawing nearer through the rush and ringing in his ears, had not called, "I'm calling the police!" David fell to the pavement and heard the spring of his bike, like the voice of someone he loved taken by kidnapers, as it leapt away forever; heard rather than saw, for his eyes were closed, revealing a pattern of explosive flowers of light, and in his mouth he tasted his own blood.

"You okay, man?" said his unseen rescuer. "They cut you? You bleeding?"

"Bike," said David. "Got my bike."

"Man, you lucky you alive," said the voice. "Them little shorties is bad. They put a old lady in the hospital just last week. Right down the block. She gone live, though."

David opened his eyes. The dots swam together lazily to form at the top of his vision. Behind them wavered and danced the image of one of the bravest men he would ever see: an old, frail black man with a cane, his white beard bobbing up and down beneath a straw hat. "Bike," David said again thickly. "Which way? Which?"

"Leave it alone, brother," said the old man, wheezing as he helped David upright. "We best get off the street, call the police. They handle it. Maybe they get you your bike back."

Shaking his head, David took a step, and then another, hearing in his mind the tortured spring of his bike, letting that sound lead him on through a world that glowed and dimmed oddly and roared like mighty unseen waters.

"Come back!" the old man cried. "The shorties kill you!"

David's staggering footsteps led him on to the bright dirty avenue, and he began stopping passersby, wiping the dried blood from his eyes and asking, "Bike? Seen my — took my bike? Got it? Seen it? Little shorties?"

But there was no help on the street. The strangers shrank back in fear, mouthed and pointed, turned their backs. Like a tortured shadow he reeled down the long blocks, imploring aid, trying to focus his eyes and to follow that sound of gears that grew louder and softer as he walked, until after a time he became aware of a police car nearby and a knot of people around it whispering as if making some hideous decision. With the desperation of his wounds and the lonely years before them, he turned to one last hope, one final samaritan, able only to ask, "Bike? Seen my bike?"

"How terrible," said the stranger, blurring and re-forming into a loving smile. "Me too."

"Find my bike. Got to . . . shorties."

"Me too. Let's find it together. What is lost shall be found. Let's go now together."

"Where —"

"In here, friend. Maybe it's in here." He was dimly aware of hands caressing him, patting him, soothing and guiding; the smile disappeared, returned, splintered, and multiplied. "What's your name?" they said.

"David. Bike —"

"What a fascinating name," said the voices, as a door closed and he was guided into darkness. "Welcome to Sunrise, David. Welcome home."

Chapter 7

THE FOLLOWING MONDAY MORNING, Gerald emerged into the lobby wearing a khaki suit and a disgruntled expression. He had slept badly and risen late to find that Handleman had eaten all the Pop-Tarts.

In the lobby, adjusting a carnation in the lapel of his seersucker suit, was Martin Grimm, president of the Park View Cooperative Board. Grimm's twenty years as a senior demographer with the Bureau of the Census seemed to have given him a distaste for individual people. On few was his disapproval showered more liberally than on Gerald Nash, whom Grimm seemed to regard as a troublemaker, a bad credit risk, and a bureaucratic parvenue. This dislike had been ignited by Gerald's initial suitability interview with the co-op board.

"Do you keep pets?" Grimm had asked him, balancing a teacup on a leg clothed in spotless white flannel.

Gerald gave what he assumed was the proper answer. "No, I don't like animals. They're a lot of trouble and they're dirty."

At that moment Grimm's sleek white Siamese tom, of whose

existence Gerald had been unaware, leapt into his lap. Startled, Gerald jumped to his feet, sending the animal straight into its master's lap, where it overturned the teacup on the flannel trousers and the off-white raw-silk upholstery. Shortly afterward the board had recorded a split decision against Gerald.

The board agreed to examine Handleman instead. For the occasion he chose an Italian suit of brown wool flecked with a faint blue, with a flared single-vent jacket and pleated trousers. What Handleman said in the meeting Gerald never knew, but the pair had been given permission to enter on solemn condition that the lease be kept in Handleman's name alone. This gave Willys leverage in his monthly wrangles with Gerald over the rent; Willys had only to consider giving notice and Gerald was forced to moderate his demands.

"Mr. Grimm, could I speak to you a second?" Gerald said.

The president's gaze swept impassively over Gerald, then dropped to the mirror-bright finish on his own black oxford shoes. "You're up a bit early today, aren't you, Mr. Nash?" he said.

"I was wondering what had happened to David. He wasn't on the elevator when I came in last night."

"David has apparently decided to move on to, ah, greener pastures, shall we say."

"You mean he quit?"

"Oh, I imagine David would regard formal notice as a minor detail. But he failed to report for work Saturday or yesterday, and we can only surmise he has chosen to . . . move on."

"Maybe he's sick."

"As it happens, Mr. Nash, our superintendent has spoken with his landlady. She said he had left without paying his rent on Saturday."

"Did you check the hospitals or the police?"

A faint smile scrolled up Grimm's pale pink cheek. "Mr. Nash, I gather that in the social milieu in which David lives, this sort of thing is far from uncommon. The landlady apparently said that he had reneged on some promises he had made to her as well."

"Had he picked up his paycheck?"

"I don't handle the payments myself. But I do know that we've had a difficult time over the years finding dependable people to work here at the Park View. David was not really the sort of employee we can hope to keep for long. A very . . . volatile young man. I understand, for example, that he made a number of unauthorized alterations in the wiring system of the elevator controls. We're calling in an electrical contractor to put that to rights."

"I still think we ought to find out if he's all right."

"I'll bring your views to the attention of the board at its next regular meeting, Mr. Nash. Of course, if you feel such personal — or perhaps I should say sociological? — concern, you're certainly free to make any inquiries you want on a personal basis, as long as you don't involve the board in any way."

"Thanks very much," said Gerald, turning away. "I'll certainly try to keep you out of it."

"Mr. Nash," said Grimm, before Gerald had gone two paces. "Your name did come up at the regular board meeting last Thursday." Grimm looked at him with a sarcastic half-smile, as if the two of them shared a private joke. "Our discussion was, shall we say, musical in nature."

"Mr. Grimm, I'm due at the office, so I wish you'd just tell me whatever's bothering you."

"Very well, then. It was agreed unanimously to ask you not to practice your accordion in the apartment."

"I don't play the accordion!"

"Really, Mr. Nash, given the number of complaints from your neighbors, it's hardly a secret."

"Maybe you should ask Willys about it."

"I hardly think it does you credit to try to throw blame on someone like Mr. Handleman. After all, there's nothing discreditable about pursuing a musical hobby, for those who have ample spare time. I myself played the French horn as a young man, before the demands of work became too intense — and, of course, my service on the board —"

"Look, I don't care about your musical history. I don't play the accordion."

"Excellent! In that case, all the board would ask is that you *not* play it somewhere else. Shall I tell them you will comply?"

"Tell the board —"

Gerald's full answer was cut off by the glass front door. Without noticing it, he nearly flattened a flower salesman from the Temple of Ray, then inadvertently brushed aside an octogenarian and took the taxi she was about to enter. When he regained his wits, he was already speeding downtown.

"Would you like to hear Soviet joke?" said a Slavic accent.

The cab license identified Gerald's chauffeur as P. I. Chichikov.

"Sure," said Gerald. "Why not?"

"Okay, Stalin shaves off his mustache," said the driver, a man of middle years, not slender but not quite fat. Balding, faintly down-at-heel, he had the look of a man who had been fired from better jobs than this one. "Nobody recognizes him. He goes to workers' tavern. With one worker he drinks vodka, they talk football, food shortage, this and that. They very drunk. Stalin whispers, 'Say, what you think of Stalin?' Worker very nervous. 'Quiet!' he says. 'Not here! Come with me!' They go in street. 'Not here,' says worker. They get boat, row to middle of river. 'Shhh,' says worker. Looks right, looks left, to see is anybody listening. Then whispers, 'Just between us — *I like him!*' "

A sudden turn onto Constitution Avenue threw Gerald against the side of the cab.

"I know a Soviet joke," Gerald said.

"Okay, so tell!"

"What's the difference between communism and capitalism?"

"Boy, that I know plenty — no, I give up."

"Under capitalism man exploits man, but under communism *it's precisely the opposite!*"

The cab screeched to a halt in front of the Department. "I don't get," the driver said, turning a flat, hostile face.

"Never mind." Gerald frantically overtipped. "I must have told it wrong."

In the center of his desk, casting petals on a draft budget guidance paper for the coming fiscal year, was a tiny nosegay of wildflowers in a cut-glass bud vase. Attached was a card decorated with multicolored balloons, popular cats, and the words

> It's nice to have a sunny day,
> It's nice to have a chance to play!
> And here's another thing that's true —
> It's nice to have a friend like YOU!

This tasteful missive was signed "Ruby Fentress."

In some confusion, he went down to Ruby's office, where, for perhaps the first time in her life, she smiled at him.

"Hello, Ruby. Thanks for the flowers," he said.

"Did you like them?" she asked, as if desperately worried about his opinion.

"They were swell. Say, Ruby, are you feeling okay?"

Maternal exasperation crossed her features. "My stars, Gerry, can't a body do something nice without being sick?"

"They're very nice."

"You're just as welcome as you can be. Now you better hurry down to the big staff meeting. It starts at ten."

This was Gerald's first notification of the meeting, which would start in two minutes. "Christ, I'd better get down to the conference room, then," he said. "Do you know what it's all about?"

Ruby's underlip poked out and her eyes glistened. "Oh, shoot, Gerry, I thought we were *friends,*" she said.

"I'd better run," he said and bolted down the corridor.

As Gerald entered the conference room, he felt a sense of expectancy, as if some great drama were about to reach its denouement there. It would be hard to imagine a less prepossessing setting for a grand climax: Room N317–A–F was windowless, green-paneled, and had a long conference table surrounded by chairs of the kind used in small-town airport departure lounges.

Already facing each other across the table were two of the five people who ordinarily attended senior staff meetings: Bradford Watkins, head of the Office of Training, Education, and Professional Development, and Jack Worthy, head of the Office of Morale Enhancement Services. They looked at Gerald and abruptly broke off their conversation.

Watkins was a plump black man in his forties, with dark, thick eyebrows and a faintly mocking smile. The federal government occupied in his life the place that other men reserve for the church, the Marine Corps, or the Los Angeles Dodgers organization. Having joined the government as a messenger with a high school diploma, Watkins had advanced within it over a quarter-century until he was the holder of two graduate degrees and the head of all the Department's educational programs, which for obscure historical reasons included an entire evening-study program offering courses in disciplines from oenology to urban studies.

In contrast with Watkins's direct path up, Jack Worthy's record was remarkable for its succession of demotions, missed promotions, and intra- and interagency transfers. A pale man with a gray goatee, Worthy had plodded to within half a decade of retirement, carrying still the burden he had brought into the civil service thirty-seven years before: an integrity he had neither the courage nor the charm to support. The years had refined his ineffectual goodness into a kind of invertebrate sanctity; his mere presence in a room could drive others into frenzies of remorse. His superiors found themselves daydreaming of ways to get rid of his reproachful presence, until it became an obsession and Worthy was transferred again.

Once he had been notified of his transfer while still in costume after playing Santa Claus at the office Christmas party, and on another occasion after bowling six perfect frames at the interagency bowling championship. Once he had returned from two weeks at the beach to find his office eliminated altogether, its doorjamb removed and the door sealed with freshly painted bricks. The men who did these things were not cruel. They wanted to provoke from Worthy some outburst, a vow of vengeance or a physical threat. But after each new outrage, Jack Worthy shouldered his burden without a word of blame, and like Bunyan's Pilgrim moved faithfully on to the next leg of the great road to his pension, until he landed his present job. His most arduous duty was selecting commissioners for the intramural sports leagues, which often occupied weeks of thought and negotiation.

"Good morning, Jack," said Gerald, thinking as he looked at Worthy of all the dishonorable or equivocal things he had done recently. "How are you, Brad?"

The two men watched him sharply. "Hi, Gerry," Watkins said. "Big day, huh?"

"Damn if I know what's going on," Gerald said, hefting his case onto the table.

Worthy smiled, as if forgiving Gerald for keeping a secret.

Gerald's ears picked up a rumble in the still air, as of an exotic army on the march with brave banners and rolling drums. Suddenly the door burst open and Baxter Muntin entered in a blast of smoke, singing in a tobacco-coarsened but otherwise tuneful baritone:

> "Oh, the drums go bang and the symbols clang
> And the horns they blaze away!
> McCarthy pumps the old bassoon
> And I the pipes do play!
> And Hennessey-Tennessey tickles the flute,
> And the music is simply grand!
> A credit to old Ireland
> Is McNamara's band!

"Good morning, gentlemen!" he cried, beaming at all present, then, catching sight of Gerald, cried, "Friend, come up higher!" He would have carried Gerald bodily toward the head of the table if the latter had not wrapped his ankles around the metal legs of his chair. So Muntin descended with a crash into the seat next to Gerald, beaming at him as if he were Muntin's long-lost son and also, on his mother's side, the lost dauphin of France.

"You seem reasonably satisfied with yourself this morning, Baxter," Gerald said.

"Gerald," Muntin said, "once, as a young Marine lieutenant, I led a rifle platoon into a small Japanese fishing village. We were the first Allied forces to arrive there after the surrender. We disembarked from landing craft, and the commander of the garrison knelt and presented me with his sword. Then my men disarmed his soldiers and placed them under arrest. We carried the flag of our country through the streets to the village hall, and as we passed, every old man, every woman, every child in that village knelt by the roadside and placed their foreheads in the dust. I have never forgotten that morning. And yet, even so, I can truthfully say that I had never known triumph until yesterday. But what am I thinking of, babbling of my petty concerns to you? You are the one to be congratulated, from what I hear, eh?"

"I really don't know what this is all about —"

"Very wise, Gerald. Keep your secret. But remember me when you come into your kingdom. Really," he said with sudden earnestness, as if this were his last chance, "won't you have a cigarette?"

Then Nancy Quoin made her entrance.

Gerald had never seen a queen. Yet ever after he would retain a vague sense of having witnessed Marie Antoinette riding the tumbrel through a jeering crowd. Never did noble or commoner mount on scaffold high, with family and fortune forfeit, never did general or statesman advance under flag of truce, reputation blasted to bloody fragments, with more grace than Nancy Quoin that day. She wore a light-brown business suit. Her blouse was dazzling white, secured by a white bow closing. She wore her half-glasses in her hair, like extra eyes fixed on heaven. And her smile, at its highest wattage yet, swept over the group at large.

"I'm delighted you could all make it at such short notice," she said, assembling four-by-six note cards neatly on the table in front of her. "This meeting is important for a number of reasons. We have some important announcements and a visitor from the State Department who has come especially to be with us. I've asked him to wait in my office for a few minutes, though, because the first item of business concerns the division family only.

"Some of you may remember that at our very first session together, I said that my most important personal goal and objective was to improve and nurture communication within the division, and to try to foster mutual loyalty and — I'm still not ashamed to use the words — love and family feeling. Well, gentlemen, it's been a long struggle, but we have made progress. As you probably know, there have been some differences within the division, and I should confess candidly that I myself may very possibly even in some small way bear a minor part of some of the blame for a few of them. No matter how small or insignificant my contribution to already existing tensions, even if that contribution may have arisen inadvertently or even out of a desire to improve things, it was not my intention and I sincerely regret it.

"The good news is that yesterday, after a very stimulating emergency meeting involving myself, the deputy general counsel, an assistant United States attorney, and a representative from the Merit Systems Protection Board, our own Baxter Muntin very graciously yielded to my sincere pleas and agreed to remain in his present position. Speaking for the Assistant Secretary, who spoke with us by a direct telephone link from the Department's field office in Boothbay Harbor, and also of course for myself, I'm delighted that Baxter will continue to enrich our interaction with his unique skills and good humor. I'm sure we all join in congratulating him — and ourselves." Here she began a small round of applause, which everyone joined but Muntin, who smiled and regally sprinkled cigarette ashes across Gerald's legal pad.

"Naturally . . ." Quoin's throat dried up. She quickly drank a little water, then began again. "Naturally, Baxter has also dropped all civil, criminal, and administrative charges against other members of the senior staff. But gentlemen, I say that it is time to put this unhappy episode behind us! Because one of the other announcements I have the pleasure of making today is that this division has been selected as host agency for a three-day conference and workshop to be held in October for a delegation of top officials from the People's Republic of China. Our conduct of this conference will reflect not only on the division and the Department but on our country as well. In fact, the State Department has formally requested that one of their Foreign Service officers be permitted to brief us before we begin the preliminary planning. Jack, would you mind stepping down to my office and asking Mr. Calvin to join us?"

The group sat in silence for a minute (except that on Gerald's right, the outwardly impassive Baxter Muntin was quietly humming "The Marine Hymn"). Then Worthy ushered in a tall young man whom Gerald recognized as Crane, the gangling runner with the pastel jogging suits. In his official attire he was more impressive: his nose was as assertive as ever, but it surmounted a suit that would have made Handleman slaver, complemented with a narrow blue Yale tie, a white shirt, black suede shoes, and the look of a noble nature thrown among thieves.

He acknowledged Quoin's introduction with a curt nod. "For those of you not familiar with China," he said, "it is a large nation located in east Asia."

He then proceeded through a summary of China's population (dense), government (Communist), economy (huge, primitive), natural resources (considerable), and strategic value (incalculable). Bradford Watkins passed into total unconsciousness; Nancy Quoin occupied herself with contemplation of her reversal; Gerald feigned note-taking; Baxter Muntin doodled page after page of cartoons representing the letter Q in situations of distress — Q's blasted by lightning, Q's pierced by knives, Q's drowned in murky pools. But Jack Worthy kept up a look of interest that led Calvin to protract his briefing to the very edge of endurance.

Finally, however, he concluded with a clear summary of administration policy toward China (warm friendship for the heroic people of the mainland in their struggle against their expansionist Communist neighbor and for the peaceful development, with Western assistance, of their socialist economy) and Taiwan (warm friendship for the plucky people of the island in their struggle against their expansionist Communist neighbor and for the continued success, with Western assistance, of their free-market economy). "I must stress to each and every one of you," he said, "that mention of Taiwan, or any hint of a so-called two-China policy on the part of the United States government, would be extremely unpleasant for our guests and embarrassing for the United States government. I strongly urge that this subject be avoided at all times. I will take any questions now."

Muntin raised his hand. "I'm puzzled by your reference to a two-China policy," he said. "Do you mean one set for everyday use and one for special occasions, or what?"

Nancy Quoin rose with a long-suffering air that, Gerald suddenly realized, came from knowing that from now until the end of time, she could not rebuke Muntin for anything at all. "Thank you very much, Mr. Calvin," she said, hustling the diplomat to the door so precipitately that his posture dissolved and he lurched out, nose foremost.

"Now," she said, "with those formalities out of the way, let's get down to the really exciting part, which is our program planning. Brad and I have done some preliminary work on a seminar I think will be a true high spot for us and for our visitors. Brad?"

"Thank you, Nancy," said Watkins. "As most of you know, the theme of our conference is 'Consumer Credit in the Emerging Nations: Flexible Policy Development and Appropriate Technologies.' I hope you'll forgive me if I say that the wealth of expertise which I have on my adjunct faculty is one of the reasons that we were picked as host agency. Our draft agenda will obviously be circulated for input from the other participating agencies — Commerce, FTC, the Fed, OPIC, the White House Consumer Adviser's Office, Fannie May, Freddie Mac, and so on — but we have a core here for the others to build on.

"To begin with, we've scheduled an opening address by Dr. Sharon Glassbinder, who is the author of two excellent books on this topic, *Give Yourself Credit* and *Charge Your Own Life.* After her address there will be a response from an interagency panel, including Henry Palmer from Baxter's shop, who'll present some of the fascinating work his group is doing on credit cards as they impact the larger question of fungibility. The next day there will be a series of workshops on the following subjects: 'Consumer-Credit Counseling at the Hamlet, Village, and Provincial Capital Level,' 'What Color Is Your Water Buffalo? or Career Opportunities in Third-World Consumer-Credit Networks,' and 'Don't Leave Your Hut Without Them: State Bank Policy Modeling for Indigenous Small-Denomination Soft-Currency Traveler's Checks.' The final morning will be devoted to a hands-on seminar on microcomputer technology as applied to consumer-credit transactions in countries where citizens are not allowed to own checking accounts. Then there is a tea-and-fortune-cookie reception and a two-minute farewell speech by our visitors, and that'll wrap it up."

"Brad," said Muntin promptly, "I'm afraid I can't let Henry do any public presentation on fungibility just now. We're readjusting the conceptual basis of that project. Sorry."

"I understood that Nancy had cleared this with you," said Watkins, turning to Quoin for support.

"Don't worry, Brad," said Quoin, not meeting his eyes. "I'm sure Baxter understands that this is an honest mistake on your part."

In the awkward pause that followed, Jack Worthy suggested that the conference room be decorated with paper Oriental lanterns.

"Okay, before we break up, I have two announcements," Nancy Quoin said. "The first is a memo I received from the Assistant Secretary after his West Coast tour this month. As you know, he is very concerned that the CATA program is running at only forty-six percent of authorized funding this FY, and even lower than that in the area of new grants. The AS is committed to the CATA program, and so is the administration. We think it's a good program, and I know you all agree. In that context, he seemed very impressed with what he saw in Gouge Eye of the lumber-mill project there, and he wants us all to break the logjam, so to speak. Do you agree, Baxter?"

"No problem, Nancy," Muntin said casually. "The papers have been ready for a couple of months. I just felt that in light of events, I would wait for guidance from above."

"Baxter, I think you've handled this just right," she replied in placatory desperation. "But now, with the AS having made an on-site evaluation and giving us written authorization, I think we can move ahead."

"No problem, Nancy — I'll have the papers for your signature after lunch."

"Actually, Baxter, as you have so wisely pointed out, this grant is a special case in many ways," Quoin said uneasily. "I think it might be better if you route them directly to the Special Assistant's office for the AS to finalize himself when he stops through before the Labor Day break."

Gerald raised a hand, intending to volunteer to pick up the papers after the meeting. But Quoin looked at him with injured eyes.

"Oh, Gerald, I'd hoped to make that announcement myself. Do you mind?"

Mystified, he motioned her to proceed.

"The last item on the agenda," she said, "is one some of you may have some inkling of, but which has become official only in the last twenty-four hours. All of us who have worked with Gerald Nash over the past eighteen months have frequently remarked that we are lucky to have someone of his talents. Well, I'm afraid our luck has run out. Effective immediately, Gerald is taking a ninety-day furlough to serve as assistant political director of the Reelection Committee. When I say that he will be working directly for Toad Earnshaw, I think that gives you some idea of the level of responsibility he's being given. We're going to miss Gerald. But we have found one of the few people in this town who could begin to replace him. Starting this afternoon, Bernard

Weisman will be coming on board as a consultant. As you know, he's left Hench's staff pending the outcome of the trial. So Gerald can go in peace, knowing that the fine work he has been doing will go forward in capable hands. I think that's all for today. Thank you all for sharing this time with me."

The others rose, folded their papers, and shuffled out, nodding deferential congratulations to Gerald.

"Thank you so much for letting me handle the announcement, Gerry," said Quoin. "I won't forget that." Then she was gone in a crisp clatter of heels and a cloud of Babe perfume.

Ruby was waiting for Gerald. "Sugar, you have two messages. Mr. Weisman says take your time, as long as you have the office cleaned out by two o'clock. And a girl named Diana said congratulations. That's what I say too, lamb." She kissed his cheek, and when he left his green cubicle forever, he bore on his face two red lip marks and a look of utter shock.

Bernard Weisman surveyed his new kingdom with wintry satisfaction. There was much to do, many things to set right, and most of all, many scores to settle.

His eye fell on a file marked "Gouge Eye Lumber Co-op," to which had been clipped a memo sheet reading "For yr. immediate action — BLM." He reached for the phone. "Baxter, Weisman here. What's the rush on this Gouge Eye thing?"

"DAS says the AS wants it ASAP," said Muntin. "I know of no reason to disoblige him. Of course, the individual involved did steal my briefcase and destroy your former boss. But otherwise it's purely routine."

Weisman hung up and looked at the file. Then, with surprising dexterity for one so pale and still, he began folding its pages into a variety of aerodynamic shapes. These aircraft he launched from his desk into the hall, where they fluttered briefly in the elegiac light and then disappeared forever.

Part Three

I was assured by a great Minister, that if the island
had descended so near the town, as not to be able
to raise itself, the citizens were determined to fix
it for ever, to kill the King and all his servants,
and entirely change the government.
—"A Voyage to Laputa, Balnibarbi,
Glubbdubdrib, Luggnagg and Japan"

Chapter 1

GERALD WANDERED UP AND DOWN Fourteenth Street for twenty minutes in a steaming drizzle, looking for the campaign office. He found that the celestial prominence to which he had been elevated was the second floor of a building whose storefront bore the legend "ADULT BOOK STORE — *All Girl Revue — Film Screenings — Filipino Marital Aids.*"

Inside the door a tiny hand-lettered card said "Reelection Committee use elevator." An arrow directed Gerald into a small, wheezing elevator that, after a surprisingly long one-story trip, disgorged him into a bare suite of offices from whose dusty walls echoed the mellow, confident voice of Toad Earnshaw.

Earnshaw was encamped in a corner office, presiding from a perch atop a worktable — so far as Gerald could see, the only piece of furniture in the entire complex. He halted the meeting at Gerald's entrance. "Well, a diller a dollar, a ten o'clock scholar," he said. "I think you know everybody."

Gerald did know almost everyone in the room. In former days some had lacked paunches, others neckties; now most had both. The women wore slit skirts and the men wore bowl haircuts.

"Okay," Earnshaw said, "now that Gerald's here we can get this show on the road." Without warning he gave an explosive sneeze, which he partially stifled with a blue bandanna handkerchief. "Sorry 'bout that," he said, wiping his eyes. "Y'all gotta have some tolerance for me, because the doctor has told me to quit cigarettes. Anyway, we're all real happy and pleased that we've been able to put together such an experienced and high-powered team. The President said to me this morning that He was impressed by the loyalty and superb talent of all of you, and that He personally will remember the sacrifice and dedication of the people who have stuck with Him. As you may have read, my leave from the White House becomes official at midnight tonight, so I'll be here full-time from tomorrow on.

"We've got to think hard, think aggressively, and do the kind of job we did four years ago. If we do that, we'll win, and win big. Anybody who doesn't believe that, just remember that if you have the faith of a grain of mustard seed, you can move mountains. Okay? There are a lot of details to discuss, but before we get into that, the Ambassador himself is going to speak to us. I don't need to tell you how many campaigns he's been through. He's waiting in the other office with his respirator. Buford, would you step around and ask him in?"

As the Ambassador hobbled to the front of the room, the applause nearly drowned out the strains of "You Could Be Dancin'" seeping up from the porno shop. The old man took a position in the center of the room and surveyed the group with the disapproving air of a prep-school headmaster.

"There's very little I need to say," he said. "Our party never loses when we have an incumbent President at the top of the ticket. There are a few simple rules. Call in the union leaders and promise to repeal the Taft-Hartley Act. Call in the corporate leaders and promise not to. Remind the middle classes that we saved them from the Depression and won the war. Give out two-dollar bills in the colored neighborhoods. There should be no difficulty. I will leave you now. Good day." He stumped slowly to the elevator, indignantly shaking off the arm of a young aide who rushed to offer his assistance.

Someone downstairs began playing "Ring My Bell." A voice said, "Toad?"

"Yeah, Buford?"

"Do they still make two-dollar bills?"

"I'll call one of our people at the Treasury and have him find out. All right, let's get down to business. Now, as I guess you all know, we've had a number of pressing concerns at the White House, and we haven't been able to get the campaign organization developed to the high level we might have wanted. So we've got to make some decisions now. I want people to take over regions and key states, to get some action going until we put the formal structure in place. Don't be shy about speaking up, now. I'll go through the possibilities, and everybody raise their hands when you think you'd like to get involved, okay?"

First he named the President's native region. A dozen hands went up. "Actually, I'd kinda figured on handling that part of the world myself," he said. "Glad to see all this enthusiasm, though. How's about New York State?"

The staffers seemed suddenly to discover something fascinating out the window, on the ceiling, or in their jacket pockets. "Come on, damn it," Earnshaw growled. "Buford, weren't you up in New York for the primary?"

"Yeah, Toad, but we lost that one."

No matter; the Empire State was pressed firmly into Buford's faltering hands. Then Earnshaw marched across the nation like a Sherman in reverse, awarding the conquered lands to reluctant proconsuls: the Midwest fell, then the West, until finally there remained only one region, the Pacific Northwest, and one eligible staffer, Gerald Nash.

"Whaddaya say, Gerry?"

"Christ, Toad, I don't know anything about that part of the world."

"Ever been there?"

"No."

"Ever wanted to go there?"

"No."

"Got family from there?"

"No."

"Ever date a girl from there?"

"No."

"Ever done any work on it at the Department?"

"Good God, no, unless you count something minor like looking over a CATA application."

"There you are," Earnshaw said with satisfaction, writing Gerald's name on his master list. "Okay, that does it. All of y'all get on the phones, soon's we have 'em put in, and get me something to work with. I want memos by next Monday, then we'll sit down together and fit it into the overall strategy. I'll try to get a couple of desks in here too. Meanwhile, we're going to hear something about strategy from the other two principals at this end. Doc, you want to read the Epistle?"

Putnam Cadwallader was a Washington lawyer. His roots lay in Darien, Connecticut, but in recent years he had begun to affect a soothing prairie accent, Stetson hats, string ties, and the self-bestowed nickname of "Doc." He rose before the meeting in a shower of light: it gleamed from his gold longhorn tie ring, his gold belt buckle, his gold presidential-seal cufflinks, his gold party-symbol lapel pin, and most of all from his small, alert, golden eyes, which darted across the room in a glow of ambition and self-satisfaction.

Cadwallader was known chiefly for his overweening humility. "I don't want any of you to think we've got this thing won just because I'm on board," he said. "Our chief worry is overconfidence. That's a problem I can help with, because of course I struggle with it every day. When you've been in this town as long as I have, you tend to get yourself a reputation that maybe doesn't have much to do with who you really are. Sometimes I read about myself and I wonder, who is this fella everybody seems to agree is so wise and compassionate and powerful and well liked? I don't take it too seriously, frankly. For example, when the press recently wrote something to the effect that my experience, my contacts, and my persuasive abilities would do the job by themselves, why, I just didn't even read it.

"Even if I were all they say I am, and I guess you'll just have to take my word for it that I'm not — even if I were twice as good as I am, which I'm not — I still couldn't do it all by myself. That's where the rest of you come in. If each and every one of us bears down and gives it everything we've got, no matter how little that may be, well, then in my own personal opinion, for whatever that may be worth, we can be a damn sight more than optimistic. All of you should feel free to call on me whenever you want. I'm not really such a formidable figure as you probably have been told. That's about all."

Next to advance was Clark Guppy, the pollster, a tall, gawky, sallow young man with large freckled hands and dark moist hair that grew straight down his neck as far as could be seen. He had once worn black Levi trousers and white short-sleeved shirts with plastic pocket penholders, but now stuck to Brooks Brothers suits and monogrammed custom-made shirts.

Striding slue-footed to the front of the room, he arrayed before him on the table a loose-leaf notebook, a statistical-functions calculator with built-in thermal printer, a carousel slide projector, and a randomly selected bound volume of *The Journal of Sociology*. He had adopted the clothing and props in self-defense after the previous campaign, during which visiting dignitaries had repeatedly mistaken him for the mailboy. Now, of course, his face and name were familiar to every American who read newsmagazines (two covers in four years), watched television talk programs (a mean of 2.7 appearances weekly over the same period) or game shows (one week as a contestant on a network program and two as guest host on a cable show), or read glossy-magazine Scotch whisky advertisements ("Last book read: *De la division du travail social* par Emile Durkheim").

"Speaking scientifically," Guppy began. Then he pitched his voice an octave lower and began again. "Scientifically speaking, that is to say, the electorate this year presents us with an intriguing set of challenges. Disparate and seemingly conflicting indices of public opinion, coupled with accelerating social change, might at first glance seem unfavorable to the President's reelection. However, interpreted from a sociological standpoint, the deep structure of the public mood is extremely promising. Let's look at the first slide."

With a whir, the slide projector displayed on the wall a table of figures with the heading "Seven-Year Gross Revenue Projections, Independent Polling Service."

"Wrong slide," Guppy said smoothly, then clicked to a two-color map of the United States headed "Areas Leaning Toward

President." According to a legend, areas in which the President was viewed favorably were marked in shades of red; those in which the challenger was favored, in tones of blue. The area within one hundred miles of the President's home town showed up as a round pink blemish on a shifting blue sea that ranged in color from baby through sky and Carolina to navy, with a few patches of purple congealed near the Great Lakes.

"Viewed in isolation, these findings might erroneously be considered cause for concern," said the pollster. "But to the specialist they are extremely promising. As the opposition commands a large lead, both in the gross percentage figures and geographically, we are given a significant tactical *and* strategic advantage. He must defend and preserve; we can attack and destroy. His campaign must be conservative and timid; ours can be innovative and bold. He must seek to remain ahead in all areas; we can pick the areas in which to make maximum effort. We can feint; he must parry. And lastly, since our gross figures are so low, we can safely anticipate change in our favor over the next four weeks — and the declines in his standing will set up what we in the profession call a victory psychology, running strongly in our favor.

"Our opponent has the misfortune of being so far ahead in the polls that a statistically significant number of respondents now actually believe him to be president already. Thus we can blame him for defects in our own record. Viewed in this light, the next slide becomes grounds for particular optimism."

That slide was a bar chart with the heading "Statistically Adjusted Indices of Voter Satisfaction with Administration Performance." On one side squatted a broad dwarf of a bar, about the shape of a cake of industrial-strength hand soap, labeled "Satisfied or not disgusted." Like a taxicab parked beside the Sears Tower, it crouched next to a soaring, graceful structure labeled "Unhappy, alienated, homicidal, &c."

"As I think even the lay people in the audience can see, this voter profile offers significant opportunities for the strategy I outlined above, particularly as large numbers of those depicted in the second bar are members of ethnic, racial, geographical, and economic groups which ordinarily cast a majority of votes for our party. Thus we must convince these groups to vent their anger at us by voting for our party.

"For voters who by education or intelligence are relatively impervious to the argument that the opposition is actually in power, we will suggest that their dissatisfaction arises not because of defects in presidential performance but because of failure or even imminent collapse of the political system itself, which enables us to run against politics, politicians, etcetera, and at the same time to win points for our candidate's candor, truthfulness, and refusal to raise unreasonable expectations. This will dovetail neatly with the opposition's strategy, which according to my analysis is the now antiquated one of promising such desirable but nebulous goals as prosperity, military strength, peace, and domestic tranquillity. A series of carefully tailored mass mailings aimed at selected higher-educated groups will demonstrate that these desiderata are not only impossible but actively bad.

"There will of course be a core of voters whom we will be unable to sway with either of the first two tracks, and so we have devised a third track which is designed to simultaneously harden our growing base of support and defuse the opposition's. This involves an implicit communication that those aggressively dissatisfied with this administration are responsible not only for their own problems but also for those of everybody else. This will have two effects: it will give our target group the chance to vote against someone — namely, their fellow citizens; and it will induce in the opposition a sensation of self-doubt which will reduce the number of them to be put in the 'likely voter' category.

"To sum up, I would say that the task before us is challenging but far from impossible. We must convince our friends that we are no longer in power and our enemies that they already are. I anticipate a period of extreme fluidity in poll readings, culminating after the World Series with a steady rise for the President and a solid election victory. Are there any questions?"

"Speaking of that," Toad said, "Buford will be coordinating the World Series and play-off pools as usual. Because we recognize that a lot of us are taking pay cuts to work in the campaign, we're going to cut it down to a dollar a shot."

Feeling like a slow student in Sociology 101, Gerald raised his hand. "I wonder if you have figures on voter preference for the President and the challenger?" he asked.

The pollster responded by thinning his nostrils, as if he had offered to perform a Mahler octet but had instead been asked for the theme from "Leave It to Beaver." "As it happens, I anticipated that question, and I do have a slide with our latest data. However, before I present it, I must note that this gross measure of voter preference is perhaps the most fluid and least powerful in predictive terms of all those in the pollster's armamentarium. It is to be viewed as a result of social trends and political strategies, not as a cause. Here is the information."

The new slide showed a small bar representing the 32 percent of the population leaning toward the President, a large bar showing the 59 percent favorable to the challenger, and a tiny bar labeled "Don't Know, No Opinion, Unaware of Election, Incarcerated, Minor Parties, Mickey Mouse &c."

"That concludes my presentation," the pollster said, hastily turning off the slide projector. "I think at this time Toad has prepared some thoughts on strong issue appeals which can be used to implement the strategy I have outlined. Toad?"

"Yes, well, on that I'm going to have to get back to the group," Earnshaw said. "As I mentioned before, we've had some urgent matters up at the White House and I haven't been able to follow up on it. Let's break up for some lunch now and then get back here and hit the ground running. Gerry, wait up, will you?"

Toad winked at Gerald as the others filed out. "Say, I'm glad as hell you're with us, Gerry," he said, stuffing papers into his briefcase. "I wasn't sure your roommate was going to give you the message. First he thought it was some kind of practical joke and then he started trying to convince me to hire him instead. I mighta done it if I didn't have such a goddamned long memory. It's a curse; my granddaddy had one too. Say — hold that car!"

Grabbing Gerald by the arm, Toad rushed the elevator, which had been filled by the younger and more athletic Bowl Haircuts but which was now gradually repacked in a round of musical status until its final passengers were Cadwallader, Guppy, Earnshaw, and Gerald.

"Ain't it good to have Gerry back with us again?" Toad asked the others as the car began its slow, noisy descent. Lawyer and pollster together allowed their heads to move through ten degrees of a nod of assent.

"There aren't many people in this town you can really trust," Earnshaw continued. "Far as I'm concerned, most of them are in this elevator. You want you some of this shit, Gerry?" Toad extended a small, colorful tin labeled "Dr. Chadband's Pure Carolina Mentholated Genuine Nasal Snuff."

"No, thanks," said Gerald. "I don't dip it, myself."

"Me neither, usually," said Toad. "I'm trying to give up cigarettes." He seized a hearty pinch between thumb and forefinger and thrust it up one nostril. The elevator ground to a halt. As the doors opened Earnshaw gave a sneeze so mighty it seemed literally to blow Gerald out of the elevator and forward into the entryway until he was halted by the arresting, cool, unexpected eyes of Diana Cazadora. She was surrounded by an admiring knot of Bowl Haircuts who seemed desperately eager to submit themselves to searching interviews with her.

"No release today, honey," said Toad, wiping his nose with his blue bandanna. "We've got a press conference at the Mayflower tomorrow afternoon."

"I'm not here on business," she said, directing her habitually inquisitive gaze for some reason at Toad's bandanna. "Gerry," she said, drawing him aside while eight pairs of eyes followed them with suspicion and envy, "I think I've found your friend David."

Chapter 2

THERE ARE TIMES WHEN OUR LIVES, like rivers changing their beds, begin to flow toward new destinations. These periods are often marked by a kind of chronological fuzziness, as if the normal mechanisms of time were suspended. Thus Margaret Luck was never able to reconstruct how Bob Zardovsky ended up crashing in her apartment on the sweltering September evening when Gerald called to ask for him.

Lately Gerald had moved, in her mind, beyond enigma into full-blown incomprehensibility, as if he were a book she was trying to read in which the key pages had been glued together. "Congratulations," she said. "Willys told me about your new job."

"I wish he'd told *me*," Gerald replied. His voice had a kind of grudging haste in it, as though he were performing some onerous task. "I wonder if you know where to reach your friend Bob Zardovsky?"

In memory it was only then that the big ballplayer materialized full-length on her couch, snoring and sweating in the evening heat. "Bob? Sure, he's here, as a matter of fact," she said. "What do you need him for?"

"A couple of things, really," Gerald said with the false heartiness of a bureaucrat with a secret agenda. "I wanted to talk to him about his grant, of course. And I need some advice about that cult outfit he was involved with."

"The Temple of Ray?" she asked. At those words the sleeping Zardovsky gave a snort and began corkscrewing himself awake. "What in the world do you want with them?"

"I don't know if you remember David, who runs the elevator in my building, but apparently they've got hold of him, and I want to get him out if I can."

"He's joined the Temple?"

"I'm not really sure about that. But he's in their building, and Bob's the only person I know who's been inside it. Can I talk to him?"

Zardovsky had pried his eyes open and seemed to be trying to remember which part of Mexico he had fallen asleep in. "*Qué pasa?*" he said. Grabbing the phone, he plunged into a conference with Gerald, from which she could make out only some references to Fritos.

"You wanna walk uptown with me?" Zardovsky said when he hung up. "I said I'd meet Gerry in front of Sunrise House and see what I could do. Afterwards maybe we'll all go eat Mexican food or something."

"Let me get my running shoes," she said.

"I got a few scores to settle with those Sunrise people," he went on. "This guy Open, he's the head man there, I owe him a couple because he tried to rip me off. And there's a little honey named Sunshine up there who likes ballplayers pretty good. I never did finish up with her."

She jerked her shoelaces, painfully tight. "Let's go. And we'll stick to main streets this time, if you don't mind."

Hundreds of people were on the sweltering streets, jostling each other for ice cream or soft drinks or shoddy goods sold by street vendors. Knots of men lounged in the parks, playing congas; cab-drivers lounged against their cabs; young couples walked panting dogs.

Bob led her into the 7-Eleven store on Columbia Road, where he bought a bagful of assorted sweets and candy bars. "Christ, Bob," she protested, "it's too hot to eat that mess."

"This is just stuff that might come in handy," he said. "That little girl I told you about has kind of a sweet tooth. Matter of fact, they all do at that place."

"What are you planning to do?"

"I don't rightly know. I'll just wing it when I see what all this is about. See, I figure if I help out your friend, then maybe he'll help me some with this grant business."

"He's got a new job now. I'm not sure he can help."

"Well, Christ, maybe he could just explain what the hell went wrong. The damn government is worse than the ball club I played for. At least when the front office cut you, they sent a telegram."

She saw Gerald in front of the shabby row house a block away. Something in his tidy stillness reminded her of a bird watching a cat prowl at the bottom of a tree.

Bob let out a whoop of greeting. "Hey, buddy!" he called. "You got 'em cornered in there?"

Gerald's eyes met Margaret's just as Zardovsky's huge paw thumped him companionably on the back, nearly dislocating his spine.

"Maggie says you've become some kinda hotshot politician," Zardovsky was saying. "Congratulations, buddy."

"I want to talk to you about that," Gerald said. "I think maybe we can work out some way to help each other."

"Christ, I'm glad to hear that," Bob said. "Tell the truth, I been kinda gettin the runaround from your friend Weisman —"

"He's not my friend," Gerald interrupted. "Let's talk about it later. Right now I need some advice on how to handle these crazies."

"Is your buddy in there now?"

"I think so. Anyway, somebody told me he was. They won't let me talk to him."

"Who you been talking to?"

"Some guy named Lightning."

"Oh, yeah — little skinny guy with about half a face at a time?"

"I guess so. Do you know him?"

"Hell, yeah. He's from near my home town."

"You think you could talk to him?"

"Hell, I'll paint my ass blue and whistle if it'll help get the gran— get your friend out. But I tell you, the best thing would probably be if you could distract them while I get in the back and check out what's going on inside there."

"I'm not sure I can keep them at the door very long. They just slam it in my face."

"Yeah, maybe we need something a little more spectacular. You don't have a coupla cherry bombs or something like that, do you?"

"Can't say I do. I never know what Willys might have, but he's gone out somewhere, and if I went into his room alone I might never come out alive."

"Maggie, you know what I'm thinking?" Zardovsky said. "I think who we need is that guy Paco. You think you could find him for me while I check out the lay of the land?"

She struck off almost at random, finding to her surprise that her feet knew where to carry her. Soon she stood in a kind of urban dream landscape, on a street where she felt sure she should find Ma Dzudz Café; but instead of the nightspot there was an unfamiliar storefront topped by a sign reading

OFICINA DE AYUDA PÚBLICA
"El Matamigras"
Abogados — Visas E.U. — Impuestas — Seguridad Social
Notarios — Servicios de Traducción
Consultantes por Negocios Pequeños
Guardas de Seguridad — Mariachi-grams
Veedores por Todas las Fiestas

She heard a voice, at once cheering and chilling, in her ear: "Hey, lady, you lookin for me? You need maybe a mariachi band or somethin? How you like our new business? I tole you I need money, so we fold up the cantina and open up this service for the community, I got some guys workin with me, lawyers an stuff like that, one guy used to be chief justice of Honduras. Also we got the FLAN office here, they send me a little money, not much, but the struggle goes on, I got out a press release and I been doin some guest spots on the Spanish radio stations and like that, you know, makin propaganda for the revolution. You doin all right? Where's Tres-Dedos? He need some help or somethin?"

With some false starts and shortness of breath, she explained that Bob needed help to rescue a friend from a house of very bad people.

"You mean those guys from the Temple of Ray?"

"You know about them?"

"*Como no?* We got them back home too. See, lady, we got everythin bad there that you got here. It's just the good stuff you people don send us."

"Can you help?"

"Hey, no sweat for sure, lady, we pull somethin together for Tres-Dedos, let me get some people together. You got a coupla dimes, lady? See, our phone got cut off, reactionary monopoly an all like that."

She followed him to a pay phone around the corner. He spoke in Spanish to several parties; she heard the repeated phrase "Tres-Dedos." Within a few minutes they were at the center of a mariachi marching band, complete with bass drum reading "Fijar su mensaje aqui/Por información llamar Paco Sanchez 555-4567." At Paco's command the band set off down the center of the street like an impromptu Cinco de Mayo parade. The musicians struck up "Guadalajara"; from somewhere came a shrill keening mixed with clucking, and she saw a fat woman in a red dress and head-scarf scurrying into the procession with a live chicken under one arm.

"Who is that?" she shouted at Paco.

He genially cupped his hand around her ear. "Well, I figure these religious guys are a li'l crazy, and maybe Hermana Eva can help us with some magic stuff."

They burst into Columbia Road in a tumult of shrieking brakes and wailing cornets.

"Viva Tres-Dedos!" cried Paco as he caught sight of Bob and Gerald, huddling together at a distance from Sunrise House as if they had beaten a prudent retreat out of range of thrown objects and boiling oil.

"*Qué tal*, Paco?" Zardovsky said. The two men slapped hands in an intricate pattern which, on Paco's side at least, seemed likely to go on all night; but Bob finally stopped him and said, "Whoa up, amigo, I want you to meet my friend Gerry Nash."

A crowd had begun to gather; they were attracted not so much to the musicians as to a truck that had veered to the curb nearby and begun disgorging television cameras and sound equipment. REACTION NEWS SQUAD said a garish legend on its side. The crew was assembling under the direction of a dark young woman who struck Margaret as oddly familiar. A little Oriental man appeared with a tray of iced coconut soda, which he began hawking in loud multilingual pidgin.

"Okay, look," Bob was saying, "you guys make a lotta ruckus out front and we'll go around back. I got a feeling somebody will let us in back there."

"What makes you think that?" Gerald asked.

"Well, you remember I mentioned I had some candy to give to your friend?"

"They didn't seem to like that."

"I got a little gal inside with a kinda sweet tooth. I bet you I can talk her into letting us in the back way. I been inside this place — it's got a back set of stairs and a whole lot of little rooms up above. They probably got your friend in one of them. My guess is he's getting a little hungry about now. But if we get inside, we gotta be quick — these guys are kinda puny, but there's a lot of 'em. So stick behind me, do what I do, keep your mouth shut, and if anything goes wrong, run like hell."

The two men moved off toward the alleyway. Margaret said quickly, "You're not leaving me out here on the street. I'm coming too."

Bob shrugged and said, "Okay, come on then. Just don't make no noise."

The musicians began a reprise of their marching songs, which blended eerily with shrieks from the gypsy witch and her chicken. Like shadows, Gerald, Bob, and Margaret slunk into the alley.

The trail led by the kitchen of a Cuban eatery, from which they were nearly blinded by saffron-scented smoke, then turned behind the row of houses. Following Bob, Gerald and Margaret stalked along a rotting wooden fence until they were at the rear of Sunrise House. "Over you go, darlin," Bob said, and boosted her over the fence. He vaulted after, and Gerald, glasses askew, puffed over last.

A half-deflated volleyball and some scraps of Oriental newspaper sat in a sodden heap in the dingy back yard. Zardovsky put a finger to his lips and pointed to the kitchen window, where a hungry little face was staring at them like Rapunzel waiting to let down her hair.

"Hi, Three-Finger," said the face. "Give me the candy and I'll be sure your friend gets it."

"I bet you will," Zardovsky said. "Listen, I gotta get in and talk to David."

"We might get caught."

"Christ, I'm not afraid of that guy Open."

"He's not elder brother anymore. Mr. Chin took him away and we're not supposed to talk about him anymore."

"Who's in charge?"

"Lightning."

"That wimp? I'll break him in half if he messes with us."

The little blonde found this prospect irresistibly amusing. She unbolted the door and they tiptoed up the stairs, Bob first, then Gerald. The little blonde seemed to object to Margaret, however. "What do you need *her* for?" she asked Bob. The big man just kissed her on the forehead, at the same time pulling a Peanut Log candy bar from his pocket. The girl unwrapped it in one gesture and seemed to be trying to cram it all into her mouth at once. As Margaret passed her, the two exchanged a glance of recognition, as if there were some bond between them that needed no explanation.

"Where's David?" Bob asked.

"In the radio room. I have the key," she said proudly. "I take care of Thunder. That's his family name." Another brief barter produced an exchange of candy for key, and the little traitor, already chewing, pointed up the back stairs.

It was hard to say what Margaret found so unsettling about Sunrise House. Its floors were worn and uneven, it was dim, the wallpaper was stained and cracked, and there was a faint musty smell that told of years of neglect; but none of these things made it any different from her own apartment. What bothered her was a silent, reverberating echo, as if the walls had stifled sounds she didn't want to hear.

They groped their way up two narrow flights of stairs in the half-light, then entered a dark hall cluttered with heaps of documents. At the far end stood an imposing, well-maintained photocopying machine. Halfway down was a door marked "Elders Only." Bob halted in front of this and fumbled with the key.

The door swung open, and there, as if imprisoned in an oak tree, was David, with a large, dirty bandage on his head but otherwise much more cheerful than the last time Margaret had seen him. He was bent over a tangle of wires with a soldering gun in his hand; without looking up, he said, "Hey, babe, you bring me that oscilloscope?"

"Hey, come on, soldier, we're bustin out of this joint," Zardovsky said.

David seemed more surprised than pleased. "Rambler, how the hell did you get in here?" he said to Gerald. "I can't get this thing fixed if dudes keep interrupting me."

Gerald squatted by David, and for the first time Margaret noticed how much they resembled each other, not physically so much as in their thoughtful, suspicious expressions. "You don't have to stay with these people, David," Gerald said. "They can't hold you here."

"Hold me? What you talking about? These are the first people to give me something decent to work on since the Nam, man. Look at this rig!" He pointed at the huge radio, its back panel open. "I could talk to God on this if I got the right atmospheric conditions."

"Lemme ask you something," Bob said. "You had a square meal since they got you up here?"

"Shit, man, I ain't got time to eat. I set a record for turnaround on a big job like this — fifty-six hours. I just put this relay in and she's ready to go. I'd like to test her out. They sent some chick out to steal me an oscilloscope. Now you mention it, I'm feeling *beaucoup* hungry."

"You better get used to it if you stay here. These folks aren't much on eating."

David shrugged. "I'll pick up something, don't worry about me."

"How much do you know about this place?" Zardovsky asked.

"What do I need to know? They got a lot of stuff that needs fixing, I'll get along. Did a lot worse out on the street."

"We'd better hurry up," Gerald said. "Those guys downstairs might catch on."

"Whyn't you go on out in the hall and keep watch?" Zardovsky said to Gerald. Gerald slipped past Margaret, waving his hands in agitation.

"Shit, old Rambler come sneaking up the back steps looking for me," David said when he had gone. "He ain't such a bad guy after all."

"He doesn't want you to end up selling flowers on the street," Margaret said.

"Are these the dudes that do that?"

"Are you kidding?" she asked. "That's the best job they have, from what I hear."

"These the ones that go around saying 'Have a nice day' and all that stuff?"

"Listen, buddy," Zardovsky said, "near as I can figure out, this is some kinda Oriental revival meeting. You won't like it, is my guess. Whyn't you come on with us and check it out a little? You can always come back later, after you pick up a coupla hamburgers or something."

The distant music fell silent. Gerald began banging urgently on the door.

"Here they come," Zardovsky said. "You wanna stay or go?"

"Okay, let's go."

The three of them burst into the hall, where Gerald, like Van Helsing with a crucifix, was standing his ground against an angry party of cultists led by Lightning, who was armed with a menacing smile and a lead pipe. But at the sight of Zardovsky the attackers fell back in confusion.

"Hey, Lightning, it's fixed," David called as they dashed toward the back steps. "You can call Jupiter on that damn thing now!"

They tumbled down the dim steps and through the yard, vaulting in a breathless rush over the fence. The cultists appeared on the back porch, hurling theological insults. "Idolators!" they cried. "Wash pots! Neurotics! Misfits! Technocrats!"

From the street came a howl of outrage and a discordant blare of horns. They turned the corner to see Lightning and Hermana Eva locked in spiritual combat.

The Temple elder was sorely wroth. He had been set at naught in his own house and shamed before his flock. It was the gypsy woman's misfortune to have offered herself on the spiritual plane at this moment. She had been taunting the cultists, dancing with her chicken and hurling curses in unknown tongues. Like many who served older gods, the gypsy made the mistake of thinking that the priests of the Temple were without power over unseen forces. These will come when called by any name, as Hermana Eva was about to learn.

"Self-deceiver! Paranoid! Narcissist!" cried Lightning in an unholy access of rage. "By the Ancient Ones of Mars, I bid you to be quiet!"

Her tongue clove to her mouth; her knees gave way, her eyes rolled up, and with a cluck of contempt, her chicken left her, never to return. As Gerald, Margaret, David, and Zardovsky approached, the mariachis began to drag her away. With a small smile of satisfaction, Lightning reentered his kingdom and closed the door.

"Mr. Beaufort is emerging now from Sunrise House," a voice said, and the group found themselves pinned in place by the cameras of the Reaction News Squad. The dark woman brandished her microphone in David's face. "You are one of the first people to emerge from this sinister cult's recruiting ground, Mr. Beaufort," she said. "Can you tell us what was done to you there?"

David smiled. "They just had a broken radio they needed fixed."

"You've been subject to some injury," she said, pointing at the bandage on his head. "Were you beaten in an attempt to get you to join the Temple?"

"Hey, that reminds me." He took the microphone from her hand and turned to look at the camera. "Listen, last Saturday I was robbed of a valuable Fuji racing bicycle about three blocks from here. If anyone has any information, I'd appreciate it if you'd call Diana at the station, okay?"

"Uh, thank you," said Diana, wresting the microphone away and turning to face the camera. "As you can see, Mr. Beaufort is a little disoriented by his experience, which we had anticipated from previous accounts of those who have become involved in cult activities. We've arranged for a specialist in these matters, Mr. Reginald Banks of the Free Thought Foundation of Santa Monica, California, to be here to help him regain his ability to think clearly. Mr. Banks?"

"Gerald," Margaret said, "what is all this about, anyway?"

"It's a long story," he replied.

From behind the camera appeared an older man, squat and muscular, wearing a navy-blue blazer, white shirt, and Royal Campbell tie. "I'm a friend, David," he said. He put his huge hand on David's elbow. "I'm here to help you learn to think for yourself."

"Aw, fuck that shit," said David, trying to pull his elbow from the man's grasp.

"Mr. Banks reports that many returning victims are hostile at first," the woman said *sotto voce* into her microphone.

"You'll thank me for this later," Banks said. He enfolded David in a broad bear hug.

David threw his frail-seeming frame into a cartwheel of flailing arms and legs. At the end of it, the big man was lying on the pavement clutching his solar plexus. "I learned that in the Nam," David said modestly, dusting his soiled black clothes. "Listen, I'll check you later, Diana. I got to get me something to eat." He set off down the sidewalk as if in search of locusts and wild honey.

"You guys help Banks out," said the reporter to her crew. She turned to Gerald. "Christ, I can't tell whether this film is ruined or fantastic," she said. "We were going to get the first film of a real deprogramming, but instead all we have is the gypsy fainting and your friend beating up Banks."

"Well, at least it's violence," Gerald said.

A short, tubby man in a blue work shirt appeared behind the reporter and tapped urgently on her shoulder. "Listen, Miss Cazadora, you don't want to give so much publicity to these guys from the Temple," he said in a nasal voice. "They're agents of a reactionary CIA-led exile movement."

The reporter turned on the intruder with blazing eyes. "Listen, if you're from Responsibility in Media, I told you before —"

"No, I'm from the Toiling Masses League. We thought you might want to do something on us. We have some interesting youth programs going at the airport and bus station."

"That's a good idea. I tell you what, let's have lunch one day next week."

Margaret had been racking her brain, and suddenly the answer came to her. "Say," she said, stepping forward, "aren't you —"

"Diana Cazadora," said the dark woman complacently. "And you must be Maggie. I'm glad to meet you at last. Gerry has told me so much about you."

It was one of those moments, also common in periods of life change, when things become suddenly, unbearably clear. Margaret turned toward Gerald, who was deep in conversation with Bob, and heard him say, "I think maybe we can swing this thing from a different angle. You want to have lunch tomorrow?"

"Bob," she called, "let's get out of here."

Gerald shied away like a nervous horse. "I'd better get home," he said. "I'll call you."

Bob, meanwhile, was staring at Diana, whom Paco was subjecting to a bilingual discourse on the FLAN. He smiled his infuriating popeyed grin and said idly, "Say, that chick is not too shabby to look at. Wonder if she likes ballplayers?"

A moment later Zardovsky found himself alone on the sidewalk, watching Margaret's retreating form. She seemed a little hacked off about something. He shook his head; she sure was a character.

He was about to start after her when a large, solid figure blocked his path. "Bob Zardovsky?" said the man. "This is for you."

"I ain't been asked for my autograph since I left Mexico. You got a pen?" But the stranger had disappeared. Zardovsky stared at the paper, which was headed with an unfamiliar Latin phrase, then shrugged, thrust it in his pocket, and started after Maggie toward home.

Chapter 3

Of THE MANY FINE QUALITIES indispensable to success in our nation's capital, none is more crucial than lack of imagination, and no group revels in it more than those journalists and pundits who are paid to imagine the future. They are by and large also unable to remember the past; whichever way they peer through their political weatherglasses, they see a land that looks remarkably like the present.

During the opening weeks of the election campaign, columnists and reporters lunched together, agreed that as the President had once been elected, he must certainly be reelected, and repaired to their computers in a mist of vermouth. The President was first considered to be even with his challenger, then to be ahead, well ahead, in a commanding lead, and finally well-nigh untouchable.

The confidence imparted by these assessments could be felt in Toad Earnshaw's office, to which Gerald was admitted the Monday following his excursion to Sunrise House. The office was as busy as the buffet table at an East-bloc embassy reception. Clean-faced volunteers were installing Toad's desk; typewriter; red, black, and yellow telephones; AM/FM stereo radio and eight-track tape deck;

electric shredding machine; bar-sized refrigerator with automatic ice-maker; wall map of the United States; hand-signed photographs of the President, the Vice President, and Jerry Jeff Walker; and wall-mounted Nerf basketball hoop.

"Well, Gerry, you got the master plan for the Northwest?" Toad asked with a lazy smile.

"Toad, I hope you're planning to get somebody who has a little more experience than I have."

"You know, I'm still not sure that you understand the philosophy of this administration, Gerry. The President believes — and I agree — that there is no problem in American politics or government that's too complex to be handled, and handled well, by a typical bright American boy like yourself. I think if you look at our appointments you'll agree that we've followed that philosophy consistently."

"Listen, Toad, I'm no expert, but it's clear to me that we do have political problems in the Northwest and that it might be a good idea to demonstrate that this administration is responsive to the concerns of ordinary people up there."

"Good thinking so far."

Quickly Gerald explained the situation in Gouge Eye and the problems the grant application had run into. "It seems to me that it might be a good chance to do something for these people and toot our own horn a little bit."

"Well, Gerry, you know as well as me that it doesn't exactly work that way," Toad said. "Of course the President is an incumbent, no doubt about that, and we plan to capitalize on that fact, but we certainly can't make any deals."

"So the answer is no."

Toad seemed disappointed in Gerald. "On the other hand, I don't suppose it's any secret that even though I'm officially on leave from the White House, I am still involved in some policy discussions over there."

"Do you mean the answer is yes?"

"Gerry, Gerry, Gerry." Toad rose to his feet, nearly braining a Duke political-science major who was attempting to polish his shoes. "I sure would be interested in hearing a more detailed oral report from you about this project in the next couple of days. Maybe we might discuss it one afternoon this week in the elevator, when I'm on my way over to my other office. Get me some names of the people out there. I appreciate your bringing this to my attention, by the way. You keep saying you don't know anything about this area, but you've already got a real grasp on the essentials of the political and economic situation. Damn fine work, damn fine! Keep it up."

At that moment the red telephone rang, setting off a near-lethal scramble for the door. Gerald left Toad bowing slightly in the direction of the receiver.

Gerald and Bob Zardovsky met at a K Street cafeteria at noon on a hot September day. The street presented a lively scene: groups of office workers spooning yogurt from plastic cups, balloon vendors aggressively demanding patronage, street vendors working the crowd, and the area's own individual crazy person, a woman with an enormous bouffant hairdo, a loud stereo box playing bouzouki music, and a huge sign that read COMMUNIST BUREAUCRATS STEAL SEX HORMONES. These quotidian sights were enlivened by a procession of disgruntled demonstrators carrying banners in Burmese, closely supervised by two dozen mounted D.C. police.

When Gerald found Bob, the big ex-ballplayer was reaching into his trouser pocket while conferring with a neatly dressed, expectant-looking man.

"What's this all about?" Gerald said.

"My buddy here got all his gas siphoned out," Zardovsky said. "I'm gonna lend him two bucks to get home to Crystal City."

"Christ, are you still working that dodge?" Gerald asked the stranger. "You might at least get a new routine."

The man seemed to remember a previous engagement, toward which he began stepping in a quiet, sidelong way.

"What're you talking about?" said Zardovsky, hesitating with his hand half out of the pocket, clutching a wad of bills. The stranger dived for the cash, but he had miscalculated Zardovsky's reflexes and was repelled with minor damage to his nose, colliding with the sex-hormones woman and caroming into one of the marchers, who began belaboring him with a silken banner.

"Let's get inside before this turns into a riot," Gerald said, tugging Zardovsky through the door of the cafeteria.

"Did you know that guy, or what?"

"Oh, sure," Gerald said. "He's kind of a local celebrity. He always gives out that rap about having his gas siphoned. These days he has to pick out-of-towners."

Gerald chose a chef's salad and a glass of iced tea; Zardovsky settled for baked pork chops with stuffing and gravy, mashed potatoes, string beans, hot rolls, apple pie with melted cheese, and steaming black coffee. As Zardovsky hurled himself on this tidy collation, Gerald contemplated his luncheon guest, feeling for some reason as if he were about to engage him in an intense and personal contest. Zardovsky had changed: he did not look fully at home — indeed, it was hard to imagine a Zardovsky who would look at home in Washington while any shred of his personality remained — but he had lost something of his gawky, grinning, rubbernecked uncertainty. Like water wearing at stone, the seductions of the capital were changing Zardovsky, making him a smoother operator and, Gerald sensed without fully understanding what he meant, a more formidable opponent.

"So you're still crashing at Margaret's?" he asked politely.

"Yeah. I wish to hell she'd get a new couch," Zardovsky said. "My back is getting shot from the sag in that one."

"How's she doing these days?"

"I thought you'd know better than me."

A certain embarrassment crept into Gerald's tone. "Well, I have this new job and I haven't had much time to keep in touch."

"Yeah, she told me about that. I couldn't figure out if this is a promotion or what."

The identical question had occurred to Gerald on several occasions, but he dismissed it now as then. "I'm not sure that term means anything in this area," he said. "I suppose if the President is reelected, this job might lead to something else. If not, it's back to horsemeat law."

"Horsemeat law? You know, you really are a character, Gerry. I mean, when I first met you, I figured you were kind of a wimp. Nothing personal, I mean, I just had that opinion. But you really hung tough when we got your buddy out of that solar-energy house. I felt like you showed me something."

"Say, thanks, Bob," Gerald said. "I guess."

Zardovsky broke into laughter. "Listen, I'm sorry, I just pop off my mouth too much. Umpires used to tell me that. I should learn something from all the stuff that's been happening to me since I got here."

"It's probably a mistake to learn too much from experience in Washington."

Zardovsky laughed again and attacked his pie. "Say, what's happened to that guy David?"

"I've been trying to call him, but his landlady was a little vague about what's going on. I couldn't get it straight if he was working in her dry-cleaning shop, studying computer repair, or working at a synagogue. I think he'll be okay as long as he doesn't walk around Sunrise House at night."

"The same goes for you, little buddy," Zardovsky said. "Them guys seem to really carry a grudge."

"They don't have fond memories of you, either."

Zardovsky laughed again, so loudly that heads turned at the tables around them, which were full of solitary bureaucrats hunched over the early edition of the afternoon newspaper.

"Listen, Bob, the reason I wanted to get together was that I think maybe this is a good time to get someone to take a fresh look at your project. It seems to me to be in line with what the Administration stands for —"

"Christ, that's what we thought too, until we started dealing with all this stuff here in Washington — first that crazy broad at your office and then this guy Hench."

"Yeah, poor guy, his trial's coming up in a week or so."

"And now whenever I call down to your old office they tell me that Weisman has the papers and he'll get back to us, but he don't ever call back."

"Bernie's handling it now?" This news cheered Gerald, as it offered him the chance to gall Weisman with an end run. "We need to take after it from another angle. Can you give me the names of some people back home we could talk to?"

"The best thing to do is just call up to Zeke's Tackle Shop and talk to whoever answers the phone. Everybody knows about it."

"I'll have to have some names, Bob. See, the White House domestic-policy shop may want to look into this whole thing."

"The White House? Why didn't you say so? Christ, then I guess they should call Mayor Ferguson. Maybe do it early in the day, before he gets over to the Sockeye Tavern. Or Jack Swanson, he's the town attorney, his office hours are Thursday afternoon. Zeke, he knows pretty much about it too, but since he broke his upper plate it's hard to follow much what he says."

Slowly they assembled a list of names and phone numbers. Zardovsky was so cheered by the prospect of action that he ate another piece of pie. "Shit, Gerry, I sure appreciate what you're doing," he said as he sucked his fingers. "I had you figured all wrong — I thought you were just another one of these government jerk-offs. Christ, there I go again, sorry, what I mean is —"

"Don't thank me yet," Gerald said. "All I can really do is pass this on. We'll see what happens."

"Aw, hell," said Zardovsky, rising in a shower of pie crust and pork. "I figure if the White House is interested, we're home free. Those people get what they want."

Perhaps, Gerald thought, Zardovsky had not learned so much after all.

Leaving the restaurant, he bought a copy of the afternoon paper to read at his desk. At the elevator entrance he ran into Toad, on whom he pressed the information he had gleaned. The senior aide seemed less cheerful than usual, and left with a hasty farewell and a disgruntled glance at Gerald's paper.

Once at his desk, Gerald turned to the gossip column. One item gained his attention: "Darlings, what has dear Toad Earnshaw been putting *up his nose* in a local porn shop? Don't Watch That Space — you might get sneezed on, sillies."

Gerald had not gotten two steps into his apartment that evening before Willys Handleman bore down upon him like a ship under sail, waving a sheaf of papers. "Look at this, Gerald!" he shouted. "I've had it with this shit!"

The offending missive was from the editor of a well-thought-of liberal magazine. He was returning Willys's manuscript of "Ten Things the Government Does Well." The editor showered it with the highest praise, using such terms as *timely, cogent, clear,* and *important.* However, he felt constrained to point out that despite its title, the article as submitted still listed only six things that the government did well, and he suggested that it would be stronger with an additional four. He concluded by urging Willys to use haste in expanding the manuscript, as the magazine would like to publish it as a cover piece in its preelection issue.

The living room was a scene of disorder such as even Willys had seldom authored. Yogurt cartons, curry containers, and coffee cups had poured their contents into an evil estuary at one corner of the once-white rug; books, newspapers, and magazines were strewn about as if thrown aside by some frantic reader. At one corner of Gerald's couch, a purple plastic-tipped pen leaked its contents onto the upholstery.

Gerald settled himself gingerly on the far side of the sofa. "I'm not sure I understand what you're so pissed about," he said. "That letter seemed pretty encouraging to me."

"What? This patronizing bullshit? These goddamn liberals are such fucking hypocrites! I've had it with all of them!"

"Willys, calm down. I really think you're taking this all wrong. Hell, I'd be happy if I got a letter like that."

"Go ahead, Gerry, take *their* side! All you limousine liberals stick together, don't you? Ever since you got this hotshot campaign job, you've turned into a real Washington fathead, you know that?"

That reminded Gerald dimly that he had been meaning to ask Handleman a question. "Willys, have you been playing the accordion?"

Willys flushed with embarrassment. "Hey, I almost forgot, it's time for 'Capital Chitchat.' " He strode over and snapped on the TV at a volume that preempted further conversation.

The program invited columnists and pundits before the cameras to agree with each other; it was beamed weekly to a nation of people who had little idea what the participants were talking about but enjoyed their air of authority. The host's opening words, delivered between the weary gasps and subverbal vocalizations that were his trademark, brought Gerald up short:

"Good evening. The presidential campaign, up to this point a somewhat sleepy affair, took on a new liveliness today when a newspaper here in the nation's capital aired explosive charges of illicit drug use by the President's campaign manager and chief adviser, Toad Earnshaw. With us tonight are some of the most respected members of the capital's press corps, who have some thoughts on this growing shadow over the President's campaign."

"What the hell?" Gerald said, incautiously seating himself in a pool of Wite-Out.

The assembled pundits were appalled at the allegations; one could tell that from their gleeful faces as they traded self-congratulation with approbation in a ritual as elaborate as the Zen tea ceremony. The professorial conservative columnist felt that this scandal was the natural consequence of theological flaws inherent in the President's anti-intellectual, evangelical brand of Christianity. The bald, ruddy conservative columnist said that this was poppycock, rubbish, and flapsauce. The deep-voiced liberal columnist suggested that the failures of this administration stemmed from its deliberate refusal to come to terms with the Washington establishment. The gravel-voiced liberal columnist said that there was a deeper issue involved, since Earnshaw had been until a few days earlier on the White House payroll and thus under the purview of the ethics-in-government legislation. The columnist who went to all the parties said that he understood now why the White House had stopped serving spirits at its receptions: they were all taking drugs instead. The columnist who never went to parties said that while he was not naive enough to think that Toad Earnshaw was innocent, Harding had been known to have a few snorts and James G. Blaine had fathered an illegitimate child and what about the military-industrial complex, anyway? This provocative remark set off a partisan dispute over the new plan, proposed by the Secretary of Gerald's Department, to replace the B-52s with invisible dirigibles.

"Say, Gerry," Handleman said casually. "What does that stuff feel like, anyway? I've never been able to afford it."

There was a knock at the door.

Diana swept in like the sirocco, in a swirl of smiles and arms. In the latter months of summer she had developed a particularly effective tan, set off this evening by a white linen skirt.

"Oh, what a night!" she cried dramatically, throwing herself on the couch (thanks to the effortless grace with which she moved, she missed both the ink and the Wite-Out and reclined between them like an enchanted princess surrounded by magic pools). "Those idiots! Morons! I'm really fed up to here with the whole thing! Gerry, I wish I'd had you with me at the station to talk to my producer. You're so good at explaining things."

Naturally Gerald began to wish he had been there as well. As so often with Diana, he was, without noticing it, drawn out of himself and into a drama of which she was the star. "What's going on?" he asked.

"They won't let me use the film of Sunrise House," she said. "Christ, we had everything in it — violence, surprise, suspense — but because it wasn't what they thought it was going to be, they don't want it now. We keep talking about opening the medium up and giving it immediacy. I think this film could be the basis of a great documentary — we could add a few interviews and some background material — but if it can't be cut to three minutes, they're not interested. If your friend hadn't beat up the deprogrammer, then we could have gone with it as an example of a grateful victim being rescued. Or if he'd gone back inside, then we could have used it to show how strong the cult brainwashing is. But they say it doesn't make any sense at all as it is and so we just have to forget it. Now they're talking about cutting short the whole cult investigation and putting me on the courts or something like that — just when I had a line inside the Toiling Masses League!"

"You know," said Gerald, "it sounds like everybody's had a hard day."

"What do you mean?"

"Well, Willys is pissed about something to do with his article, and I've just had to sit through 'Capital Chitchat' and hear the stupidest discussion about Toad Earnshaw."

"What about him?"

"This idiotic thing in the afternoon paper. They were trying to blow it up into some kind of scandal."

"Gerry," she said with a kind of prim compassion, "it might be better not to talk about that. I mean, if they do switch me over to the courts, I might end up covering it."

"Covering what? There's nothing to it!"

"You may be right," she said, as if humoring him. "But I think we ought to wait and see what happens."

Gerald had enough wit to realize that when Diana voluntarily let him off a hook, he ought to accept. "All right," he said. "Are you sure you don't want a drink?"

She smiled so broadly that the evening entered a whole new phase. "I think we ought to get drunk," she said impishly.

Handleman rose like a preteenager leaving a movie theater at the onset of "mushy stuff." "I'm going out for a little while," he announced.

"God, what a relief," Diana said while Gerald scrounged under the sink for the bottle of Bombay gin. "I like Willys, but sometimes he wears me out."

"You should try living with him all the time," he said.

"I don't think it would work. I can't stand Indian food."

Wine works swiftly on a willing heart. Soon they were sitting on the floor exchanging confidences. "Gerry, do you think I should quit my job?" she asked him.

"Quit your job? Why?"

"I just wonder if it's all worth it — all this hassle with the producers and running around with the cameras. I really want it to mean something, not just to me but to people I respect — to you, for example. Does it?"

There is a time for honesty in every relationship. Looking at Diana's suntanned legs, Gerald concluded that this was not such a time. "Of course it does," he said. "I think it's pretty damn impressive how well you're doing. You've only been here a few months, and you're in the thick of things, everybody knows who you are. I think you've really just started. The sky's the limit."

These words, more potent than poetry, seemed to blend with the gin; but as their lips were meeting, Diana was seized with giggles.

"What's so damn funny?" Gerald demanded.

"You're sitting in the curry!" she said. "It's all over your pants!"

"I guess I'd better change, then, hadn't I?"

This strange day thus had for Gerald a satisfactory conclusion. Indeed, several.

In the darkness of the bedroom, he noticed that Diana's glittering cat-eyes seemed somehow to be gazing beyond or through him toward a future he could not imagine.

The next day the papers were full of the Earnshaw scandal, which was promptly dubbed Nosegate. Gerald continued to regard the furor with mild exasperation, an emotion that lasted through the news accounts, the editorials, the columns, and the cover pieces in both weekly newsmagazines, right up to the moment when the attorney general named a special prosecutor.

Chapter 4

A S THE FALL BREEZES SWEPT AWAY the poisoned, stale air of late summer, Washington changed from a tropical inferno into the graceful capital of a temperate country. For the weary slaves who toiled in the mills of government, it was as though they had labored up a long, brutal slope until they found themselves at the summit, looking down on a new and glorious city.

The Detroit Tigers were playing Kansas City on Monday-night baseball. KC was in a hot division battle and the game would be important; to Bob Zardovsky, it was a chance to see his sometime drinking buddy "Hubba Hubba" Hernandez, who was on a late-season tear, having hit safely in the past twelve consecutive games.

Zardovsky was firmly established in front of Margaret's TV with a supply of Pabst beer in the refrigerator when, for the first time in their friendship, Margaret offered to do his laundry for him. (It would have been hard to distinguish solicitude from self-preservation in this gesture, given the advanced state of fermentation of Bob's jeans.) She staggered off to the basement laundry room as the pregame show, an interview with Hernandez, began.

It took all Bob Zardovsky's faculties of concentration to follow

Hubba Hubba's remarks, which were confined to estimates of the weather, his own swing, and his contract. When Margaret reappeared, waving a crumpled piece of paper under his nose, Zardovsky was perhaps a bit short with her.

"Pay attention, Bob," she said. "I found this in your jeans."

He glanced at the sodden document. "Oh, yeah, some guy gave it to me a while back and didn't wait around for me to sign it."

"Sign it? Bob, this is a subpoena!"

"Say what? I thought he wanted my autograph."

Margaret studied the smudged print, unfolding it carefully under the table lamp. "No . . . My God, Bob, it says you're supposed to testify in federal court tomorrow! You're a defense witness in the Hench trial!"

"Is that a fact? What a kick! I never was a witness before, except one time in Oaxaca, which I couldn't follow it too good, and I guess it doesn't really count if it's your own trial —"

"Bob," Margaret said gently, "I'm not entirely sure I'm up to hearing this story right now."

He turned to look at her face, frowning over the dingy subpoena in the lamplight. Something in her manner took the sting out of being silenced. Her face had become a part of his inner landscape, as important in that jumbled country as Merida or Crater Lake: the fair, reddish tone of her skin; the humorous, quiet, gray-blue eyes; the laugh furrows around her eyes and mouth; the unruly thick blond hair streaked with fine gray strands which he had never noticed before and which, to his surprise, were in some indefinable way alluring. He laughed and said, "Damn, Maggie, you're a character, you know that? You want a brew?"

"Bob, you have to testify tomorrow morning. Aren't you nervous about it?"

"Hell, no. All's I have to do is go down there and tell 'em what I seen and heard. I watched Perry Mason enough times."

"Don't you want to talk to a lawyer?"

"What, and miss the game?"

"Christ, I don't see how you can just sit there. It makes me nervous just to think about it."

"You worry too much about everything, Mag. You know, I reckon you'd feel better if you got out and did some kinda workout every coupla days."

She squirmed as if embarrassed. "God, don't I know it. But I'm afraid it would kill me because of the cigarettes. I used to go to a yoga class at the Y, but even that was too much."

"See, that's your problem, though, is you do all this weird imported stuff instead of something real. I mean like yoga and hypnotism and all this shit. You don't need to float in the air or anything, all you need is to run a mile or so or punch a speed bag or something. You know, I bet I could help you out if you wanted. Some of the guys on the ball club used to get pretty slobbed up over the off season, drinking too much and smoking and all. I could show you some stuff that would get you squared away in no time."

"Okay," she said, "let me change my clothes."

"You mean you want to work out right now?"

"Sure," she said. "Why not?"

Hernandez was due up in two batters and Bob Zardovsky wanted to watch and see if he had improved his swing any. But then he figured, what the hell; rarely did anybody in Washington seem so eager to do anything physical, unless you counted going to restaurants or playing tennis. So he said okay.

She came back in running shorts and a T-shirt that said PUBLIC-INTEREST LOBBYISTS DO IT IN THE SUNSHINE. Meanwhile the lead-off hitter had singled, and the second had executed a smooth sacrifice bunt down the first-base line to move him to second. With one out, Hubba Hubba waddled to the plate like Villa advancing on Torreón.

"Okay," said Bob, keeping his eye on the screen, "the first thing is to get you loosened up a little, so do some four-count jumping jacks, where you jump on one and two and then bend to your toes on three, hands on hips on four, okay? I'll count off for you, slowly. One . . . two . . . three . . . four . . ."

The first pitch was high and looked like breaking inside, but just caught the corner for strike one. Hernandez gave the umpire a sour look but didn't say anything; he couldn't take a chance on getting the heave. The second pitch was wild and nearly got away from the catcher. That made an even count, and the pitcher was rattled. He sent a fast ball just outside, and Hernandez, too eager, smacked it into the stands behind the third-base line, moving the count to one and two. The pitcher checked the base runner twice and then went into his motion.

Unfortunately, Margaret, whom Zardovsky had completely forgotten, picked that moment to collapse.

He rushed across to where she lay sweating and coughing, her face red and blotched; he cradled her head and shoulders gently, lifting her slightly off the floor. "Hey, I'm sorry, whyn't you tell me you were getting tired?"

"I hate it, I hate being this out of shape," she said when her breath returned. "I used to be a jock. You must think I'm a total flibbertigibbet."

"*That one is going downtown! Holy cats, look at that ball, past the second deck and still rising! Hubba Hubba Hernandez hits his thirty-second home run of the season and look at this crowd!*"

"Maggie, I like you pretty damn fine the way you are."

The phone rang, and she made her breathless way across to it.

"Hi, Gerry, how are you? I was thinking about you today . . . Oh, sure, I see. Hold on." She held the receiver out to Bob. "It's for you."

"Bob, I just wanted to bring you up to date on what we're doing," Gerald said. "The plan is for the Vice President himself to make the announcement during his swing through there early next month."

"Far out! Sounds like we're home free! I'll call out there and tell the folks."

"Actually, Bob, we'd like to sit on this thing for a week or two. It'd be better if there weren't any leaks at this end, where the press would get on it. You see how heated up they can get over nothing at all . . ."

"Oh, sure, I get it, I won't say nothing to nobody."

The Tigers won, five–two, and KC dropped back a full game in the standings.

Like many swimmers before him, Bob Zardovsky found that the riptides of justice bore him inexorably toward a strange destination. He could never afterward say the word *truth,* or meet a lawyer, or see a certain type of blue-backed typed document, without an involuntary shudder, like that of a Carpathian peasant asked about the castle on the hill.

At the courthouse he was led before an assemblage of well-

dressed people, all looking at him with rapt but impersonal attention. With the exception of Buster Hench, who looked older and
somewhat fuddled, no one in the audience — neither the lawyers
in their grim blue suits at the counsel tables, nor the reporters
jammed in the seats with notebooks and sketch pads, nor the jury
in the box, the only group at ease and informally dressed — was
older than he. For comfort he turned back to the judge sitting behind and above him, but this personage seemed far more interested
in the ceiling of the courtroom than in Bob Zardovsky, and was
eying the tiles above him as if one were imminently threatening to
come loose and dash out his legal brains.

Bob Zardovsky felt a sudden stab of helplessness, realizing that
he was required to sit before these strangers, subject to their
searching gaze, for as long as they chose. Weary eons of captivity
reached out for him with bony legal hands, and, horribly rapt in
their contemplation, he missed the first question, which when repeated was "State your name."

"Robert Zardovsky."

"What is your occupation?"

"I'm a sawmill hand."

For some reason this occasioned enormous laughter among the
crowd, who seemed to have some prior knowledge about him and
his life to which he was not privy.

"Mr. Zardovsky, I ask you now if you are ever known as or go
by the nickname of 'Three-Finger'?"

"Yeah, but I have four."

"Mr. Zardovsky, did you go to the office of Representative
Hench earlier this year and represent yourself as a major-league
baseball player?"

"Naw, I came for the lumber co-op."

"You did not tell Mr. Bernard Weisman that you were a professional baseball player?"

"I guess I said I used to be one."

"Mr. Zardovsky, I show you now this photograph taken of you
and Representative Hench on the occasion in question. Do you
recognize it?"

He studied the shot of himself and Hench, both of whom
seemed to be in some earlier, simpler stage of life: the Congress-

man pompous and self-assured, Zardovsky cheerful and relaxed. "Yeah, that's me and him, all right."

"Do you have any idea why that photograph was taken?"

"Naw, I never did get that part of it, unless it was supposed to be some kind of souvenir for me."

Once again laughter flooded the courtroom.

"Mr. Zardovsky, approximately one week later, did you visit a nightclub in the company of Representative Hench?"

"Yeah. I wish I'd of stayed home, now."

"Just testify to what you did, please. Do you recognize this photograph?"

"Yeah, that's me and Mr. Hench again."

"Did you tell Ms. Deborah Vartan, who took this photograph, that you were a pitcher for the New York Yankees?"

"Who, me? Naw, Mr. Hench told her that."

"How did he get that impression?"

"Christ, I don't know. I think he made it up."

Laughter again.

"Did you endeavor to induce Representative Hench to drink excessively on that occasion?"

"Hell, no, he wasn't consulting me or anybody else. He was buying the drinks, and then that little guy who came up —"

"Objection, your honor," said the opposing lawyer, a young man with a nasal voice and large, clear-rimmed glasses. "I understood that both parties had stipulated as to the relevance of this matter."

"Sustained," said the judge, bringing his attention down from the ceiling to play in its unbridled majesty on Bob Zardovsky. "The jury will disregard this testimony. Mr. Zardovsky, you will confine your testimony to what you yourself did and said."

"Okay, judge. What was the question?"

"Did you endeavor to induce Representative Hench to drink excessively on that occasion?"

"Naw. I was drinking beer myself."

"How many beers did you drink?"

"A dozen or so."

"And did you then suggest that you and Representative Hench should leave the club?"

"I guess I suggested going for a pizza."

"And did you go for a pizza?"

"Naw, 'cause, see, when I went for a cab he disappeared with the little —"

"Mr. Zardovsky," the judge said, again landing his gaze on Bob's neck, "please confine your answers to yes or no."

"He disappeared."

"Disappeared?"

"Well, see, he was with this little g—"

"Your honor!"

"The jury will be excused."

The jury was escorted from the room, darting reproachful looks at Zardovsky. He felt like a rude guest at a party who has spoiled the treat for everyone.

"Mr. Zardovsky," the judge said, "I am instructing you not to continue to wander off the point of your answers in this manner. If you do, I will be forced to take measures to prevent you. Do you understand?"

"To tell the truth, judge, I sure don't. See, there was this little —"

"Mr. Zardovsky, I am not going to repeat myself. For the time being and unless it is absolutely necessary to do otherwise, I want you to confine your answers to yes or no. Do you think you can do that?"

"Well, sure, I guess so, but I wish —"

"If you feel you can do that, Mr. Zardovsky, then please begin now. All right?"

"Well . . . yes."

"Marshal, you may bring in the jury again."

In they came, in single file like obedient children, looking speculatively about them as if wondering what adult mysteries had been discussed while they were led out by Nanny.

"Mr. Zardovsky, did you leave the nightclub at the same time as Representative Hench?"

"Yes."

"And he was then intoxicated?"

"I guess — yes."

"But you have no idea how he got from the nightclub to the house in upper Northwest."

"I don't even — no."

"Mr. Zardovsky, can you tell us the extent of your professional relationship with the Federal Bureau of Investigation?"

"Say what?"

"What is your relationship with the Federal Bureau of Investigation?"

"I try to stay out of their way."

"And what was your relationship on the night of the incident?"

"Christ, none."

"Mr. Zardovsky, you have described yourself as a sawmill hand."

"Yeah, except I used to play ball."

"Would it surprise you to learn that the only sawmill in Gouge Eye closed fourteen months ago?"

"Hell, no! That's what all this who-shot-John has been all about from the git-go! Haven't you been listening to anything I said? See, I came here to get a grant —"

"So would it be fair to say that you came to town to obtain funds fraudulently for a defunct sawmill, that you gained access to Representative Hench through a false claim to be a major-league baseball player, and that you then led him directly into a compromising situation set up by the FBI? And that at that point your memory suddenly shuts down?"

"Hey, listen, I can't follow any of this, and besides, I remember what happened, it's just that he went off with — I mean, he disappeared."

"That will be all, Mr. Zardovsky. If the government has any cross-examination?"

The small young man did not even look at Bob Zardovsky, as if he were not worth noticing. "Mr. Zardovsky, have you ever been employed by the FBI or any other government law-enforcement agency?"

"One time I applied for work as a ranger."

"Yes or no?"

"Naw, they rejected me 'cause of my hand."

"And you were not so employed on the night in question?"

"Naw."

"Have you ever met with or been coached by agents or employees of the FBI or the U.S. Department of Justice?"

"Coached? No, we had one trainer in Merida used to be a *federale* —"

"Thank you, Mr. Zardovsky."

This little fellow seemed somewhat more reasonable than the defense lawyer, and Bob Zardovsky was moved to offer a suggestion that might help clear up the confusion these young people seemed to be in. "Listen," he said, "if you want to get to the bottom of this thing, I think you ought to find that little g—"

The crack of the gavel cut him off. "Mr. Zardovsky," said the judge, "if you say one more word I will hold you in contempt of court! You are excused as a witness."

In the huge corridor Zardovsky felt as drained and shaky as if he had just been shelled off the mound. He began to doubt his own memory, as if the person who had given the testimony could not be the same person who had lived his life. There weren't any showers, apparently, so he decided to go back to Maggie's and get some sack time.

It was something of a surprise to leave the courthouse and find a pleasant fall day outside. He bought a hot dog from a vendor and was considering another when he realized that a fairly foxy tall girl with pale blond hair was looking at him with an expression of intense interest. He gave her a big smile. She was dressed nicely, in a silk blouse and a slit skirt; he judged that she was probably some kind of secretary.

"Aren't you Mr. Zardovsky?" she asked, as if his appearance were the fulfillment of her fondest prayer.

"Sure," he said. "You want an autograph?"

The notion seemed to surprise her, but she said, "Oh, yes, would you, please," holding out to him a narrow steno notebook of the kind he had seen sportswriters and secretaries writing in.

"What's your name, little darlin?" he said.

She laughed merrily, as if he had said something charming but absurd. "Just put 'With best wishes,' " she said.

He signed while she circled around him nervously, as if afraid that someone would spot them. "Are you going uptown?" she said.

"Yeah, I reckon."

"So am I! Let's share a cab, can we?"

Bob Zardovsky was beginning to recover his good humor. "Sure thing!" he said. "I'll go flag one!"

"Never mind, there's one here," she said; a taxi drew up as if it had been waiting. "Where are you going?"

"Just ride me up to Dupont Circle. I'll get a hamburger and a beer and go home from there."

The driver serenaded them with a cassette of Indian sitar music. The girl posed prettily on the cab seat. At second look she wasn't as young as he had taken her for, but she was still nicely put together. He was beginning to pick up a taste for older women, maybe from being around one all the time. "Say," he said, "do you like ballplayers?"

This struck her as another witty remark. "Were you really a baseball player?"

"Sure," he said. "Three seasons with Merida. Before that I was just in the rookie league. I pitched to Hernandez plenty of times."

"What do you think will happen to Hench?"

"Christ, I don't know. Poor guy. He just had a coupla bad breaks."

"What's going to happen with your sawmill project?"

"Well, things are looking up — but say, I guess I shouldn't say anything about that."

As they drove uptown, he expanded on his baseball career and his impressions of Washington. It was a long time since he had met someone who was just interested in him and his opinions and not in playing some kind of game with him. A girl like this one restored his faith in human nature.

But when they got to the Circle, she turned down his offer of a hamburger. "I've got to get back to work," she said abruptly. "It's been nice talking to you." She gave the cabby an address on Fifteenth Street.

He shrugged; this wasn't the first time a girl had changed her mind on him. At least this way he wasn't out cab fare.

"Piece of cake," he told Maggie when she got home from work. There wasn't any ball game on TV, so he held her ankles very carefully while she did a few sit-ups, then they went up to the Cuban joint. After a few beers, the whole business seemed funny to both of them.

He was sprawled on the daybed, snoring his way through a dream in which someone was asking him questions about his ERA and then refusing to let him answer, when she woke him the next

morning. "Bob, did you give an interview to the morning paper?"
"Hell, no," he said. "Christ, I don't even know who their baseball writer is anymore."

"Not the sports section," she said, unfolding in front of him a page layout with a photograph of himself above the headline "Power Base: Mystery Fixer in Hench Case Poses as Bush-League Has-Been."

Under it he read, "Not since Edward L. Doheny, millionaire oil speculator and bribemaster behind the Teapot Dome Scandal, described himself to a Senate committee as 'an improvident sort of a prospector' has a key figure in a Washington scandal adopted such a modest façade.

"To hear Robert 'Three-Finger' Zardovsky tell it, he's just a 'sawmill hand' who used to be 'a fair country ballplayer until my arm went bad on me.'

"Otherwise, says Zardovsky, he'd be in major-league baseball today, instead of in major controversy as the shadowy figure behind both the Buster Hench bribery case and the 'Briefcasegate' scandal which flared briefly at the new Department.

"Behind the 'aw, shucks' manner and the muscular physique lurks a cunning mind with a flair for mystery . . ."

There followed three paragraphs of quite flattering physical description, followed by a dozen-odd more that quoted the remarks he had made to the pretty girl in the taxicab, interspersed with unflattering suggestions about his motives for telling such transparent lies.

"Christ, you mean that broad in the taxicab was some kinda reporter?" he said incredulously.

Maggie asked for a description, and he gave one which seemed to be rather more detailed than she wanted.

"She's one of the best-known reporters for the paper."

"Well, she didn't tell me that."

"She probably assumed you knew who she was."

"Ain't that backwards? I thought reporters were supposed to recognize other people."

"Bob," Maggie said in a tone of grudging approval, "I don't think you're ever going to catch on."

Chapter 5

WORKING IN THE REELECTION COMMITTEE headquarters was like traveling in an antique Pullman car: too rocky for comfort, too loud for thought, and too risky for long-term planning.

Gerald's first assignment, to write a master campaign plan for the Pacific Northwest, was also his last. After that, all was frenzied activity of which neither the origin nor the purpose was ever quite clear. The plan never did get written, at least not by Gerald, though he could not have sworn that it was never written by anyone. The entire idea of the master plan acquired such mythic force through Toad's incessant reiteration that Gerald came to believe that it existed somewhere in the campaign headquarters.

It might have been in the piles of papers that washed over his desk daily, many of which he read without understanding and others of which he initialed without reading. Or perhaps it was among the loads of papers he took home at night to read and never could finish, which got tangled among Handleman's papers until Gerald was never sure that what he brought back to the office was what he had taken home. (On one occasion he received a stinging memo from Doc Cadwallader, the slick lawyer, for having mistakenly included in a list of talking points to be supplied to state officials the partial draft of a ferocious essay Handleman was composing for God knew who on Rumania's short-term bank debt.)

Gerald derived peace of mind from realizing that even though the work he was doing seemed irrational, incoherent, and largely useless, the chain of command of the Reelection Committee (of which he had latterly been promoted to the title of special assistant to the executive director) had become so thoroughly snarled that he had no way of being sure that somewhere else in the organization someone was not doing something worthwhile.

The chaotic situation was made no clearer by Toad's legal difficulties. As an eyewitness to the alleged incident (which continued to pop up in the newspapers nearly every day, crowding off the front page such ephemera as the candidates' speeches and wars in Islamic countries), Gerald had been called in for an interview by Toad's lawyer, a walrus-mustached bald man with a reputation as a master courtroom tactician and a skilled helicopter pilot.

Gerald was ushered before the presence by a whispering junior associate and served coffee in a bone-china cup by a deferential secretary. The lawyer listened in silence. Finally he flickered his eyes resentfully and said, "Snuff, huh?"

"Yeah, that's right. He was trying to quit smoking."

"I see. Well, if that's your story, you stick to it. I'll call you if we need you." Apparently they never did.

Meanwhile, Toad's appearances at the headquarters became less frequent, and Gerald's work assignments became more nebulous. He became known throughout the headquarters as a person of vast authority whose work was too secret to be discussed. Gerald regularly asked Cadwallader, Clark Guppy, and anyone else he could find to give him some work; they repelled his requests with faint, cynical smiles, as if avoiding a trap of the utmost subtlety.

Handleman began dressing himself more or less normally in the mornings and going out, though where and to do what were never quite clear. He hummed as he departed. A repairman arrived one morning, and by evening the broken recliner had been restored to its original upright condition. On another occasion someone delivered six especially fine custom-tailored fall and winter suits.

Once Gerald came home early and found Handleman deep in conversation with Diana; he could not shake the impression that the subject had been hastily changed when they heard his key in the lock.

One early-October Saturday, Diana picked him up in front of the Park View for a picnic at Great Falls, a park in northern Virginia. He almost failed to recognize her: everything about her was new, from the sporty yellow Volkswagen Rabbit convertible to her modish tank top and tailored gray sweat pants to her hair, which had been shorn short and fluffed front and back, giving a faint suggestion of electricity passing through her body.

"What in heaven's name?" he said as he climbed into the passenger seat of the little car.

"Diesel," she said. "Great mileage."

"No, the hair."

"Oh, yeah," she said negligently. "The station's playing around with a 'punk news' concept. What do you think?"

"Makes you look younger."

Gerald was hard put to be sure whether her new hairstyle was making the difference or whether it was something new in her manner, some readiness, as if she were a caterpillar who had begun to feel somewhere at the edges of its cocoon a slight fraying that promised freedom.

He felt a sudden and strange gust of compassion for Diana. What did it cost her to keep herself so tantalizingly near but so precisely out of his reach? These thoughts were unfamiliar ones, and as so often when we allow our minds to stray from the small path they walk like prisoners in an exercise yard, there came into his consciousness a thought that had been blowing around its walls and battering its shutters: he saw that wherever her lonely pilgrimage was carrying her, he was now, as he had been before, not a destination but a resting place, a way station on that wild and exotic route.

In the parking lot Gerald shouldered the picnic hamper. "What did you cook for us?" he said.

"I was going to cook, but I ran out of eye of newt. So I got two box lunches from that new wine bar on Connecticut Avenue. There's a good bottle of Chardonnay with them. I covered a strike at that vineyard," she said. Then, "I'll leave mine if you'll leave yours."

Like reflections in an upwardly mobile mirror, they were both strapping beepers to their waists. "Jesus Christ," he said. "A two-beeper picnic. I can die happy."

"What do you say we can them both, just for a couple of hours?"

The bargain was to his advantage; Diana's beeper was quite likely to go off, while his had only sounded once, when Clark Guppy had called to ask where Gerald had left the owner's manual for the shredding machine. "What the hell, I guess they can live without me for an hour or so," he said, and tossed it under the seat.

The park was a network of steep trails winding around rocky creeks and waterfalls. Diana, who operated by a kind of mysterious celestial navigation, quickly found a narrow, weedy track that led away from the traveled areas, across a wooded ridge, and down a rocky slope to a small pool. They spread their cloth on a shady promontory overlooking the water.

The wine bar had packed some kind of paté, Russian salad, crusty rolls, and cold chicken. The water made a cheerful sound, just loud enough to wrap them in a tiny world of their own. Yellow sunlight filtered through the birch leaves. Gerald felt the doors of thought once again edging open, admitting long-buried memories and regrets.

"Diana, what were you doing in that physics class?"

She was stretched full-length on the rock, her back supported against the slope, eyes closed, hands laced behind her head. Her face was in repose, and Gerald noticed the fine lines drawing downward around her mouth, as if traced there by the strain of keeping secrets. "What class?"

"The one we met in — you know, Physics for Poets."

"I thought you picked me up in the occult bookstore."

"I picked you up? I thought it was the other way around."

"I do not pick up men. There is no need for it."

"I first noticed you in class. I used to try to get there late and get a seat near you, in the row behind."

"I wondered why you were such a pushover that day."

"You seemed to recognize me right away."

"I know a good thing when I see it," she said. "I thought the rest was just a coincidence."

"You said you didn't believe in coincidence."

"That's why I was in that class. I wanted to find out about synchronicity and so on. I didn't get much out of it."

"All I can remember about it is that some physicists believe there are particles that travel faster than light and move backwards in time."

"Tachyons," she said. "I don't believe it, myself. Nothing goes back."

"What about you and me?"

"Especially not us, Gerry."

This theme blew through the conversation like a north wind. Diana's face made an appeal to him; she reminded him at that moment of a deer that had dashed from cover straight toward the hunter and stopped, flanks heaving, nose flared, eyes wide. Or was Gerald the hunted, being offered amnesty, allee-allee-ox-in-free, an end to snares and delusions if he wanted it? Who can say that the right word at that moment, if Gerald had known it or been given it by a friendly spirit, if he had heard it in the wind or the cry of the birds or the distant sound of a stone striking a stony floor, might not have altered forever their odd, unbalanced love?

"Do you want to go swimming?" Gerald asked.

They changed in the bushes. Diana wore a racing swimsuit, built for speed and not style, but her sleek lines gave it the air of a garment donned for swimming in enchanted pools and moats. She burst out laughing when Gerald appeared. "Where did you get that thing, at a retirement-fashions store?" she asked, pointing at his swimsuit.

"It's from L. L. Bean," he said. "Black Watch tartan. You don't like it?"

"*Like* is a broad term."

"Oh, come on, let's go." The water reached their knees. Cool streams fed the pool, but the eddies were warmed by the sun. They lay across bands of temperature, which gave them an expansive feeling, as if the tiny pool had grown huge, and they with it, to the size of continents and archipelagoes. Gerald rested his head against a rock and closed his eyes, and presently felt a feather-light tickling on the soles of his feet. "What are you doing?" he asked, opening his eyes; but Diana was across the pool, sunning herself on a rock, and his feet were under siege from a score of tiny silvery fish, each a half-inch or so long, nibbling politely.

"Sharks!" he cried. "Rescue! Help!"

"What are you bellowing about?" she said, leaning idly toward him. The fish broke and scattered, and he signaled her to come down beside him and be quiet.

Presently the fish returned, drawn now toward Diana, and began their infinitesimal nips at her legs. "Are you going to devour me?" she asked. "What a wonderful way to die!"

Gallantly Gerald scattered the attackers with his hand. "Are you looking for a way to die?"

"I spent a lot of time working on it in the past."

"That's not really the way I remember it."

She sighed, an unfamiliar, aching sound. "What do you know about it anyway?"

"Oh, Jesus Christ!"

"What's wrong?"

Wordlessly he held up his dripping billfold, which he had put in the pocket of his swimsuit and forgotten. Diana flopped in the shallow water, laughing at him and scattering the fish. "I knew that bathing suit would get you into trouble!"

"We should be getting back," he said.

Gerald modestly hid to slip on his trousers, but Diana dressed in the sunlight, slowly reassuming her stylish, remote identity. When she picked up her top and slipped it over her head, a patrol of Boy Scouts crested the ridge and marched past her, eyes right, forever to be tantalized by the thought of what they had almost seen.

"It speaks well of the discipline they learn," Gerald said.

She laughed, fluffing her new hairstyle with her fingers. "Or perhaps I'm slipping."

"You couldn't prove it by me."

"No," she said as if disappointed. "I guess not."

At the car they heard the shrilling of a beeper, forlorn and insistent.

"Damn it!" she said. "They said they wouldn't call me unless it was for World War Three."

"Diana," he said in some puzzlement, "it's mine, not yours."

* * *

It was an emergency meeting, with Doc Cadwallader in the chair, Clark Guppy by his side, and four Bowl Haircuts in the choir.

"Nash, glad you decided to call in," the lawyer said coolly. "You'll be sitting in for Toad. I understand he's closeted with his lawyers. He's going before the grand jury on Monday."

"Again?" Gerald said. "This is the third time."

"I've been around this town a long time," the lawyer said evenly, "and if I've learned anything, which some people might dispute, I have learned that you can't neither hurry a proud lady nor a grand jury. You better look at this."

He threw Gerald a fresh copy of a quarterly magazine that had been liberal when that was fashionable and was conservative now. The cover bore the headline "Special Election Issue: *Seven Things the Government Does Badly,* by Willys A. Handleman."

Gerald idly wondered what the *A.* stood for. But he had not spent half a decade laboring in the bureaucratic vineyard for nothing; he quickly sorted out his possible responses and selected that valuable standby, brazen gall.

"I don't get it," he said. "What does this have to do with me? I didn't have anything to do with it."

"Of course not," said the lawyer. "Jesus Christ, who the hell ever heard of this guy? But look at Number Seven. It's on page eighty."

Gerald leafed through the tract, admiring the ease with which Willys had converted the first six items in the catalogue, originally intended to illustrate governmental competence, into examples of the opposite. The main technique seemed to be the insertion of the word *not* into otherwise intact sentences. He skipped forward to the offending passage and saw the heading "Lemon Socialism, Pacific Style" above a caustic description of the Gouge Eye People's Lumber Co-op Number One, cited as a premier example of government boondoggle, which would subsidize inefficiency, increase the creep of socialism and statism into the midst of our free institutions, pose a major threat to the play of the free market, imperil our relations with Japan, and worst of all, unfairly victimize the helpless Total Energy Corporation. The project was represented as a corrupt brainchild of the "notorious backroom fixer, 'Three-Finger' Zardovsky, one of the least known and most powerful of Washington's invisible liberal masters."

"Christ, Handleman," Gerald muttered, "still stuck for numbers, I see."

"Say what?" said the lawyer.

"I said, their numbers are all wrong."

"Who's going to know that? Listen, we got lucky to get this advance copy before it hits the papers — and before we stuck our necks out with the announcement. I happen to know that this thing has already been bought to run in the Sunday paper. And it's bound to show up on 'Capital Chitchat' too. So you see the position we're in. I need you to get back to your friends and tell 'em to sit tight until after the election. Then we'll see what we can do. But for God's sake tell 'em to keep it quiet. If they pop off their mouths, tell 'em we'll remember it for a long time."

"If we win," Gerald said, almost reflectively.

"Oh, don't worry about that," said the lawyer. "I've been in this town a long time, and some people say I've learned a thing or two, but I can tell you I've never seen the columnists more favorable than they have been in the last few weeks. Oh, I grant you, the other fellow looked pretty good in the debate — where the hell did he find out all that about the fucking Rumanian bank debt, anyway? — but the people who know what's what agree we're right on the money. Listen, get busy on this, would you, Nash?"

And so the grant announcement was postponed a third time.

One must be careful frolicking around the countryside. That night Gerald came down with poison ivy across both shoulders and his back.

Chapter 6

LIKE MANY OTHERS SENT TO WASHINGTON on temporary missions, Bob Zardovsky found it impossible to leave before election day. He was suffering from a mild case of that disease that ravages so many souls along the Potomac: pursuit of a goal that seems at one minute impossible and at the next almost within reach. Those minutes can add up to a lifetime.

As best he could tell from talking to Zeke, the rug had been pulled out from under the grant for no reason that anyone could understand, the Vice President's visit had been canceled, and the elders of the co-op had been informed in convincing terms that if they said anything to anyone, the grant proposal not only would be postponed but would have a stake driven through its heart for all time to come. Gerald was suddenly unavailable, having been promoted after the indictment of Toad Earnshaw to the exalted post of deputy political director — a change that interposed a battery of secretaries with extensive vocabularies of negation between him and Bob Zardovsky.

But Bob lingered through the bright, brisk days of fall, watching colorful leaves and fashionably dressed women scampering along the grand avenues and listening to the drone of helicopters and the purr of limousines slicing through the crisp daylight breezes, the gargle of sirens drifting on the chill night winds. In the fall sunshine hung a sense of some appointment waiting for him, some unfinished business that kept his thoughts of leaving distant and vague.

The newspapers suddenly decided that the election was a spectacle of high drama. Skillful columnists predicted in successive columns victory for each party, both times with extensive and spurious reasons concocted minutes before deadline. Others complained loudly that the election was a bore and that the candidates must do better in future; still others berated the electorate for its shallowness, or their colleagues for their pigheadedness, or past generations for lack of foresight, or present generations for lack of knowledge, or future generations for lack of memory. And so the election season closed in a soggy tangle of newsprint, aviation fuel, and clichés.

Election day dawned cold and dark, with winter suddenly in the air and the sky full of a moist, cold cloud cover pressing down on the city like a thumb. Bob walked up the hill with Margaret that morning. She was going to vote at a school near Columbia Road. "I reckon we better get there early," he said. "Seems like from the papers that every vote counts."

"Easy, Bob." She extricated her arm and slowed her pace. "Given the way I'm voting, it won't make any difference in the presidential race."

"How's that?"

"Bob, this is D.C. It will go for the President by four to one or so. The only suspense on the ballot is the vote on the call for a UN plebiscite to make D.C. an autonomous trust territory. And anyway, if you're so concerned about every vote counting, what about yours?"

"That's all taken care of — everybody votes down at Zeke's, and I just asked one of the guys to do it for me. It ain't so formal back home as it is here."

At the polls the line was already out the door. Two white stripes had been painted on the pavement to keep campaigners at a respectful distance from the voting. Behind one was a file of Temple of Ray members carrying American flags and patriotic signs; behind the other, a circle of pickets from the Toiling Masses League with signs reading REPUBLICRAT SHAM ELECTIONS HIDE FUSION POWER FUTURE. Most of the voters were black. As Margaret and Bob neared the line, a white man so apologetic as to be nearly nonexistent appeared from behind them and thrust pieces of paper into their hands: flyers touting the presidential challenger. "*We* have to stick together," the gray little man said, pulling his chin back with such force that he retreated out of their sight.

"Wait here, Bob," said Margaret, crumpling the flyer. "It shouldn't take too long."

He fell into conversation with the pickets from the Toiling Masses League, who seemed to know all about him as someone who had visited humiliation on their hated rivals in the Temple. "We're going to be on TV soon," a familiar-looking tubby fellow with a beard explained. "So if you want to raid us or something, you might want to do it in the next month or so. It'd be good publicity for both of us."

"I sure appreciate the offer," Bob said genially. "Might do it, 'cept I've had all the publicity I can use for right now."

"Oh, yeah, I guess you intelligence types don't want your names in the paper."

"I guess that's a compliment," Zardovsky said. "Anyway, it's the first time I've been called an intellectual."

This struck his new friends as the height of wit; they began describing to Bob their demand that the government build home fusion reactors for every citizen. "Sure sounds like a good idea," he said.

"Pass it on to the people you work for," suggested the tubby guy.

"To tell you the truth, they hardly got enough money to keep the company going."

"Budget cutbacks, huh?"

"I guess you'd call it that. Christ, just last month — but I forgot, I ain't supposed to talk about that stuff. Just forget it."

This struck them as highly significant, and they all winked at him solemnly.

"Bob, can't you stay out of trouble for ten minutes?" Maggie's voice said from behind him.

"Voter!" the pickets hissed at her. "Collaborationist! Republi-crat! Energy offender!"

She pulled him away. "What is this affinity you have for crazy people?" she asked.

"Oh, come on, they seem like pretty decent guys."

"I guess that answers my question." She fumbled a cigarette from her purse. "Don't say anything, Bob."

"I ain't bugging you, Maggie. You're the only one who's down on yourself about smoking."

She had progressed to fifty jumping jacks, thirty sit-ups, and even half-a-dozen pull-ups; but she invariably collapsed after a quarter-mile when he took her out for road work. It didn't bother Bob; he thought she was looking pretty good these days, and he didn't mind saying so, even if he was her coach. But she seemed to regard ciga-rettes as a sickness of the soul that would not be cured short of death.

"I wish I didn't have to go to work," she said. "I'm so damn sick of my job I could spit."

"What-all are you doing?"

"Supposedly we're trying to put together some criteria for rat-ing the past Congress and have them in place so we can get our lobbying strategy worked out for the new one. I'm supposed to be watching the races where our key people are up for reelection. But actually all we do is listen to the all-news radio and place bets on who'll control the Senate. The whole place just makes me bored. Why don't you come downtown and eat lunch with me?"

"Why not? Can we wait until after the 'Morning Movie,' though? It's something about a talking mule."

The spot Margaret picked for lunch was the most desirable piece of real estate in the entire superheated Washington market. Built over a subway station, it was an indoor mall that might serve, when this phase of our civilization mercifully draws to a close, as a monu-ment to a society that leapt as one into the oral phase. Gracious metal tables, topped with umbrellas to protect patrons from what-ever precipitation might fall from the ceiling, occupied the areas between small carry-out restaurants, from which a hungry office worker could buy Coney Island hot dogs, Southern fried chicken, Mexican tacos, Italian pizza, Chinese egg rolls, Italian chocolate,

Japanese sushi, Danish ice cream, Indian tandoori chicken, frozen yogurt, baked potatoes with choice of toppings, tofu burgers, salads, chocolate-chip cookies, cheese, vitamin supplements, fresh-baked bread, hot pretzels with mustard, or cigarettes.

Margaret arrived shivering and bought a salad and a cup of decaffeinated Italian-roast Ethiopian and Kilimanjaro-blend cappuccino topped with freshly ground imported cinnamon. Zardovsky settled for two tacos, a slice of pizza, a side of coleslaw, and a vanilla milkshake. She was scanning the early edition of the afternoon paper, which contained absolutely no information of any value about the election. Voting was reported as heavy across the country, as it always is in the morning, but the one actual return was from a small New England town that had returned one more vote for the challenger than census officials believed there were people alive in the town. She fiddled with her lunch.

"How was the office?" Zardovsky asked.

"Boring."

"Christ, Mag, would you lighten up for a minute?"

She smiled ruefully. "I guess I'm not much as a lunch date," she admitted. "I spent all morning pretending to work, but what I was actually doing was fantasizing about quitting my job. It feels so goddamn useless. We've worked for three years to get CATA criteria loosened a little bit, for example. So what? You still haven't got your grant, and now we're going to have to start all over with a new Congress and maybe a new administration. And the truth is, I don't care anymore. I'd like to pack my bags and split town and get a job as a waitress or an auto mechanic or something."

"Hell, if you're a good mechanic you can always find work."

"I'm not a mechanic at all. The only job I'm really qualified for would be modeling for 'Wrong Way' in a stop-smoking clinic."

"You don't really want to leave town, do you? I thought you liked it here."

"Christ, no. I'm sick and tired of talking about real estate, or having people ask me who my boss is as if that's the only possible thing of interest about me."

"Well, what about your boyfriend? You don't want to move away from him."

"Have you seen Gerry around lately?"

"Hell, he's just busy with this reelection stuff. That'll be over today and then he'll be back in action."

"Oh, I don't think he's been out of action, Bob," she said darkly. "Shit, all of a sudden I just feel old!" And suddenly, quietly, she began to cry.

Zardovsky was nonplussed. Handling crying women was not his strong suit, and Maggie had never before seemed like the type to get so down. "Listen," he said in some desperation, "did I ever tell you about the time in Potosí that the wrestling bear got loose in the visitors' dugout?"

She wouldn't meet his eyes, but she smiled wryly. "Bob, I don't want to offend you, but I'm not really ready for baseball stories right now."

When baseball failed, only food remained. "Listen, why don't you come on home early tonight and I'll cook some dinner and we'll watch the election returns on TV and make animal noises?"

"Thanks, Bob, but last time you cooked in my kitchen I had to sandblast the countertops. I'll get something at Larimer's and cook dinner. I'm glad to have somebody to watch with."

"Sure, that's the spirit! We can get barfing drunk."

She dabbed her face with a Kleenex. "What a great lunch for you," she said. "I'm sorry to carry on this way."

"Hey, no sweat. That's what friends are for."

"Yeah," she said. "Well, thanks a lot, pal."

Zardovsky huddled inside his parka and walked with his eyes on the pavement. The wind stung his face and set motes of light dancing in his vision. In the gloom he walked amid phantoms: the woman with the bouffant hairdo lurked somewhere at the edge of his vision, and on the other side a familiar figure seemed to be asking for gasoline money; a pair of bright eyes hurtled by in the wind, and through a doorway he thought he glimpsed a pale strange woman goggling in surprise; someone else seemed to be walking behind him, though when he turned there was no one there. He saw another apparition on the pavement, a prosperous figure in a camel's-hair overcoat, white scarf, and Homburg hat, smoking a huge black cigar. The figure grew more solid, more enviable in its confidence, sangfroid, and genial interest in the world around it, until he felt compelled to pursue it up the pavement, calling, "Hey, Willys! Hey, wait up, buddy!"

Handleman turned to him with what seemed like fear.

"Hey, little buddy!" Zardovsky said. "Long time no see! How the hell are you?"

The fearful look was replaced by the effusive friendliness people reserve for someone who has just accepted a bad check. "Pardon my glove," Handleman said as they shook hands.

"Where you been keeping yourself, anyway?"

"Oh, you know, this and that, busy, deadlines —"

"Yeah, you and old Gerry are two of a kind that way, I guess. We haven't hardly seen him neither. How's he doing?"

Handleman shielded his eyes with a hand in fawn pigskin. "Well, candidly, you know, tell the truth, frankly, I haven't really seen as much of him as maybe I might like, you know, busy, honestly, lots of work."

"I been trying to call him just to find out what happened with our grant proposal and so on."

"Yeah," said Handleman. "I was sorry to hear about that. Tough break."

"Well, we'll work it out. Maybe they'll give Gerry a coupla weeks off before he goes back to his job, we can work out a new approach."

"Oh, he'll definitely have time off, no doubt about it. Listen, Bob, I've got to run right now, but give me a call later on. Maybe I can help you out when this is all over."

"Say, thanks, little buddy, that's right kind of you. You walking uptown?"

"No," said Handleman firmly. At that moment a large black limousine pulled up to the curb. A figure inside it was vaguely familiar as well. Zardovsky's eyes stung as the car engulfed Willys and drove away.

Zardovsky retied the drawstring of his hood and plunged back into the wind. As he passed slowly up the street, a faint image paced silently some way behind him, like a shadow, or an illusion of the gloom.

"This ought to be fun," Zardovsky said, settling himself in front of the television with a Pabst beer.

"What? I can't hear you, Bob!" called Margaret, who was out in the kitchen putting a chicken casserole in the oven.

The TV newscaster directed at Bob a look of disapproving solemnity and then said, "Good evening. This is the special election roundup, Ed Hackett reporting. If early polls of voters today are an indication, the news tonight is grim for the President. We'll return to those poll results in a moment, but first let's take a look at the early vote returns."

"Where have I seen that guy recently?" Zardovsky muttered.

Maggie came in and settled herself on her India-print cushion with a glass of white wine. "That'll be ready in about an hour," she said. "Don't let me forget."

The coanchor was saying, "As you can see, here at network election central we have no returns at all — none from the industrial Northeast, where the polls closed just minutes ago, none from the South, and none from the Midwest."

Behind him was a board decorated with zeros in all columns. "Looks like some batting averages I seen," Zardovsky said.

Then a gong sounded and figures appeared in some of the windows. "Here's our first projection," the announcer said. "With a little over one point five percent of the votes counted, our network computer now projects that the state of Rhode Island, with its four electoral votes, will go to the challenger. This, as you can see from our Electoral College board, gives him an early lead of four to zero. Now that's a lead which may lengthen as the evening progresses, if our network exit polls are correct. Isn't that right, Ed?"

"Ken, that's right," said the first anchor. "As we wait for more returns, I'll review very quickly the results of our exit polls, which show a strong trend in every region of the country running toward the challenger and against the President. This trend runs across usual geographic, ethnic, and economic lines. Now I understand that Diana Cazadora is at the President's headquarters and will shortly have a statement from officials there, and we're going to her live. Diana?"

"I know," Bob said. "He was the guy with Handleman today."

Margaret didn't hear; she was glaring balefully at the woman on the screen. "What the hell has she done to her hair?" she said. "It looks like she caught her toe in a light socket."

Bob Zardovsky thought that the woman looked pretty fine — her face flushed with excitement, her eyes sparkling as if she had caught on the wind the faint scent of prey. But he sensed that now was perhaps not the time to dispute the issue.

"Ed, I'm here at the ballroom which the President's campaign has rented for what officials still predict will be a victory celebration tonight. Behind me is the door to the office suite where the top officials of the campaign committee have met to consider the early reports coming in from around the country — reports which, as you have indicated, suggest that celebration may be the last thing on anyone's mind. I've been told that an official of the committee will make some kind of statement here in just a minute, but I don't know what he will say or even who it will be — whether it will be campaign manager Toad Earnshaw, who, as you know, returned to work last week when the charges against him were dropped, or someone else in the hierarchy of the campaign. But as I said, we do anticipate that someone will be here almost immediately."

As she spoke the double doors behind her opened, and there emerged, at something between a trot and a stumble, Gerald Nash, his glasses slightly askew, his hair tousled, and his blue-and-yellow foulard necktie neatly looped over one buttoned wing of his blue shirt collar. Zardovsky had the definite impression of a hand at Gerald's back, propelling him into the view of the cameras.

Diana moved toward him with smooth, predatory haste, saying, "Ed, we have here Gerald Nash, deputy political director of the campaign committee. Gerald, it's good to see you."

From a shaky beginning, during which he wore the expression most people feel on their faces during dreams of being in public without their clothes, Gerald now began to rally. "Diana, good to see you."

"Gerald," she said, "as you may have heard, our initial exit polling results show a strong trend against the President, and our network computer has just projected the first state to the challenger. I wonder if you at the committee feel that the show is in effect over, or if you are somehow managing to cling to some faint shred of hope?"

Gerald blinked into the cameras with an owlish look. "Diana, I haven't seen your data, of course, but we have our own poll results showing this to be a very close contest indeed, and of course we haven't heard even from the major states of the Northeast, where we expect to do well, or from the South, so all in all we feel we're still very much in the contest, and we expect —"

But Diana was staring into space like a cat, as if some secret wisdom had just come to her. "Gerald," she said, adjusting her earplug, "I'm sorry to interrupt, but I've just learned that our computers have now definitely projected the opposition to carry New York, New Jersey, Connecticut, Pennsylvania, Florida, and Massachusetts, for a total of one hundred twenty-eight electoral votes, so far, to zero for your ticket. I wonder if you have any comment on that?"

Some sage has suggested that in the future each of us will be famous for fifteen minutes, and if so, Gerald Nash still has twelve minutes coming.

"Gerald," said Diana quickly, "we're going to cut away to the challenger's headquarters now, thank you very much, this is Diana Cazadora at the President's headquarters, over to you, Bill."

The scene shifted to what might have been a TV preacher's vision of Heaven: everyone was happy, well dressed, white, and middle-aged.

"Poor Gerald," said Margaret, resting her face on her knees.

"Oh, I don't know," said Bob. "It seems to me he did all right. He should have fixed his tie, though."

She laughed as if this notion held some rich memory for her. "No, I think he should have stayed inside the office."

"Well, hell, all his friends and folks back home got to see him. One time I was on 'Wide World of —'"

She jumped to her feet. "No baseball stories, all right? I've got to check the rice. Call me if anything major happens."

For the next twenty minutes Bob drank Pabst, calling Margaret every five minutes or so as the newscaster, with the flourish of a game-show host, awarded another state to the challenger. Finally Margaret emerged with plates of food. Zardovsky wolfed his, but she sat without lifting a fork as she watched Ed Hackett summarize the carnage thus far.

"Here we are, still relatively early in a remarkable political evening, watching vote totals pile up in an astonishing landslide for the opposition ticket which has produced a veritable cloudburst of votes from all over the country, burying the President and many others of his party in a political sweep such as this country has not seen in nearly twenty years. To summarize briefly by region, the President has lost the Northeast, he has lost the Midatlantic states, he has lost the South, he is in the process of losing the Midwest, and the early returns from the West do not look favorable. With us in the studio to discuss the meaning of the election returns are some senior members of the Washington press corps who frequently appear on 'Capital Chitchat.' "

The silver-haired, urbane conservative columnist said that the vote was predictable because of the President's quaint religion. The gruff conservative columnist said that this was flapdoodle and moondust. The deep-voiced liberal columnist said it was because of the President's isolation from those who really knew Washington. The columnist who never went anywhere reminded his peers that there had been landslides before. The columnist who went to all the parties said that maybe for one thing a man would be able to get a drink at the White House for a change.

Zardovsky ate steadily through this drivel, then through a commercial for California wines, then through an interview with Clark Guppy, who assured Diana Cazadora that he had privately predicted the landslide months earlier. Doc Cadwallader, interviewed separately, echoed this version of events, with himself as the font of prophecy. Then the challenger's campaign manager told another interviewer that he had privately predicted it; then members of Congress said they had; then state and local officials of both parties said they had; then the correspondents agreed with each other that they had.

Margaret grew quiet and pale; she fiddled listlessly with her food. She seemed to be making some hopeless plan or plotting a long and desperate journey. "Do you have a cigarette, Bob?" she said at last.

"Naw, Maggie, you know I don't smoke."

"Yeah, of course. Well, listen, I better go out and get a couple of packs, won't be a minute."

"Go out? Christ, Mag, it's fucking freezing out there."

"I won't be long, I'm just going over to the Circle."

"Wait a minute." Zardovsky scanned the room. "Thought so — there's half a pack over there by the radiator. You left 'em there yesterday."

"I'm out of matches, too. I'll be right back." She went to the closet to get her coat.

"Hey, you can light 'em on the stove if you have to. Come on and eat your dinner, and we'll get a little drunk."

"Absolutely. I'll be right back."

"What the hell is this? If you want to go out or something, maybe I'd better come with you."

"Oh, no, no need, I'll be right back —"

"Maggie, what's going on?"

She walked to the door without meeting his eye. "I've got to make a phone call."

"Use the phone here."

"Bob, leave me alone, I want to call Gerald."

For some reason this idea enraged Bob Zardovsky. "Call Gerald? What the hell for?"

"Bob, let me go, I won't be long."

"You're going to leave me here with the fucking TV to go call Gerry? How will you find him?"

"I might just jump in a cab and go down to the headquarters."

"Maggie, that's the dumbest thing I ever heard of."

"It's not anything to do with you —"

"The hell with that! You're leaving me here without even a ball game on the tube to go chase that nerd-nose across town! This really pisses me off! Here I've been listening to you talk about how he doesn't call you and you have no future with him and all this jazz, so you're going to dump me and go find him! So who am I, Mr. Dumb Asshole or somebody?"

Maggie was looking at him wryly. He was raging back and forth across the apartment, feeling that though he was no longer under his own control, everything he was saying and doing was according to some script written long before and not revealed to him until now.

"Bob, you sound jealous," she said gently.

"I'm not jealous, I'm just pissed off. You think I'm just a big dope, I guess, sitting here and swilling beer. It's okay to go out for a pizza or something with me, but when things get tough, you want some wimp in a necktie. You're a dope, you know that? Here you are, a great-looking broad, smart as hell, a real character — you could do a lot better than that guy Gerald."

She looked at him as if considering some new possibility for the first time. "Like who, Bob?" she said softly.

"Well, Jesus Christ, I don't know. I mean, maybe . . . well, shit, like me. That's who, like me."

She stood for a moment, half in and half out the door, bulky in her down coat, while Bob Zardovsky felt his face flushing. This was unfamiliar territory for him. Ordinarily women did the talking in his life, and this declaration had forced its way out of him without any prior warning. Now he felt embarrassed and at a loss, sixteen years old again — a feeling that grew when she threw back her head, shaking loose her thick hair, and laughed. He felt like six kinds of idiot, thinking that a smart girl like her would have any interest in a four-fingered lumberjack like him. Then she unzipped her coat and laughed again.

"Well, I'll be damned," she said, closing the door. "When did all this happen?"

At midnight they realized that the TV was still babbling news of disaster and defeat. Margaret ate cold chicken during a recap of the congressional races. Among the new members of Congress were two vegetarians, a transactional therapist, and (from Buster Hench's old district) a fundamentalist funeral director.

She put the set out of its misery and led Bob to the window. Grayness caught the lights of Washington and threw them back to earth. Everywhere around them the city heaved and sighed, stirring in noisy confusion like a feverish patient, past the crisis, who cries out in his sleep. The spectacle seemed far away, as if they two were the only people awake in a world of dreamers and the mad. The city, with its mighty dome and its proud monuments, was surprised, surrounded, and changed by forces it did not understand.

And so were they.

Part Four

This *favourite* is hated by the whole herd, and therefore to protect himself, keeps always *near the person
of his leader.* He usually continues in office until a
worse can be found; but the very moment he is discarded,
his successor, at the head of all the Yahoos in that
district, young and old, male and female, come in a body,
and discharge their excrements upon him from head to foot.
—"A Voyage to the Country
of the Houyhnhnms"

Chapter 1

WHEN IS WASHINGTON MOST FAIR?

Some praise her in spring, when gentle rains give way to pink-and-golden sunsets and soft evening breezes whisper of the South. Some praise her in fall, when the north wind scatters bright leaves across her circles and the night tastes of adventure and apples. But her full squamose blossom is unveiled only in that rare and special seventy-five-day Indian winter between the election and the inauguration of a new President.

Call the season transition. Then her people, from deputy assistants to hot-dog vendors, gracefully change long-standing allegiances, break solemn vows, rupture lifelong friendships, take up new sports and hobbies, redecorate apartments, buy new wardrobes, and dissolve unsuitable marriages. Hotels and photocopy shops are full. Rumors whisper like spring breezes; résumés fly like autumn leaves. In the corners of hotel lobbies, the conference rooms of think tanks, the antechambers of senatorial offices, the parlors of Georgetown homes, the newsrooms of publications, and the faculty rooms of private schools form competing shadow governments, which engage in complex conspiracies, utter savage threats, take brutal vengeance, execute hostages, slay entire bureaucratic tribes, and sow official cities with salt — all in conflicts that, in the end, may have no bearing at all on influence or power.

Ancient courtiers, shopworn assistants, incompetent deputies, laughable ex-speechwriters, famous scapegoats and whipping boys grin at themselves in mirrors, seeing no reason that their reflections should not be washed clean by undeserved preferment. And in the midst of this ghastly marketplace, the servants of the departing leader pass like ghosts with noiseless, uncanny tread.

In late November a ghost named Gerald Nash received an invitation to visit his old Department. The occasion was an awards ceremony. Those outside government often do not realize that it is not only the uniformed services that value ceremony, tradition, and decorum; the civilian agencies have their own heroes, victims, martyrs. cowards, and traitors, and their own rituals to honor the brave and commemorate the lost.

The solemn assemblage convened in a gray-green, windowless auditorium in the Department's headquarters. It was a tattered, motley band of appointees, civil servants, friends and family of those to be honored, and bums looking for a quiet place to sleep. There were no reporters, and indeed no one of any consequence in the new Washington; the occasion had the air of a family reunion in a house about to be foreclosed. Presiding was not the Secretary (who was closeted with his advisers, trying desperately to place an article explaining that he had privately argued against every tenet of past administration policy and had instead urged a set of measures roughly identical to the platform of the victorious challenger), nor the Deputy Secretary (who had taken to the Maine woods the day after the election with a pair of L. L. Bean gum-boots, an Eddie Bauer parka, a Coleman stove, and a tattered copy of Thoreau), but the Assistant Secretary for Evaluation, Training, and Morale.

Impressive in his store-bought double-breasted blue serge suit (of a type known in his native region as a burying outfit), spread-collar, white-on-white rayon shirt, buffalo-nickel cufflinks, and me-tallic four-and-a-half-inch blue-and-silver necktie, he stood behind a blond wood podium and opened the obsequies with a nod to the

conductor of the U.S. Merchant Marine Concert Band. This gleaming aggregation, in tribute to the Assistant Secretary's heritage, performed a medley including "Wildwood Flower," "To Canaan's
Land," "When the Roll Is Called Up Yonder," and "They Cut
Down the Old Pine Tree," then concluded with a selection of
marches, including "The Stars and Stripes Forever," "The Washington Post," and "Columbia, the Gem of the Ocean."

Such music has the power to grab the heart and turn it to
thoughts of service and sacrifice. Gerald heard the ensuing oratory
through a mist of exalted regret. The Assistant Secretary recapped
the story of evaluation, training, and morale throughout all of
human history, beginning with the civilizations of the Fertile Crescent, marching briskly through Egypt, Israel, Greece, and Rome,
lingering lovingly over the administration of Andrew Jackson,
pausing wistfully at the army of northern Virginia, saluting the
Tennessee Valley Authority, and concluding with events of a few
days before the recent election.

He then awarded the Department's Bronze Shield to his loyal
Deputy, Nancy Quoin, and its Silver Palm to Jack Worthy and
Brad Watkins; after which, by her own most urgent request, Quoin
herself made a special award of the Silver Scroll of Merit, with clus-
tered quills, to Baxter Muntin. Then Gerald stepped forward to
accept the Medal of Distinction, Second Class, and he took the
bauble with none of his usual irony, weighing it on his palm as
something that, however slight, was still enough for now.

After a concluding medley — "Yankee Doodle Dandy," "On
Wisconsin," and "Stayin' Alive" — the assembly rose. As Gerald
pocketed his medal, he felt his elbow trapped in a viselike grip.
"Come on, Sunshine, we got a staff meeting to go to," said the
Assistant Secretary's voice. The AS called most of his staff by such
affectionate nicknames in order to avoid learning their real ones.

"I'm not on the staff anymore," Gerald said.

"Hell, won't none of us be much longer."

"All right," Gerald said. "It's not like I have much else to do."

No sooner had the Assistant Secretary loosed his left elbow than
his right was enfolded in a better-padded but no less strong hand.
"Gerald, my dear fellow," said Baxter Muntin. "What a wholly
unexpected pleasure! I saw you on television, you know, and I only

regret that your brief appearance did not bring you as much profit as mine did me. Will you have a cigarette?"

"No thanks, Baxter, I don't smoke."

"You know, I have a feeling that smoking may become quite chic again under the new administration. So many fashions change, and we poor civil servants must try to adapt to the changes."

"Why is it, Baxter, that I feel so little anxiety about your ability to handle the transition?"

Muntin laughed. "Because, as I have often said, you are far too intelligent for government work, which is best left to drones like myself. But I must say that I'll feel more pain than I had ever anticipated when I bid farewell to the Deputy Assistant Secretary. I've become quite fond of Nancy over the past few months. It's been a veritable love feast around here — pity you weren't here to take part."

"I can imagine. Has Nancy been ironing your shirts for you?"

"Unkind, Gerald. But I have found her most eager to please — now, you know, more than ever. The poor woman has the quaint notion that she can keep her job. She's been producing back-dated memos faster than the mint makes nickels."

"Listen, the AS wants me to sit in on the senior staff meeting. You want to go up together?"

"Gerald, since the election I've begun to feel more relaxed about our regular staff meetings. Give me a call if you're down this way again, Gerald, and do write if you get work." Executing a smart about-face, Muntin lumbered majestically away.

Conference room N317-A-F, in all its dingy splendor, was so familiar that Gerald might have been returning to the same meeting he had left two months before. Watkins and Worthy were in their accustomed places, while Harry Palmer sat in Muntin's seat and Bernard Weisman sat in Gerald's. Nancy Quoin had moved to the right-hand side of the place of honor. The Assistant Secretary, hitching up his trousers, settled into the chief position, gesturing Gerald to take the place at his left.

"Well, chickadees," the AS began, "we have a couple of quick items on the agenda."

"Sir," Bernard Weisman interrupted, "before we go any further, I have a question."

"What's on your mind, Sunshine?"

"Sir, I'm not sure that strictly speaking it's in order for Nash to be in on the business part of the meeting, as he has no official status in the division at this time."

The Assistant Secretary sighed. "Sunshine, I don't know who's got status and who doesn't, but I dimly recall that when I left for my tour of New England last summer, George — I mean John . . . I'm sorry, what is your name, child?"

"Gerald, sir."

"Gerald here was my special assistant, and when I got back he was gone and you claimed you were my special assistant, and nobody had ever talked to me about it."

"Sir," Nancy Quoin said reproachfully, "there is a memo on this subject to you in the file."

"Every time I turn around there's another memo in the file. I'm not criticizing anybody, I'm just saying that I still extend recognition to Gerald, and he's here in case I need some special assistance."

"Sir," Weisman said relentlessly, "as you may or may not know, there are guidelines on questions of this sort, designed to insulate the division from undue political influence —"

"Well, if that's your concern, Dudley, we're off the hook, because I believe if there's anyone in six states with less political influence than yours truly right at this moment, it's probably Dooflop here. By the way, I saw you on the TV election night, thought you looked mighty dapper. Who was that lady I saw you with, anyway?"

"Sir," Weisman bleated a third time, "I still have serious questions about this procedure, and I'd like to have my objection noted in the minutes."

"Great day in the morning, I didn't even know that there were minutes for these little get-togethers."

"Yes, sir," said Nancy Quoin. "You'll find the procedure explained in my memo to you outlining the staff list for the meetings. I keep the minutes and distribute them to the participants, with one for the file, of course."

"You write up the minutes?" asked the Assistant Secretary, seemingly touched. "Well, that's just fine. I didn't even know you could type."

A brief silence followed this remark.

"The first item on the agenda," Nancy Quoin finally said in a somewhat stilted tone, "is the status update on the OPPE Fungibility Project. I had hoped Baxter himself could brief us on that, but of course I'm delighted that he's sent his capable deputy, Harry Palmer. Harry?"

"Thanks, Nancy," Palmer said briskly. "The FP has been evolving rather rapidly since the — in the last few weeks. In fact, we are in the process of substantially broadening the range of views to be represented in the final action plan, and of making some very determined outreach to the private sector to make sure that the end result of our project is not simply another wasteful layer of government regulation and restraint on the business community. There's also been some shift of outside personnel, and we have regretfully accepted the resignations of Mrs. Guttmacher, Professor Farben, and Dr. Trivet. An intraoffice task force is now working with representatives of the Transition Office to come up with suitable replacements and to draw up a new conceptual basis for the FP. Pending the release of the conceptual section of the document for divisional, departmental, and interagency review, the project-planning process as such is in abeyance."

"I'm glad this subject came up," said the Assistant Secretary. "Can you just explain to me what exactly this project is supposed to accomplish?"

"Well, actually, sir, at this stage of the process I don't really think I can."

"Moving to the next item," said Nancy Quoin smoothly, "the Assistant Secretary has indicated that he has some divisional concerns he wants to discuss. Sir?"

"Thank you, dear. I really only have one, which is that according to the preliminary figures I got last week, the CATA program is still running at less than sixty percent of budget authorization. One grant I specifically authorized has still apparently not been funded. Can someone explain to me what gives?"

"Nancy," Weisman said, "why don't you handle that?"

"Oh, yes, certainly, Bernie," she said, shooting the special assistant her best surreptitious dirty look. "Some of the staff felt that in view of some subsequent events, which of course you could not be aware of at the time you verbally authorized the grant, the project in question might involve the division and the Department in undue controversy, and it would be best to extend the application-review process until we could get some guidance as to the future direction of the program."

"I don't know what could be so damn controversial about working pulpwood," said the Assistant Secretary. "I've been out to see those folks, they're good people and they got a nice little town out there. I'm damned if I see why we should keep money in Series E bonds while their sawmill goes down the drain."

"Sir," said Weisman, "I think it may not be quite as simple as you seem to think. This grant application has some distinctly unsavory aspects, in view of Congressman Hench's involvement. Admittedly, his conviction has been set aside by the court of appeals on the grounds of probable government misconduct by this man Zardovsky, but that to me is just a further reason to wait for the results of the new trial."

"Bernie, I couldn't agree more," said Quoin hastily. "As you and I have discussed in our exchange of memos earlier this fall, many of the senior staff feel some concern about CATA and the overall direction of the division and what we felt were some political pressures coming to bear on the ongoing policy-planning and grant-review processes. This grant is one example, and another is the conference with the Red Chinese. As I'm sure you know, sir, this group was unanimously opposed to our participation in that conference on the grounds that it would disrupt our warm ongoing interagency cooperation with the government of Taiwan."

"That's right, Nancy," said Brad Watkins. "I believe you have my memo on that subject, written at the time."

"Yes," said Quoin, "and Bernie and Baxter have mine —"

"And you have ours," said Weisman.

"So, in conclusion," said Quoin, "we felt we might be drifting along that road again here."

"Nancy," said Harry Palmer, "I'd like to add that many of us at the staff level at OPPE felt there were policy concerns about the overall suitability of this type of project. We have asked the general counsel's office to attach an opinion on some of those questions in terms of a reading of the authorizing statute as amended. I know

Baxter routed that request directly to Mr. Seitz, but as far as I know there's not been time for a response — it's been less than three months, after all."

"All in all, sir," said Weisman, "I think it's the sense of the staff that it would be better to wait on this particular project. Does that clear up the question?"

The Assistant Secretary had listened with his chin heavily cupped in his hand. Without opening his eyes, he said, "Maybe I'm not making myself as clear as I thought. I didn't ask for the sense of the staff. That grant is approved and I want the papers on my desk by two P.M. today. Is that clear now?"

"Oh, yes, sir," Nancy Quoin said sweetly. "But would you mind putting it in writing for inclusion in the file?"

"You know, Tinkerbell," the Assistant Secretary remarked in a conversational tone, "if you really think you can hold on to your job, then you don't have the brains God gave a June bug. But hell, yeah, you can have it in writing, and anybody else who's squeamish can have a carbon. I'm going to get that grant out of here, and if anybody tries to stop me, I'm going to commence flaying skin, and I won't stop until they carry me out on January twentieth. Anybody got any other business?"

As usual, this was Jack Worthy's moment. "I don't suppose," he said in a voice that carried no hint of prospective reproach, "that you'd like to hear about the plans for the division Christmas party?"

There was an impatient shifting of bodies. But the Assistant Secretary, who knew how to add stars to his heavenly crown, smiled broadly and said, "Jack, I'd surely admire to hear about your party."

When the meeting ended, Gerald felt a rush of sentiment: gratitude for the medal he had received, admiration for the odd superior he had served, and dim love for the dingy bureaucratic outpost where he had labored with a kind of passive distinction. He went toward Nancy Quoin, who was conferring in whispers with Weisman, intending to wish her all the best in whatever she did.

But Quoin and Weisman walked past his outstretched hand as if it did not exist, and vanished indignantly down the hall.

Chapter 2

GERALD WOKE THE NEXT MORNING to the unfamiliar sound of Willys Handleman singing "Lady of Spain" in a passable light tenor. He stumbled into the living room to find his roommate dressed in a white shirt, red-and-white boxer shorts of the type bought only by women to be given as gifts, and black calf-length socks. Handleman was daubing Meltonian cream wax on a pair of Italian shoes, and other footwear was ranged before him: black wing-tips, cordovan tassel loafers, brown deck shoes, even a pair of black suede slip-ons with matching brush, all sparkling in the cold morning sunlight.

Gerald was less sure than ever what Handleman did. By day he disappeared from the apartment; at night he read books about wine. His former rancorous envy had disappeared, replaced more and more by a kind of solicitude that made Gerald uneasy.

"Good morning," said Handleman, administering a final ferocious brushstroke to the tongue of the left shoe. "You slept right through the news. It's nearly ten."

"How do you expect me to wake up if you don't yell at the TV? Was there anything I should know?"

"Not much that's important — from your point of view, I mean. The President-elect announced a new cabinet-level position to direct the budget cuts."

"What's he going to call it, Lord High Executioner?"

Handleman smiled with patronizing politeness. "Director of Difficult Decisions."

"Three-D, huh? Who's the lucky fascist?"

"They haven't announced that yet. The other news was an earthquake in Albania."

"That must have interested you. What will it do to relations between Hoxha and the Yugoslavs?"

"Who cares?" Handleman rose and carefully dusted his thighs, searching for traces of shoe polish. Then he donned a pair of gray-blue wool slacks, slipped on the Italian shoes, and carefully collected the other pairs and his polishing gear and took them to his room.

Gerald watched in some amazement. He could not recall ever having seen Handleman clean up anything without loud curses and threats of violence.

Willys returned, wearing a natty blue sport coat with a faint gray stripe and a taupe checked tie. "Well, I'm off," he said, throwing a camel's-hair topcoat negligently over his shoulders. "What did you say you had on today?"

"Nothing this morning," Gerald answered. "I'm having lunch with Toad, and after that we're all going over to help clean out the headquarters."

"Give my best to Toad," Handleman said. "I've been worried about him. He's such an unusual and interesting guy — I do hope he finds something that's suitable for his talents. Tell him to call me if he needs anything."

"I'm sure he'll appreciate hearing that. Where is the morning paper, by the way?"

"I used most of it to shine my shoes on. I saved you the want ads, though."

Handleman disappeared through the door, then poked his head back through. "Oh, I almost forgot. Diana called and said she had to go to New York."

"What for?"

"She didn't say. She said she'd call. But Margaret wanted you to meet her at the bookstore for a drink tonight at six." Handleman snapped the brim of his Borsalino hat and vanished again.

Gerald met Toad in the hellish anteroom of the restaurant. Toad had shaved his goatee and now wore a Fu Manchu–style mustache. He offered the headwaiter the customary five-dollar bill, but the great man hastily muttered, "Put that thing away, whaddaya think this is, the Mexican border?" Gerald and Toad were denied access to the basement dining room and unceremoniously led to a tiny table in the bar, between the men's room and a maintenance man mopping the floor with ammonia solution.

"We got no beer in the can and no chicken salad," said the waiter briskly. "All's we got is corn beef and sauerkraut."

Like many from his home region, Toad seemed to be at his best when enduring indignity. As the waiter snatched away their menus, he smiled genially and lit an Old Gold.

"You back on cigarettes?" Gerald asked.

"Hell, yeah," said Toad. "They're gonna kill me someday, but they won't get me thrown in jail."

The food arrived cold. Toad munched thoughtfully while discussing his future plans. "I figure I'll go back home and make a country album. Hell, maybe I'll get back in the mobile-home business. Or some damn thing. But anyway, I'm getting out of this town, and if it's half as glad to see the last of me as I am to see the last of it, then they'll be dancing in the streets . . . Gerry, you know, you did a damn fine job for us under difficult circumstances. I know it and He knows it. And you know, He would like to do something for you to show His appreciation."

Gerald, feeling some relief, began to make grateful noises.

"The problem is," Toad continued, "there's not a damn thing He can do for you or anybody else right now. So good luck to you in whatever you do."

"You through yet?" asked the waiter, lightly sprinkling coffee on Toad's chino trousers.

"Reckon I was and just didn't know it," said Toad, rising. He and Gerald exited through the crowd of gray-clad men pleading to be allowed to descend. As they passed, Gerald saw a distinguished party passing down the broad stairway: newscaster Ed Hackett, Baxter Muntin, and Willys Handleman, genially applauding some witticism, head thrown back in laughter so that he caught Gerald's eye. The group passed into the warm regions below.

The headquarters was like a house where a powerful but unloved relative has died; there was some formal mourning, some spontaneous relief, and some uncertainty about whether any of the inmates would ever see each other again, or want to. At midafternoon a technician arrived to remove the telephones. Clark Guppy and Doc Cadwallader departed shortly afterward, darting suspicious glances at each other like characters from *Treasure of the Sierra Madre* on their way to check stashes of gold.

Toad settled into the work, his mind already roaring down country roads and shooting holes in mailboxes. As he worked he sang, "I ain't going to work tomorrow, and I may not work next day." Gerald, working beside him, found that using his muscles stimulated odd feelings, reminding him of parts of himself he had not used in some time. All his thoughts and plans, his ambitions and fears, fell away as he lifted and toted, descended and climbed. He was more than anything relieved that Diana was gone for a little while, as if someone had announced a brief time-out in a desperate struggle. From there he progressed to vivid, unbidden images of Margaret: her thick hair, her fine skin, her soft, solid body like a safe harbor at the end of a dangerous voyage. By the end of the day he was swimming in desire.

They were to meet at the same combination bookstore and bar. It was the end of the trading day; rumor-mongers and influence-peddlers were offering distress prices on their unsold wares. Initials filled the air: DAS, LA, EOB, NSC, OMB. Most prominent in the babble of rumor was Three-D, the promised Director of Difficult Decisions. The afternoon paper reported that the President-elect (still on vacation at his bungalow in the Virgin Islands) had promised to name "an individual of unquestioned reputation and wide experience," and in his short walk to the bar, Gerald overheard whispered reports that the nominee would be the president of Southern Methodist University, the chief executive officer of the

Bank of America, the general president of the Laborers' Union, the commander-in-chief of U.S. forces in Europe, the anchor of the evening news, and the commissioner of baseball.

He pictured an unhurried night ahead — dinner at some quiet, dim bistro; some good talk, in which he would finally open up as he knew she had long wanted him to; and, of course, the unhurried finale. He was so absorbed in imagining the latter that he did not even recognize Margaret. "Gerry?" she was saying to him. "Wake up, Gerry!" Maybe it was her clothes: a heavy padded parka, blue jeans, and gumboots; maybe it was her hair, longer and wilder, almost as if she had just woken up; maybe it was her expression, less wistful and tentative than he remembered.

She was being pursued by a recruiter from the Toiling Masses League, a chubby, bearded young man wearing a jacket and a Wharton School of Finance tie. He was trying to force on Margaret a color brochure denouncing solar power as a Jewish plot. "Listen, we have a great new line," the young man was saying urgently. "Oil companies are progressive. We're swinging right."

"Beat it, comrade," Gerald said.

"Red-baiter!" the man hissed, retreating. "Zionist! Liberal!"

"My hero," said Margaret.

Under her gentle, ironic gaze, he swelled with solicitude and lust, mixed with the desire to bury his head in her lap. Instead he bought her a glass of white wine.

"We've had a shakeup at work," she said, sipping. "They're getting ready for the new administration by cutting back on bureaucracy. A lot of functions are being shipped out to field offices. It's a good idea — some of us have been arguing for it for a long time. But it means my job disappears. So I'm getting out of town."

Gerald felt the kind of thoughtless freedom that steals upon us at odd moments, in which everything about our lives begins to seem not only expendable but easily so. Mentally he cast aside Washington, his apartment, his career, Diana; the idea of clearing out appealed to him, as an open road of a kind he had not pictured in many years — since, he suddenly realized, Diana had disappeared a decade before, taking the open road with her.

"That sounds great," he said. "I'll come too."

She smiled gently. "What a sweet idea," she said. "It wouldn't work from your point of view, though. See, I'm going out to the West Coast for a while."

"I'm serious, Maggie. You shouldn't have to go off alone. We can buy a camper and live on the beach. Or maybe we'll sell soft ice cream, or get into the movies. What the hell, Maggie — I'm sick of Washington too. The goddamned rat race is turning me into an old man. I know it's frustrated you too — we haven't had much time together. I want to talk to you about that tonight. But I think it's a great idea. Let's go somewhere and really do something new. Wherever you say."

She held her wineglass between her cupped hands very carefully, as if it might break at a breath, and she spoke to Gerald the same way. "Gerry, dear, I'm very grateful to you. You were nice to me when I felt like an old lady nobody wanted. And I will miss you, sometimes. But what you need to know is that I'm going out west to live with Bob for a while, until I figure out what I want to do. That's why I wanted to see you." She kissed him on the cheek, then set her glass down on the bar and waved somewhat nervously at someone across the room. "In fact, Bob's here now, and I've got to go. We're going over to that Spanish place. Goodbye, Gerry. Let us know where you end up."

Across the bar Bob Zardovsky was waving at Gerald, grinning his mad, goofy grin. Margaret made her way through the crowd toward him, and they slipped out the door.

After a minute or so the man on Gerald's right, as if taking pity on him, said, "Okay, you didn't hear this from me, but the latest word is it's going to be the cardinal of Omaha."

Around him the traders drank and bellowed; outside the night closed in.

Chapter 3

Just as Jack the Giant-Killer, preparing to descend the beanstalk with the singing harp, might look around the giant's castle with an unexpected stirring of regret, Bob Zardovsky began to feel a kind of affection for Washington as the site of a portentous and magical chapter of his life.

One sunny December morning he and Margaret were sitting in the apartment, surrounded by boxes, lists of things to do, and empty Mateus wine bottles, waiting for someone to show them a used van they had read about in the want ads. Maggie wanted to take to the open road in a silver bus with a stereo and a sun roof. Bob had begun to discover Maggie's true self: though on the surface she seemed like one of these Washington types, real intellectual and serious, always reading *Time* magazine and watching public TV, underneath it all she was really a normal American.

Zardovsky took a cavalier attitude toward all non-baseball-related material possessions, and during his baseball career had repeatedly abandoned sodden heaps of comic books, frying pans, broken transistor radios, back issues of *Hustler*, bathing trunks, suntan oil, and sombreros. So he was mystified by Maggie's anguish at the thought of parting with her Maxfield Parrish print, or the bone-china ashtray her great-aunt had given her, or her collection of toy cats, or her wok.

"We got fry pans in Gouge Eye," he said. "And most people just flip their ashes in their beer cans."

"All the more reason why they need someone to bring ashtrays."

"That's what I'm telling you is, you don't —"

"Bob, I don't expect you to get it on the first try," she said. "But I seem to keep changing my life out of all recognition every couple of years, and if I don't bring these things along, I might forget who I used to be, which might not be so bad except someday I'll want to collect my Social Security."

"Social Security? Maggie, you know, you really are a character."

The doorbell rang. When Bob answered it, a smiling head insinuated itself through the opening. "Please, I come to show the van," said the visitor, a small man with dark hair and wary eyes who seemed reluctant to come all the way into the apartment, as if afraid of a trap. "You come with me, I show you. Is beautiful car, not use much, very nice." He took Zardovsky by the arm and tried to hustle him out the door.

"Whoa up, cowboy," Bob said. "You better show it to the lady, she's the one buying."

This answer seemed to discomfit the stranger, but he recovered quickly and said, "Yes, of course, very nice car for lady. I show you."

They descended to the street. The stranger's van was custom-painted with a scene of minarets; below them was some spray-painted Arabic writing and the scrawled slogan DEATH TO GREAT SATIN.

"Please, you are no offend?" said the stranger anxiously. "Is just for business, this writing. I throw in free paint job, no extra charge. You see motor — excellent. Factory air. Pile carpet, eight-track AM/FM stereo, front and rear, tinted sun roof, cruise control, power lock. Please, you try."

"What the hell have you got against satin?" Zardovsky began. Margaret made shushing noises.

"All right, I throw in roof luggage compartment, no charge.

Also is undercoat. I throw in free American flag decal and front license. You drive, you like, we talk price. Please, sir, you drive."

"One of us has to stay here," said Margaret. "The phone company is coming to take out the phones."

"Yeah," said Bob. "Tell you what, I'll take it for a little spin and tell you what I think. After all, once we get her out on the highway I'll be the one behind the wheel."

"Bob," said Margaret patiently, "wrong again."

She got into the van with the little stranger, who shot Zardovsky a sympathetic look, as if they shared a common dislocation.

He heard the telephone as he mounted the stairs, but he assumed it was someone from Margaret's office calling with another idiot question. It seemed the organization had not realized how much it depended on her until it fired her; now most days there was at least one frantic call asking for the location of a file, or the explanation of some procedure, or suggestions about where to find essential information. Zardovsky went to the kitchen and took from the refrigerator a cold Pabst beer and a light midmorning snack of leftover chicken hash, cheddar cheese, and banana bread; but the phone kept shrilling, so he strode over and picked it up, intending to give the caller a thorough kick in the ear. "Who the hell is this?" he asked.

"Mr. Robert Zardovsky?" said a female voice.

"Yeah."

"Hold please for the Assistant Secretary."

"Hello? Is that my old friend Three-Finger?"

"Fuckin' A! I mean, pardon my French, hi there, how the hell are you? Sir, I mean. How are you, I mean. Everything okay? Given a lot of grants lately? And stuff, I mean."

"Thank you for asking, Three-Finger," the voice said, pausing oddly over his nickname, almost as if reading it off an index card. "I'm just fine. I hope you are well?"

"Oh, hell, yeah. Everything's great! With me, I mean — oh, well, I mean, I'm sorry about the election and all."

"I have a suspicion the Republic will survive for a few years longer. But of course I'm not quite out of work yet, and as a matter of fact there are a few things I wanted to do before I go back home, and one of them was to call you and tell you that I have finally arranged for your grant to be funded and that the check will be issued today."

For a second or two Bob Zardovsky almost couldn't remember what grant the caller meant.

"Holy shit," he remarked.

"You should be getting a registered letter to this effect in a day or two," the voice went on. "And of course the top copy is being sent to the officials of your co-op out at Zeke's. The official announcement will be made tomorrow here at the Department, and if you'd like to join me for the occasion, I'd be delighted to have you. I'd like to buy you some lunch to repay you for the fine hospitality y'all gave me when I visited your fine community, Three-Finger."

"Say, listen, I'd like to come on down, but it seems to me that every time I get near this thing, something goes wrong. So maybe if you just pretend I don't exist until sunset tomorrow, we can finally get it locked up and I can go home a happy man."

"That's an ambition I approve of," said the Assistant Secretary. "Well, give my best to all your colleagues."

"You come see us next fishing season."

"That's mighty kind, Three-Finger, but once I get back to the mountains, you're going to need the Eighty-second Airborne to get me out again. God bless you, and have a pleasant day."

What happened next, in memory at least, resembled one of those scenes in old movies where all the characters jump around with jerky, mechanical haste. The Assistant Secretary hung up the phone — indeed, from the sound of it, he hung up twice. Bob Zardovsky was capering oxlike around the apartment, thinking that after months of delay, confusion, and embarrassment, everything seemed to be going his way at once, in much the way he remembered his control coming back to him with a rush after one or two rocky innings sometimes, when the doorbell rang and a voice said, "Special delivery for Mr. Zardovsky."

He threw the door open, and perhaps unfortunately resisted the impulse to throttle the letter-carrier there with a friendly bear hug. "Shit, that was pretty damn quick," he said.

"Sign here," said the carrier, a thin, vaguely blond young man whose uniform seemed to have been fitted for him before he went on a diet. He thrust a clipboard into Zardovsky's hands while he reached into his leather bag. "I have the letter right here."

"I never turn down an autograph." Zardovsky signed the form with a flourish and offered the clipboard back, saying, "Here you go, buddy, and you have a nice —"

But the mailman had pulled from his bag a cold blue snub revolver. "Put your hands behind your head and walk in front of me," he said in a somewhat shaky voice.

"Hey, what is it, do I owe postage due or something?"

"No arguments, you narcissist!" said the intruder. "Get moving!"

With the pistol nudging his back, Zardovsky paced quickly down the stairs. In front of the house a panel truck was double-parked. It bore the inscription PHOBOS & DEIMOS FLOWER ARRANGERS.

"Get in the back and lie down," said the voice behind him.

"You're not a postman at all," Zardovsky said with his customary rapid deductive reasoning.

"Move it, *now!*" He was shoved into the van and knocked to the floor. He felt someone binding his hands behind his back, and a gag was roughly thrust into his mouth.

"Elder brother," said a voice, "there's a van following us. It has some kind of Arab writing on it."

"Sons of Ishmael! Terrorists!" said a familiar voice.

Zardovsky found himself looking into a flickering, sinister smile. "Hello, Three-Finger," said Lightning. "Welcome home."

Chapter 4

NANCY QUOIN SAT IN HER OFFICE checking and recheck-
ing a troublesome equation. On one side were the results of the
November election; on the other, the mortgage payments on her
new house in Montgomery County. By no stretch of wishful thinking could the figures be brought into balance. If on January 21
she found herself out of work, she could not hope to earn by her
old consulting practice anything like enough to keep up her share
of the monthly payment, set in a moment of optimism at a figure
slightly lower than the debt service on the gross national product
of Burundi. So she had begun an attempt to bring herself, her
words, and her past into conformity with the new administration.
Need, muse of last resort, can make dreamers of the most prosaic
of us. Nancy Quoin was hoping to keep her job.

The obstacle to this dream was the Assistant Secretary, who since
the election had shown a disturbing sense of duty. Like a faithful
steward awaiting the master's return from a far country, the Assistant Secretary could be found early and late at his desk, counting silver talents, sorting keys, preparing lists, checking records,
and most ominous of all, granting money. The Assistant Secretary

had become in her mind the very embodiment of everything she most loathed about the patriarchal system: he was patronizing, obstinate, old-fashioned, and more important, an obstacle to her advancement.

But Nancy Quoin, like molten lava, oozed relentlessly through any opening. At present she was smoothly rewriting the record of her tenure in office, putting her endeavors in the most favorable light possible. File folders were piled on every surface, towering over the potted plants and ferns. Before her on the desktop passed the high points of her career: her attempt at rewriting the departmental personnel evaluation forms, with the full texts of the general counsel's opinion disallowing the psychosexual questions; the aborted affair of the travel downhold, with clippings of the publicity that resulted when her orders had been misinterpreted as preventing employees from traveling by subway; the heated memos following her edict that only decaffeinated beverages could be served in the Department's cafeterias; the attempted ban on sexist music during the lunch-hour coed aerobics classes, including the petition defending Donna Summer, with 5000 signatures collected by a publicity-seeking disc jockey in Kansas City; and best-documented of all, the Muntin matter.

In Quoin's agile mind, this last dispute had rearranged itself into a major triumph of her management style — a painful but necessary growth process that had helped a valuable but troubled executive regularize an untenable position. Muntin himself she now thought of with an affection so thorough that it almost completely disguised the fear beneath.

As she reviewed her career, she was eating a carton of kiwi-fruit yogurt and listening to classical music on the radio. The music — romantic, exotic, and warm — lulled her into pleasant reveries of success. She was somewhat jolted when it was replaced by a discreet and breathy voice.

"That was the Polovtsian Dance Number Two by Borodin, played by the Yerevan State Chamber Orchestra, Arnos Stephanian conducting," said the voice. "And now, the news at one. A bizarre standoff developed today between District police and members of the controversial Temple of Ray cult, who are said to be holding one or more hostages in the Temple's headquarters in Adams-Morgan. Witnesses reported seeing cult members enter the building holding at gunpoint a man identified as Robert Zardovsky, a former baseball player who was charged by defense attorneys in the recent trial of former Representative Buster Hench with being an undercover agent for the federal government. When police attempted to free Zardovsky, the cult members threatened to kill him unless the government revealed what they called, quote, the full extent of the conspiracy by Zardovsky and government intelligence agencies to infiltrate our Temple and heap scorn and desecration on the Ancient Ones of Mars, unquote. Police units have surrounded the building and are negotiating with the cult members, but report little success. Government agencies contacted by the Associated Press deny that there is any reference to Zardovsky in their files.

"Elsewhere in the news, spokesmen for the President-elect denied reports that the head coach of the Green Bay Packers is in line to be named Director of Difficult Decisions, the new cabinet-level supervisor of budget cutbacks. But they did say that the final decision would be forthcoming within a week, as soon as the victorious candidate returns from his lodge in the Sangre de Cristo mountains."

Who can see inside the human conscience? What motivated Nancy Quoin to do what she did next? Was it concern for an innocent man threatened with death by arbitrary and dangerous forces? Did she imagine some advantage that might come to her from acting in the midst of urban drama? Or was she simply seized by the desire to be at the center of the stage? In the files she had studied was a reference to Zardovsky, who had been named in television reports as the culprit who had passed on Muntin's briefcase to her. Other files, to which Quoin had no access (the Department had been organized so that the departmental police, and particularly the obscure Office of Security Information, could be reached only through Muntin's office), were cited. And in those files, it was reported, was "information derogatory to subject individual and his relationship to extremist religious groups."

At any rate, Nancy Quoin attempted to do a good deed. Therein lay her newest misfortune. She gathered the files together, and pausing only for a final spoonful of yogurt, rushed clattering out the door.

Chapter 5

THE SIEGE OF SUNRISE HOUSE offered the occasion for a bravura performance by the federal and District governments, the D.C. and park police forces, the local and national press corps, the diplomatic community, and the service sector. In their cumulative splendor they quite outshone Sunrise House itself, much as the majesty of Washington overshadows the drab nation it governs.

The District police were manning barricades; bellowing through bullhorns; controlling, misinforming, infiltrating, and photographing the crowd; installing communications systems; assuming sniper positions on nearby buildings; tending to drug-sniffing and bomb-detecting dogs; conferring with psychologists, hypnotists, and deprogrammers; drinking coffee; and eating doughnuts.

Reporters and camera crews were transmitting over two-way radios; interviewing spurious eyewitnesses; offering bribes to anyone who looked important; attempting illegal entry into nearby buildings; lying to each other; confusing the public; and engaging in meaningless and futile derring-do on rooftops.

The mayor of Washington was smoking a particularly large

Jamaica cigar (ring size 49) as he conferred with the director of public safety, interrupting the discussion only to thrust himself into photographs and television shots.

Investigators, consultants, and staff aides from the seven congressional committees (House side, five; Senate side, two) that claimed jurisdiction over the ongoing investigations of the Temple of Ray were mingling with federal marshals, FBI agents, Secret Service agents, representatives of NSA, CIA, INS, IRS, the Treasury's Alcohol, Tobacco, and Firearms Division, and the Humane Society, and private detectives retained to find beloved family members, pets, and portable property that had fallen into the clutches of the cult.

Ambassadors of three Asian nations (from left to right: Communist, nonaligned, and pro-Western) had parked their diplomatically immune limousines in a bus zone and were vying for the honor of mediating the dispute; the chief of station for Rumanian intelligence was assuring reporters that the chairman of the Communist party of the USSR was feeling much, much better these days; and an assortment of souvenir and refreshment vendors was catering to the bodily appetites of the crowd.

And, of course, the action was attended by a large and enthusiastic crowd of the curious, the bloodthirsty, the idle, the dishonest, the larcenous, and the lost. It was a good crowd for such a cold, threatening day, boisterous but good-natured. Lost in it was Margaret, the only real eyewitness (the van vendor had disappeared on hearing the word *police*), who had been shoved away from the police command-and-control center by the reporters, city officials, and consultants. (Among the latter group she had seen, with the kind of guilty inevitability common to nightmares, the lisping hypnotist who had tried to rid her of the smoking habit.)

Morning wore into afternoon. The wind rose. Free-lance bookmakers in the crowd began offering odds on the outcome, but Sunrise House remained shut and silent, and Margaret was left alone with her unsettled feelings. The sudden explosion between her and Bob had come as an unexpected and mystifying gift. It had seemed a lark, like dyeing her hair red or buying a pair of thigh-high boots. Suddenly she had to ask herself if what had seemed so improbable, so comic, might not be a real treasure.

Zardovsky was an oaf and an ignoramus, and unsuitably enough, she loved him.

By two o'clock she had realized that the police had no idea what to do and were most likely to do something dramatic but fatal to all involved. She went looking for help.

Once again the little storefront had been transformed out of recognition, this time with a new, more elegant façade and a discreetly lettered sign that read

TARGAVERDE CHILD CARE SERVICES
"Convenient Care Options for Professional Families"
Reliable Infant Nurses and Housekeepers
Licensed Day-Care Center
After-School Enrichment Program
Van Service to and from All Private Schools
Major Credit Cards Honored

A well-dressed young woman greeted her: "Good morning, and welcome to Targaverde. How old is your child, please?"

"I'm not a mother."

"We are presently accepting applications only for experienced live-in child-care specialists. Can you provide three written references?"

"I'm looking for Paco."

"Mr. Sanchez is in a staff meeting just now. If you'd like to wait in our lounge, we supply complimentary coffee and *The Wall Street Journal*."

"It's kind of an emergency. Could you tell him Margaret Luck is here?"

"Very well. I'll see if he can speak with you."

After a few minutes, Paco emerged, wearing a navy-blue pin-striped suit.

"Hey, Margaret, good to see you," he said hurriedly, sweeping her into a tiny office. "I'm kinda in a time bind here today, you know, we got an accreditation inspection comin up. You like the new operation? See, we found a way to fulfill a need here and make some money for the cause too. A lot of our ladies been makin money this way, but they get ripped off. We find work for them, we pay them good, we guarantee service for the parents.

We're mostly doin a service for your community. Maybe we build some good will too. You know, to show our revolution has a place for the private sector. We need to get the word out because we gonna win soon, we really had some big victories lately. Up here we got a terrific cash flow — stick around and I show you the pre-school when the kids get back from the Smithsonian."

Quickly she explained why she had come. Paco frowned judi-ciously when he heard that Bob was in the hands of the cult. "I tell you, Margaret, Hermana Eva don't want to mess with those people no more. She was laid up for three weeks and finally had to take up a new line of work. She's workin here, actually, with the three-year-olds."

"Well, can't you come and bring the musicians or something?"

"Tell you the truth, we don handle the mariachis no more. They got themselves a MESBIC loan and they're openin their own club. But I like to help Tres-Dedos. Tell you what, lemme finish settin goals and objectives for the professional staff. I got to do that before the franchising consultants get here. Then I come up there and see what I can do. See you later, maybe."

When she got back to Sunrise House, the Toiling Masses League had arrived in force and were hurling taunts at the cult head-quarters. Listening to a transistor radio, she learned that police had established communication with the cult and learned of their demands. The President-elect had given reporters his opinion that the police should simply storm the building. Rumors were sweep-ing the crowd: Zardovsky was an agent of the FBI, the CIA, the KGB, the Centers for Disease Control. Street odds on a SWAT raid before nightfall had fallen to three to two on a five-dollar minimum bet.

Never before had she felt so lost or friendless or confused. The city she lived in seemed to have become a mindless and threaten-ing beast, which could devour Zardovsky's death as a mild prelude to the serious excitement of Inauguration Day. She knew of no one she could talk to and no one who would care. The only thing that kept her from panicking was the knowledge that no one would pay the slightest attention to her if she did. So she did an unusual thing (for her): she prayed. Not knowing to whom she was appealing, not having a real hope of being heard, she sent out a call: *Let something happen. Let somebody help. Break the rules if you have to, but save Bob.*

Few people ever viewed Nancy Quoin as heaven-sent, but she arrived on the scene shortly afterward, bursting wildly out of a cab, wearing a camel's-hair topcoat, waving a sheaf of papers above her head, and gibbering wildly. After a frantic parley, the police parted the barricades for her; TV cameras and microphones turned toward the hurried conference in the command post; bookmakers started to revise the odds. All this attention was probably what distracted the patrolmen on the barricade and indeed kept everyone but Margaret from noticing when David Beaufort walked boldly to the front of Sunrise House.

David was, as usual, dressed in black; he also wore a black hat with a broad brim. Beyond his clothes, however, he carried no staff or symbol of authority — only the air of a man who has slept on the mountaintop and been fed by ravens.

Nancy Quoin was making a statement to the press. No microphone recorded what David said; he never entered the official accounts. Margaret saw him raise an accusing finger at the blind eyes and bolted door of Sunrise House, and heard him call in a hoarse, penetrating whisper: "Lightning! I want to talk to you!"

Nothing stirred in Sunrise House, but the blind façade changed, as if something inside were listening. "You better shut me up if you can, Big Brother!" David called out quietly. "I ain't no gypsy witch-woman. You better do something about me fast or forget it, because I'm going to wise up these poor suckers you got working for you. Listen up, people — these priests are just hustling you! They say this place is a temple, but it ain't nothing but a whorehouse! Lightning says these Ancient Ones can hear you and see you and mess with you, but they ain't doing squat to me! Why don't they blow my ass away? Are they drunk, or strung out, or what? Maybe their radio broke again! I tell you what, they ain't no Ancient Ones! They isn't but one God, and He don't live on Mars and you don't need a radio to talk to Him! He don't want people being kept as slaves and starved and beat up on and generally fucked around with! Any of y'all that want to live better clear out now, because God is going to come down on this place and burn it to the ground. Lightning, Daybreak, all you turkeys with the funny names, you can't do nothing about it! It's over for you! Hang it up! Clear out and don't look back!"

The television cameras, having recorded Nancy Quoin's statement, now turned back to Sunrise House. David stepped back, shrugging his shoulders as if he no longer felt any responsibility for what happened next. A voice inside Sunrise House screamed, "Fire!" and suddenly the boards flew off windows, the doors gaped, and the smiling, starving captives, terror and joy mingled on their pale and frantic faces, scrambled out into the December sunlight, hit the ground running, and scattered to the four winds. Last to come, hobbling, was Bob Zardovsky, leaning heavily on the arm of his old friend Paco Sanchez and waving his pitching arm to acknowledge the cheers.

Police and reporters rushed toward the big ex-ballplayer. Seeing Margaret, Zardovsky waved and grinned his goofy smile, then disappeared under the pack. Paco broke free.

"See, lady, I tole you I would do somethin if I could. So I got inside — shit, I tore my suit too, and this is a good one, I got it at Joe Bank. I had to distract everybody so I set that fire, and that worked real good. Then I got Tres-Dedos and we just walked out — everybody else was all runnin around like they'd been bit by a snake or somethin. This might be good publicity for us, too — you know, parents don like those cults. So lemme go talk to these TV people." He ran back into the pack, showering business cards in all directions.

For some reason, Margaret seemed to be the only person who had noticed David's assault on the cult. He was standing quietly by the porch, his hands in his pockets, watching wisps of smoke curl out of the windows of Sunrise House. The smoke, through a chain of associations of which Margaret was not consciously aware, sent her fumbling in her handbag for a cigarette. She lit up and inhaled deeply, then went over to David. "That was very brave," she said. "I wonder what would have happened if Paco hadn't set that fire just then?"

He turned toward her with a look of affection blended with pity. The discontent and hunger were gone from his face; in their place was a kind of smoldering glee. His eyes drew Margaret in and would not let her go, as if in each pupil burned the image of a bush. "Hey, Maggie," he said casually, taking the cigarette from her nerveless fingers. "You don't need that shit anymore. I'll check you later." His dark form disappeared casually down the street.

Later that evening, in a hastily arranged ceremony, Margaret Luck and Bob Zardovsky were married by a justice of the peace. Among the guests at a small celebration at a popular new Adams-Morgan nightspot was the Assistant Secretary for Evaluation, Training, and Morale, who came especially to make a formal announcement that the Gouge Eye People's Lumber Co-op Number One had been awarded a Community Action Training Allocation of $250,000.

At midnight the bridal pair walked home through the streets of the city and saw distant flames reaching toward heaven. Not until the next morning did they learn that the ancient row house recently known as Sunrise House had burned to the ground. Nor could they know that nothing would be built there for many years to come, nor that Margaret Luck, doomed to a long and interesting life, would never touch a cigarette again.

Chapter 6

As the bright, cold days of December ground mercilessly toward the new year, Gerald Nash began to feel that he had walked without volition or understanding off the edge of the world.

His former colleagues moved smoothly into the think tanks, lobbies, law firms, universities, advocacy groups, magazines, newspapers, and broadcast media of the capital. Others left on tours of the world, or announced their intentions of founding large families in wilderness cabins, or accepted posts as investment bankers in New York. Toad Earnshaw announced a plan to start a chain of franchised chicken-and-rib restaurants; Clark Guppy accepted a lucrative polling and public-relations contract with the government of Paraguay; Putnam Cadwallader proclaimed himself head of a new political action committee designed to eradicate all trace of the outgoing administration from public memory. But Gerald Nash seemed to know too much or too little; to have too much experience, or not enough, or the wrong kind; to be overqualified, or underqualified, or just unwanted.

In short, he did not find a job.

After a few weeks, he humbled himself to visit the offices of the Equine Defense Fund. His former boss, a lanky society matron with a pronounced chin, greeted him warmly until the talk turned to employment.

"Well, it's awfully kind of you to think of us, but of course we can't really offer you a salary that would match what you were making with the government," she said.

"I'm not worried about that. I took a pay cut once before to work here."

"We couldn't possibly think of asking you to do that twice. It's a very generous offer though, really."

"Then accept it."

"Oh dear, much as I'd like to, the problem is, you see, you don't have just the right kind of experience for the job."

"What in the world do you mean? I had the job for two years!"

"Exactly what I mean. You see, we're in the process of reorienting the fund to bring it into tune with the times. In the past we've been too tied to the outdated regulatory model. We need more emphasis on private-sector initiatives — voluntary agreements with industry groups and self-regulation in general. But you're terribly sweet to have thought of us, and of course we wish you the best of luck in whatever it is you may end up doing, and do let us know what it is."

She walked him to the door, holding his elbow rather firmly, as if afraid he would try to bolt to his old desk. "I saw you on TV," she said. "You were marvelous. All things considered, I mean. And who was that divine girl?"

"A friend of mine. I think."

"How is Willys? We all miss him so much — except for the cleaning people, of course."

After this interview Gerald found himself waking late in the still, bright apartment, breakfasting on half-cartons of yogurt and leftover fried rice, and drinking fruit-flavored soda-pop in front of the midday news (this lapsed more and more often into an absorbed viewing of "All My Children").

Diana's mysterious business trip was extended repeatedly. She communicated from time to time through odd, intense phone calls. Her voice seemed to be coming from another planet, a world from which he was barred, but he did not question her any more than a starving man dreaming of bread wonders about its fiber content.

One morning he slept particularly late, caught in one of those interminable dreams that hold a sleeper for hours if he does not wake at his regular time. It was a buzzing, grim scene of water, sky, and merciless, mysterious wisdom. He was swimming in cold and choppy seas, at night and far from shore. In a far bay he could see the tiny lights of dwellings, the huts of a fishing village where the people fished by day and sewed their nets by hand and from which, for reasons unclear, he had been cast away into the silence of the sea. Again he heard the rumble of some message from God or the dolphins, but he could not make it out. The dark waters were alive with giant shapes; he felt inhuman mouths gaping under his feet. He saw the hard twinkle of the lights, the cold glimmer of the stars, both equally unreachable; he gasped in despair and plunged under, but emerged instead, gasping, into his pillow, hearing the rumble of the television in the next room.

Handleman had not slept at home in weeks; Gerald was suddenly glad of his company. He threw open the door and said, "Willys, where in the world have you been?"

He found Diana perched on a chair in front of the living-room window, which she was trying to measure with a metal tape measure. She wore a belted beige dress with a short skirt and a high collar; the skirt had ridden up, exposing her elegant thighs in black stockings.

She nearly lost her balance. "You scared me, Gerry!" she said. "I didn't know you were here." Over the weeks she had taken more and more to black eye makeup — part of the punk look at the station — and her face was now totally unreadable.

"What are you doing?"

"Oh, nothing, really. I just wondered if there should be new drapes here." The tape measure disappeared into its housing with the flick of a serpent's tongue.

"How was New York?" he asked.

"Big." She jumped gracefully down from the chair and turned off the television with a prim motion, as if it should not be allowed to see what was going to happen. "Want some coffee?"

"We don't have any. I've been drinking Willys's Postum, but that's about gone."

"Actually, I just brought some — and a new coffee-maker."

"Really? Is it a present for me?"

"Well . . . for the apartment. Let me fix it." She dashed into the kitchen.

He dressed with more than usual care, like a man going to an execution: tan chino trousers, a white shirt with a faint blue check, a pale blue sleeveless sweater, and suede shoes.

"It'll be ready in a minute," she said when he emerged. They stood awkwardly in the airy living room, as if they were the only guests at a gummy cocktail party. "I was sorry about election night."

"Yeah. My mother called the next day and asked when you were going to let me finish my statement. She was pretty miffed when I said never."

"Your mother never liked me anyway."

"That was a pretty good assignment."

"It was really a thrill to work with Ed Hackett."

"Is he an okay guy? I guess I've always been prejudiced because Willys is always so down on him."

"I think Willys is rethinking his attitude."

"Willys seems to be rethinking his attitude on a lot of things," Gerald said.

"Yes." She smiled for the first time that morning. "You know, that's what makes Willys so interesting. He's always up to something new."

"Well, it isn't dull. Anyway, it's hard for me to get too down on Willys — he usually seems to be having such a hard time."

"Do you know what time it is?" she asked suddenly, as if reminded of something.

"Ten of eleven."

"I've got to get across town to the press conference. They're announcing the Director of Difficult Decisions in twenty minutes."

"They finally found somebody, huh? Who's it going to be, Richard Petty?"

"My guess is it's going to be a real surprise."

"You're covering it for your station or the net?"

"The net. It's my last assignment with them." She looked away suddenly, letting her eyes sweep over the cityscape below the window. "I was up in New York and then out in Idaho interviewing for a new job."

"Idaho? Who is it with, 'Potato Week in Review'?"

"No," she said, standing at the window with her back to him. "See, there's a new network starting up, New Harmony Satellite News, and I'm going to anchor the Washington segment of their morning show."

"No kidding? That sounds terrific! Who's behind it?"

"It's owned by the Fourth Planet Education and Research Foundation."

"The Fourth Planet . . . Holy Christ, Diana, that's the Temple of Ray! I heard about them on TV — shit, it was one of *your* reports!"

"I know," she said. "After I did that show I met a few of the top people there, and I think I really gave a misleading impression of what they're all about. And of course they've promised me complete journalistic freedom. It's a wonderful opportunity, Gerry — we'll reach thirteen million homes at first, and more than that pretty quickly. It won't be on around here, of course, because we don't have cable, but you may be able to see it where you are."

"What do you mean? I'm not going anywhere!"

"What? I'm sorry, I'm confused, I thought Willys told me something about your leaving."

"Diana, what in the world is going on here, would you tell me that?"

She stepped over and gave him a dark, warm kiss tasting sweetly of poison. "Gerry," she said, "you're a wonderful man. I'm so glad we found each other again, even if it wasn't for very long. That was something I really needed, and it meant a lot to me — more than you know. I've enjoyed it. Goodbye."

It was like the moment when the doctor or lawyer tells a truth one has known all along, which has stolen softly into the soul until it can never be questioned. He realized helplessly, and even with a touch of satisfaction, that Diana was going to get away scot-free once more. "Listen," he said, "don't you think you ought to explain things a little more than that?"

"I have to run. I really do. But Willys has promised to talk to you." And she was gone all at once, in a dark whirl of legs, leaving a rushing wind that seemed to carry away some part of his being forever; and the robbery was so sweet that ever after he could not distinguish the pleasure from the pain.

He wandered through the bright apartment as if through a desert. Nothing outside — not the cold, windy day, nor the city which lay at the foot of the building, nor the world beyond it — seemed to exist, as if his appointment with destiny still lay within these white walls and high ceilings. After a blank time, he was recalled from his fugue state by the smell of fresh-brewed coffee.

In the kitchen he found a shiny, expensive Japanese coffee-maker. As near as he could tell from the cryptic bilingual markings, it could be adjusted in advance to grind and brew fresh coffee at an appointed time. He poured some into a cup; it was spicy and light. India Mysore, said a brown paper bag on the counter.

Without knowing why, he wandered into the living room, turned on the television, and subsided into the white armchair, glued to a rerun of "Happy Days." But after a few mercifully mindless minutes, the Fonz was replaced by Ed Hackett.

"Good day," said the image, fixing Gerald with its eyes as if what followed were intended most particularly for him. "This is a network special bulletin. Just a few minutes ago at his transition headquarters here in Washington, the President-elect went in front of reporters to announce the eagerly awaited identity of his Director of Difficult Decisions. He told the press that what he called, quote, the single most important appointive post in the executive branch, unquote, will be filled by Washington journalist Willys A. Handleman. Though little known outside the capital, Handleman is a prominent figure in conservative circles here. Diana Cazadora, a personal friend of the new director, was at the press conference today and is here in the studio to give us some background on this crucial appointment."

The camera pulled back to reveal Diana, her dark eyes unreadable and hypnotic. "That's right, Ed. Though you called Willys Handleman a journalist, it might be more correct to call him a political analyst and thinker, and he has in the past few months become one of the most influential members of a growing intellectual movement that has questioned the bloated, wasteful social programs of previous administrations. Handleman worked as an adviser to the President-elect's campaign and helped prepare the candidate for the debate, but he especially impressed the President-elect with an article published this fall, entitled 'Seven Things the Government Does Badly.' Since the election he has been a high-ranking though unofficial adviser to the transition team. Those of us who know him personally have long been impressed by his understanding and insight. Now it seems he will become a prominent figure on a national basis. Ed?"

"Diana, I wonder if you could tell us a little about his philosophy."

"Well, Ed, when you say philosophy, like many members of his generation, he has been evolving politically over recent years, and in addition he has a very strong streak of good old American pragmatism. He does believe that government should spend less, and should spend money only where it is efficient. According to the article I mentioned recently, that means not spending money for public welfare, housing, so-called hunger programs, health and safety regulation of industry, transportation, environmental protection, or community development."

"Excuse me, Diana, but what does that leave?"

"Well, Ed, military power, nuclear energy, and law enforcement. I suspect that given Mr. Handleman's views — and, of course, those of the new President — we'll see a shift in emphasis to the private sector. One of the ideas Mr. Handleman discusses in an upcoming article, for example, is letting the market handle decisions like, let's say, what drugs can be sold, on the grounds that dangerous or ineffective drugs will not achieve a durable market share. Also, of course, there is the idea of privatizing the currency through competitive mints, which Mr. Handleman has not fully endorsed as yet.

"Mr. Handleman will have the support of a very able bipartisan staff, by the way. Today he announced that his deputy will be Bernard Weisman, the respected former Hill aide and more recently a top official in the new cabinet Department, which Handleman has vowed to abolish. He said today that he is also planning to make use of a fascinating new study done under Mr. Weisman's supervision as part of something called the Fungibility Project, whose final report, to be released early next week, will suggest that the best way to evaluate any government program is according to how much money it makes for private industry.

"But Ed, I don't want to give our viewer the idea that Willys Handleman is some kind of sterile economic theoretician or bureaucrat. Everyone who knows him has remarked on his warm, fun-loving, social side. For example, he's recently become a regular at Status, the glittering, exclusive nightspot owned by Congressman 'Honest John' LaVache, who is one of his close personal friends. That's one example of how he'll help the new administration find its way in this town, which as you and I know, Ed, can sometimes be somewhat treacherous for outsiders. In fact, you might say that one problem of the outgoing administration was that it just never found its Willys Handleman, and so it was never fully accepted by the political and journalistic communities here."

"Diana, did you say that Handleman sang a song for the press conference today?"

"Not only sang, Ed, but accompanied himself on the accordion, which he plays remarkably well — and by coincidence, Ed, that is the President-elect's favorite instrument. Mr. Handleman today played and sang the old standby 'There'll Be Some Changes Made.' All in all, Ed, it was one of the most intriguing press conferences I've ever attended, and if I can editorialize just a little here, a very heartening change from the traditional stuffy Washington briefing to which we've all been subjected a thousand times."

"Well, thank you, Diana, and while we have you here on camera, I must break the news to our viewers that you're going to be leaving us shortly for a new job and new responsibilities. We are brokenhearted to lose you, but of course we wish you well in your new life."

"Ed, just let me say that it's been a privilege to work with you in particular and I hope we can do it —"

But Diana's farewell speech was never finished. Without fully realizing it, Gerald Nash had grasped a book lying beside the chair (*The Wealth of Nations,* he noted as it flew through the air) and flung it into the screen of his color TV. Gerald jumped to his feet and shouted, in a voice so loud and angry he did not recognize it at first as his own, *"YOU GODDAMN FUCKING HYPO-CRITICAL IDIOTS!"*

At that moment he heard a key in the lock. He walked to the door, hurled it open, and screamed, *"YOU LYING ASSHOLE, I OUGHT TO BREAK YOUR FUCKING NOSE!"*

"Control the impulse, Mr. Nash," said Martin Grimm, the co-op association president. Behind him were three men in the uniform of a local moving company. "I had not expected — or should I say, dared to hope? — to find you here," Grimm said.

"Keep your sarcasm to yourself, Grimm. You want to tell me what the hell you're doing coming into my apartment?"

"Strictly speaking, from a legal point of view, it really isn't *your* apartment but Mr. Handleman's. Of course I have his permission, in writing, to be here. As of tomorrow, I'm pleased to say, this apartment will be the property of Mr. Handleman — under the lease he has the right of first option on the property, and I believe he is signing the papers this afternoon to exercise the option. All of us in the association are pleased to have a man of Mr. Handleman's reputation as an owner. And I must say that it does him credit that he has hired these gentlemen to assist you by taking your items of furniture to any reasonable destination. You see, the decorators are arriving tomorrow morning, and Mr. Handleman prefers that they start with a clean slate, so to speak. I rather imagine that applies to yourself as well, Mr. Nash. Naturally I will be deeply grieved to see you go."

The telephone rang, and Gerald fled toward it half gratefully.

"Gerry — hi, buddy," said a familiar voice.

"Willys, what the hell is going on?"

"Didn't Diana explain?"

"Not exactly."

"Listen, I'm real sorry I couldn't say anything sooner, but we had to keep tight security on the whole business. I'm sure you understand; after all, you used to be in the same position — well, maybe not this high up, but . . . Listen, I'll pay the first month or two of storage, don't worry about that, it's just that we couldn't get this guy for another couple months if he didn't start tomorrow and he's very good, the First Lady recommended him actually, he does all their vacation homes and he's redoing the Residence after the inauguration. But anyway, I wanted to talk to you before the reporters started calling. I think the best thing to do from both our points of view would be just to say nothing, frankly. If you want, I can have our press people put something together down here and release it — it'll get good play, and the exposure will be good for you. I know you haven't found a job yet — the Equine people called me, I did what I could but really, you weren't right for that job, I'm sure you understand — but I thought if you needed something to tide you over, I'm putting together a little collection of some of my pieces, the publisher wants to get it out quickly, we're going to call it *Money and Power*. Some of the pieces are a little dated, you know, and I need somebody to take a month or so and get them squared away."

"You mean like what you did to the 'Seven Things' piece?"

"Exactly. That's why I thought of you first, you understand how I think and where I'm coming from. It would be mostly re-wording things, making them compatible with what we're doing now. So if you want to have a crack at it, I could get a couple of thousand for you up front, and a place to stay — one of our senior people has a hunting lodge on the Eastern Shore, terrific place, we worked up there sometimes during the campaign, real peaceful, no phone or anything. But I need to know right away."

"Willys, what is this shit with my apartment?"

"Oh that, listen, it just fell into my lap, see, the owner it turns out is one of our people, he's getting some DAS job at State — nothing important, some shit about human rights, I think — but he wanted to get rid of it and I had to move fast. You know the lease is in my name and I figured, you being between jobs and all, you might be glad not to have to get half the rent up for a while. Anyway, we thought Diana might be going to New York, but with this new job she's staying around so she's going to move in — I don't know how long we can pull that off, really, the President is pretty strait-laced, so I guess we'll need to get married in the spring, I'll let you know when . . ."

It was not clear at what point in this monologue Gerald set down the receiver and walked away. When he came to himself again, Martin Grimm, with atrocious glee, was supervising the removal of his bed, his desk, and his bound volumes of *The National Journal.* "Would you like the movers to pack your clothing, Mr. Nash?" he asked.

Gerald slipped on his overcoat and wandered out the door, with no earthly destination in mind.

Epilogue

But for my children, I would have them keep their
distance from the thickening center; corruption
Never has been compulsory, when the cities lie
at the monster's feet there are left the mountains.
—"Shine, Perishing Republic,"
by Robinson Jeffers

THE FRAIL AND GRACEFUL EARTH, girdled in green and white, turns toward the light. Her children live and die by the line of sunlight. And in our story it has turned, rising out of the Pacific and bending inexorably across Asia, to bring the dawn of the twentieth day of January.

Of those we have followed through nearly a year of life, the first to see sunrise on this day is David Beaufort. Daylight finds him climbing an olive-colored hill, and the dawn comes with a roar and crash: the noise of Israeli airplanes dropping bombs somewhere to his north and west. David's ears are strained for any sound: the chatter of small-arms fire, the crackle of orders across the portable radio he carries on his back. David Beaufort is back in uniform, wearing the fatigues of the army of Israel and marching north into Lebanon.

It is a strange fate for him, but God has led him to it for reasons of His own, and David does not question his Creator. He has learned a new language since escaping from Sunrise House; when he uses it on the radio, the sounds burn his tongue with the same fire he felt when he faced down the elders of the Temple of Ray.

This new life is dangerous, and hard, and lonely too. Sometimes it feels ridiculous, and sometimes it feels unjust. But when has Yahweh been kind to those he loves?

Sunrise next passes over the oceans to find Nancy Quoin in her mortgaged bathroom in Montgomery County, throwing up.

Never one to buck a social trend, Nancy Quoin is suddenly, happily pregnant. This condition, which for a decade she has feared as the direst threat to her career, has come instead as its salvation. Today she begins work as associate publisher of *Executive Mother* magazine; this afternoon she will meet with the venture capitalists who are to underwrite her chain of Dress for Success Maternity Boutiques.

There is only one cloud on the unlimited horizon for Nancy Quoin. She has been subpoenaed to testify before the LaVache committee (until recently the Hench committee) about what its chairman calls "the theft of important government documents." For Nancy Quoin's one ineffective attempt at a good deed, she will pay with lawyer's fees, public scorn, and gray hairs. She will never make such a mistake again.

Sunlight marches west and finds a Kentucky mountain where a former Assistant Secretary is hiking with his dogs, Dixie and Trigger. The growing daylight picks out each pine tree on the mountainside. The former official knows each tree by history and habit, like old relatives or friends. He feels, for the first time in two years, that he is where God intended him to be. Already his time in Washington is fading like a magnificent dream; soon there will be no trace of it except a tattered postcard collection his nephews will inherit. The dogs course ahead, searching for rabbits; their master walks behind them on oil-resistant soles; their three minds are utterly and gratefully blank.

Further west, in a new city by the Gulf, where oil tankers throng the docks and the air is thick with chemical fumes, Gerald Nash sits on the side of a bed in a furnished studio apartment. He is staring at the color television, on which is the image, like a distant bad memory, of Diana Cazadora, hostess of the New Harmony Satellite Network's "Sunrise" show, interviewing Willys Handleman, the U.S. Director of Difficult Decisions.

Gerald has found a job. He starts today as policy-planning director of Harbor Legal Aid.

"Your experience really isn't right for this job," the director had told him the day before. "Our practice is involved with defending the interests of our deaf and mute clients. Do you think you can learn sign language?"

"I'd like to learn a new language," Gerald had said, as he gingerly took up a copy of the book the director had given him. His hands made tentative passes in the air, expressing unfamiliar concepts: *I think. I feel. I want. I love. I am.* As he signed them, in his heart he heard the distant sound of a small stone striking bottom, and it pointed him for the first time toward home.

"Mr. Nash? Are you listening? I said one thing that works in your favor is your Washington experience. I have a feeling that we're going to have some trouble with these budget cuts. Do you have any lines in to this guy Handleman?"

"No," Gerald had said quickly. "I never knew him at all."

Sunrise next travels toward the Pacific, and near it finds Margaret Luck already drinking instant coffee and poring over the chaotic ledgers of the Gouge Eye People's Lumber Co-Op Number One. She is in her new office, a drafty cubicle in the old lumber mill where she will keep the books, draw up the checks, keep track of inventory, and try to prevent disaster. It is the kind of work she tried to foster when she worked for the Coalition on Industrial Alternatives, but it feels different now that she is actively engaged in it: messier, less inspiring, slower, more painful, less certain of success.

But Margaret is reasonably content. She has run a mile and a half and eaten a good breakfast; outside the window she hears her husband loudly cursing a piece of equipment frozen from rust and neglect; her feet are warm. Margaret has decided never to think further ahead than that. Having twice chosen the course of her life, only to see it veer of its own accord toward another destination, she has now relinquished any anxiety about what fate holds in store. She makes no plans, she never worries. It is a piece of wisdom she has learned, without knowing it, from Bob Zardovsky. It is the only present he can give her; it is the only thing he has; but it is more than many people ever get.

Zardovsky himself is occupied with machine oil; he's wrestling with a decrepit fork lift, drenching it, himself, and his environment with WD-40. His deformed hand can still grip a spanner; he knows now that his future lies with tools and not with baseballs. He has bid farewell to the old dreams; life offers him machine tools, refried beans, and love. His mind, like a tranquil bay after a mysterious storm, has grown smooth and still again since his return from Washington. As it has done so, it has rearranged the image it carries of his time in Washington, until by now he thinks of it as a time when a citizen asked his government for help and the government gave it, just as it should. The rest — deception, betrayal, danger, frustration — has been forgotten; it is no longer useful.

By the time daybreak has found Margaret and Bob, it is nearly time for festivities to begin in Washington. Paper lanterns and balloons festoon the trees; Muzak serenades the sidewalk; fireworks burst in the broad, blue, chilly sky. It is inauguration day, that magical moment of liberation that frees the old administration to begin disowning its mistakes and the new one to begin repeating them. A mammoth parade is planned, and in it will march a string band, dressed, as is their custom, in Indian regalia (the Navajo nation, in protest against this plan, has sent east a marching band dressed as bankers, but these troublemakers have been arrested at Union Station); the Olympia Marching Band of New Orleans, a famous black jazz band, which will insist on playing funeral marches along the entire route; the Mormon Tabernacle Choir, which will ride a flatbed truck and sing *ad nauseam* the "Ode to Joy"; the precision glockenspiel squadron of the U.S. Naval Observatory, chiming on the quarter-hour; the Alcohol, Drug Abuse, and Mental Health Administration's fife, drum, and bugle corps; the Veiled Prophet of Korasan; and the fabled Marching Mariachis of the U.S. Immigration and Naturalization Service.

A delegation from the Temple of Ray was to attend, carrying American flags and signs reading PATRIOTIC ANCIENT ONES HAIL MARTIAN–AMERICAN FRIENDSHIP, but the members unfortunately became involved in a renewed outbreak of the sectarian violence that has recently shaken the Washington nest; partisans of the Three-Fingered God have come to blows with the heretics who worship the Dark Prophet. This doctrinal dispute will not be resolved for several decades, and in the course of it three provincial governments in Asia will be overthrown and several U.S. corporations will become embroiled in proxy fights. The demigods who inspired the dispute will never hear of it at all.

Across town the delegates from the Business Executive Roundtable for Economic Growth and Space Warfare (formerly the Toiling Masses League) are buttoning their vests and adjusting their briefcases. They will not carry signs but will quietly seek donations for their new causes: tax breaks for nuclear power, and a crash program to build a huge space magnifying glass that will focus the sun's rays on Russia and burn it to a crisp.

At the embassy of a small Central American nation, the ambassador checks his necktie. Paco Sanchez has never attended a ceremony of state, but as newly named ambassador of the provisional revolutionary government, he is determined to make a good impression. It will be a nervous afternoon, however; no one is quite sure what the change of administration will mean for the revolution, except probably nothing good. He will appear on "Sunrise" tomorrow, to plead his cause to the American people; but in the embassy safe are his stock certificates in Targaverde Enterprises, which went public, to great acclaim, the week before.

For one Washingtonian, today is a workday like any other. In his grand, windowless office, Baxter Muntin sits in shirt-sleeves, tie loosened, in front of a typewriter. He is writing a memo to his valued friend the Director of Difficult Decisions, who has asked him for suggestions about what can be done to dismantle the new Department where Muntin works. In response Muntin has produced a thirty-page discussion of each of the Department's functions — its little-known police force, its dirigible factory, its new Office of Fungibility Assessment, and all its other programs, with their administrative and clerical support staffs — and concluded that the national interest will be threatened if cuts are made anywhere but in the Community Action Training Allocation program. That is where a show of determination will produce a good example for the bureaucracy and people alike, and Muntin recommends that the program be abolished altogether, that no new funds be appropriated, and that already appropriated funds be impounded.

But more is needed to symbolize the change. Muntin recommends that Handleman's office bring suit to recover some funds already spent, on the grounds that they were given out improperly. To this memo he appends a legal opinion that outlines a possible suit — admittedly a legal long shot, but with some chance of success and every chance of publicity — asking for return of granted funds, civil penalties, and punitive damages from the former Assistant Secretary, the former Deputy Assistant Secretary, former special assistant Gerald Nash, the Gouge Eye People's Lumber Co-op Number One, and most particularly the controversial Bob Zardovsky.

Muntin's eyes gleam as he types the latter name. He rubs his hands as if in anticipation, then lights a cigarette with his M-1 battle-tank lighter. Smoke wreathes his smiling face, and his fingers fly across the keys.

From sea to shining sea, the American Republic sprawls under the sun in gaudy and defenseless joy. No danger or decay can threaten it while Baxter Muntin is on guard.